TALES MY BODY TOLD ME

# Tales My Body Told Me

A NOVEL BY

## WAYNE COURTOIS

LETHE PRESS
MAPLE SHADE, NJ

## Tales My Body Told Me

Published in 2010 by LETHE PRESS
118 Heritage Avenue • Maple Shade, NJ 08052-3018
www.lethepressbooks.com • lethepress@aol.com
ISBN: 1-59021-247-9
ISBN-13: 978-1-59021-247-9

Portions of this book appeared, in different form, in the webzine *Velvet Mafia* (No. 14, 2005) and in *Hot Gay Erotica*, edited by Richard Labonté (Cleis Press, 2006).

This is a work of fiction. Names, characters, places, and incidents are products of the author's imagination or are used fictitiously.

Set in Minion, Myriad, & Humana Serif.
Cover art: Ben Baldwin.
Cover and interior design: Alex Jeffers.

---

LIBRARY OF CONGRESS CATALOGING-IN-PUBLICATION DATA

Courtois, Wayne, 1954-
Tales my body told me : a novel / by Wayne Courtois.
    p. cm.
ISBN 1-59021-247-9 (pbk. : alk. paper)
1. Gay men--Fiction. 2. Psychotherapy--Fiction. 3. Maine--Fiction.
4. Satire. I. Title.
PS3603.O887T35 2010
813'.6--dc22

                                2010016876

For Ralph, my one and only

# Acknowledgments

Thanks to Steve Berman, Ben Baldwin, and Alex Jeffers. Thanks also to Greg Wharton, who made useful comments on an earlier version of this novel.

Special thanks to my partner, Ralph Seligman, who let me borrow numerous items for this narrative—including his birthmark.

# I. A Pardoner's Tale

# Chapter 1

**Have** you ever tasted a young boy's skin?

When you were a young boy *yourself*, I mean.

In the roughhousing of youth, did your lips ever brush against the nape of a neck—a tanned, salty strip of boyskin, slightly greasy at the hairline? Did the tip of your tongue sense an *earthiness*, the essence of the planet?

Wrestling, did you ever get a thrill from being trapped in an armpit? Locked in a leglock, never wanting release? And did you ever, when throwing a boy to the ground or getting thrown yourself, let your mouth glide across a forearm, or maybe (oh maybe, just once, by the swimming hole) a bare chest?

It's the stuff of my dreams, in this ancient house where the wallpaper's bumps and bruises look like varicose veins and the smells are just as homely: must and camphor, lemon cough drops, the onion-and-boiled-milk of chowder. The staircase leading from the front hall to the second floor sags slightly, and tepid air leaks from the floor vents like an invalid's last gasp.

Outside, in the town of Two Piers, the Ferris wheel and Tilt-a-Whirl sit empty at the edge of the beach, their cars covered in canvas, their bright spokes pitted with salt. A sign reading **ICI ON PARLE FRANÇAIS** blows along the boardwalk. The sea lies alone, unvisited,

3

a smudge on the horizon. The one remaining pier, its mate having washed out to sea ages ago, sits uneasily in heavy winter surf, its pilings groaning and creaking in the cold.

These things are as lonely and as far removed as my former life, which seems to have given up on me. I can't hear it calling anymore.

**After** a long night I wake up wrapped in my sheets. I reach for the blanket, but it's slithered away. I'm a mess, leftover dream images crimping my consciousness like things too hot to touch. And here's Brian at the foot of my bed—there are no locked doors here—pulling back the curtains.

"It's Sunday, Paul," he says. "Pancakes today."

After a couple of tries I manage to clear the cobwebs from my throat. "Pancakes? With blueberries?"

His shoulder-length red hair, which he usually wears tied back with a rubber band, is hanging loose, framing his sweet smile. "Blueberries, Paul? In the middle of winter? I don't think so!"

I laugh. "I don't know why, I just thought of blueberries, for some reason." A lot of things still confuse me, including the exact circumstances that brought me here. Brian says it's normal, nothing to worry about. ("Take a pill. A white one.") Many guys "blank out" their first encounter with East Oak House; it's traumatic, after all, to commit to changing your whole life. ("Make it two white pills.") The blanking out is a voluntary act of the mind as it prepares to abandon one way of thinking for another.

Once Brian has left I put my slippers on, throw a robe over my pajamas, and make a stop at the second floor bathroom, remembering to knock first. I face the man in the mirror, a middle-aged dad from a TV sitcom, the kind of guy who looks best on a small, black-and-white screen. That he stares so impassively as I pee, or that he moves when I do, ducking his head as I spit out toothpaste, is a bit disconcerting. Yet a curious sense of control keeps me heading for the back stairs, down to the kitchen.

Brian's pouring pancake batter onto the skillet. I take the half-gallon orange juice jug from the fridge and fill the six small glasses on the table. "Why six?" I ask.

4

"We'll have a guest this morning," Brian says. "Someone who may be joining us."

Sometimes I blush when Brian looks at me, I feel it in my cheeks. So much for control. I look down at my outfit: the standard-issue pajamas, chalk-blue hospital scrubs, and a white robe as threadbare as an old washcloth. "I should have showered and dressed before breakfast."

"Nah, don't worry." Brian is still smiling. "That's 'past life' thinking, Paul. You look fine."

I feel better, at least until Davy and Aaron and Todd appear. Davy and Aaron have showered and dressed, wearing the loose clothing that's preferred here, oversized sweatshirts and sweatpants. Todd's still in his pajamas, like me, but they're nice ones, cream-colored with a subtle red-and-black print. They even look like they've been ironed, for Christ's sake. And his slippers aren't the mangy-looking things I'm sporting but stylish and gleaming, made of the kind of imitation leather that makes you wonder why they bother with the real stuff. Not a scrap of skin shows between their uppers and the hem of his pajamas. As for me, I'm grateful, after we've said our good mornings, to take a seat and hide my hairy white ankles from view.

"We were going to have a guest this morning," Brian says, carrying a platter of pancakes to the table. "But he's late. You know what that means, he might not show. So I'm not holding up breakfast."

Mixed reactions around the table. Aaron and Todd look slightly disappointed, while Davy, who is blond, skinny and nervous, looks relieved. I'm pouring syrup on my pancakes and still brooding, for some reason, about blueberries—big ones clumped together in thick syrup, like pie filling. It doesn't matter, it's not important. I shake my head, clear away the image.

"Anybody have a dream?" Brian asks, as he does almost every morning.

"I did," Davy says, raising his hand as if we're in class. "I had a dream about Sean."

Ah. Sean, the ex-lover. Swiveling our heads in unison, we smile politely.

5

"We were in a room. A totally white room, like in an art gallery or something. We were, uh, naked. And he was holding a cat in his arms. A black cat."

"And what were you doing?" Brian asked, knowing from experience that Davy, always so quick to volunteer, usually needs prompting, as if raising his hand took all of his energy.

"I was—leaning in, I think."

I get his quandary—it's tough, the way perspective shifts in a dream, hard to describe unless you're a cinematographer.

"I was about to kiss him, and then the strangest thing happened.... It was like this guy comes into the room, and it's me. Another me. And this me takes the cat from Sean's arms and throws it out the window."

Brian beams approval, even though he knows—he *must* know— that Davy's full of shit. He's only regurgitating this week's lesson: that if you can master certain powers of concentration, you can change your dreams. To my surprise this was meant quite literally: if you're asleep and having a dream that's ominous or discomfiting or just plain scary, you can—because you are master of your mind—enter that dream *without waking up* and *change the outcome*. It's all a matter of concentration, and with practice anyone can do it. I stare at my silverware, wondering how I managed to reach middle age without ever learning this. I've wasted a lot of time on nightmares filled with pain or incoherent, erotic urges that twist and turn like the sheets I wake up in.

Davy has more to say, no doubt, about his naked ex and the black cat. But my silverware-staring has yielded strange fruit, and I can't help crying out. "Wait," I say. "Wait, wait, wait." I tug on Davy's sleeve.

"What is it?" he asks.

The small hairs on the back of my neck are rising. "Does my fork match my spoon match my knife?"

"What?"

"My fork match my spoon match my—"

"Take it easy, Paul."

*Take it easy*—how many more times am I going to hear that? Doesn't anybody understand why I'm upset? My *knife*, my *fork*, my

6

*spoon*—in a house where no two plates or glasses match, where every blessed cup and saucer has come from a different garage sale, it's *impossible* that two pieces of silverware would have the same pattern, let alone a spoon *and* a fork *and* a knife....

"I see what he means," Brian says. "It's true, they all have the same pattern. What are the odds?"

Now they're all peering at my silverware. "Huh," Aaron says. "I've never seen two alike before, let alone three."

They not only match, they bear the initial *C* in Old English. Now what does that mean? How sad that someone who went to the trouble to get monogrammed silverware is now forgotten, only his initial left behind.

Brian laughs. "Well, don't worry, Paul. Just because your tableware matches doesn't mean you're a fag."

*Har har har.*

"Yeah," Todd says, "it doesn't mean you don't like pussy."

This kind of talk is allowed, to an extent. Not that we're intended to be sexist pigs in training, lacking appropriate respect for women; it's just that...well, we're just *guys*, that's all, and that's what guys are like. Todd ought to know—Todd of the tall slender frame and sarcastic voice, Todd whose skin holds a deep boyish tan even in the dead of winter.

I wrote about Todd in the journal I keep, the one nobody knows about. I call it the Dirty Gray Notebook (tip of the hat to Doris Lessing). In fact, I write about all of my housemates, even Brian; but Todd, the big, competent man-boy, was the first I put pen to paper about: *It's precisely the nape of his neck that I love to suck and lick and nibble at. It gives me that little-boy feeling again. There's nothing better in the world—unless it's the smooth, salty edge of his shoulder blade or the funky shallows of his navel. Surprisingly strong, he slings me up against the headboard, excited to see my shoulders thump wood. If I look scared, so much the better, for it's all about power, just like those boyhood games. "Go ahead," I tell him, raising my knees toward my bruised shoulders. "Fuck me, hurt me, leave a mark that'll never go away." He lowers his face toward mine, having something to prove with his tongue, turning my mouth inside out, marking his territory from bi-*

7

*cuspid to tonsil. When I can't stand waiting any longer I beg. "Fuck me, you know you want to, your balls are gonna burst, give it to me…!"*

*When he's good and ready, he does.*

"Hey, Paul?" Aaron asks, barely concealing his mirth. "Do your sheets match, too?"

You ought to know, I should tell him. I've been knitting dreams about him, too, in the Notebook—Aaron and his J/O fetish. *Whenever we're in the same room I try to keep my hand in his line of sight, my fingers lively. Wiggling, stretching, curling, cupping handfuls of air like scrotums, playing with pencils or pens. What do you know, the sexiest part of the male body is that old opposable thumb and forefinger! Aaron blushes even more easily than I do, and when he sees my suggestive digits he can't look away.*

*One evening at supper, while Brian is holding forth on some topic or other, I catch Aaron's eye in a way that's become so easy, leading it down to table level, where my hand oh-so-subtly caresses the salt shaker. Now I'm looking away, my hand acting entirely on its own, fingers gliding just the teeniest distance up and down the smooth glass cylinder. You wouldn't even notice it, if you didn't have lust for what fingers can do. As Brian talks on, as I nod very seriously, the speed of my hand picks up, my fingers are almost grasping the shaker now—the kind of shaker that has, conveniently, a metal top that bulges out over the narrow glass neck, so that it's easy to tease its edges, stroke its apex…I can almost feel it engorging, getting ready to spurt a fountain of white stuff…. One more squeeze, nearly but not quite lifting the shaker free from the oil-cloth, and there's a gasp from Aaron's end of the table. I shift my eyes just in time to catch his guilty glance, and I know I've got him.*

*A few hours later I'm in his room, breezing through the door as if I own the place. He's under the covers, pretending to read, a book propped up on his belly. "Don't you ever knock?" he asks, but he's not fooling me—he's more relieved than anything when I close the door behind me. And he doesn't put up a fight when I tenderly pinch his blanket and sheet and pull them down. His birth-giving position is appropriate, for a spanking-new hard-on is crowning, raising its eye to the wonders of life. Reaching for it, I watch the magic lantern show in Aaron's eyes, an endless loop of fear-disbelief-shame-resignation-desire. "Easy," I tell*

*him, reassuringly, my tender grip on his shaft the very definition of easy,
oh how easy it is....*

*"I was just...." He says.*

*"Yes, I see what you were just. Where is it?"*

*"Where is...?"*

*"The bottle."*

*Under his pillow, that's where it is—hand lotion, not the best prod-
uct for the job, but it'll do...and be so reminiscent of that night under
the moon, years ago, at Boy Scout camp...those first exciting touches.
He's never lost the excitement of those greedy male hands holding him
down, stripping off his shorts. Which is why I kneel above him, taking
control, forbidding him to use his hands. Making his cock a monument
to the sticking-place where fantasy and flesh meet, and he will never
forget it. Never forget me. It. Me. It.*

*"Don't," he says, writhing and thrusting whorishly.*

*"Oh, you were* made *to be played with, hard guy, made* for *it...." I
am reassurance, threat, cool voice of wisdom; more than half whore as
well, a slut with itchy palms that'll do anything to keep the greased-up
miracle going. "Ooh, Aaron, I love your shaft, so hard, so long, and look
at that fat slick dickhead, I just want to work it...." He groans, loving
this kind of talk. "Slick, and so hard...just* begging *for it...."*

*"Please make me come," he pants.*

*"You really get wet, don't you, Aar? I put out a lot of precum my-
self...."*

*How long can I keep him on edge, begging me to bring him off? Oh,
for days. Months. Years. A cock, after all, is made to last a lifetime.*

9

**S u d d e n l y** the doorbell rings, and Brian rises to answer it, each
movement graceful and assured. When he's been gone a few seconds
I realize I've been holding my breath. I force myself to relax a little
and smile across the table at Aaron, who's brushing crumbs from the
front of his sweatshirt. He looks up, meets my eyes, glances down
to where my right hand is caressing the salt shaker, fingers gliding
the teeniest distance up and down the smooth glass cylinder. Oops.
Didn't mean to do it, I swear. My face is just starting to burn when
Brian returns with our guest, a slim young man in his twenties with

a mustache and dark, heavy eyebrows that give him a skeptical look. I'm glad his seat is down at the end of the table.

"Everybody, this is Kent," Brian says. "Kent, meet Davy, Aaron, Todd, and Paul."

Kent nods, just once, a lock of dark brown hair falling across his forehead. He smoothes it back, using only the first two fingers of his left hand. A delicate gesture—tellingly so. I glance at the others, who are smiling calmly. Kent sits down and, with some effort, moves his heavy captain's chair closer to the table.

"This is a typical Sunday morning," Brian says, returning to the griddle to pour out more batter. "Up at nine, something special for breakfast—and these pancakes *are* special, if I do say so myself. Uh, we don't have religious services here, I think I told you that."

"Yeah, I don't care about that," Kent says. His hands grip the armrests of his chair, his eyes keep shifting toward the corners of the room. The judgmental side of me observes that he'd be more at home sipping a bloody Mary or mimosa. When he glances at me I look down, as if I've dropped something—hardly the proper thing to do. My face turns red again. When I look up there's Kent staring in dismay at the two golden pancakes Brian is sliding onto his plate. "I forgot to tell you," Kent says, "I already ate breakfast."

Brian laughs. "It's all right, Kent, we don't put anything in the food. Have some coffee, anyway." He fills Kent's cup from the carafe and takes his seat at the head of the table. "And think about this." He leans forward, steepling his fingertips as he makes eye contact with Kent. "Everything that worries you about your life…all the complications, the pain, the guilt…all of it gone. Does that sound like a better world?" He pauses for a beat. "You bet it does."

Brian's a force to be reckoned with, all right, his blue eyes so startling in their intensity that they help make up for the rest of his face—the blunt nose, the weak chin that always has a few scrapes on it, as if he shaves with a razor made for larger, more challenging chins. He's someone I long to be, never got the chance to be, or can't stand the thought of being. No wonder Kent is squinting at him in deep concentration. Or maybe his contact lenses are bothering him.

10

"Now," Brian says, "I'm not telling you it's easy to change, but in the right environment it can be done. And we have that right here at East Oak House."

Kent's eyes, breaking loose from Brian's to glance here and there across the tabletop—at a fork, a red-and-white-checked napkin, a tub of low-fat margarine—seem not so much to be staring at things but looking within, their restlessness a symptom of the urge to change. It's almost too private a thing to be witnessed, and I look down into my lap again.

Brian sees it's time for some light conversation. "Well, let's talk about some of the things we do for fun."

"I've been reading Chaucer," someone pipes up. Oh, it's me. "*The Pardoner's Tale.*"

Like everything else I say, this has to be explained by Brian. "We make our own entertainment here," he says to Kent, "and we're getting ready for an evening of reader's theater. Paul's doing some Chaucer, and—"

"I'm doing Robert Frost," Davy says. "'Stopping by Woods on a Snowy Evening.'"

Sometimes Davy is so cute that I want to put him in a headlock and rub my knuckles on his scalp. Hey Davy, that's a poem we all learned in the second grade, can't you do something a little more ambitious?

Todd, by contrast, announces that he's doing some Shakespeare. Unfortunately he has a manner of speaking that makes everything he says sound sarcastic. "From *Julius Caesar*," he says, and it's hard to know whether to take him seriously.

"And I'm doing some *Leaves of Grass*," Aaron says.

All of our heads turn toward him. Really, Aaron? Walt Whitman?

"What?" he says, the corners of his mouth twitching. Like me, he's easily flustered. He uses his fingers for almost all food, including his pancakes, which he's rolling up and eating dry, without butter or syrup. For me there is no "what"—it may be a stretch to put Aaron together with *Leaves of Grass*, but I wouldn't mind a bit of Walt. Who cares if he was a card-carrying queer, long before that concept even existed? Chaucer's Pardoner was probably a member of the club as well.

Since our literary discussion seems to have ground to a halt, Brian takes the opportunity to ask Kent if he wants to take a tour of the place. As Kent gets up I get a good look at him again. His button-down shirt is open at the neck, revealing a nice serving of chest hair, and his jeans define the trunk of his body a bit too well. A ring of keys hangs from his right-side belt loop. In the old days that would have meant he liked to get fucked—do key codes still apply? And what kind of language is that—*he liked to get fucked, he liked to give head, he liked j/o, water sports, fisting?* It's not so much that it sounds obscene, it's just—dated somehow. Old and quaint-sounding, like Chaucer's English.

"Be right back," Brian says, and they disappear up the back stairs, around the corner from the kitchen. I'm ready to take my coffee into the den, the only room where smoking's allowed, but for the moment it feels good to sit and bask in my relief that our initial encounter with Kent is over.

Todd gives a nervous cough. "He seems nice enough," he says, sounding sarcastic

"He didn't seem as nervous as I was," Davy says. Like you *are*, I'm thinking, watching his orange juice tremble as he raises it to his lips. Sometimes I shake the way he does, after too much coffee. The sugar I've had doesn't help, my thoughts are racing in a familiar way. The sugar high is something I've used all my life as a coping mechanism, but what a foolish trick. More often, these days, it only leaves me confused and tired. Which doesn't stop me from helping myself to another cup of coffee with two heaping teaspoons.

12

"Seems like Dwight's been gone a long time," Aaron says.

"I miss Dwight," Todd says. "I mean, as a friend."

I miss Dwight too. He came here not long before I did, and already he's gone. Well, recovery is different for everyone, as Brian would say. In group Dwight had a nice self-deprecating sense of humor, kind of like mine but without the pathos. He was so fair his hair was almost white. The Dirty Gray Notebook points out that *his chest hair, almost white as well, was thick and lickable. Nipples so sensitive, breathing on them made him sigh. When his dick was hard it was the darkest part of him. His dickhead was like a knob of putty stuck slightly off-center. I liked to ride it while he bucked like a bronco. "Fuck me, stud. Fuck me till dawn and I'll slap your tits, just the way you like it."*

*Dwight taught me so much about tits: working them with slick fingertips, I caused different parts of him to twitch—his buttocks, his feet. And he never failed to look at me with gratitude that I had so quickly found his weakness, his obsession, his reason for living.*

But what was his reason for leaving? Of course there's only one reason to leave. On the morning he made his decision he gave us a speech about life and change, presenting his case with sincerity and skill. But why he chose that exact time to go…wracking my brain gave me no answers, and if I were really honest I wouldn't need one. Instead I would admit the truth: he left because he didn't need us anymore.

"Been a while since we had anybody new," Davy says. Does he know that he's tapping his fork with his fingernail, making it *ting-ting-ting* against his plate? "Not since Paul."

Oh great, everyone looks at me. I try to smile and feel it misfire. No doubt my mouth looks as insincere as Todd's voice sounds. They know that, when all is said and done, I'm different from them. I keep to myself too much. Yes, this is a place for healing, you're supposed to be self-absorbed; but it's also a place for—oh, that word—*sharing*. Sharing and caring. Ditties run through my head all day: *Oh, we share and care in our underwear.*

I glance at Aaron, who's smiling at me, just slightly. Like Dwight he's almost painfully blond, especially in the fluorescent light of the kitchen—his eyebrows like frost, his lashes like attenuated snowflakes. Almost an albino. There's another dimension to Aaron, too, for if you took his wintry paleness away, painted his eyebrows and lashes brown, his blue eyes hazel, you'd have Eric, my ex-husband.

Oh, he's here, Eric is—in my dreams, the ones I never talk about. He hovers over me, his features as clear as the media player of memory can make them, and his Spanish accent keeps on ticking when I turn the volume up. His words and actions are limited, though, as if I've run short on disk space. Often he's naked, I see the freckles on his belly, the dick I know as well as my own, the dime-sized birthmark on his hip. He peers at me, as if at his own reflection in a mirror, and asks something like, "Paul, what are you doing?"

13

"What the fuck do you think I'm doing?" I ask gently.

His lower lip trembles. "Come back to me."

"Come back to *you*?" I sweep my hand in dismissal, forcing him to step back. "*You're* the one who left *me*, in case you've forgotten. You cheated on *me*. Then you left me."

He raises the back of his hand to his mouth just as a sob tears it open. "No! That's not true, Paul!" The vehemence of his words—he's practically screaming—wakes me up. I lie in the dark, trying in vain to think about what's true and what's not. Wondering where my husband is now. What's become of the king-size bed we shared. What's become of our cat, whom I would never throw out a window, not even in a dream.

Davy gets seconds on orange juice. I warm up my coffee from the carafe. By the time we've sat down again Brian and Kent return, single file, Kent ducking into the kitchen as Brian, behind him, asks, "Well, what do you think?"

"It's pretty nice," Kent says.

So young. He looks young enough to be in high school, and he speaks—shades of Todd!—like a kid talking to a teacher, saying the right words but really thinking *You're full of shit*. Oh, he likes to get fucked, all right: somehow it comes through in his bright smile and untrimmed mustache. How about that mustache? He's neat enough in other ways, why doesn't he keep it straight-edged? He must think that ragged fringe curling against his lip looks sexy, and damned if it doesn't. One unkempt detail can go a long way. I know you, Kent: you're a little sex machine, working your sphincter around a lubricated shaft like you were born to it. In mouth or ass you can take two cocks at once, sucking them up like a Dirt Devil. I see you, I recognize you even from my humble vantage point—middle age, chalk-blue pajamas, white hairy ankles and all.

I wonder what Brian has seen. Does he feel that Kent is a good candidate? Hard to tell from his expression. "Well," he says, sticking to the script, "I'm going to leave you all for a bit, so you guys can, you know, talk amongst yourselves." He takes his coat from the rack and edges through the kitchen door—making a show of leaving the house so that Kent won't think he's hiding somewhere, listening.

14

Taking his seat at the table again, Kent looks at each of us in turn, seeking eye contact. Soon I'm trapped in his steady blue gaze; if my head were snatched away my eyeballs would stay in place, hanging in midair. Yet I return his gaze very calmly. Let him accuse me of hypocrisy, it wouldn't be the first time. He should have been here when our last guest came through—a little shit with a shaved head, his salt-and-pepper mustache giving away his age. Rodney, his name was. As soon as the five of us were alone, Brian having slipped out the kitchen door, Rodney let us have it. "Fucking hypocrites!" he screamed. "You'll never change, you know you won't, you CAN'T. But once you're completely brainwashed you'll be just like your creepy 'leader,' telling guys they can get rid of their gayness, a GOD-GIVEN gayness, by the way. So don't talk about God, you pathetic bastards. Just FUCK OFF, okay? Fuck yourselves, if you're not fucking each other!"

Looking back, I'd say we did very well. Not a lip trembled, not an eyelash fluttered as we sat and listened to Rodney, who was shaking so hard he nearly fell off his chair. We didn't argue, didn't cry—okay, one tear appeared on my cheek, but it dried up quickly—and didn't correct his notion that we talked about God. As he'd already been told, God doesn't enter into our affairs. Poor guy—he must have suspected that the minute his back was turned we'd beat him with Bibles. Sitting, staring calmly, our advantage was almost unfair. No wonder he finally bolted to his feet and ran, leaving the kitchen door open, his footsteps crunching through fresh-fallen snow, his car roaring furiously as it overtook the stop sign at the top of the hill.

For another minute, we just continued to stare. Finally Dwight, who was still with us, said, "Jesus fucking Christ." It was enough to release the tension, we laughed as if it was the funniest thing we'd ever heard.

Now Kent is giving us the hairy eyeball. I plant my feet flat on the floor and take a swig of coffee. Another outburst is unlikely; Rodney was an anomaly. Guys are too thoroughly screened to fake their way in here—though how or when I was screened I cannot say. Sure enough, Kent's voice is soft as he asks, "So you guys aren't…?"

We sit perfectly still, as if we've put our heads together and decided to let composure speak for itself. Even Davy manages not to fidget.

"Nobody likes to suck dick? You don't even like to look at pictures of naked guys?"

Continued composure. Unruffled feathers.

"Jesus," Kent says, "don't you guys even *beat off*?"

My composure breaks, in the form of a short, sharp laugh that sounds and feels more like a sneeze. No one else's breaks, though. Davy speaks up clearly and calmly. "You might not believe it now," he says, "but it's possible to lead a life where you're not obsessed with sex all the time. It's possible."

Kent sticks his tongue in his cheek, rolls it around as if tasting something new.

"We're not, like, monks or anything," Todd says. "It's not like we're giving up sex forever, or anything like that." To my surprise Todd has found a new way to overcome his habitual sarcastic tone: by growing louder. His next statement fairly booms. "It's just that some of us would like to get married, have kids."

Kent sits for a moment, considering. He looks down at the floor. The table leg squeaks, he must be rubbing his boot against it. "I haven't been doing much with my life lately," he says. "Not really."

"You can do something here," Aaron says. "We can help you. We support each other. We're doing it."

If there's a double meaning to *We're doing it*, it doesn't show on Aaron's perfectly sober face. Now an awkward silence points out that I'm the only one who hasn't added to the pep talk. Isn't there *something* I can say? I don't have to search my thoughts too far before I come up against a wall. It's a high, blank wall, but at least I know what's on the other side: grief, a whole shitstorm of grief and loss and despair. When I speak it's to that wall, as if I might break through it, then level off the sea of muck so that I could, for the first time in what seems like years, glimpse the horizon.

"Do it, Kent," I tell him. "Do it now, while you're still young enough that you haven't ruined your life yet, or anyone else's. Do it before so much time has passed that you don't know if you can. Do it so you don't have to learn how scary that is, or what it feels like to live with so much regret."

More silence, but of a different kind. Kent seems about to speak, his lips trembling; instead he just looks at me while I blush for the third time this morning, feeling it like a warm dry cloth laid over my face. I've done what had to be done, what could only be done by me—the oldest man at the table, the one with more gray hair than anyone else.

Brian would be proud.

**Sunday** breakfast is always followed by free time—a reminder that we are "free" from the burdens of churchgoing and other religious rot. I head for the den, where I can stare at the book-lined walls and smoke one cigarette after another. The only other smoker in the house is Brian, who keeps trying to quit. He'll duck into the room, light up and start pacing, biting drags off his fag, crushing it out when it's half gone. I said to him once, "If you're going to smoke, you might as well enjoy it," then wished I hadn't, for he looked even more ashamed. Maybe he feels that, as an expert on quitting queer life, he should set an example in quitting smoking as well. If you can forsake blow jobs, doesn't it follow that you can stop sucking on Marlboros? Yet I'm glad—secretly glad—that I'm not the only smoker in the house.

I don't see Brian during this Sunday morning smoke because he's left for the supermarket, to get supplies; Kent has already decided he'll be moving in tonight. So I sit and smoke and listen to the vague winter complaints of the house and Davy's noodling on the piano in the living room. Todd and Aaron are probably upstairs, reading or perhaps writing letters with the standard apologies: *Sorry you can't visit me here, sorry we can't even talk on the phone, sorry I can't even give you the address. Sorry, sorry, sorry. Those are the rules....* Rules, that is, meant to protect our privacy, and our safety in this little Maine town where the locals would torch the place if they thought it contained homosexuals, recovering or not.

The slamming of the kitchen door wakes me. Christ, have I been dozing with a lit cigarette in my hand? I check my hand, my lap, the chair, the floor, the ashtray. Nothing burning. The kitchen noise means that Brian is back from his shopping, I couldn't have slept very long. Long enough, though, for a thousand tiny dreams, and I close my eyes to try to recapture some. It was also a dream that was troubling me when I woke up earlier this morning, I'm sure of it. Dreams

17

are nothing to worry about. Still, I'd like to know *exactly* what it was I'd seen in my sleep, and whether or not it has just revisited me....

Something brushes my cheek, startling me again. Another nap has come and gone, an extremely brief one, and though I didn't feel the familiar *oops-I-left-a-cigarette-burning* panic, there's panic in me just the same: *what* could have touched me? I look around for the winter housefly (rare) that might have settled on my face; I wave my hands, seeking out the draft (not so rare) that might have caressed me. Nothing doing. But now I *know*: something touched me during the night, too. Brushed my cheek, and more—left me twisted in my sheets, too. It was no delusion.

As I sit and smoke my fourth cigarette of the day, I pick my way through the minefield of what I like to call my consciousness. Some crap is always on the edge of exploding, and if it should all blow at once—all the events, say, of the last six months or so—it would leave a Paul-sized crater where I used to be. Should I confide more in Brian? He already knows what a mess I am, but he doesn't know...everything. *I* don't know everything. Does anybody?

Not that he doesn't *think* he knows everything. *How smug he sounds, calling me into his office on the first floor, just beyond the living room. "Come on in, Paul."*

*His bare chest is coated with curly red hair, and I know that under the desk he's naked as well. Out of sight, maybe, but I can smell his hard dick. It sets me to salivating.*

*"How old are you, Paul?"*

*"Uh...forty-five. I think."*

*"You realize your life may be two-thirds over? Two-thirds! Think of it!"*

*"I guess I'd rather think of it as half over. That's assuming I'll live to be 90, which, I admit, isn't too likely...." I'm mumbling. I hate when I mumble in front of Brian, it makes me feel like a bratty kid who's been brought before the principal.*

*"Whether it's half or two-thirds, Paul, the key word is 'over.' What are you going to do with what you've got left?"*

*His blue eyes are so bright; they are (a) his most prominent feature, followed by (b) his curly ginger mustache and (c) his Adam's apple, like a tonsure among the bristles his razor didn't quite reach. From there my* eyes slip easily down his chest. His nipples are hard, and why wouldn't they be, it must be twenty below outside and this is far from being the warmest room in the house. If I pressed my palm against the window-pane near his right shoulder it would probably stick, fast-frozen. Just the thought of it makes my hand cold, I slide it under my thigh as I stare at that perky right nipple and try to decide, for the hundredth time, if it has a telltale hole from an old piercing.

"Look, Paul," he says when I am obviously at a loss for words. "Look. Is this what you want?" With a push against the floor he sends his chair rolling back, and I have to stand up now to see that he is indeed sitting there naked. He spreads his knees, lifts his pelvis. His hard cock strains against his flat, hairy belly; his balls are tight and wrinkled, his scrotum reacting to the chill in the air. His hands with their long, sensitive fingers appear on either side of his bush, framing the goods. "Is this what you want?"

Drooling, I watch a delicate finger trace the length of his cock. His other hand appears beneath his balls, and they respond, descending in the warmth of his palm. Making a circle of his thumb and forefinger, he slides it over his shaft, moving up and down like a magician proving that the audience volunteer has no strings holding him up. He is not quite jerking himself off, just keeping enough contact to ensure that his cock stays its hardest. "Look, Paul. Take a good look." His fingers move across his balls, poking and tickling them while his other hand takes a firmer grip on his shaft. "Is this what you want?"

My dick is speaking for me, pitching a tent in my sweatpants.

"Or how about this?" He lifts his knees, raising them nearly to his shoulders. While I can't quite see his asshole, that's clearly where the tip of his middle finger is headed, inserting itself as his tongue barely protrudes from his mouth, as if the two are connected. "How about it, Paul? This is all there is, isn't it? The be-all and end-all. You'd give up your whole life for it. In fact, you already have."

Now I ask again, as I light cigarette number five: Does anyone know everything?

As if in answer the doorknob rattles. When the door swings open I expect to see Brian, hunchbacked with guilt, fitting a cigarette to his lips. Instead I see a cigarette, but the man it's attached to is Kent. He's startled to see me, his eyebrows go up—or rather eyebrow, for it's

19

more like a single straight line hooding both eyes. Ordinarily I like the feral look of excess hair in a few well-chosen places, but right now it only makes me nervous.

"Sorry," he says.

It takes me a moment to respond. "That's all right" is what finally comes out, though the pause before it makes it sound like a lie. "I just came in," I explain, "to look for a book." Yet it must be obvious, from the pack of cigs beside me and the butts in the ashtray, that I came here to smoke and smoke and smoke.

Kent doesn't seem fazed by my awkwardness. He nods, lips his cigarette and lights it, and I'm lost, watching him. No sultry jazz musician ever handled his mouthpiece the way Kent handles a cigarette. He takes a drag, rolls the taste around with his tongue and lets it go, his lips puckering the smoke into a thin line like steam escaping through a fissure. He nods, as if in silent agreement with his coffin nail, takes another drag and exhales through his nose, blinking rapidly. Finally he looks at me again, takes a step in my direction. Then another. My back stiffens against the chair—*What am I afraid of?*—and I think I might actually cry out till I see he's only heading for the ashtray by my right elbow.

"Sorry to interrupt you," he says, mixing his ash with mine.

"Oh, no, not at all. I was just…." What? Haven't I already told him I was looking for a book? I stare at my lap, but my eyes refuse to focus. Do I even know how to read?

"I'm moving in tonight," he says. "Just thought I'd look around a bit more."

I smile, or try to, as his bright blue eyes zero in on mine. "Sure. Fine. Welcome." Did that sound friendly? And why is he *still* looking into my eyes, even as he takes another drag? Finally I have to look away, my face flushing again for no reason. We're just a couple of guys having a conversation, no big deal. It happens all the time around here.

Except that it doesn't. Not like this. Even when I first met Todd and Davy and Aaron and Dwight, there was nothing like what I'm feeling now—as if I've not only *thought* of doing wrong, but have already done it. And Kent knows.

20

That's it! Kent *knows*. He knows that something brushed my cheek in the night, and then....

And then there were two bodies, and a lot of grappling under the sheets, as if we were trying to catch a mouse, not each other. Hands that hadn't felt another male in ages stumbled upon dimly remembered erogenous zones. The clumsiness, the desperation, the accidental roughness was part of a thrill that did not, could not last long once hands found hard cocks, hot and slippery, achingly touchy. The explosion that followed was potent and copious, I thought the sheets would melt, the air ignite.

Then there was my door closing gently, and bare feet crossing the hall, scurrying off to...where?

Kent can see all of this in my eyes, I know it. So I ask him, silently, *Where? Who? Which door closed softly in the night?* But he only smokes, and stares, and reads me like the books I'm feigning interest in. It's time for another effort to make all this seem natural, but as seconds tick by the chance to redeem the moment moves at warp speed, out of sight. He crushes out his cigarette and says, "Okay, see you later...Paul? Is that right?"

I nod. "Paul." The name that sounds like a funeral bell. "See you, Kent."

The door is about to close behind him when he pauses again. "Say, can I ask you something?"

To pose that question is *already* asking something, a pet peeve of mine. But I try to put on a bright smile. "Of course."

"That guy who left recently? Dwight?"

I don't know why, but his question disappoints me. I guess I expected something more personal. Had a good answer, too: *Six inches, Kent. Versatile, yes, extremely so. I swallow, too. Always have. In for a penny, in for a pound.* "What about Dwight?"

"Did you know him? I mean, did you get to know him before he left?"

*Sucking Dwight's chest hair while he moans, polishing his off-center knob till he begs me to bring him off.* "A little, I suppose." Enough to know that Dwight had a problem. Not that half the world isn't disturbed—no, three-quarters of the world, at least. With Dwight it was

21

anger. "We're all angry," I told him once, knowing that the anger that had once motivated me was gone, leaving me hollow.

*I rock him in my arms as he cries. "I can't do this anymore," he says. "I can't, I can't."*

*"Baby, hush." I hold his scrotum, warm his balls in the palm of my hand. A final pearl of cum leaks from his slit. "You can do anything you want, I don't mind."*

*He nearly chokes on tears. "That's not what I mean!" Heaving himself up, he turns toward the door as if he might step like this, naked and still semi-erect, into the hallway. Instead he raises his pale fist and slams his knuckles into the wall. "Shit!"*

*"Baby, baby." Arms encircling him from behind, my fingertips soothing his tits. "Let me sell you a pardon. I'm the only one who can, you know...."*

*His fist slams the wall again. The ancient plaster crumbles, but that's not what I'm worried about. "Honey, don't," I tell him. "That's your jackoff hand, you don't want to...."*

Kent voice intrudes. He's still questioning me, but it's hard to follow. It's too much like having a real conversation, I'm not used to it. "Excuse me?" I ask.

"I asked you if you saw him leave the house. Dwight."

"I don't see...."

"On the day he left. Did you actually see him go?"

"Well, no, I don't think I did." Actually I know I didn't. No one did, we didn't even know he was gone till Brian announced it at breakfast. "Why do you ask?"

"Oh, no reason."

As if such a question could fail to have a reason. I'd sneer at him if he wasn't so cute, standing there with his little package pointed at me. *"Mind if I ask you a question, Kent?" "Why, not at all. Eight inches. Get your trick towel ready, I blow a wad like you've never seen. But you have to fuck me for a good hour first."* He seems about to shut the door, then pauses again.

"Have you ever seen *anybody* leave the house?" he asks.

Well, I've seen Brian leave the house, and come back, too. You can smell the cold air clinging to his parka. And Riley, our gopher and handyman—he comes and goes, too. But it's too late to give an answer like that. I've let a pause slip in, a long enough one to reveal that I know what Kent's really asking. Which leads me, somehow, to Chaucer.

I want to tell Kent about *The Pardoner's Tale* and what it's about: three guys, three 'rioters' in a tavern, getting drunk as usual, when they learn that a friend has been killed by a thief named Death. They go off in search of Death, to give him what for, and an old man directs them to a tree, telling them they'll find Death underneath it. But instead they find piles of gold under the tree. They decide to carry it off, but not until it gets dark. One of them goes back into town for some food and drink. While he's gone the other two start plotting: when their friend gets back with the provisions they'll kill him, so they can split the gold two ways. And when the guy gets back, they do. Kill him. But then they drink the wine, and what do you know, the guy had poisoned it so he'd have all the gold to himself. So they all end up dead. It's just like they were told, there's Death under the tree.

I want to tell him, but I can't. He's so young. And Dwight's the only one who's left since I came here, so how could I know...?

"Okay," he says, sounding as if he's humoring me. "Okay, Paul. See you later."

Wait, I want to call after him. I didn't tell you everything after all. Somebody keeps coming into my room at night. It's not a dream or a fantasy, it's real. But Kent has closed the door behind him.

Now Brian comes in, his cheeks still flushed from being outside. Agitated, he bounces on his heels a few times, *and just when I think he's going to take out a cigarette he takes out his dick instead. This is made easier by the fact that he never wears underwear, though I feel like asking him, Gosh Bri, doesn't that ever cause a problem, I mean what do you do about those embarrassing pecker tracks on your jeans? But as usual he starts talking first. "You want this, Paul? You want it? Tell me how bad you want it." His fist moves so fast he's going to tear that big dick right off, I've never seen him so horny, his prick so hard. He's going to jizz any second,* which doesn't stop me from getting out of my chair and walking right through him.

**It's** almost midnight. In the room next to mine Kent is pumping seed for all he's worth, masturbating so furiously that he can't sit or

23

lie or stand still. He's reeling about the room, crashing into furniture, panting and cussing as his shoulder nicks a wall or he stubs his toe on the rug. Throwing himself to the floor, thrusting his hips in the air. Of course I can't see this but I can hear it and picture it. We've all been through the same thing. He's draining himself of spooge, he'll find it hanging from the ceiling in the morning, obscuring the corners like cobwebs. It's a strange ritual, because you can't really drain the body of anything: given the minimum daily requirements of nourishment and oxygen and warmth, it will just keep on making more. But it's the symbolism of the act that counts, and I understand symbols very well.

I have in front of me the edition of *The Canterbury Tales* that I took from the den, illustrated with faded woodcuts of the pilgrims, including the dour, elongated Pardoner. At one time his profession had been an honest one; the Church even commissioned folks to roam hither and yon, selling pardons for sins. But by Chaucer's time the profession had become corrupt—so much so that George Lyman Kittredge called the Pardoner "the one lost soul among the pilgrims." Irredeemable, because he's not only a cheat and a liar but also, it turns out, a homosexual—at least most scholars think so. There's the telling detail that he travels with a male companion, and also he's referred to as a "mare"—slang for you-know-what. Plus he looks like a fairy, a little too light in his medieval loafers.

So I feel for the Pardoner, who pardons others falsely and slavishly while clutching his own sin tight to his chest. He keeps me company as I make this effort to remember, to create a record for myself alone, an understanding of what's been happening to me over the last several months.

This afternoon I woke from a long but unfulfilling nap to a winter twilight that was just a few shades lighter than midnight. I sat up, sensing not only the house but the whole little town settling around me. Creaking footsteps in the kitchen, the wind whistling through a crack in a funhouse wall. Even the sea made its presence felt, the cold surf dragging like slush across the sand. Heightened senses for sure, thanks to a dream that wasn't the usual obscure teaser but vivid as life itself—a life I've known elsewhere. I listened, I crept to the window, looked out at the back yard with its few bare oaks. I closed my eyes and another scene appeared, as clear as Eric's face and voice had been as he'd called, *That's not true, Paul!* It was the sea I was looking at—not a winter sea but an autumn one, viewed from the window of…a diner. I sat alone in a booth, eating pancakes. They were real diner pancakes, hot from the griddle, topped with blueberries in a deliriously thick syrup, like pie filling—hell, it probably was pie filling. The sugar high mingled with a caffeine rush as I refilled my mug from the thermal pot at my elbow.

That was it. No action, and no meaning, really, just a snapshot from my mostly unremembered recent life. But it gave me hope that I might be able to piece my story together, after all. Throughout the evening, a dull Sunday evening of dinner and playing cards, pieces of the past kept floating past my eyes, adding to my conviction.

It's a story full of reeling that I have to tell, like the jackoff scene next door, with more than its share of stubbed toes and bruises. And other things, things I can only trick out vaguely from here and now. Perhaps the most persistent is a restless shadow in my memory—something emptied of life that nevertheless keeps moving, senselessly, rhythmically, in the darkness.

# Chapter 2

**Yesterday** morning, sometime after breakfast, I found myself walking along the second floor hallway of East Oak House without quite knowing how I got there. I was sitting in the den one minute, and the next I was staring at one of the watercolor landscapes that struggle to break up the pattern of the oatmeal-colored wallpaper. These skips and pops in the vinyl of my daily life are a pain in the ass, but Brian says they're to be expected. Anyone making a major life change, etc.

One thing I haven't discussed with Brian or the others is the ache that I sometimes feel—a tenderness, a soreness. All this talk about healing is enough to convince you that you really do have a wound throbbing away inside. Even Brian feels pain, the pain of old memories, the sear of regret: it's there in his eyes. But my achiness—it's as if I've got something in me, not from the past, but from the future. A message yet to be delivered creeping through my innards.

How long have I been at East Oak House? Time is de-emphasized here; the yardstick that measures every move in the outside world is taken out only occasionally. No calendars hang, few clocks tick. I haven't been wearing my watch…come to think of it, where is my watch? And whose hand was that, this morning, pressing against the wallpaper? Why, it was my own hand, holding me up, bravely trying

27

to steady me as the carpet shifted beneath my feet. A moment of
wooziness, that's all. Still, it was the strangest hand I'd ever seen, so
pale and bloated, a crustacean without its shell.

Kent is with us now, making five of us instead of four—six, counting Brian—and relieving me of the duty of being The New Guy. I'm
part of Brian-Todd-Aaron-Davy-Paul, and Kent is the interloper.
This morning Davy's at the stove scrambling eggs, plying his spatula
against the skillet like an ice scraper. I take orange juice and pass the
pitcher to Aaron, whose hand shakes as he pours. He's wearing a pale
yellow sweatshirt I don't remember seeing before. It makes his blond
hair look a little darker than usual, with a reddish cast. His eyebrows,
too, are reddish, and his eyes, the tip of his nose. A cold?

Kent holds his hand over his glass, he doesn't want juice. *Drink,
man,* I'm thinking, *you're probably dehydrated.* Over the past few days
he's kept up the ritual masturbation, the purging of seed that's meant
to mark our first twenty-four hours here and no longer. *Ka-thwacka
thwacka thwacka* goes his headboard against my wall, and I'm thinking, Good Christ, he's making enough noise for two people, or two
rutting wildcats. But at least he's doing it in bed now. Keeping his
jizz in one place—in a jar, maybe. I tried doing that as a teen, jacking
off into one of my mother's empty prescription bottles. My cum, so
mysterious and fascinating when fresh, soon deteriorated into a thin,
bitter-smelling liquid that begged to be thrown away.

We had our night of reader's theater, Davy with his rinky-dink
Frost poem and, much more interestingly, Aaron with selections
from *Leaves of Grass.*

> *The untold want, by life and land ne'er granted....*

That line brought it back to me, the episode on the bus, the old
man on the floor. The driver and his mirrored sunglasses. I hadn't
pictured anything from the past that clearly in a long time. It practically wrecked my concentration when it came time for me to read, I
spat out Chaucer as if I had a pussful of cracker crumbs, doing no
justice to his harsh, guttural tongue. Then, of course, I had to tell the
story in today's English. "So there was death under the tree, after all,"
I concluded, and swept my eyes across a cluster of blank looks, Chaucer and Whitman being pretty much in the same ballpark with this

group. It was Todd who saved the night with his scathingly sarcastic reading from *Julius Caesar.* Tripping off his tongue, "Friends, Romans, countrymen" sounded like "Fags, rimmers, men-with-cunts…." Best of all, of course, was that he had no idea how he sounded up there. He thought he was Olivier, or at least Richard Burton, not Don Rickles. It didn't matter to me, let him have his illusions.

I sat there and thought about the untold want.

**It's** late summer, and I'm standing at the bus stop, sweating in my lightest jacket at 7:30 a.m. The sign above the bank blinks 84 degrees already. This stretch of Main Street, two blocks from the townhouse where Eric and I live, has something for everyone: besides the bank there's a drugstore, a firehouse, a sub shop, and a branch of the Public Library, all keeping a low profile in a mainly residential neighborhood. Morning traffic is sparse, pedestrians few. You can set your watch by the moment the college boy in shorts comes loping across the street to get the sub shop started up. I think of him, affectionately, as Baloney Boy.

You can also set your watch—almost—by the appearance of the Number 57 bus at the corner, making the turn onto Main like an ice skater whose routine is all technical tricks and no style. The big honker glides down the slope with an almost palpable sense of relief, hissing to a stop. I slip the pass from my shirt pocket to show the driver as I board. He nods at me and I grab an overhead bar, swinging my briefcase and gym bag in one hand for balance as the door hisses shut and the floor lurches beneath my feet. It's one of the newer buses, with tinted windows and air conditioning that works. I welcome the cool, thinly populated darkness, the feel of slippery contoured plastic under my butt. Directly behind the driver sits a blind man with a harnessed Labrador at his feet. Two women sitting behind me are trading office gossip in clipped, bitter tones.

"Of course *she'd* be the one to work late…."

"And *he'd* be the one to take credit for it."

Yes, yes, *he she, he she.* We dogleg from Main onto Ward Parkway, then back to Main again, just south of Brush Creek. The little river, ignored in most parts of Kansas City, becomes a star as it enters the Plaza district, adorned by graceful pedestrian bridges like combs in

29

a coiffure. In gratitude the river ripples and sparkles—a sight that, combined with the coolness and the gentle rocking of the bus, makes me feel I've slipped from my workaday life into a split-second vacation, and had better make the most of it.

Making the most of it means napping. Not so long ago I was in the king-size bed that Eric and I share, and the alarm startled me from a sleep I thought I'd never shake off. I shuffled to the breakfast table and sat wagging my head like an old dog over cereal and coffee—wagging alone, since Eric was sleeping in. He needs the car today for a dental appointment, so here I sit, drifting off in a half-assed fashion, picturing him in bed, rolled up into a ball, a few loose curls winging from his head.

We keep to ourselves, Eric and I.

The bus lurches to a halt at 47th Street. It's the first busy stop on the northbound route, with few passengers leaving but plenty climbing aboard. Like most of the riders they're older people, or perhaps younger ones who look older than they are. Some wear fixed smiles as they pay their fares and make their way down the aisle. Others face the task of finding a seat with wide-eyed astonishment, as if they have no idea how they've come to this, boarding a city bus at an ungodly hour. The younger—or younger-looking—men sneer at their surroundings, their eyes half-closed, lips curled. Blue-collar workers not planning on riding the bus forever, they slouch down the aisle, attractive in rough, subversive ways. Eric hates tattoos, but I'm susceptible to a well-placed panther or eagle, or those sharp, abstract designs that suggest the wearer is part animal, part plant. Then there are the pleasures of a well sculpted beard and/or mustache and/or sideburns.... No, riding the bus isn't all bad.

Not for a while, anyway. At 39th Street there's another crowd scuffling and fidgeting at the curb. They're itching for a fight, I can see it in the whites of their eyes. The women board with arms akimbo, elbows running interference as they push their large frames down the aisle. One young woman has a baby in a stroller, another has both a baby and a toddler, one in the crook of her arm and the other bouncing along behind. But if the women are more aggressive this deep into midtown, the men are less so, staring at the floor with their shoulders slumped, enduring the indignities of squeezing through narrow spaces. These men are past cockiness or surliness, past all pretense of *making the best of it*. And if some of them look strung out, all I can think is that maybe I'd be strung out too if I were in their shoes.

A few blocks from this bus stop is where Eric and I had our first apartment together, in the little neighborhood known as South-moreland. We had more friends in those days, too. Then Hal moved to Seattle and Michael to Denver, both of them seeking something new, something better than Kansas City; Tom and David pulled up stakes and left for Houston, where Tom's job had been relocated; and Faye, Eric's close friend and co-worker, died of cancer. These shock waves knocked us around as we clung to each other, settling into a trough of relative calm between jolts. And as I turned forty, then forty-one, I wasn't as sure of myself as I used to be. I started watching my back. There was something out there waiting for me, some agent of change with my name on it. I had seen the unpredictable too often not to try to factor it into my predictions.

Meanwhile our apartment complex fell on hard times, thanks to a new owner, a depraved-looking former judge. Paint peeled, steps broke, grass and weeds grew wild. By the summer of 1997 we gave up wondering why the owner didn't want to protect his investment, and started looking for a place to buy. Which is how we ended up in our small, cozy condo south of the Plaza.

And without planning to, or even wanting to, we keep to our-selves.

The bus lurches forward, and those still standing grab desperately for seats before they can be thrown off their feet. It's like a round of musical chairs, except that everyone ends up seated. The spot next to me, in fact, remains vacant. Of course my bulk takes up more than its fair share of space, but that can't be the only reason why I'm sitting next to an empty spot. Maybe I look snobbish in my jacket and tie. Or maybe I look like a salesman ready to push some long-term disability coverage on the first stooge who comes my way. It all becomes moot when we reach the next stop, where the number of new passengers means I'm sure to get a seatmate, however reluctant.

The old man who slides in beside me wears cast-off clothing, a light-colored windbreaker and green polyester slacks that expose

31

his thin, bare ankles. His longish white hair, combed straight back, has streaks of color I can only call phlegmy, as if someone has used him for a spittoon. His eyes and nose are runny, his upper lip slick and shiny. He looks straight ahead, without a glance in my direction. Which is all very well except that I can't return the favor, can't ignore him as he ignores me.

The truth is, he smells. There's nothing ordinary about his smell, either; it's not the body odor familiar to public transit riders everywhere. I can't put a name to it, partly because it's not constant. I'll get a whiff—enough to send my eyes rolling up into my head—and then a brief respite, perhaps due to the vagaries of the ventilation system. Then, *wham!* I'm holding my breath, looking out the window, expecting the Four Horsemen of the Apocalypse to come charging down the grassy knoll near Linwood Boulevard. *Something* apocalyptic is coming, surely—something to warrant this end-of-the-world stink, this sulfur-and-brimstone abomination. Death itself is in the air, the death of something that had smelled bad even when it was alive. Meanwhile my seatmate sits and sniffles and blinks his watery blue eyes like any other passenger. Studying his face as often as decency and the absence of whiffs allow, I decide he's in a normal frame of mind—*oriented times three*, as they say at the Clinic where I work. He's even better off than me, in the sense that he's not asphyxiating.

Soon, having traveled some of the longest blocks of my bus-riding life, I'm mouth breathing, and not being very subtle about it, when my stop comes into view, near the corner of 31st and Main. Thank God! I hope my seatmate will sense my stirring and swing his legs around so I won't have to step over them and perhaps brush up against…. But he doesn't move when I do, not even when I'm halfway out of my seat, and his eyes are closed. "Excuse me, sir," I say once, and then again, crouching painfully, half-sitting, half-standing, as the bus begins to slow down for the stop. Oh God, I'm going to have to *touch* him. Should I prod him with the blunt edge of my briefcase? That wouldn't look very nice, would it? The proper thing would be a tap, just a one-fingered tap on his shoulder.

It's not anything to do with the other passengers, the driver, or the gently swaying bus that causes what happens next. It's my finger, just the pressure of my finger on the man's shoulder, that sends him crashing to the floor. A collective *gasp* rises around me as I let my briefcase and gym bag fall, nearly tripping myself up as I try to get to the old man, to see what he's doing down there, as if some harmless explanation might be at hand—a sudden yen on his part, for example, to stretch out in the aisle for a more comfortable snooze. Kneeling beside him, I shout at the knees and pantlegs of the curious closing in, with their suffocating body heat: "Get back! Give him some air!" Talk about foul—how *hideous* these people are, so desperate to get a look at someone collapsed in the aisle. I'm desperate too, for more than a look; I want him to *be all right*, and if the laying on of hands will help I'm ready to put mine wherever they have to go to pull him upright again. Yet I can't touch him. Small enough to lie on his side in the aisle with room to spare, his knees drawn up and spine rounded in the fetal position, with his left arm and hand extended over his head, finger pointing toward the rear of the bus, he looks…*peaceful*. His face is relaxed, eyes closed, a thread of drool trailing from his lower lip to the filthy rubber mat.

"Stand back! Please!" The driver, a stocky black man in mirrored sunglasses, sounds a lot more official than I did. Looks it, too, in his blue Metro uniform with the peaked cap which, like the sunglasses, adds to his inscrutable look, like Claude Rains in *The Invisible Man*. But does he truly understand what's happening? Before I know it I'm babbling: "This man needs help, he fell, he's lying here, what's wrong, what can we do…?" I'm ready to perform mouth-to-mouth, clap electrodes to his chest, use my fountain pen as a tracheotomy tool. I'm even ready to shove the driver out of the way, for he's on the floor now, too close to the old man, giving him no room to breathe.

Before I can say or do anything more the driver stands, wipes his palms on his uniformed hips. "He's gone."

"What do you mean, he's not gone, he's right…oh." I sink down from my half-crouching position—which was not, come to think of it, much different from the old man's—into my seat again. The driver makes a sign—crossing himself in an abbreviated way, or blessing the body, or just waving off the old man's stink—and returns to his seat, where the radio is squawking. No need to tell others to stand back now, a dead body isn't as interesting as one that's alive and suffering. Maybe, by not even breathing, I can turn back the clock a measly

33

fifteen minutes, and the old man will still be alive. Then I can act, call for help before it's too late. I'll be able to *change the future*, the way idiots in science-fiction potboilers are always trying to do. But dead is dead, that fragile strand of saliva hanging from his lips tells the whole story. It occurs to me to say a few words—another convention from popular culture—and the words that come to mind are by Walt Whitman:

> *The untold want, by life and land ne'er granted,*
> *Now, Voyager, sail thou forth, to seek and find.*

These lines get quoted quite often in one gay context or another, and why not? They have an excellent gay pedigree: written by Walt, plus lending the title to a terrific Bette Davis picture. Whether the pedigree is relevant or not, the words seem appropriate. An old man who has died filthy and stinking on the floor of a city bus must have borne more than one untold want.

The driver gets off the radio and comes toward me again, standing a respectful few seats away. "You don't have to stay here if you don't want to," he says.

"Well," I tell him, "nobody *has* to stay here." I look toward the back of the bus, to the others who, like me, can't just abandon a man who has just died. But at some point, whenever the driver opened the doors, every single solitary soul fled. Through the window I see that my fellow travelers have crossed Main and are now standing on the southbound side of the street. Where do they think they're going? Back home, to take the day off? *Every-man's-death-diminishes-me* has become *great-excuse-to-call-in-sick*. I can hardly do the same, I'm only two blocks from the Clinic, where I have HIV education slides to prepare. Yet I can't move. I look to the driver, who seems alarmed, or at least his eyebrows do, furrowing above his sunglasses for the first time: maybe he has a dead body *and* a nutcase on his hands.

"It's not your fault, you know," he says.

"I know that." Am I snapping at him? "I just happened to be here. Just sitting beside him, that's all. It could have happened to anybody."

The driver nods, backing slowly toward his seat. His sunglasses keep staring. The part of my mind that's not quite working knows that, if it were functioning normally, I'd be finding this driver attractive, I'd be mentally undressing him by now. His uniform gives him the kind of package that unwraps easily. Those Mapplethorpe photos, the black men with the dicks hanging out of their pants.... Poor funny mind! I look again at the fallen man, who probably lost control of his bowels at the moment of death; but who's to say he hadn't lost control long ago, there might well be a diaper under the swollen seat of his pants. Something had to account for that stench which, truth to tell, is more becoming to a dead man than a live one. The stench that is now telling me, *Go away. Put this behind you.* I look toward the driver again; he's in his seat now, but his mirrored eyes are reflected in the rearview, aimed at me. How many times have I seen a bus driver look up like that, searching for a troublemaker, a disturber of the peace, a nutcase?

I get off the bus. Behind it, a light blue Taurus with a flashing amber light on the dash pulls to the curb: a Metro road supervisor's car. An incident report would be filled out, an ambulance is already on its way. I drag my feet toward the crosswalk, half expecting someone to call me back, to re-establish my role as crucial to the scene, a key to closure.

Maybe this is how you become a nutcase: you begin to believe, *sincerely* believe that everything happening in the world is happening to *you. Nerts,* says the world, *it's all in your head.* And you find yourself explaining, right back at the world, that everything *really* is happening to you. Otherwise why would you cling so to events, and why would they return the favor, coming back to you in the middle of the night when you close your eyes and hope for sleep and instead see an old man tipping over, his unforgettably round shoulders tilting toward death? Why would you feel that it's your own familiar world tipping over, crashing to the floor because the future has tapped you on the shoulder?

Why, Walt? Why, Bette? Why, why, why?

**It's** after breakfast now and I'm in the den, smoking and undressing Kent with my eyes. He hasn't yet taken to wearing sweatpants like the rest of us; he showed up this morning in the tight jeans he came in with, walking like a guy who's saddlesore, picking delicately at his crotch when he thought we weren't looking. Of course he was pale,

35

who wouldn't be after spraying so much jizz around—enough cum to amaze even him, the boy-toy of New England. Looking around his room he probably thought, Christ, I've slimed the place, it reeks like an old porno theater where the seats don't get cleaned.

It's not hard to picture Kent naked: his trim torso, with enough definition to make it memorable. Big, sensitive nipples—why not?—and a mischievous furrow of hair leading from his pecs down to his navel and picking up again below that, beelining to his bush—a creeping Charlie. Yeah, they call it a treasure trail too, or a nature trail, but creeping Charlie is the name I prefer, I don't know why. Oh yes, he's easing himself into an armchair, definitely sore, the tender rim of his German helmet probably chafed, and I'm sending him telepathic messages of sympathy and advice: more lube, plenty of it. And look into some sweatpants. Please.

"So," I ask him, "how are you settling in?"

He winces again, shifting to get his cigarettes from his pocket. The one he shakes loose is a bit crushed, curved like a half-erection. He lights it, takes a drag, lets it out, picks a fleck of tobacco from his tongue. "Did you feel funny," he asks, "when you first came here?"

"I feel funny every day," I tell him, trying to suppress a laugh. Just then I catch, even through the combined smoke of our cigarettes, the slightly brackish scent of male skin and seed. Maybe that house rule is wrong, the one about no cologne or scented after shave. There are more seductive aromas by far. As my nostrils dilate I ask him, "How do *you* feel funny?"

He shivers, as from a sudden chill. "Oh, it's nothing." he hugs his upper arms, briefly buries his nose in the fuzz of his forearms. I could watch these antics all day. "I just wonder if everything here really is the way it seems."

Okay, so he's figured me out. He's read my thoughts. He knows I've stripped him naked. Maybe he knows about the dreams I've been having, too. Can it show on my face that it happened again last night—the sudden heart-thumping flurry, the clawing and grasping that leaves no marks, except…well, yes, there were three faint red lines on my shoulder this morning, but so what? Who's to say I didn't scratch myself sometime in the night? As for the sheets, so I have wet dreams, so what? There's nothing wrong with that. Perfectly natural.

So I can return Kent's gaze without cracking. No, he doesn't know my thoughts—or what I've written about him in the Dirty Gray Notebook.

The scene takes place in this room, between the two of us, and it begins with a confession: *"I can't self-suck anymore," he says.*

*"Beg pardon?" I ask.*

*"I used to be able to self-suck."*

*"I've seen pictures of that. It always looks a little strained, too awkward to be all that pleasurable."*

*"No, man, it's a trip, sucking yourself off! You ever try it?"*

*"Well, this is probably the kind of thing where size matters, and since I can barely find my dick with both hands...."*

*"I'm just not that limber anymore. It ain't fair."* He gets out of his chair, pulls up his t-shirt with one hand and shoves the other down the front of his pants. *"Shit, I'm getting hard again, just thinking about it."*

*Okay, it* would *be hot to suck yourself off. Never mind how you'd look, curled up like a caterpillar that's been poked with a stick. And not to be able to do it anymore.... I slide forward in my chair. "Bring it on over here."*

*The quickest decisions men make have to do with sex, you can measure them in nanoseconds. He pulls out his double handful of dick and I see how chafed he is, poor thing, I was right about his German helmet. This calls for great delicacy, and a mouth that's less dry than mine at the moment. I raise my coffee cup and take in a lukewarm mouthful, the dregs from the bottom of the pot—a funky rinse if ever there was one, but it's not like I'm trying to kill germs. Kent walks toward me with his jeans around his knees, it's impossible to manage a walk like that without looking silly but damned if he doesn't almost pull it off. His engorging dick is moving faster than his legs, reaching me l-o-o-o-n-g before the rest of him does. I reach around, take a firm grip on his asscheeks and guide him in. His relief is immediate, this is what he needs, a wet (who cares if it's coffee) mouth that knows how to suck. His knees buckle, he damn near falls on top of me but I'm with him, sliding down so he can brace his hands against the back of the overstuffed chair. Now I'm the one who's nearly curled up like a caterpillar, but who gives a fuck, I've got dick in my mouth, a real lip-stretcher, and the smell of his bush up my nose. My left hand encircles his balls as my right tenderly grips*

37

*the length of shaft that won't fit in my mouth. His thighs shake as if he's on one of those exercise machines with the vibrating belt. He tastes, not surprisingly, like the sea—the brine and mucus of that life-giving stew.*

*Amazing how much cum he's got in him. I expected a small, somewhat dry load, the kind you get in the morning from a guy who's been coming all night, but whoosh, he's gushing, my mouth brimming with incoming tide.*

*"Holy fuck," he says. "That was great."*

*Wiping my chin, I look up at him. "Okay, so now you know. I'll never be an ex-queer."*

*Carefully he puts himself back together, handling his privates as if they're made of glass. "So fucking what? There's no such thing as an ex-queer."*

**It's** time for group. The living room is big, but not too big: we have to spread out, we need our space. Todd and Davy are on the sofa, but at opposite ends of it, a safe expanse of rust-colored cushion between them. Kent sits like a teenager, one leg thrown over the arm of his overstuffed chair. Brian is on the piano bench, facing us, his back to the keys. Aaron sits in a Boston rocker like the one my mother just had to have after JFK was killed. It doesn't look comfortable, its seat too close to the floor, its back too spiny, but then Aaron doesn't look comfortable either, he rarely does.

"Well?" Brian asks. "Any dreams last night?"

I haven't contributed in a while, though there's that one dream I've had a few times. *Uh-oh, watch out,* my inner censor is saying. But could there really be any harm....

Now everyone's looking at me. Did I say something?

"A recurring dream, Paul?" Brian asks. There's a slight edge to his voice, as if he's really asking why, if it's a recurring dream, I haven't mentioned it before.

"Well," I backpedal, "I think it's a recurring dream, but there's always so little I remember afterwards." It doesn't sound promising, especially to me, but everyone is still looking, there's no way not to move forward. "It's about...I'm on the beach at Two Piers, and it's night, and I'm not alone but I don't know who's with me. We're down by the pier, and there's only the moonlight—too dark to see much of

38

anything, really. Then suddenly there's something close to me. A dark shape moves, pushed against a piling by the waves. Somehow I know it's a body, a dead body."

"Wow, that's creepy enough," Davy says.

"Okay," Brian says. "So what would you change about this dream, if you could step in and change it?"

"Well, I'd like to know, first of all, who it is who's with me. I'd either want to find that out or not have the second person there at all."

"If you could see the person who's with you," Brian asks, "would you know who it is? Or is it a stranger?"

It's hard to recover that dream-feeling, like trying to recall a taste that's too delicate for memory. "If I could just turn around in that dream, I think I'd know who it was."

"Maybe you don't really want to know," Aaron says.

"Another question," Brian says, "just as important, if not more so—who is the dead body?" We sit in suspense, the five of us, for Brian has asked the question as if he also has the answer. "I'm going to surprise you, Paul," he says, scooting forward on the piano bench. "I'm going to tell you that I think the dead body is yourself."

Why am I not surprised?

**Later** in the afternoon I'm lurking in the second floor hallway, hoping to catch Todd and Davy at something. Okay, I admit I didn't really *see* anything the other day. Neither has said a word to me about it, or acted as if anything at all happened. Which only encourages speculation. Maybe Todd reminded Davy of a former lover, or vice-versa. Maybe their moment was *so* sudden that they don't know themselves what caused it. Or maybe it was a planned thing, right there in the open, the chances of getting caught adding to the thrill.

Todd and Davy were only silhouettes in the light from the window as they faced each other, down at the end of the hallway, and it was impossible to tell what their hands were doing. But it wasn't what they were doing that gave them away, it was what followed, their hasty cover-up when I appeared at the top of the stairs. Todd had definitely had his right hand down the front of his sweatpants, I could tell that much, making the unmistakable gesture of adjusting his crotch. And Davy...Davy was standing a little too close to that gesture. Always

primed for sexual speculation, my imagination buzzed like a vibra-
tor in overdrive. Had they been playing with each other? Comparing
sizes? Had they even *gone down on* each other, right there in the
hallway? It had to have been a sudden urge for them to take such
a risk, but what inspired it? Had they been giving each other come-
hither looks that I'd been too dense to notice? Wouldn't Brian have
noticed?

I moved toward them, those two transgressors with the very
shape of guilt in their postures, but not to confront them. I went only
as far as the door to my room, giving them a little wave as I passed
through.

I didn't wait to get my own thrill out of that surprise sighting: as
soon as I was in my room with the door closed I threw myself on the
bed and shoved my sweatpants and briefs down to my ankles. Just
now there were two guys out in the hall *doing it,* fer Chrissakes, my
fevered imagination cried, dictating my next Dirty Gray Notebook
entry:

*In Davy's room, Todd strips off his sweatshirt. How often Davy has
admired that chest, Todd barefooting it down the hall to the shower
with a towel wrapped around his waist; or on that morning when they
were dismantling the Christmas tree and Todd suddenly stripped off
his shirt as he did just now. Stands there with his hair ruffled, blinking
rapidly, and in two quick steps Davy's there, burying his face in Todd's
chest hair, running a hand down his spine, finding the waistband of his
sweatpants and push-pulling them down, his underwear too. Todd's
cock springing up, Todd prying off his sneakers and stepping free of his
clothes. Davy in a spell, can't even raise his hands toward his own shirt,
it's Todd who finally pulls it over Davy's head. Chests pressed together, Todd's tongue in Davy's mouth, energized cock whipping at Davy's
crotch. It's up to Todd to stop and slide Davy's sweats down too. Cocks
nuzzling each other like friendly dogs. Davy all dizzy, nearly losing it
on his way to the unmade bed, not understanding why he can't even
walk till he realizes his sweatpants are around his ankles. On the bed
now, on his back, and Todd takes hold of the sneakers and pulls them
off, then the sweatpants, and he's looking at Davy naked and saying
"Oh Jesus Christ." Todd sinking down against the edge of the bed, taking
Davy's cock in his mouth, and Davy can't move, can only be moved, put*

to use, *sucked and finger-fucked till he starts to writhe, to beg Todd for more, more and more and more....*

Now, Paul, reach under the bed and get your jackoff towel, quick. Good thinking, because in a few seconds I'm coming like a fountain. When I'm finally done I'm staring at my handful of hot jam and recalling how, for a period of some years, I used to eat my cum after jacking off. My wide reading in erotica told me other guys did it—some even kept their loads in baggies in the freezer, just right for midnight snacks—and it never seemed strange until now. These days I have no taste for my own spooge. So it goes with sexual behaviors, appearing and disappearing like sun rays on a partly cloudy day, testaments to the randomness of the universe.

After an orgasm-induced nap I wake with a strange memory pulling at me. Oh yes, that business when we were taking down the Christmas tree. Todd and Davy and Aaron and Dwight and Brian and me, about a week and a half after New Year's. The artificial tree had an odd shape, much wider than it was tall, and an odd color, an attempt at blue spruce that looked more like a weathered gray. The wire branches were hooked at the ends, the hooks fitting into holes drilled in the upright wooden pole; and the rule that things are easier to tear down than to put up didn't apply here, since each branch had to be wrestled from its hole, just as it had had to be wrestled in. It seemed like there were a thousand of those feisty branches, and tugging them free was hot work in that front room, the one spot in the house that tends to be overheated. I was sweating myself, quite uncomfortably, when Todd suddenly straightened up and pulled his sweatshirt off.

41

The rest of us looked up from where we knelt on the floor, and we all must have had the same look on our faces, prompting Todd to say, "Well, it's *hot* in here," as he tossed his sweatshirt aside. Then we all looked down at the same moment. It was comical, not only afterward but at the time, at least for me. It wasn't as if we hadn't all seen each other partly naked before, wrapped in towels on our way to the shower. What made this occasion different was—well, what was it? At the time Todd wore, not the usual sweatpants, but bluejeans with a thick leather belt, and there was...something aggressive in his half-nakedness. My eyes itched from wanting to look at him, to steal the longest possible glances at his torso. His nipples were medium-sized, firm, with playful black hairs that spread upward and fanned out, making fields of his pecs, places to suck and lick. We were all glancing at him, even Brian, while Todd just stood there with his hands on his hips, somewhat embarrassed and yet, judging by the slight outward thrust of his chest, cocky too.

"It *is* warm in here," Brian said, and he peeled off his t-shirt, no doubt aiming to defuse the situation by baring his own soft-look-ing chest, its tiny nipples a deep pink, the few hairs that sprouted around them much lighter than the hair on his head. Not to seem prudish, Davy and Aaron and I took our shirts off too. No one was going to get turned on by me unless he had a vanilla-pudding fetish, but that didn't diminish the pleasure I took in watching the others. Todd was a stud, no question, but Davy, like his Florentine namesake, had definition and symmetry and the smoothness of cool, lovingly handled marble. Aaron, in his blond bearish way, was more sturdy than studly, but wasn't that what you wanted sometimes, someone you could throw yourself onto and wrap yourself up in without wor-rying about scratching the finish? And Brian—well, Brian was Brian, untouchable and, in so many ways, unfathomable. Who knew what kind of lover he'd been in the old days, before…? *Before sanity set in,* was how he'd put it.

Dwight was wearing sweatpants with one of the button-down shirts he favored—because, I was certain, they allowed him to bare a wedge of chest hair. It was so pale, that hair, and so abundant that his torso, as he slowly unbuttoned his shirt and stripped it free, seemed wrapped in cobwebs. The glances that we shot each other tried des-perately to be matter-of-fact, but fell so wide of that mark that I ex-pected to hear them thudding against the oak floor. I turned away, finally, when I felt myself getting hard.

My memories of Christmas Day itself are vague, like my memo-ries of the days before that. Come to think of it, I'm becoming not very good at remembering, each afternoon, what happened to me that morning. I do remember talking a walk late on Christmas after-noon—the only time, I think, that we were all outside together. Snow fell the night before, the fresh powder lay undisturbed on the street. It was a gray day, and yellow lights shone from the other houses, all of them, like East Oak House, large and set well back from the street. It was so cold my nose felt like it was in a vise. I couldn't even breathe through it, I was huffing the zero-degree air with an open mouth. My jacket was warm but not warm enough, I had a heavier winter coat somewhere…and my gloves, where were they? With a start I realized I had left Kansas City for Maine in October, and had brought some cold-weather gear with me but not the heaviest kind that I would wear in the depths of winter. Was it *possible* that I had been in Maine this long? And how long was it that I'd been at East Oak House? Lost in these speculations, I was barely aware of the others, how they kicked through the powder and made brave, lame jokes about the weather, as if we weren't the loneliest group of people in this lonely little town.

**G r o u p** again, and time for Kent to tell his story. He's sitting Indian-style on the sofa, a huge mug of tea on the end table next to him. He must have nuked it good, it's still steaming. He bites his lower lip, shakes his head. "I still don't know if I can talk about it," he says.

"But it's important that you do," Brian says. "Remember, we're not here to judge. Take all the time you need."

Kent takes a sip from his mug. "Well." Sucking in his lower lip, biting it again. If he's not careful he'll get that enviable beestung look. Finally he says, "I had…a brother."

Oh-oh. Already things don't look good. Naturally I'm excited— I've heard the others' stories *way* too often. Kent is sighing, adjusting his seating position, gulping tea for courage…and I'm wondering when I last saw my own older brother, Glen. It couldn't have been that long ago, since he lives in Portland, seven miles away. I should be able to remember, but I'm not surprised that I can't, because (a) I can't remember shit these days, and (b) I don't hold onto memories of Glen if I can help it. Not for the reasons Kent has for trying to forget his older brother, if his squirming and eye-rolling mean what I think they do, but for the opposite reason—far from being "interested" in me, even though he's gay also, my brother has always kept me at more than arm's length. No wonder I identify more with his long-suffering partner, Mark.

43

Okay, back to Kent and his nemesis sibling, Scott, five years his senior. Turns out that Scott, poor thing, has a drinking problem. Comes home far too many nights so blotto that he passes out in the hall, and it falls to Kent to help him up the stairs to the bedroom that they oh-so-conveniently share.

Kent is blinking back tears, his hands fairly fluttering at his knee-caps. "He stunk," he says. "My brother stunk of whiskey. And his hands…as out of it as he was, he couldn't keep his hands off me while I was trying to get him into bed. At first I thought it was because he was dizzy, he had to hold onto me to keep the room from spinning or keep from throwing up or something. The main thing was, I was able to peel his hands off me and get back into my own bed. Then the one night came when I managed to get him into his bed and he started thrashing around. 'Too hot,' he kept saying. Well, before I'd always taken off his sneakers and left it at that. Now I thought, well, maybe I'd better try to help him out of his clothes."

Uh-huh. Looking at Kent, I'm finding this 99 percent hard to believe. I'm betting he was a sissyboy from the word go. His kind of swish is bred in the bone. There was no miracle, no conversion at the hands of a blotto brother.

"I wasn't too good at undressing him," Kent said. "He wouldn't move at all. I ended up just unbuttoning his shirt and loosening his belt."

Oh, so that's the way it is. A striptease. More skin exposed, no doubt, in the next installment.

Kent doesn't disappoint. "The next time he was thrashing around, saying 'Too hot,' I got impatient with him. I unbuttoned his jeans and pulled 'em off."

Ah, there we go. And then…?

It takes Kent a while to get the next words out: "He was…erect."

How strange that word sounds in this atmosphere. Clinical and cold, yet setting off sparks, I'm sure of it, in every one of us, including Brian. Whoever designed the male sex organs was a true joker. It took a jack-in-the-box mentality to come up with a swelling member, a gimmick designed to inspire awe in the dumbstruck teen. Kent, I'm right there with you: I see that sweaty, circumcised giant straining against Scott's jockey shorts. What to do? Fight or flee? I see the trembling hand reaching for the waistband.... Is it really as easy as this?

The one-eyed monster nods: *even easier.*

Davy looks away, toward the bricked-up fireplace that's been painted over so many times you wouldn't know it was there if not for the mantel, still uselessly hugging the wall. Todd is studying the carpet between his feet. Aaron stares miserably into space, wishing he were anywhere else but here. Brian wears his clinical, tooth-pulling smile.

Kent doesn't stop with the briefs; he gets his brother's shirt off, too. Arranges the bigger boy to make room on the bed, then strips off his own sleeping gear (pajamas? underwear?), sobbing all the while, and stretches out beside Scott. Before long they're spooning, Scott's prick pressing into Kent's butt-crack.

And all is lost, as simply as that.

"I don't feel good," Kent says. He's truly pale.

"Take it easy, Kent," I tell him. "It's hard, what you just did." If we weren't sitting so far apart, I'd put a hand on his knee.

"That's right," Davy says. "It's affected all of us."

"But what's even more affecting," Brian says, holding up an instructive index finger, "is that Kent came through it. He's on the other side now. We all are."

Those are genuine tears in Kent's eyes. He's trying to blink them away, trying to smile at Brian, and his expression is so much like that of a child who's experiencing more feelings than he can name that I have to look away.

45

**That** night I have an out-of-body experience. A dream, but a consciously constructed one. Out of my own body but into another's—that of Scott, the drunken older brother. Scott the schemer, Scott who is not truly drunk at all. Scott who swishes whiskey in his mouth like Listerine, rubs dirt on the knees of his jeans as if he's stumbled several times on the way home. Scott who knows that, if he pretends to pass out in the hall, his sexpot brother will drag him up to bed. And it gets better: if he pretends that he's hot, kicks the bedclothes aside, Kent will undress him too. How sweet it is, pretending to be nearly unconscious while Kent puts his hands all over him. Kent the Kind, Kent who would do anything—*anything*—for Scott. For me.

When the dream is done I wipe my hands on the towel I keep under the bed. And sell myself a pardon.

**A** month or so after the old-man-on-the-bus incident, I'm at the gym, changing into my sweatpants and t-shirt in the seedy locker room. At one end of the room there's a urinal against the wall, with a sign duct-taped over it that reads **PLEASE DO NOT PUT GUM IN URINAL**. Nearby another sign is posted in the one toilet stall: **PLEASE DO NOT THROW PAPER TOWELS IN TOILET**. The correct response to these requests, apparently, is to chew gum till your jaw aches, spitting the wads rapid-fire into the urinal while pitching paper towels into the john with both hands. As for the lockers, many of the doors have been bashed in, a few even torn from their hinges. When does this bashing and tearing take place? I never see anyone taking out his aggression on the lockers; judging by their improbably twisted and dented remains it might be something to see, like hurricane footage on TV. I'm sure, though, that the straights are responsible for all the bad-boy stuff at the gym. Gum-spitting, towel-throwing and metal-wrenching just aren't in the gay repertoire. When *we* shuck our sweaty workout clothes we fold them into neat squares, instead of scattering them in a circle like animals marking their territory. *We* don't leave gobs of shaving cream in the sinks, or use spray deodorants that leave ill-smelling clouds hovering near the ceiling. *We* don't leave the showers dripping or faucets running, and we know that the chrome handle on the toilet isn't just for decoration.

On this particular day after work I'm all by myself in the locker room, which doesn't happen very often. Contemplating the silence, I take a moment to zone out in front of the mirror over the sinks. When someone comes in I dash away as if the glass has suddenly turned radioactive, bend over my gym bag and rummage through it. It's a black leather bag that, like me, has seen better days. Two of its zippers are broken, yet I can't part with it. The leather is as delicate to the touch as my dear departed mother's pie crust.

I yank out my sweatpants and t-shirt, and when I happen to glance up I flash on the man who just entered the locker room after me. He's

46

going into the toilet stall, and I catch only the back of him—dark skin, a white t-shirt and red sweatpants, a shaved head. I hang up my jacket, take off my shirt, slide my jeans down, concentrating so on the tasks at hand that it takes me a few seconds to hear the sounds of a continuing splash from the toilet stall: whoever it is in there, he's only peeing. I'm dressed, except for the sneakers, when the flush comes. Then the snap of the stall door, the creak of its hinges, the running water in one of the three sinks. This man has not only flushed the toilet but is now washing his hands. That should qualify for a gold star, or something. Now he dries them, judging by the creaking and complaining of the paper towel dispenser. Another gold star. (The preferred method of drying hands, on those few occasions when hands are washed, is to wipe them on the seat of your sweatpants or shorts.) Shifty-eyed from changing clothes in that locker room for so long, I can see, while tying my sneakers and without turning my head, that the man is taking a lifting belt from one of the lockers and strapping it on. In addition to providing back support, the belt offers fringe benefits: cinching the waist, accenting the crotch. *Shift, shift* go my eyes, noticing that he's glancing at me, too, only being more obvious about it. Something is charging the atmosphere; my mouth has gone dry, it's taking me way too long to get changed. I have to grab my sweat-towel and dash.

"Do die dere?"

His words stop me, and an automatic response percolates up my throat—*Hi, doing okay, not bad*—even as I realize I didn't understand him. Well, the automatic response would still work—he'd understand that I didn't understand. But maybe he needs an answer to something important, at least to him. And when a stranger asks a question, even a panhandler, I have to answer. It's the way I'm made.

I look at him, see his face for the first time—green eyes?—and he jerks a thumb toward the toilet stall. "Do die dere?"

"Beg pardon?" Another archaic expression, one from the vaults, but it's automatic too. A function of class, I suppose, though I don't like the sound of it, it seems to put distance between us, the well-bred me and this earthy-looking black guy who's jerking his thumb toward the toilet stall as if he's asking my opinion of the leak he just took.

He smiles, smiles as if he knows everything I'm going through. "Did you write that in there?" he asks.

I know instantly that he means the latest message scrawled on the inside of the stall door. There are three messages, each written by a different hand in ball-point ink. The first one reads:

*YOU FAGS ARE GONNA DIE!*

I was surprised when I first saw it—not by the sentiment, but that it would manifest itself in that way. And yes, the staff had tried to scratch it out, scrub it away, but it was still readable. (The simple expedient of painting the door had never occurred to them.) There had been no attempt to scratch out the response written below it:

*True, as we all must die, someday....*

The words of a wistful fag, if ever I heard any. And then there was the third remark, written below that one:

*Yeah, but wouldn't it be GREAT if all the REDNECKS kicked off FIRST, so the REST of us could have a little PEACE??*

Okay, it's true—I wrote that one. It was my first time ever defacing a toilet stall, though I'd certainly read a lot of remarks over the years, contemplated many makeshift sketches, marveled at the tenacity of those who scratched their messages in with the tip of a penknife, or those bold enough to use thick markers. My law-abiding inner nerd had always kept me from responding before. But here in this locker room it was different: it was as if a few pen scratchings were all the voice I had. Plus, of course, I was angry at the dumb jock who'd taken his best shot with an anonymous threat—a redneck and a coward, to boot. The only thing I felt fairly sure of was that this particular redneck no longer belonged to this gym. No raging homophobe could survive in this fairy playground; sheer disgust, if nothing else, would eventually take him elsewhere.

Anyway, the real question, the burning question of the moment was, how did this man know that *I* had written that response? I just looked at him, open-mouthed, waiting for him to explain.

His smile, which has always been there, grows wider. "You always got a pen in your pocket when you come in here."

48

True enough—when I come in after work I tend to have a pen or two in my shirt pocket. But as an explanation it's hardly good enough. "Lots of guys have pens in their pockets."

His smile shifts, takes one step across his face—it's now a *knowing* smile, the smile of someone who knows you more than you know yourself. I consider his features, really studying them for the first time—I've seen him at the gym before but have never taken a good look; he's existed, like the other characters around here, only in the corner of my eye. He's black, but on the lighter side, so it doesn't surprise me that his eyes have a lighter cast, too—definitely more green than brown. His mustache and goatee are short and lovingly tended— that in itself might be a tip-off that he's gay; among the straight jocks it's a badge of honor to have sloppy-looking facial hair. His shaved head makes his age a mystery: even with the few lines under his eyes and the specks of gray in his beard, it's impossible to tell how old he is. And something else about that shaved head piques my curiosity: I have never touched a man's shaved head, never pressed my palm against a completely bare neck while kissing....

Look away, Paul! How could you even think...not that it doesn't happen a hundred times a day, in the most casual manner, with guys I see in the cafeteria or on the street. Not that I can't see an attractive frame without imagining what it would be like to wrestle it down to the horizontal. It's part of being gay, isn't it? I have to accept that at every chance my libido will run out and play, like a puppy that never tires of chasing things. It's not *all that pleasant*, either, being forever caught off guard, sitting poker-faced at some meeting when the urge comes to mentally undress the guy at the end of the table, or speaking to staff at a nursing home and finding myself unable to stop glancing, skimming, darting my eyes toward a white-uniformed crotch in the third row as I categorize the horrors of HIV. No doubt I've pondered the issue of the shaved head before, my horny mind leaving no aspect of male appearance unexamined. But the fact remains that I've never touched a completely bald one; so I have to turn, red-faced, away from this man without even answering his question, pretending instead to find fault with my right sneaker lace, parking my foot on the wooden bench to loosen and retie it. Several seconds, then half a minute goes by, plenty of time for him to make an exit.

49

But he hasn't moved one developing muscle. If he'd blink I would feel it, so tense is the funky fluorescence between us. Finally I look up, as he knew I would. It's not just his half-smirk of a smile but his whole face that knows. He knows that I wrote that message on the wall. He knows that I'm attracted to him. He *knows, knows, knows,* all he does is *know,* like some workaholic oracle. He knows, not only what *is,* but what's *going to be.* And he seems…he seems to want me to know, in a not-unkind way, that…I have no surprises for him. He knows all about me, starting with my name. And if I had to name him I would say…yes, Richard Roscoe. *Richard Roscoe.* Staring at (not into) his green eyes, I realize I saw him not that long ago, though at the time I couldn't see his eyes, nor his shaved scalp.

*It's not your fault, you know.*

That's what he said to me, smiling not unkindly. We had a corpse between us at the time, quite a foul-smelling one, and Richard's eyes were behind mirrored sunglasses, the top of his head covered by the navy blue uniform cap of a Metro bus driver.

But to really remember Richard I had to go back farther than that, to the days when Eric and I lived in the little neighborhood known as Southmoreland, when I worked at the Rockhill Medical Center. In those days I took the bus to work all the time, it was just a few short, pleasant stops on the Rockhill run, which was Richard's run back then. I saw him every morning, five times a week; and though we barely exchanged more than a few words he was more of a fixture in my life than most of the people I knew, people who would die or move away or get so lost in their own lives that I couldn't keep track of them. "Hi, Richard!" I'd pipe up, climbing aboard, and he would flash me his smile—he had the mustache and goatee back then, too—and I would think, What a nice smile.

Did my horny mind think on from there? Of course it did, undressing the driver was a standard activity in bus riding.

It just never registered that he might be undressing me too.

We are interrupted now, as a sweathog still panting and grunting from his exertions pushes through the door. A real jarhead, snorting like a bull, hawking and spitting at the urinal. His obnoxious, unsexy self has defused the charge in the air, and what a skirmish of feelings this brings, relief and disappointment duking it out to see

50

which one gets to leave a taste in my mouth. Richard cuts his eyes toward the door, and with a twitch of his satisfied smile and a last tug at his lifting belt he swings across the room, leading with his crotch, a most becoming bulge. Except for my remark about lots of guys having pens in their pockets—an observation that wasn't accurate anyway, not at that club—I haven't said a word to him. Didn't even do as much as our friend at the urinal here, who is moved to say "Shit" under his breath as he relieves his bladder. Didn't acknowledge that, yes, I saw him recently, he was driving the Main Street route now, wasn't that *weird* the morning the old man dropped dead. Sure as hell didn't refer to the old Rockhill Road days, how I was often the first person he picked up in the morning for, oh, say, about three years. Didn't say so much as *How have you been?* or the question that was really burning a hole in my mind: *Hey, am I just finding out after all this time that you're gay?*

Well, it doesn't matter. There's not a speck of significance in what has or hasn't just happened. Even my overactive brain, which throws heaps of its own cells at just about anything, can recognize a non-issue now and then.

When I leave the locker room I turn left, into the cardiovascular area, rather than right, into the training room where Richard would be lifting weights.

I go through my workout without paying attention. Time passes all on its own, till I find myself sitting on a blue mat on the red carpet, having finished my stomach crunches with no memory of having done them. Only the sweat on my face, on the front, back, and underarms of my tank top, proves I've done what I set out to do. Graceless as usual, slightly light-headed, I haul myself up off the mat, inhale a half gallon of water at the drinking fountain, and plod down the hallway to the locker room. It's now the busiest place in town, too many guys trying to get to their lockers at once. It reminds me of my days in New York, where my constant occupation was *trying to get away*—from the overcrowded streets and subways, the noisy apartment buildings. In the locker room impatience is a way of life again, because nobody can wait to get his clothes and get the hell out. I stand outside a cluster of guys bobbing and weaving, choreographing their elbows and hands so that even in their haste they don't touch

51

each other, emptying their lockers as if the metal's red-hot, then trying to dress while compressing themselves into little capsules of flesh, the better to avoid brushing against strange male skin. Finally I get to my locker, yank my bag out and retreat to the other side of the wooden bench, where I strip off my workout clothes in record time, ready to dash to the shower and then home. But all three showers are in use, so I can only sit on the bench and wait. It's not my favorite thing to sit naked in the locker room when it's full of flying hands and bodies. But I don't swoon, either, if someone accidentally touches me. I don't mind a stray jab or pat, a palm glancing off my shoulder, an accidental tickle. Very rarely I have even let myself be clumsy, nearly tripping over the bench and grabbing somebody's tricep to steady myself—*Excuse me, I'm sorry*—and why not, at busy times like this you can almost smell the homophobia in here, so why not make somebody jump by coming too close....

Today, though, I only want *out*, and I grab the first shower that frees up, even if it is the one with the most tiles missing from the wall. At least the soap dispenser has soap in it, a minor miracle.

Once outside, in the parking garage, I stop just briefly, to light a cigarette. As a smoker I feel that I'm constantly under surveillance, that it's just a matter of time until some pumped-up jerk will come breezing past me, sneering: *what a fuckin' idiot.* But I can't help it, the cigarette after the workout is so good, the mentholated smoke filling my freshly-exercised lungs as if it were a little health treatment in itself. Oh man, that life-threatening little surge of nicotine makes me feel *more alive*...for the moment, anyway. And, really, I have to admit (with the help of the little surge) that when it comes right down to it, I *like* the gym. In spite of my cantankerous musings it feels good to get some tension and anger out in a physical way; it's good that I can come here and, ninety-nine times out of a hundred, be *left alone*, free to shut others out and to be shut out in return. Yes, my cigarette and I are jaunty as we make our way past the rows of cars, each parking space in shadow where it meets the concrete wall, the whole place half-lit and spooky.

Walking past vehicles. Square footage, horsepower, ability to kill... it's not surprising that SUV's are popular among the gym rats. I also see a lot of trucks, the aggressively tall ones with privacy glass and beds that are—oh, I don't know, a hundred feet long. But shouldn't a truck look like a truck, show some signs of hard use? These are just pretty boys with brass knuckles, male aggression with optional vanity mirrors. Here's one with a sticker on the rear window—these little square items are replacing the old-fashioned bumper sticker—that says **IF YOU'RE NOT OUTRAGED, YOU'RE NOT PAYING ATTENTION.** So the driver of this glossy vehicle is not only in a rage, but wants everyone else to be, too. Yet he can afford a $30,000 truck—what's *he* got to squawk about?

Walking, walking. Swinging farther along this first row of cars than I thought I would. But the walk back to the car always seems longer than the walk in. The dark red butt of the Cavalier that Eric and I have nicknamed Maurice (pronounced "Morris" in proper E. M. Forster fashion) should be peeking out at me any second now. Yet it doesn't, and doesn't. My cigarette is long gone, my steps quickening as I reach the end of the ramp, confronted by every make and description of car except my own.

Okay, so I parked in the left-hand row of cars today, something I rarely do since I find it easier to back out of the right-hand one. I retrace my steps, scanning the other row, beginning to feel like a fool even though there's no reason to, it's not as if I'm being watched. Still I feel foolish, even as my shame is tempered by a sharpening sense of dread. What if the car isn't here? Yet it has to be. I reach the end of the row again without finding it, and still refuse to believe it's gone. I walk back a few cars, then all the way back to the end of the line again, all the time saying to myself, What? What? Well, I will have to keep walking, that's all, up and down the lines of cars till I find it. So I walk, and walk, my self-consciousness gone since I now feel I am justified in looking as if I've lost my car. Why can't I spot even the smallest sign, the merest speck of metallic red?

Red. I stop short, slap my hand against my forehead. So that's it—I can't find my car because I've been looking for the wrong one, the one that drowned in the flash flood that Eric and I got caught in.

It happened two weeks ago, after a Sunday afternoon at the supermarket. It had been a week of heavy rainstorms, and the latest had come while we were inside the store. As I drove us home we saw a lot of water gushing down gutters and gathering at intersections.

53

You're not supposed to drive through standing water, I knew that; but I had driven through two such intersections with no harm done, and the last crossing was so familiar—so safe and sleepy, just a couple of blocks from home—that I *trusted* it.

The car plowed through several inches of water with no problem, and I patted its dashboard ("You're a good boy, Maurice"), not knowing that I'd soon learn the downside of turning a car into a pet. For as I completed the turn the water seemed to be *deepening*. Not just placidly sitting there, taking a rest, but *still rising*. Suddenly there was nothing but water around us, spreading in all directions. Then all four tires lost contact with the street; and though the car didn't float for a more than a few seconds I got the willies from my scalp to my toenails.

"Water's getting in," Eric said, his voice breaking.

Yes, a muddy pool was rising through the floorboards, a few things floating in it already, some loose cassette tapes, a pocket pack of Kleenex. We sat and watched the water rise, and Eric burst into tears, the knuckles of his right hand pressed against his lips. Each time I recall that moment there's a clench in my gut, an urge to either strike out at something or pull something close; I want tenderness, I want violence, I want to stomp out the sense of uncertainty that haunts me now.

The first order of business, as the surprisingly warm water rose around our feet, was to get the hell out of the car. I opened my door, swung my legs out over the street and stood, slamming the door shut again. The water was up to my knees. I moved slowly, not knowing whether the flood had turned the street as slimy as a creek bed, willing me to slip and be swept away among all kinds of horrors: dead animals, sharp objects, every known and unknown germ. Keeping an eye on the twigs and leaves swirling around me, I tried to place Eric. He should have been about where I was, trying to head toward a patch of dry sidewalk about twenty feet away. Yet there he was, still in the passenger's seat, flailing his arms and barking out sobs, unable to move his submerged feet. So instead of making a beeline for the sidewalk I waded through the milky soup toward his side of the car, yelling "Open your door!"

He tried, working the handle furiously, but the door wouldn't budge, the water was too high now.

"Try the other side!"

Eric struggled across the console as I retraced my unseen steps back to that side of the car, but its door wouldn't open now either.

"Roll the window down!"

He knelt on the bucket seat and poked his head and shoulders through the opening. I grabbed him under the arms, not sure how this was going to work. The things you *don't* do with your lover: I had never tried to lift him before. "Careful," he said, and I was, fearful of giving his back a twist that would send him crawling to the chiropractor. But he used enough of his own steam to pop out into the water like an easy delivery. With an arm around each other's shoulders we waded toward higher ground, the sidewalk that ramped up like one of those islands in a pet turtle dish. It was heaven to stand on dry ground, even with my soaked jeans weighing me down, my squishy sneakers feeling like clown shoes. Eric stared at the car with one hand over his mouth. With water almost up to the door handles, it didn't look like Maurice would survive.

We didn't want to leave the car there but we had to get going, to see if our house was all right. We were only two blocks from home, all of it uphill; it wasn't likely we got flooded. But it never seemed likely, either, that we could drown on our friendly neighborhood streetcorner. How normal everything looked on our block: the water merely trickled through the gutter, there wasn't even a puddle in our driveway. Inside—the bright carpeted hall never looked so good—we stumbled on sloshy feet down to the basement, where a few drops had stained one wall, not even enough to reach the floor. Maddy, our cat, had followed us down the wooden stairs and was sniffing our soaked legs with mixed revulsion and fascination.

A change of clothes and two cups of tea later, we were back at the flood scene. Not forty-five minutes had passed, and all the water was gone. The car, which I remembered as being far from the sidewalk, actually sat close enough to the curb to pass for a bad parking job. The street was almost *dry*, holding no memory of when it was a muddy river. Thus the true meaning of "flash flood": it comes and goes so quickly that it takes a miracle of lousy timing to get caught in one. Eric paced around the car, opening the doors, letting out the last of the water.

That car had been our first large purchase together, an affirmation of our bond. Bills of sale, closing papers, even supermarket receipts—what else does a gay marriage have? And what were we supposed to do now? The trunk of the car seemed dry enough, the groceries unharmed; should we schlep them up the hill? Are we *sure* the food hasn't been contaminated in some way? And what about our flood-soaked clothes? Should we burn them? As we paced around the car these unspoken questions pecked at us, along with the one dreaded duty we had to perform, like it or not. We had to try to start the engine. "Oh God," I moaned, knowing that its little electronic brain was dead. I fished the keys from my pocket and slid into the now-spongy driver's seat. Applying the key to the ignition, I steeled myself for the next sound I'd hear, which at best would be no sound at all, at worst the sound of a beloved machine drowning, the watery gasp of a friend going down. I closed the door. Eric stood outside my open window, grasping its edge with white knuckles.

The afternoon held one more surprise: when I twisted the key the engine turned over and stalled, in a not unheard of, reasonable way—as if the car had only suffered a momentary setback. The smell of gas told me the engine was flooded—ha, ha—so I pressed the pedal into the oozing carpet. I tried again. And again. It *almost* caught, and Eric and I exchanged a look. One more extended try, and at last the engine coughed to life. Eric let go of the door, grabbed it again, not knowing what to do. "Get in," I said, and in a minute we were chugging up the hill toward home.

We kept the groceries—storing them in our fetishistic fashion, so that you could reach into the refrigerator blindfolded and know what you were grabbing—and put our flood-soaked jeans and sneakers into the washer. Our car, ruined or not, sat safely in the garage.

"I'm sorry, honey," Eric said.

He was standing in the arch between the dining room and living room, and I was too preoccupied to know what he was talking about.

"I just panicked," he said. "I'm sorry."

He was looking directly into my eyes, his expression soft and solemn, and I saw—not for the first time—how beautiful he was, how gentle and kind. I wanted to hold him, to clutch him against me as if the two of us, two broken pieces, could make one whole.

A few days later, at the car rental lot, the little blue Plymouth Neon looked fine from the outside, but—talk about smells! The rental agent had already skipped back inside when we opened the doors and the odor of pot smoke nearly bowled us over. I could only say, "Cheech and Chong were here."

"Unbelievable," Eric said. But his expression showed mixed feelings, a hint of longing amid the disgust. I felt it, too: a tug from the past. We had both smoked our share of grass in the days of youth and risk, before we knew each other. The smell was even stronger than the stale cigarette smell in the car rental office, and really more disgusting; but if there was a joint in the glove compartment I'd have willingly split it with Eric then and there. Neither of us made a move to get in, though. We were stuck in a mature-adult moment: not even degenerates like us wanted a car that reeked of cannabis. We looked longingly over the rest of the lot, but the demand for rental cars had left nothing else but a little white Neon with a flat.

"I guess that smell will go away," Eric said.

I got behind the wheel of the Neon while Eric slid into our old car. We'd been driving around with the seats sheathed in old dry-cleaning plastic, and though we kept the windows open I noticed, when I first got in the car in the morning, how the smell was getting a little worse each day. It still wasn't awful, not as bad as I'd feared it would be, but it wasn't nice either. There were *things* in the car, that much was certain—bacteria and other pests building up power, holding rallies, marching with little signs that said LET'S GET TOXIC! It was the end of the Cavalier. Never mind that the car was running perfectly, it was still the end. The insurance company had totaled it, and on Saturday a big flatbed truck would pull up to the curb, and the car would be driven up the ramp, and that would be the last we'd see of it.

The little blue Neon is a lot easier to find than the car I thought I had. As I hoist my gym bag onto the rear seat that smells as if it's been doused with bong water, it occurs to me that the boy and girl who worked at the car rental place must have taken breaks in this

57

car. Together or separately, they would sit in some secluded corner of the lot and get stoned to the gills, and that got them through the long tedious hours behind the counter. Probably, if they did manage to take any breaks together, other things also took place on the back seat of that car. The sudden thought of that startles me and I jerk back, bumping my head on the doorframe. The tips of my ears begin to burn hot. Was it the thought of two toasted kids fucking in the car that brought on my sudden embarrassment, or just the fact that I had bumped my head, a head unfamiliar with this tiny vehicle and its tiny doors? And why would that embarrass me, unless….

Unless I'm being watched?

For someone to get a good look at me he'd have to be close by, in a vehicle that's been backed into a space—no sense straining to see in a rear-view mirror. Only one nearby vehicle meets the criteria, the orange truck that's across from me and three cars to the right, and I can't be sure at first whether that's someone's head in the cab or a shadow. But the more I stare, the more sure I am that someone is staring back; and at last there's movement, someone resettling himself in his seat, his head moving just slightly—watching me, all right. In an orange truck. Not orange, really, but red, a faded red, unlike the shiny cherry finish on the newer trucks. The glass of this one isn't tinted, either; if he were parked one space closer, in the light, I'd be able to see him clearly.

What do I do? It's obvious as I stand here, staring frankly at this man who is staring at me, a man whose features I can't make out, that I only have two choices, advance or retreat. I can't imagine doing either. Suppose I were to walk right up to that truck, to confront him? What would I say—"Stop looking at me"? Christ, I can't be a complete paranoid idiot, can I? But he's seen me looking at him, how would it look if I ran? If the laws of my egocentric universe tell me that I've put him there myself, have wished him into being, it doesn't detract from the absurdity of the situation, the futility of wishing. "Water's getting in," Eric said, and his shallow gulping sobs followed. There is only fear and failure in life; and this man, looming behind the wheel, his eyes in shadow—okay, it's Richard Roscoe, I might as well admit—has yet to learn that there's nothing but foolishness in sitting in a parking garage waiting for someone to come along.

It's time for me, the patron saint of foolishness, to tell him so.

I take one step toward the truck and the dome light in the cab comes on: he's cracked open the passenger's-side door. I see his eyes just briefly before he ducks back into shadow behind the steering wheel. A ballsy move, opening that door, as well as an unwelcome reminder that he's been watching all this time, clocking my frustration as I fretted up and down the line of cars. "Huh," I tell him, under my breath. I turn around, unlock the Neon's trunk and toss my gym bag in. When I slam the lid shut the car bounces a little, like a pet that wants to play. Now a young woman is near, practically on top of me, her sneakers barely registering on the concrete, one of those trim young women with feathery hair who exercise in eye makeup, this one in pink tights under a pink windbreaker, her gym bag a darker, shocking pink. Her Toyota starts with an alarming roar and almost immediately backs up—I have to jump out of the way—and zooms off down the sloping floor to the next level. Meanwhile, several cars down on my side, two straight exercise buddies leap into their jeep, laughing like hyenas. The jeep also backs from its space as if fired from a cannon, and off it zooms, perhaps in pursuit of the feathery blonde. I look at Richard, still sitting there under the light, his hands on the wheel, and I shake my head in a way that seems ambiguous even to myself—am I saying "No," or do I have water in my ear from the shower? Of course I mean *No, I'm not coming over there, this is a public place, everybody passing by, who do you think you are, who do you think I am?* It makes no difference to the figure behind the wheel, as unmoved and unchanged as a cardboard cutout, so patient as the dome light wears down his battery.

59

I look at my feet, scuff my shoes against the concrete. I see myself walking over there and asking Richard, very politely, to leave me alone. I hate the confrontation of it, the weirdness; but the alternative is to stand in the garage shuffling my feet all night. So I look both ways for pumped-up speed demons and make my way over to the truck, slowly, my hands in my pockets.

I plan to speak to him with my feet firmly planted on the ground, but the truck sits too high, the door handle practically at eye level. When I swing the door wider I can barely see him. Very conscious of my blue suit as I get more intimate with what promises to be a filthy vehicle, I step up onto the running board—are they still called running boards?—and slide carefully onto the seat, meaning to perch there in a manner that is in no way suggestive or even friendly. When I look at him there's alarm on his face, as if he wasn't prepared for this moment after all.

"Shut the door," he says, pointing a finger at the dome light.

I do as he says, but slowly, wanting him to get the drift that it's a little too late to be inconspicuous. Closing the door cuts off the dome light, of course, but I'm not ready for the way his face falls into shadow as if a shutter has clicked into place; not ready to see his lap, the sweatpants more successfully red than his truck, sitting in a rectangular wash of brilliance from the small square garage light. There are smells, too, lagging behind my sight but now catching up: a cruddy essence of dust and dirt and worn rubber; the greasy, brackish tang of fast-food bags balled up underfoot; the wintergreen bite of liniment. The closeness of the air, the humidity, his illuminated crotch (Christ, he didn't *plan* that, did he?) make me speak up in a voice unfamiliar to myself, practically whining—okay, whining: "If this is what you wanted, for me to come over here, you've got a strange way of making invitations."

"You don't recognize me, do you?" he asks.

"Of course I do. You're Richard, the bus driver."

"You remember me from Rockhill?"

Yes, yes, the Rockhill bus—having gone over all this in my memory, it's tiring now to have him bring it up. I'm *not* a past-dweller, I don't dote on the old days when the Rockhill bus stopped right at the front gate of our complex, the figure of Richard immaculate as the doors hissed open, the spit-shine on his black shoes, three gold-braided **DISTINGUISHED DRIVER** patches sewn to his navy blue sleeve, mirrored sunglasses giving back a tiny, intense world. Sometimes there were only the two of us on the bus for the length of my ride; they shut the route down entirely when the old Medical Center closed. I usually had my nose buried in a book as I waited, marked my place with my thumb as I climbed on and flashed him my monthly pass, and started reading again just as my fanny hit the seat. I was aware of him, the name Richard, the flash of his lenses in the rear-view mirror, the way he said hello. My usual weakness for black men only doubled for black men in uniform—any uniform. But I had my book, and I didn't like to talk much in the morning, and besides, I never spent too much time fantasizing about the young black bus drivers. They all seemed so unimaginatively, irrevocably, boringly straight.

Now unrecognizable Richard in his tank top and sweats rests a dark hand on his illuminated thigh as he says, "I'm not the same guy."

I have to give him credit, he's kept up with my thoughts. "So what happened?"

"Left my wife and kids three years ago."

"That must have been tough." Not wanting to sound sympathetic, but what else can I do?

"Tougher on me than it was on them, I'm pretty sure," he says, fingering the keychain that hangs from the ignition key. Is that a tiny rainbow flag on it? "But you—I knew what you were all about the first time I saw you."

I keep looking at the keychain, the little rainbow that travels along in his pocket when he goes to the gym. Of all the queens who traipse in and out of there, secure in their varying degrees of fairydom, how many carry as much as a gay-themed keychain? Some may act out in the locker room when the coast is clear, and some may reveal themselves on the gym floor by talking with their friends in voices hushed but far too animated; but there are no rainbow flags or stickers or decals gracing their clothes or gym bags, no pink triangles on their chests or in their pierced ears; no linked male symbols, the circles and arrows, attached to the chains around their necks. You wouldn't catch *me* dead with any of that stuff, no more than you'd catch me on the workout floor in a t-shirt reading **LET GO OF MY EARS, I KNOW WHAT I'M DOING.** This keychain, now, with that ripple of rainbow… suppose something like that fell out of your pocket while you were changing up? Never mind how "out" you were, you'd be *embarrassed.* Richard would be embarrassed—though maybe, just maybe he's still too naïve to realize it.

"What did you just say?" I ask.

"I said, I knew what you were about the first time I saw you."

That tiny smile, crossing his face as quickly as a pulse—is he *gloating*? I picture myself as he would have seen me boarding his bus, a

61

bearded fortyish man in a suit or, in cold weather, a tweed topcoat and Stetson fedora. Nothing mincing or fairyish about him. On the other hand, the books that I had my nose in might have included *States of Desire* or *The Trouble with Harry Hay* or even *The Male Couple's Guide to Living Together*. I never censored my reading matter on the bus—it wasn't required, somehow, just as it's not required for the gym rats who keep all clues off their attire and accessories to keep their cars and trucks equally symbol-free. Here, in the parking garage, are the rainbow decals, the pink triangles, the SILENCE = DEATH stickers, the proudly entwined circles-and-arrows that never make their way inside. My own car, back when I *had* my own car, sported a rainbow-striped license plate frame. So at least our cars are liberated, have staked a claim on public life. "You've got a nerve," I say to him, and there's no acting to it, the corners of my mouth droop honestly with the disappointment and unhappiness of it all.

"No offense," he says. "I just…." He waved a hand vaguely between us. "You know."

I know that I'm going to keep my ugly mood going. "Have you ever noticed that people only say 'no offense' when it's already too late?"

"Yeah." A gentle blinking of his eyes, I can just sense it on his dark face. "Me and my big mouth, huh?"

If there was ever a time to bolt, it's now—when it's not too late to rewind the last two minutes, pretend they never happened. Making a quick exit from a strange vehicle isn't something I'm used to, not in recent years anyway. Where the hell is the door handle? I ought to be able to feel it with my elbow or forearm, but there's nothing there except some unpleasantly soft upholstery.

"You like black men?" he asks.

Now I know why everything he says sounds so *wrong*: it's because I can't see his eyes. It's the eyes of black men that get to me first, as proven by Burke Robbins, the man I originally came to Kansas City to live with. It's taken forever to learn how to keep him out of my thoughts, most of the time anyway. It helped that I saw him at the funeral of a mutual friend a few years ago. By that time he was no longer the twenty-five-year-old with the glistening Jheri curls and dimples in his cheeks. His hair had been cut brutally short, and—

62

even allowing for the fact that we were at a funeral—he didn't look like he smiled much any more. Maybe his rancid past had caught up with him. Of course, I wasn't the 32-trying-to-look-25-year-old stud I used to be, either. But since then I haven't been troubled by dreams of Burke, or random urges to see him again. I've washed that man right out of my pubic hair. Now, Richard's eyes aren't brown like Burke's, they have a green cast—the green of water clear enough to show the ocean floor, its secrets open to snorklers and glass-bottomed boats. The interesting thing is that I can picture his eyes quite clearly even though I can't see them now. Which means that he's taken root in my memory—not the Richard of the navy blue uniform and mirrored sunglasses, but Richard in the locker room, in his gray tank-top and red sweats. Richard and his green eyes asking, "You write that in there?" He has a place in my head now, this Richard who left his wife and kids so he could sleep with men. That's something else about black guys I've known, they would not say "guys," which is a white guy's word, but always "men," the phrase *black men* sounding as if it's got an extra syllable in it, the way Burke would say *black-uh-men*, and Richard's got it too: *You like black-uh-men?* The more I chase these thoughts, the more important it becomes to keep my poker face—to not give anything to this black-uh-man who's already got something and seems to know it. And I ask, in the spirit of not really wanting to know, "What do you want?"

Richard says nothing, doesn't move a muscle—none that I can see, anyway. Then his right hand, which has been resting on the seat next to him, comes to life, glides silently toward his crotch. It seems to want to tug at the waistband of his sweats, but no, it's the hem of his shirt that it's after, fingers curling around it, lifting, raising the shirt to bare his belly, his chest. It's no still life: the movement of his generous chest betrays his quickened breathing, and on the portion of his face that I can see, his lips have parted.

What can I do but take him in. It's not even a question. His hand—having bunched the shirt into his armpits so it won't slide down—drifts slowly over his pecs and down his middle, but it's not necessary, my eyes can follow the trail by themselves, up and down and up again. No standard weightlifter's body, at least not yet, but I like it all the better for that; there's no thin-skin-with-bulging-veins

63

look, no tiny waist with abs stamped out of tin. There's meat on his bones. The skin of his belly, not flat yet compact, slightly sagging at the edges…his chest, strong yet soft, hanging like a skinful of ripe fruit…I'm ready, more than ready to believe that he doesn't want anything from me after all, he wants only to give.

None of this is fair.

I'm not myself, sitting here. Not Paul in the presence of this miracle, not Paul who would be offered up flesh like this. And surely not Paul who would take it, burying his face in that paper-bag-brown warmth that's as fragrant as fresh bread. Richard caresses the back of my not-Paul head, his hands slightly rough with callus. He moans, not out loud so much as through his skin, the vocal cord of his body trembling, twanging. I stroke his nipples with my mustache. His hands are around my shoulders, my hands cup his rib cage tenderly. The old chassis under us squeaks, springs in the seat complain. A glance at the windshield shows how steamed up we are.

When I've licked and sucked and nibbled on every bare inch of him I can reach, I'm reminded—by my hand, which has wound up on his thigh and now slides farther up than I intended—that there is more. How could I forget that there's more? It's as if each moment of touching him has been enough, a miracle in itself that doesn't need more.

"Ah, Jesus." I straighten up, my shoulders snapping and cracking like twigs on the forest floor, neck complaining. "Jesus God." I can't bear to look at him but I do. His parted lips have dried in the shape of O, his chest is heaving, and now I'm wiping my mouth with the back of one hand and feeling for the door handle with the other. Then I'm gone, in a scrambling departure that doesn't take into account the height of the truck or the running board.

I should have landed on my can. Instead I'm on two unsteady feet, in an underground evening grown unseasonably cool. Looking around with the eyes of a just-hatched chick, I see that (a) the parking garage is even uglier than I remembered, more gray and grimy than it has a right to be; and (b) a whole lot more cars have left, and I didn't notice a thing. I walk, first in the wrong direction, toward the gym, then in the other, looking *once again, dammit* for the red car that is no more, remembering a second later to head for the blue Neon.

He never did ask me why I have so much trouble finding my car.

As I get behind the wheel of not-my-car, my body feels all wrong in my blue suit, as if someone else is wearing it. How is it that my body's become full of fetid swamps exposed to the air when I move my arms or part my legs? In my rearview mirror I see Richard still sitting there—not his face but the shape of his head, the shape of patience itself. *Fool* is the word that lobs back and forth through my head, like a tennis ball or handball or any of those other kinds of balls I've never handled. *Fool! Fool!* After a couple of minutes, I still haven't looked for my car keys. It would be a miracle if they were still in my pocket, if they haven't fallen out in Richard's truck. Wouldn't it be funny if I had to go back. I practice a laugh, but only manage to bring up something vile from the pit of my stomach, sour and burning in my throat. The swamps reach deeper than I thought, right into my gut. I flip down the visor to find the optional vanity mirror, but this funky car doesn't have one. In the rear-view mirror I look moist and disheveled but haven't sprouted the revolting features of a demon. I look like Paul.

*Fool.*

Paul.

*Fool.*

I'm busting out, standing in the empty space next to the car—it's surrounded by empty spaces now—and shaking like a wet dog, shaking off the hallucinations, swamps and swamp critters that were crawling all over me. Where it seemed cool a moment ago it's now unbearably humid, too much for a man to take. I grab at my neck to loosen my tie, forgetting that I took it off much earlier, that it lies folded on the back seat. I unhitch two more buttons on my shirt. Slick air itches across my palms. My glasses steam up at the edges. I'm looking to Richard's truck, its red so painfully flat, and at the same instant I hear…a sob catching in someone's throat, or a car door slamming or brakes squealing or someone shouting up on the next level, any of the spooky amplified sounds that make up the language of the parking garage. "Wait." Yes, that's me talking, but it's a swamp-thing's voice if I ever heard one, croaking as if it's half submerged. "Wait!" That's better, I sound almost human. "Wait!" I say a third time, though the truck shows no signs of leaving. I move toward it, my

steps so irregular that at times I seem to be moving backwards. Another fluorescent light, triggered by motion, comes on over my head,
throws everything into sharper relief. I reach the truck, pull the door
open.

I climb in as if I'm being rescued, but it's a short-lived relief: my
door has not quite clicked shut, the dome light is still on, and he's
looking at me as if I'm the white, educated, privileged mockery of
everything he's ever done or wanted to do.

"Don't make fun of me," he says.

Fun of him? When I'm the one who's made an ass of himself?
"What are you talking about?"

He wipes the back of his hand and wrist under his runny nose,
then turns to look out his window, the back of his head somehow
signaling anticipation, as if a parade might come marching down the
aisle. I'm trying to think of something to say when he turns back and,
in one motion, launches himself across the cab. And I'm saying *Hey*,
or maybe it's only *Huh* as he damn near knocks the wind out of me
with his bulk and strength, his randy odor filling my nose, his body
heat percolating through my white shirt, his arms wrapped so tightly
around me that he can grab his own wrist behind my back, squeezing
hard as he digs his face into my shoulder. His sobs are not only grief-
stricken, they sound pained, his lungs or windpipe bleating for help;
I put my arms around his torso, my palms on his back. He's heaving
and shuddering but I hang on, our combined bulk rocking the truck,
providing a misleading show for anyone passing by. The door handle
that I couldn't find before is pressing into my ribs in a most obnoxious way, and since the door isn't quite closed there's every chance
I'll spill out onto the concrete any second; but for once, please God,
let me not think about myself so much. The man who's gripping me
as I haven't been gripped in a long, long time is *hurt*. Good Christ,
maybe this is the first time he's dared approach a man. Look at his
actions, see what he's done—how can anything be driving him *but*
desperation? I sink my fingers into the thin skin of his tank top, and
he's not crushing me now because I'm melting under his heat and
pressure....

His mouth on mine. Breath, tears, life itself. If male mouths aren't
meant for each other, then how come...? Now my libido's pound-

66

ing on its not-well-fortified door. From far away, creaking springs, the rattle of the keychain against the dash, a rustle of paper on the floor, feet scrabbling for purchase on the seat. Ungodly creases in my twisted blue suit.

By the time he stops crying his pressure has put my arms to sleep, I can't feel my hands against his back. I'm half on the seat, half on the floor like one of Dali's melting timepieces, and there's a jellylike feeling in my groin, a tenderness around my balls as if I'd just had the orgasm my thoughts were racing toward. He pushes himself off me, one hand on the back of the seat, the other on my window. The soaked collar and neck of my shirt are losing their heat, it feels as if I've got a tepid dishcloth around my throat. And that just-after-sex feeling persists, the only way my body knows how to respond to an experience this physically profound.

I'm looking up at the back of his head. He lifts his hand repeatedly, I picture his fingers uselessly dabbing his face. My right arm comes alive, tingling as I reach back to find the clean handkerchief in my hip pocket, unfurl the soft square and tap his shoulder with it. "Here." A glimpse of his face as he takes it, a sliver of profile like a waning moon, the darkened, puffy flesh under his eye. He gives his nose a healthy blow.

When enough time has passed that something has to be said, I search for a remark that will help him save face. "Bet you haven't had a good cry in a long time."

He wags his head.

"Feel better? I usually do, after...." I slide myself upright carefully, mindful of the odd angles my back is moving through. I brush my sleeves with the edge of my palm. He doesn't quite look at me. The drill is familiar: instead of having our own little focus group, going over the past few minutes to analyze what they did and did not mean, I'll return to silence and he'll be grumpy and sulky, our shame the kind that's built into men like a secondary sex characteristic. If you're a gay male, with a full set of feelings, then you learn to recognize this shame. You learn to wait, on the edge of the mattress, or the car or truck seat, or against the back wall of a bar, and not say anything more while the man you're with pulls himself together. Meanwhile you pull yourself together as I'm trying to do now, raggedly,

67

straightening the legs of my slacks so they won't look so much like I've fucked in them.

Outside, I use the pay phone near the gym's front door. The quarter and dime feel too big, like toy coins, as I push them into the slot. Eric answers on the first ring, his "Hello?" hopeful and anxious.

"Hi, honey. I'm sorry, I had to work a little late, so I'm just now getting through at the gym. I hope I didn't worry you."

"Oh, that's all right," he said, worry still coming through in his relief, haunting the wires.

"I'll be right home. Do we need anything, should I stop somewhere?"

I don't hear his answer over the sound of Richard's truck, which has roared to life and bolts from its space now, turns in a radius I wouldn't have thought possible, its little round taillights slipping from view. "I'm sorry," I tell Eric, "I didn't hear you."

"I just said all I need is you."

Well, there it is. He's not the kind of man you cheat on. He can make it hurt too much, without even trying. "I'll be right home, baby," I tell him; and if my voice had been a swamp thing's before, it's a mechanical squeak now, the phoniest of sound effects.

# Chapter 3

I woke up this morning with a leftover dream-thought whispering in my ear: *Suppose Old Joe is real?*

To which I replied, without moving my lips, *That way madness lies. So scram.*

Old Joe is the resident ghost at East Oak House. He makes all the odd noises that can't be explained away, and even some of those that can. When he's not rattling the pipes or creaking the floorboards he's outside, pitching icicles off the roof. All just a silly running joke, of course…at least in the daylight. But at night….

I want to mention Old Joe at the breakfast table, but before I can Todd drops a bomb on us. "Brian's gone for the weekend," he says.

"Without saying anything?" Davy asks, his voice squeaky with anxiety.

"Family emergency," Todd says. "In Rhode Island."

"Rhode Island?" I ask.

"Nantucket."

"Oh, please, Todd, don't do me like that. You know what limerick is racing through my mind…."

He gives a rare, full-throated laugh, showing his teeth. "Do I ever!"

Brian's departure may have been sudden, but like any good father leaving the boys home alone he's left us a to-do list, written out in his elegant fountain-pen script on greenish notebook paper. The kitchen floor, for example, hasn't had a good scrubbing in a while.

"We'll do it right," Davy says, his anxiety lessened now that we have an agenda. "Everything gets moved out, into the hallway."

"Everything" consists of table, chairs, a few smaller tables, telephone stand, rack of cookbooks…. I'm afraid Davy's even going to insist on moving the fridge. He seems satisfied, though, when everything else is gone. Amazingly, I'm even fired up about the task. "I'll scrub," I announce. "Who's with me?"

"I am," Todd says.

We fill buckets with hot water and lethal ammoniated suds. Stout wooden brushes with thickets of bristles: hey, this is a man's job. Never mind that I haven't scrubbed a floor on my hands and knees in years. Somehow it feels good to get down to it, even my knees aren't complaining too much.

The off-white linoleum is shot through with fake gray "cracks." They're supposed to lend a marbled appearance, and though they don't quite make it, you have to admire their capacity for hiding dirt. How long *has* it been since this floor was scrubbed? "Jesus," I'm saying with each sweep of my hand, my brush sopping in filthy surf.

"Disgusting, ain't it?" Todd says. Like me, he's wearing bluejeans today. His aren't the Loose Fit that I favor for myself. And on his hands and knees like that, with his butt up in the air…. *Not a good idea, hon,* I want to tell him. *Think you could point that in another direction?* But he's oblivious, humming along with the Oldies station on the radio. "They call me the Wanderer…." Who knew, who fucking *knew* that these fucking songs would be around for fucking *decades*? And when did I last hear this one? Probably yesterday, they seem to play it every hour.

Sounds of industrious cleaning drift in from other areas of the house: Davy is vacuuming the downstairs, Aaron upstairs. And Kent is…I don't know what Kent's doing. I don't need to know, I'm not in charge here. Which leads to an interesting question: with Brian gone, who *is* in charge?

Against the mopboard now, under the sink. Out of curiosity, I open the cupboard. The usual assortment of cleansers, a few stiff rags. Enough room for me to wriggle inside a bit, turn my head and look up at the underside of the sink.

"Hey, Todd," I call out. "Look at this."

There's nothing to look at, but I don't tell *him* that. Still, "What is it?" he asks, in the skeptical tone of one who's about to be swindled.

"Oh, just...something interesting."

Creaking sounds as Todd makes his way across the floor, still on his hands and knees. He opens the cupboard door next to mine and sticks his head in. "Okay, what is it?"

Pointing as well as I can in that cramped space: "Up there."

In order to see, he has to do what I've done: crawl into the cupboard, wedging his shoulders and torso around so he's right next to me. "I don't see anything," he says.

Okay, this is what I wanted: Todd next to me, in tight quarters. Todd in his maroon t-shirt, slightly sweaty under the arms, grunting, his breath hot as he wedges even more of himself in.

Todd's sex life started out fast and easy, with Karl and Danny, a couple of guys from his high school swim team. These three knew what they wanted, and pursued it with the sense of entitlement that comes naturally to those who own the pool—keeping quiet about it, of course. Then came the day when one of the boys' fathers, returning unexpectedly from out of town, caught them in bed together.

The scandal was kept quiet, too. Todd and his lovers faced, not public humiliation, but rather a steady stream of mealy-mouthed threats, low rumbling warnings, and whispered exhortations from their parents, who were scared to death that their sons might really turn out to be queer. With an adaptability that would stay with him throughout his life, Todd began dating the most desirable girl in his class. His transition from boys' toy to Homecoming King, complete with a Queen on his arm, was so swift that the old just-a-phase-he-was-going-through chestnut got hauled out and dusted off, and made his straight future possible.

Except, of course, that it wasn't possible. Even as he donned his butch crown, his thoughts weren't on Queenie at his side, but rather on Karl with the big cock. He bided his time, avoided any serious

71

entanglements with girls and, as soon as he reached his majority, got Karl again. Only now, with Karl's cock in his bed, he found he couldn't stop thinking of Danny with the versatile dick. And so it went, from Karl cock to Danny dick to Wally willie to Randy rod, world without end amen. Like the character in *The Boys in the Band* who said—rather thrillingly, I thought, when I first heard it—"I want them all, and I'll have them all."

Now, staring at the dark underside of the sink, he says "I still don't see anything."

I'm taking him in. How massive he seems, how strong his male scent. Our shoulders rub up against each other. Do I dare to try anything? My heart hammers at the thought. This isn't just my dirty mind working, or my dirty notebook. This is *real life*. After all, I could dream up a better place to meet than this.

*Cry if I want to, cry if I want to....*

Where the hell is that coming from? Oh, the radio. Another song that they play seventy-five times a day. I know most of the words—more than I want to. It distracts me so much that I get claustrophobic all of a sudden. I want out of this tight space, and I want to shut that fucking radio down. It's tough to move, as if I've swollen while lying here; and when I try, I bump my head against a pipe.

"Hey," Todd says. "You all right?"

Wriggling out onto the kitchen floor as gracelessly as a newborn, I notice how the light of day, which usually fills the kitchen to the brim, has gone dim somehow. "Of course I am. I just bumped my head, that's all." It's really poor, this noontime overcast light—unless it's my vision that's covered the sun with a scrim of dirty dishwater, as I recall an afternoon that seems to have taken place in a former lifetime.

**It's** Thursday afternoon, 5:15 sharp, and I'm pulling into the permanent shade of the parking garage, searching for a spot near the gym entrance. As usual I have to park some distance away, but that's all right. I grab my bag from the back seat and lock up, whistling a happy tune and pocketing my keys as I head for the double glass doors. At the last minute I turn and, instead of proceeding through the gym entrance, pull open the door to the concrete stairwell. Three quick flights up and I push through onto a parking level that looks deserted—or is it? It's agony to wait till my eyes can adjust to the gloom of a far concrete corner, where—yes!—a shadow appears, shaped like an aging pick-up truck that would, in better light, be a faded red.

Some rituals become second nature so soon that it's hard to explain how they ever began. Did 'we'—i.e., some combination of the rational thought processes of Richard and myself—decide that I would always park on the lower level and he would park up here? True, the seclusion of this particular spot does approach the ideal—the offices on this level close at five and clear out quickly. But who am I fooling by pretending to head for the gym, swerving at the last minute toward the stairwell instead? Why don't *I* park up on the third level too? No one would notice, no one would care. But the thought of our two vehicles in such proximity—it's more bothersome, somehow, than the very real proximity of our flesh. Equally noxious is the idea of making out in my spiffy new car, which is not really mine but mine and Eric's. So I take the stairs and stand blinking in the gloom, nearly swooning with anxiety till I see the truck's shadow.

We are free here, as free as we can be in the cluttered cab of his truck, where there's every chance that I'll rise up from crouching over his cock to find an Egg McMuffin wrapper stuck to my knee. Forget about traces of lipstick and mascara, the traditional foes of straight husbands; I have to worry about errant streaks of mustard or barbecue sauce. I can find more faults, too—the dashboard clock that's six hours slow, the ashtray overflowing with candy wrappers, the ten years' worth of grime shrouding the rear window. But when I'm here with him, and he's stripping off his tank top and pulling down his jeans, none of it matters, not even my own dress slacks, which will end up in a puddle on the floor, to be shaken out and dusted off once we've done what we need to do.

73

Soon I'm on my way home, with something new to think about—a proposition Richard just made—and something new to play with, the black jockstrap he was wearing, which I've stuffed in my gym bag along with the workout clothes I haven't worn in weeks. The jock was a great touch; far beyond reading my mind, Richard's learned how to brush his fingertips across the Braille of my libido.

When I come in the house from the garage Maddy meets me in the kitchen. He's meowing, so before I look I know his food bowl's empty. He's probably complained to Eric too, but I can tell that Eric's on the phone upstairs—with his parents, no doubt. The sounds of rapid-fire Spanish tap on the ceiling. I wash and dry Maddy's bowl while he rubs against my legs. He's a healthy cat, but only because we take better care of him than we do of ourselves. Twice a day he gets his insulin shot, and we feed him only the hypoallergenic lamb-and-rice that he does best on. I fill his bowl, then fetch a 3/10cc syringe from a plastic bag in the cupboard, his bottle of insulin from the butter compartment in the fridge door. I roll the little cold bottle between my palms, mixing up the fluid without causing bubbles. The needle pierces the rubber seal, the tiny graduated cylinder fills—does anyone else ever notice that insulin looks like cum, or do other people have such thoughts? It's easy to shoot Maddy while he's eating; I pinch up a bit of loose skin on the back of his neck, and the needle's so fine he never feels a thing.

The Spanish gets louder as I pass through the dining and living rooms. Eric's in his study at the top of the stairs. He tends to be loud when he's talking to his parents, because they can't hear very well over the phone; but tonight he's louder than ever, standing with his back toward me, one hand holding the phone, the other raking through his hair. Ten to one his parents are giving him a hard time about something. Glad he can't see me, feeling I need an overhaul before I present myself, I continue on to the bedroom, where I peel off my suit, hang it in the closet, and throw my shirt in the laundry basket.

Whenever anyone asks how Eric and I have managed to stay together for ten years, I spill the secret: separate bathrooms. Looking at myself in the wall-sized mirror over my sink isn't my favorite thing to do, especially when naked; but now it seems some inspection is necessary, some verification that I'm still Paul—Paul-the-Fool, Paul-the-Ingrate or whatever I need to call him, but still Paul. Unfortunately, the vast, fleshy, hairy image in the mirror reminds me of no one I want to *meet*, let alone *be*. A flat affect doesn't help; telling myself to cheer up doesn't, either. *C'mon, Paul, show those pearly whites.* How can I do that, knowing what those pearlies have been nibbling on so recently? I grab my toothbrush, look at it, put it down. Fetch Richard's jockstrap from my gym bag, which I've brought into the bathroom with me, and press it against my face. His proposition—

74

"I want you to come over to my place"—was as inevitable as it was impractical, and the hundred different reasons why I can't go pale before the certainty that I *will* go. I *have* to go, and it has to be this Sunday afternoon. I realize this with a kind of vertigo, for here I am at home—a home that I've achieved through compromise and co-operation, a home as real as any I'll ever know—and yet no part of it seems as real, as miraculous, as totally deserving of my devotion as these few square inches of cum-soaked cloth that I'm stretching over my nose and mouth like a surgical mask.

The tiny room holds most of what I need to subsist for a time—cigarettes, books and magazines, a radio, and oh yes, bathroom facilities. As in any good bomb shelter, there are probably other provisions around, a chocolate bar or two among the creams and ointments in the vanity drawers. I finish one cigarette, then another. It's past time to decide what we want for dinner, putter around in the kitchen, look through the day's mail—any number of things. But the life of the household is stalled, becalmed. Everything that I know about unfaithfulness to a partner I've learned from books, movies, TV, and other second-hand accounts; and nowhere have I been told what it's like, this dreadful afterwards, this *being alone with yourself* and suffering for it.

**O n** Sunday afternoons I usually take a shower before I go the gym—though I'll be working up a sweat and showering again before too long—and today is no exception. Except that today, of course, I'm not going to the gym, I'm going to Richard's, so I brush my teeth extra hard. I've been using a new kind of toothpaste lately, and now I notice, for the first time, that the tube has a warning label. Jesus Christ, life isn't complicated enough, now you have to keep your *toothpaste* out of reach of kids under 6? At least this new formula is multitasking, it handles everything from breath cleansing to tartar control. I scour around as if my life depends on it, jamming the brush so far back in my mouth it hurts. I want to believe that this magic potion really can do anything—even take, *in advance,* the taste of illicit cock from my mouth.

I bring my bag downstairs at two o'clock, an hour earlier than usual. Eric is sitting on the sofa with a bowl of popcorn in his lap, watch-

75

ing Animal Planet, his favorite cable channel. Like me he's spent the day in t-shirt and sweatpants, his hair still askew from last night's sleep. The kernels of popcorn are too big for his small fingers, they keep plopping back into the bowl. One falls to the carpet, but Maddy, curled up at his feet, isn't interested.

"You're early," Eric says.

*Emergency Vets* is on, a show about dedicated docs who heal maimed and injured animals, or at least get them into rehab. Your heart goes out to the suffering beasts, even though you know that by the end of the half-hour the beagle will learn to walk again, the cockatiel will find its voice. Now I'm looking at a snake that's become lethargic and won't eat, perhaps because it's swallowed something it shouldn't. A reassuring lesson to be learned from this show: animals always have a reason for what they do—just as there's a reason why I'm leaving earlier than usual for the gym. I open my mouth, but like the snake's it doesn't seem to want to work right.

"Fitness test," is what finally pops out.

Eric's forehead wrinkles. "What kind of test?"

"Oh, you know, where the trainer takes your measurements and goes over your exercise plan and gives you a whole lot of new stuff to do." In point of fact I've been overdue for a fitness test by at least a year, but Eric doesn't know that. "So I'll be longer at the gym than usual, I don't know how long." How do other people manage this kind of deception? According to popular culture, people lie to their spouses all the time. Half of all the plots of stage, screen and literature turn on it. Surely I've lied to Eric in the past; the white lies that keep a relationship running smoothly have tripped off my tongue like declarations of love. I just never lied on this scale before. "I feel like going and getting it over with," I tell him. That much isn't a lie, I *do* want to get it over with.

The worry-wrinkles in his brow haven't totally faded. "Are you okay?"

It's not the way I spoke that makes him ask, or my strange urge to go to the gym early; I know from experience that I must have some kind of *look* on my face. Sitting in the living room, walking down the street, shopping at the supermarket—I never know when Eric will ask me what's wrong, because I'm wearing a *look*. Something has crossed my mind—some random unmoored *irritation*—and my face has clouded over, the corners of my mouth turned down. Usually I can snap out of it, shrug or wave to show Eric that nothing's wrong, not really. Only now the look isn't so easy to shake off. I turn away, as if one of the CD's in the rack next to me has spoken my name. I run a finger down the titles, not really reading any of them. If there ever was a time to confess, it's now. It's early enough to be forgiven without too much pain changing hands. It's my chance—the *one chance*, also familiar from stage, screen, and literature—to alter the course of the story. I hesitate for so long, standing with my leather bag in one hand, that it's as good as admitting that something's wrong. A lump in my throat is just waiting for my lips to open so it can burst into the room. Yet whatever form it would take—a cry of relief, a wail of sorrow—must be avoided at all costs. I shrug again, wave my free hand—*nothing's wrong*—and go over and kiss him, quickly, and stroke Maddy, who has moved up from the floor to Eric's side.

Once I'm in the car I let out some hot stale breath, all that's left of the pending explosion. That moment in the living room took some years off my life. Before I know it I'm angry, pounding my fist on the wheel. It's good, this anger: it gets me going, like a fourth cup of coffee, out of the garage and onto our sleepy side street, deserted on a Sunday. Richard lives out by Bannister Mall, which means I have to head east for several miles along Blue Parkway, a stretch of road where there's some round-shouldered ruin on every other lot—fly-blown roadhouse, tumbledown motel, adult bookstore-and-peep-show in a tin shack. It all smells of feckless, human-sized failure, as homely as a sad country song that's painful to listen to, but you listen anyway because the lyrics hold an unexpected truth. I could park my new, shiny car in any of these weed-choked spaces and paste my shingle to the windshield: **45-YEAR-OLD WITH TEARS IN HIS EARS WILL CUCKOLD DECENT PARTNER FOR FREE.** Get out the barbecue, Ruby, and the malt liquor, too, while you're at it—there's a new show in that patch of goldenrod down the street.

Blue Parkway finally leads to I-435. My radio, tuned to the oldies station, fades in and out as it always does on this stretch of highway. I turn the radio off and listen to the muted *whoosh* as I pass every vehicle, even the bouncing tractor-trailers, in a Sunday rush hour of

77

my own making. Richard, this is the first and last time I'm meeting you like this, it just can't be done. Yet I can't deny the thrill of it. To be alone with you, to stretch out naked with you on an honest-to-God bed—I've been waiting for this for more than one lifetime. No Blue Parkway entrepreneur ever harbored a sweeter or more sordid dream.

He lives in an apartment complex, one of those huge places built on the cheap but, for many, a step up from humbler beginnings. There are no dangers to be found on a cul-de-sac with a swimming pool—no crack, no drive-by shootings, none of the temptations of the streets. There are signs of families here as well as single adults: a tiny playground with a sandbox, a slide, and some tubing to crawl through. It sits empty on a Sunday afternoon, everyone gone, perhaps, to visit relatives.

I find Richard's building without too much trouble. It helps that his truck is parked near the stairs. It strikes me that I've never taken a ride in it—not the kind that involves distance, anyway. Though I've seen it travel at least as far as the exit of the parking garage, it's as if, suddenly, I can't believe it moves on its own. It must be the hand of God or some other unlikely force that picks it up and moves it from one place to another. This thought makes me bark with laughter. I take the stairs to the third level and ring his doorbell as if I do this every day, as if I already know the layout of his apartment, the contents of his kitchen cupboards, the view from his living room balcony.

When he comes to the door I brush past him as if there's someone else I came to see. I've no idea what he's wearing, whether he's excited or anxious. The apartment's like the first one Eric and I shared: combo living room/dining room, kitchen on the right, hallway to the left. Two bedrooms, probably, one large and one small. The place came furnished—with administrative decisions. The oatmeal color of the carpeting and wallpaper means no offense, but offends anyway: nothing should be *that* neutral. It's all as clean as bachelor quarters tend to get, though it smells a bit musty, like an air-conditioned motel room. Right now they could bottle that scent and sell it, for it's nothing less than *erotic*, as stimulating between the legs as it is dismaying to the nostrils.

78

I spin around to face Richard: His expression is composed yet tentative, like a recipe he's never tried before but hopes will suit the occasion. He wears his trademark sweatpants and tank top, and glancing down I see his bare brown feet. I've seen them in the locker room before, but to see them now, in this space of freedom and possibility, is unbearably arousing. I'm ready to bust out laughing at the outrageousness of being here, at learning the secret that sin is just plain *fucking joyful* after all.

A smile plays at his lips. He's reading half my thoughts and guessing at the other half. "Can I get you something?" he asks, raising one eyebrow. "I've got iced tea."

"What else have you got?"

He shrugs. "There's always beer."

"Great!" The idea of drinking beer with him is, like his bare feet, unbearably sexy. Who knows what will turn me on next—the dust on the mantel over the fake fireplace? The half-closed living room blinds that make the windows look drowsy?

"Here you go."

He hands me a bottle of Rolling Rock by the neck. I don't normally drink beer—never acquired a taste—but when I do it's still a treat, sinfully cold. "Nice place you've got," I tell him, and wipe my mouth with the back of my hand.

"Yeah," he says, and swipes a hand across his large, luscious lips. He's luscious all over, like fruit from the market that looks even better when you get it home. This plain setting suits him right down to the ground, and he's confident as he leads me down the short hallway to see his workout room, with a bench and free weights, and beyond that his bedroom. I *think* it's his bedroom. It's hard to tell because it doesn't have a bed, just a big sofa against one wall and some uneven brick-and-board shelves that hold books, CD's and a small stereo system. The lack of a bed throws me off; I forget to say anything till we get back to the living room, and then I only repeat myself: "Nice place."

He sets his half-empty bottle on an end table. There's a sofa here too, all sharp vinyl edges. He sits, pats the space beside him. It's the same gesture I use to get Maddy up on the sofa with me. As soon as I sit he puts his arm across the back, as if he's about to give me some fatherly advice. It's overwhelming, the heat of his body, his smell of Ivory soap. But I must have a *look* on my face, for when I finally glance up a jab of his chin invites me to come clean. Apparently my fucking joyfulness has faded. After a couple of tries all I can say is, "This isn't easy."

"I know," he says, but he doesn't know. He's not in a strange place, with a husband that he's lied to waiting at home. Or could it be that this place is, in its way, strange to him too? A framed photo on the end table shows a pretty young black woman and two dimpled boys who favor her. It must have been hell to leave them, no matter what he says.

His hand settles lightly on my shoulder. "We don't have to do anything if you don't want to."

"Oh, yeah," I tell him. "Yeah, we do."

I press my face against his chest. This will never be undone.

**Later** I'm stumbling naked into the living room, seeing by the clock over the fake fireplace that it's been only an hour—is that possible?—since I arrived. My mouth and throat are so dry they hurt. I move on to the kitchen for water, helping myself to a glass from a cabinet, immersed in the strangeness of the room. I fill the glass from the tap but only drink half of it, enough to dispel the dehydrated feeling. I've just put the glass in the sink when a cat, a short-haired orange cat, comes around the end of the counter, rubbing against the corner and purring. Where has the cat been all this time? I have to remind myself that not all cats are like Maddy, who comes to the door to greet strangers. "Hi, kitty," I say to this one, and he closes his eyes for a second, a signal of love and trust. Since I've made it to the kitchen, that inner sanctum, I must be an okay guy. Or maybe being naked has something to do with it, if cats even notice that kind of thing. More likely this one is just hungry. I spot a plastic one-piece food-and-water bowl across the room, beside the refrigerator. The bowl is almost empty, but there are a couple of teaspoons of pale brown mush left. The cat looks at the bowl, then looks at me as if he's mistaken me—a huge white flabby object—for his owner. Embarrassed by his mistake, he scoots away.

I stop at the bathroom to pee. The toilet seat lid and tank are up-holstered in red plush, one of his efforts to soften the atmosphere of the place. Or maybe it's a contribution of a former lover. I know so little about Richard, just the outline of his life—his job, the wife and two kids he left behind. In the bedroom, during our thrashing around, I found myself at one point with my chin nearly resting on his nightstand, and there was another picture of his kids, playing in a park or back yard. Then I was snatched away from them, just as Richard's life had snatched him away.

Standing naked in someone else's living room for the first time in years, I take a moment to try to reconstruct what just happened; it was impossible, during the course of events, to absorb it all. Strange-ness hits me again, this chair, that braided rug, and what am I looking for? Oh, my cigarettes, on the orange coffee table. It's not convincing as wood, this table, just as his bed was not convincing as a bed—it was the sofa, after all, that folded out into a bed. When he tossed the cushions aside and yanked the contraption open, I thought, Oh shit, I know these so-called beds, right under that wafer-thin mat-tress there's an iron bar that'll break my back. He gave me a look that said, Sorry, but this is it. That raised eyebrow again. I'm standing there with my dick sticking out of my jeans—what am I going to say? I shuck them off, throw my t-shirt on the floor. He takes my forearm and pulls me over. I need a place to put my glasses, end up tumbling them onto the night table, near an alarm clock with huge red digits. Now that I've entered this contest without reading the rules, there are things I should explain. My hands shake as I try to sketch in the air how unsure I am, how unlikely it is that this will all turn out, but he's not only read the rules, he's inventing new ones. His hands shake too, sparking off sex. My awkwardness pitches me off balance, the bed makes a sound like a trash can full of jingle bells, but the impact's not as bad as…hello, he's still with me, hovering weight, searching tongue, hot hands squeezing as if he can't believe I'm real. And why should he, when his hands, his breath are transforming me into something I've never been before?

"Hey," he calls out to me now, alerted by the flick of my lighter, "bring your smokes in here."

He's lying on the edge of the bed, facing the photo of his kids dressed in their Sunday best. The striped ball on the grass between them looks nailed to the spot. Is the nightstand, next to this bed and the things it has seen, an appropriate place for this photo? How would I know? It seems he's communing with them, having a private moment. Then he turns to face me, in his hand a yellow, boomerang-shaped ashtray that he places in front of him. I pass him the cigarettes and he shakes one loose, reaches for my lighter. As he takes his first drag his chest expands, his nipples, their color barely perceptible, rising. He shifts closer. His big cock lolls around like a drunken invertebrate. I smoke, aware of my own chest rising and falling, and for a few moments we're lost in the great lie that smoking is sexy. "I didn't know you indulged," I say, startled by my own voice, that it still sounds like me.

"Only on special occasions," he says, smoke leaking from his mouth.

He makes eye contact more often than anyone I've ever met, perhaps because he knows—have I told him?—his green eyes are captivating. *Have* I told him? What have I said to him, ever, about anything? He raises a hand, strokes the side of my face. Goosebumps swarm over my backside. Not long ago I was dripping with sweat, my face mashed against the mattress. Feeling his hands, his sweat. There are as many ways to say please as there are things to ask for, but I never…never begged like that before. Not with anyone. Never went to jelly like that, turned myself inside out for cock.

He knows it, too. He's swaggering, if a man who's horizontal can swagger. He takes a drag, exhales, holds his free hand out to me as you would to a stray dog. And damned if I'm not sniffing it. Does this remind me of anything? Maybe a hundred things. There's only so much memory can pick up, rolling back over the years like a lint brush: a few flashes, some textures, the quality of light in a forgotten room—someplace in New York, maybe, where I had so much anonymous sex, so many connections fragmenting in my memory because they were just bits and pieces to begin with. And the whole point of each one was…what? That there would be *others*, already standing in line, each holding a torn ticket?

82

I shake my head at him. "Jarred a few things loose." Thump the heel of my hand against my temple.

"Pardon?"

Did he just say *Pardon*? "Jarred a few things loose," I say, wagging my head again, and worry crosses his face, as if I might be talking about my teeth. But his hand is still hanging there so I go back to it, licking it, savoring its salt.

"Shit," he says, realizing the cigarette in his other hand has about burned down to his fingers. So has mine. My hand seems so small and white next to his as we crush the butts deep into the ashtray.

I lie back and close my eyes. How easy it would be to drift. A groan of plumbing, a hoot from the parking lot, a siren somewhere—sounds more lulling than distracting, like the scent of his sweat, not sour, more like the smell of baking bread. If I could stay like this, with time just once refusing to unfold, the red digits on the bedside clock as still as if painted on, then I could rest.

But instead of rest comes a dream. I'm driving, the speedometer needle twittering upward at the lower edge of my vision. Straight ahead is a blurry stretch of road where something's waiting, and it won't wait for long. The collision will leave nothing behind but dust and ashes, a scatter of smoking parts. And I can't slow down, the needle only moves one way.

I wake with a start. Though I couldn't have been asleep for more than a minute, it was enough for Richard to drift off too. He wakes with a smooth unfurling of his eyes.

"Ahem," he says, holding his hand out again. "Where were we?"

I'm sucking his thumb, deeply, seriously, as if I could make it come.

When it's time, I pull on my clothes and look around as if it's a motel room I'm leaving, with little chance of reclaiming anything I might leave behind. Richard has left for the bathroom, so I have privacy for the call I have to make, my fingers trembling over the dial-pad of Richard's cordless phone.

When Eric's voice comes—"Hello?"—it takes more than a beat, more than two, for me to answer. "Hi, honey," I say. Is it my imagination or does my voice sound far away, even to me?

"How was the test?" he asks.

83

My legs go out from under me, placing my sore butt on the edge of Richard's jingly-jangly bed.

"Did it wear you out?"

That second question nearly does me in. How come nobody told me how hard this was going to be?

"Hello? Can you hear me?"

I take a deep breath, the only thing I can think of to do, and when I let it out some toxin seems to go with it, leaving behind a spot of calmness like the eye of a hurricane, enough for me to remember: the fitness test, that's what he's talking about. "Oh, hey, it was rough," I'm telling Eric, "but I feel good. Nothing like a, a tough workout."

"Are you ready to go to dinner? Want me to wait for you outside?"

Okay, okay, time for the next lie, a way to explain that, while it usually takes me five minutes to get home after I've called from the gym, this time it will take longer. "Oh, no," I tell him. "Actually I have to go back inside, they reminded me my contract's about to expire so they're writing me up a new one. It shouldn't take too long."

"Okay, if you say so."

Thank God, this torture is over, I can return to where I am, I can wrap up my visit here, I can get back to my life—but wait, wait! Eric hasn't said "Love you," which means it's up to me to say it first. But I've returned to where I am, I'm not in that limbo where I learned to speak glibly, and though it sickens me to admit it I don't want Richard, who is out in the living room now, to overhear me say "Love you" into the phone. So I just say, "'Bye, sweetie," and hang up.

I paste a smile on my face for Richard, who is standing by the door, ready to usher me outside—but not before he gives me a long, probing kiss. Slightly dizzy, I follow him onto the breezeway to the top of the stairs. "Hey, listen," he says as we're standing at the brink, his hands in the pockets of his sweatpants. "This should've been longer. We should've had more time."

My touchy side surfaces—is he blaming me for having to leave? I could remind him that it's lucky we got together at all, though "lucky" can't pass my lips right now. I have to get home, I have to see Eric's face before I can believe in luck again. At the same time, I know what Richard means. In a perfect world we'd have more time, and I wouldn't have to lie, and Richard and Eric and I would all be content. We have to salute the flag of happiness, even if it will never draw nearer than the horizon. Anyway, this is a unique occasion; I'm standing outside Richard's apartment, the place where he *lives*, and he's bidding me goodbye with a look of regret, satiety, fear, and hope. At one time, prior to Eric, this forceful, well-endowed man with green eyes and handsome brown skin might have been my savior; even now, in this wetting-my-pants rush to get home, I can't take it for granted that he thinks I'm worth reaching for, patting my shoulder, the best he can do in this public spot. I pat his shoulder in return. "It's been great," I tell him.

He moves his lips in the slightest suggestion of a kiss. "See you Tuesday," he says.

The wooden steps seem flimsier on the way down. Their paint is a bit worn, chipped at the edges. In a small patch of gravel by the landing sit three fresh, startlingly brown dog turds. Nearby, the open door of a laundry room releases odors of chlorine and scorched lint. I know this, the homely life of the apartment complex, the sights and smells of semi-privacy; it reminds me again of the place where Eric and I started out. Strange how, in the equilibrium of the moment, my life with him and my afternoon with Richard both make sense.

Wired, I drive out of the cul-de-sac as sensitized to every pebble on the road as the princess to the pea. The radio is way too loud, and when turning it down doesn't help I switch it off. It won't work on I-435 anyway, and before I know it I'm at the Bannister on-ramp. Tractor-trailers are everywhere now, I no sooner leave the ramp than a big mothering honker bears down on me from behind. I slow down, forcing him to pass. If he's trying to make up for lost time he's doing well, flying low at 80 in a 65-mile-an-hour zone. "Jesus *Christ*," I snarl at him, feeling the suction as he pulls past. A few seconds later another aggressive grill fills my rear view mirror. Out of nervous habit I reach for the radio knob again. I want to hear something, anything, even if it's the *rama-lama-ding-dong* of the oldies station. What do you know, the signal's still clear, and they're playing "It's My Party," as they do so often. The girls singing *cry if I want to, cry if I want to* sound as if they wash their hair with Prell, drink sodas at the corner drugstore, and don't have a clue that they're singing about anything as ugly as betrayal.

Before I know it I'm slowing down, pulling into the emergency lane and stopping. At this moment there's no traffic in either direction, my friends in their semis have vanished over the horizon. *Cry if I want to, cry if I want to* breathes its last. I close my eyes, press my fingers against my temples and rub. Something about the wavering yellow stripe at the edge of the lane has stayed with me, sickening me. If I could concentrate, find something to center on, I could make the dizziness stop. The problem is, I'm confused about where I'll be when I open my eyes. Will I be back in Richard's bed, waking from a post-coital dream? Perched on the sofa in my living room, watching Animal Planet as if none of this ever happened? I'm onto something here, it's crucial to follow the exercise through. So I concentrate, probing and pushing till I can not only place myself in another time and place but in another *body*. The body of…Eric. Eric at his computer desk, staring at a screen that shows stacks and columns of playing cards, one of his inscrutable solitaire games. The hand on the mouse clicks away, making cards fly. There's no point to this scene, except that… *something is about to happen.* Since there's nothing to see except the computer screen—card, cursor, card, cursor—I sharpen up my hearing; and sure enough, there it is: the phone ringing.

The phone sits on its own little shelf attached to the side of Eric's desk. But he doesn't pick up on the first ring, or even the second. There's only one reason for that pause, and there it is: the little white rectangular thing that sits in front of the phone. It's about the same size as the kitchen timer we keep near the stove, with the same kind of little screen. Only this screen shows—oh, Paul, how could you have forgotten?—an unfamiliar phone number, and underneath that number, as clear as can be, a name that appears as **ROSCOE RICH- ARD**.

So what do we do, Eric? Let the call go, assuming it's a wrong number, or pick up? Well, it is about time Paul was calling…in fact it's past the time when he should have called from the gym…and so on impulse we pick up. And here it comes, the all-too-familiar, Cicero-addressing-the-Senate voice of Paul. "They're writing me up a new contract," says this idiot, casually betraying ten years of trust.

I open my eyes, unbuckle my seat belt and throw the car door open so fast it rebounds, clipping me in the shin. I barely make it to the guardrail before I heave my guts out onto the bright green grass. I've eaten nothing since breakfast but a banana, a cup of yogurt, and a beer; but I know, as I watch the thin pale mixture trickle down to the earth from which it came, that there's something else there, after all—the taste of Richard Roscoe, a taste that's been haunting the back of my throat for weeks.

On the road again, I take the Blue Parkway exit, which leads to a wooded intersection. On one corner there's a general store in a log cabin, or a building made to look like a log cabin (which works for people like me, who don't know the difference). At the entrance stands a sign-on-wheels advertising a sale on 80-pound sacks of dog chow. I pull in, making sure that the card hanging on the door says **OPEN**.

The owner stands behind the counter, a newspaper spread flat before him. An older man with slicked-down hair so white it seems to disappear into his skin, he looks at me with eyebrows raised, mouth open. I foresee a short visit, a matter of seconds before I'm told, politely or not, to hit the road. But he just looks at me as if he's never seen a pale, heavyset, stressed-out guy with traces of puke in his beard. So I ask my question: "Do you have a phone I can use?"

He stares for so long that I begin to wonder if he's the aging white version of a wooden Indian. When he finally nods his head slightly toward the center aisle, I look back and there it is, on the rear wall, past sacks of dog chow like body bags. I move toward it, dread weighing me down. It's like one of those scenes where the condemned man shuffles toward the electric chair. My stomach lurches again, and I wonder why they never show a condemned man throwing up. Doesn't anyone ever hurl on his way to the chair, especially after one of those heavy last meals? And what's with my heart? It seems to be expanding with each beat, pushing out the front of my shirt in a cartoon parody of fear. I guess a heart attack on the way to the chair is also possible. But I make it—or make it as far as picking up the receiver with one hand and searching for coins with the other. Beads of sweat trickle down the back of my neck, and I'm seeing a lot of floaters, like a stampede of one-celled animals. I listen for the dial tone, then drop silver. After one ring I know it's no good, and hang up. It's getting later every minute, and I have to have something in

87

mind to say. In what seems like a lifetime ago I said something about having to renew my contract at the gym. As so many losers have said, it sounded brilliant at the time. Now I don't have the heart, not to mention the brain, to come up with further excuses. I'm going to have to tell Eric the truth.

But *not right now*. For now I can just call, reassure him that I'm on my way home, and get a feel for what kind of mood he's in. Explanations can come later. I drop the thirty-five cents again and dial. If the caller I.D. says **PAY PHONE** he'll pick up. He'll have to.

One ring, and another, and a third. After the fourth ring, the answering machine comes on. There's Eric's voice, slow and solemn: *and we, will return your call, as soon, as possible.* There's still time for him to pick up, I'm not about to let go of the line. "Eric? It's me, honey...pick up. Are you there? Pick up...I'm still here...Honey?" Stupidly I raise my voice, as if that will make a difference: "Eric? I'm on my way home!"

This time I hate to hang up, to cut off a connection that's getting me nowhere yet seems like my last chance. My mouth goes dry, the floaters return and my heart's trip hammering again, my body unwilling to follow where my train of thought has gone, suddenly and painfully: *Last-ditch effort. Damage control. Salvage therapy.* No, I can't think in terms of losing Eric; if I do I'll break down completely. For a minute I pace up and down, wringing my hands, past shelves of dusty canned goods. Jesus Christ, there still aren't any other customers here, this place must be failing. Well, it's Blue Parkway, after all.

Somehow I decide, with my short-circuiting brain, to call Richard. As I dig for additional change this seems more and more like the thing to do.

He picks up on the first ring. "Hello?" How formal that one word sounds.

"Richard? It's Paul." No doubt I sound businesslike too. I have no warm feelings at the moment.

"Thought you might call," he says.

"Do you know what's happened?" I ask, as if my scenario—Eric's spotting Richard's name on the caller ID and assuming the worst—is now as well known as yesterday's news.

"I've got a pretty good idea." His speech drags a bit, as if I've awakened him from a nap. "You've got caller ID at home, huh?"

Having my worst fear confirmed by his sleepy voice feels even worse than I imagined. "So Eric called you?"

"Somebody called, asked for you. I said you weren't here, and hung up." The hesitation in his voice hints at a longing to say something more. Finally he says, "I shouldn't have said that. I should have just said, 'Wrong number,' and hung up."

"It doesn't matter." My eyes are closed; I realize I've had them closed ever since I dialed his number. "The end result would be the same."

"Where you calling from?" he asks.

"I'm on the road. I haven't been home yet. I've got a feeling Eric's not there. I called and got the answering machine."

"You don't think he's on his way *here*, do you?" For the first time he sounds alert.

"No. He could have looked up your address, but I doubt it. I don't see it happening." Of course I don't, I have my eyes closed. "Anyway, I'd better get off the phone." With that I cradle the receiver, still with my eyes closed, perfectly catching the hook on the first try. This is good, because I've got a notion I'll be doing everything by feel from now on.

**It's** the stillness of our house that gets to me—the instant announcement of silence. If the walls and floors suddenly went transparent it would be no clearer that the place is empty.

Yet it can't be. Clutching my gym bag—a prop I just won't let go of till the curtain rings down—I race through the living room to the stairs. "Eric?" The study door is closed. I swing it open to find his chair empty, his computer turned off. Sitting there like an innocent bystander is the caller-I.D. device, but I don't have the heart or nerve to look at it. "Eric?" I knock on his bathroom door, open it to the usual clean-smelling orderliness. "Eric? Maddy?" No one in the bedroom, either. Where could he have gone? Why can't I even find the *cat*?

I go back downstairs, slowly, trying to think. The "redial" thing on the phone would tell me if he called a cab or a friend to pick him up, but I don't have the heart to try it. If only I could find Maddy, then I could convince myself that everything's all right. But he's not in any of his hiding places, the holes in the cat tower, the space behind the sofa.

Think, Paul, *think*. Maddy's bowl is still on the floor, still with food and water in it, isn't that a good sign? And if his insulin is in the fridge, *as of course it is*, then everything is definitely all right. I open the fridge door with a recurrence of that swoony feeling, as if the cat's cold body might be stuffed onto the second shelf, between the yogurt and the Cool Whip. Raising the lid on the butter compartment, I find the insulin gone; but wait, wait, maybe I didn't put it back in the right place after shooting Maddy this morning. Which reminds me of another way to find out for certain if Eric has left and taken the cat with him: I let the fridge door close and open the cupboard near the wall phone.

Maddy's box of syringes is gone.

He not only left me, he had to take the cat.

Wandering back to the living room, I find it ruthlessly intact, like a little museum exhibit, with its scatter of newspapers and cat toys. And, as in a museum, I can hardly just go in and sit down. I back away, shaking my head. Better to leave it all—the butts in the ashtray, two empty coffee mugs, the cable box tuned to Animal Planet. Seal it up until the weight of time wears it down to what has been its true essence all along: that of a human-sized, round-shouldered failure.

**"He's** all right," Todd says. "He just hit his head."

I'm sitting on the kitchen floor, beside the sink, and Davy's there, squinting down at me. Aaron's there too, just standing with his mouth open. It must be Kent who's still vacuuming upstairs; the drone of the Electrolux is slightly disturbing, like a dentist's drill heard from the waiting room.

"I'd just as soon you all not...stare at me like that."

"Oh." Davy jumps, as if I've really accused him of something. "Well, back to work, I guess." He and Aaron leave the room as if they're yoked together.

Todd isn't convinced that he needs to stop staring. "You look really pale. Maybe you should lie down."

"Yeah." I think of white pills. Two of them would knock me out for eight hours, but I don't want to be out that long. Or do I?

**A b o u t** our rooms. Davy's is a pigpen. There's no one to tell him to pick up his clothes—Brian's not our house mother, after all—so they collect in layers until even Davy's sick of it and has to make six trips down to the laundry room. Aaron's room is messy too, in a different way. He's a reader, like me, so there are books and magazines strewn around. The *Playboys* that pile up in the front room tend to gravitate here: he really does read the articles. (I go for the Forum and the party jokes, myself.) Todd's room, on the other hand, looks like something out of a military school dorm. There's even a footlocker—a *footlocker*, for Christ's sake—parked at the end of his bed. Not much of a reader, he puts together model airplanes—I guess Riley gets them for him— that look nothing like the models I made as a teen, all crooked wings and misbegotten globs of glue. No, Todd's look professional, and you really have to wonder about a guy who's as neat as this.

Now, Dwight's room, which is now Kent's room, was funky. Its brackish smell—there I go with the sea analogies again, I just can't help it—was traceable to his rumpled bedclothes that I visited more than a few times—yes, I admit it—when he wasn't there. I loved the way the powder-blue bedding got pushed around by his body. I ran my fingertips along the mysterious depressions, picturing his thighs *here*, his ass cheeks *here*…here his heels, here his elbows. I imagined I saw the delicate tracks his sleep-erect cock had left. His pillow smelled of hair and breath. The funk continued on the floor, where the thick wool socks he favored lay with their gaping tops askew like a crowd of fish-mouths exhaling the sultry stink of his feet. Not for the faint-hearted, but what the fuck, I crawled on my hands and knees among those socks, the grays and greens, the navy blues, and discovered, through frank assessments made by trembling fingers, that he used them to *jack off* into. Each one bore a crust inside, like a hidden prize. From there it was a short trip to his white briefs, which had a gray cast, like rain clouds. What would he have thought if he'd found me, sitting in the middle of his bedroom floor with his Fruit-of-the-Looms stretched over my head like a ski mask, the better to sniff and lick the crotch?

91

He would have bust a gut laughing, I'm pretty sure.

Only Brian's room remained unknown to me, until that day when we were sitting around the front room, waiting for him to get back from town so we could start group, and Davy said, "I've been in Brian's room."

"Bullshit," I said.

Davy was sitting Indian-style on the sofa, with the latest issue of *Playboy* on his lap. Trying to take interest in naked women who looked less real than vinyl blow-up dolls. "No bullshit," he said. His eyes were definitely somewhere else, and I realized, with not much surprise, that he had a crush on Brian like the rest of us did.

"So spill," I said. "All of it. Tastes, smells, and what have you."

Davy laughed, partly from shock—did Paul ever stop? "Well, I didn't taste anything. But there was a scent in the air. Incense. What's that one that begins with *p*?"

Penis, of course, was my first thought. "You don't mean Patchouli?"

"That's it."

"Yuck. Too sweet."

"I think that's what it is. He uses lotion, too, this skin lotion that has a smell to it. Big old bottle. Vaseline Intensive Care."

"Oh Christ." In my excitement I got to my hands and knees, rump wiggling like a dog's. "You know what he uses that for."

A blank look.

"Oh, Davy, he *jacks off* with it!"

"Okay, Paul." This admonition was familiar. It meant *Okay, Paul, you've had your fun, you're gonna have to stop now. All kidding aside, let's remember what we're all about here. Maybe you need to go to your room for a while.*

I pressed on anyway. "Well? What else?"

"Nothing else."

"Bullshit."

"A crucifix on the wall."

"You don't say."

"A creepy one. Lots of blood."

"A Catholic upbringing. There are always remnants."

"But we don't talk about God here."

"All the more reason why he'd have a private shrine. Any candles?"

"I've said too much. Way too much." He closed the cover on the curvaceous babydoll spread across his lap.

"But you didn't explain one thing," I said. "What were you doing in his room in the first place? Were you lost?"

He shot me a look that said it really was time to shut up now.

Then there's my room. A dull affair. No dirty clothing strewn around; I stow it in a duffel bag I found somewhere. Some books on the desk, but nothing like the unkempt piles I have at home. Had at home. When I had a home. See, that's part of the problem. My room has no lived-in feel because I resist seeing it as my room. It's as if I still have one somewhere else, *which I don't*. Even the closet: I can't seem to keep more than two shirts hung up at the same time. The rest are folded, ready for the suitcase.

Perhaps the bed is all that counts. Twisted blankets, skewed sheets—there's a touch of Paul in here somewhere, perhaps no larger than a grain of sand. Pulling the bedclothes up over my nose and mouth, I sense my scent. A scent that has no smell, at least not to me; it's more like a temperature, the feel of air that's been inhaled and exhaled a million times till there's hardly anything left in it—no nourishment, no relief, just the inside of my body turned out, my abused lungs, my scandalous mouth, my leaking dick. *Ahhh.* I may not live here, but I can sleep here. Which is what I'm doing, following Todd's suggestion that I lie down. (Of course I had to have lunch first—two peanut butter and jelly sandwiches, a glass of milk, and three cigarettes.) It's a sleep that's not quite sleep, dozing on a cusp where my consciousness teeters, trying to decide whether to let go completely.

Soon my curiosity gets the better of me: the house is *too* quiet. I put on my slippers and pad downstairs, to find the others sitting around in the den, each with a section of newspaper. We're supposed to have Group this afternoon, it was on the list—after the kitchen floor and running the vacuum and cleaning our rooms. I didn't clean my room, and I doubt if anyone else did. If chores can be blown off, I guess Group can, too. Except that I've got something to talk about. So I offer, to these paper-covered faces, a question I hope doesn't sound too shaky: "Hey, how about Group?"

93

"Can't we take a day off?" Kent asks, not bothering to set his paper down.

"Yeah," Davy says. "Brian's taking the weekend off, so why can't we?"

*But the list*: it's on the tip of my tongue. I can't say it, though—it's too much out of character for me to want to stick to someone else's schedule. Still, I need Group. In a place where I'd least expect it—under the kitchen sink—I have discovered something: that Eric didn't betray me, it was quite the reverse. Now I need confession and absolution, words I've never taken quite this seriously before. I'm about to broach the subject again when Todd, who's been reading the TV section, pipes up.

"Look. Tonight, on Channel 8. *The Haunting*. Any of you guys seen it?"

Yeah, about a dozen times. "No," I tell him, "and I don't want to."

"What's the matter, you scared?"

There's a macho challenge if there ever was one. *Hey, you! Scared of a movie? Scared of the dark? Scared of your own shadow, nancy-pants?*

Davy chimes in. "That's a hell of a scary movie."

Kent's frowning. "What is it?"

"*The Haunting*," Todd says. "With Julie Harris and Claire Bloom."

"Who are they?"

Me (depressed): "Oh Christ."

"Sounds like a chick flick," Kent says.

"Doesn't scare me," Aaron says, not looking up from his book.

All right, so the score is: Todd is challenging, Davy is respectful, Kent is disdainful, and Aaron and I are both lying—me, because I have seen it before, and Aaron, because he's scared witless. The way he uses his eyes, or fails to, gives him away.

Yet, in spite of our differences, I could swear we've all just moved closer together.

Davy licks the tip of his pencil and says, "It is a great movie. One of the best of its kind."

Kent's still sneering. "One of the best chick flicks?"

"Okay, you son of a bitch," Todd says. "I dare you to watch it, then tell me it's a chick flick."

94

This challenge brings a gleam to Kent's eye. "You're on."

"Ten o'clock," Todd says.

Oh, good. Ten o'clock. That means the movie will be over at midnight—a great time to be scared shitless.

The TV room is really just an alcove off the living room. The TV set dates from the days when they were disguised as pieces of furniture: the old console has an Early American look, it even sits on little carved legs. A VCR sits incongruously atop it, but doesn't work. So we're stuck with whatever happens to be showing at any given time. Not that we watch TV that much; our viewing habits are irregular. For a while Kent displayed an unhealthy fascination with "Bewitched," which resembled Aaron's obsession with "I Dream of Jeannie." Todd, as he tells it, was a "Law and Order" addict for a long time, but went cold turkey shortly after moving in here. Aside from occasional shows I remember from childhood—Eric and I have sat through more than one "Twilight Zone" and "Get Smart" marathon—I haven't been much for network TV, preferring to watch videos. I last saw *The Haunting* in its VHS incarnation. Indifferently formatted, with no remastering of sound or picture, the flick still packed a wallop. Mercifully, I was able to go to sleep after seeing it—the opposite of the experience I had as a kid.

**It's** almost ten. Davy, who with great effort has dragged the green wingchair into the alcove, pipes up again, "Would Brian want us to watch this?"

I have a Bronx cheer with Davy's name on it. *Now* he brings up Brian, after a day that began with cheerful cooperation and lapsed into neglect. Not only did we not do Group, we didn't follow Brian's dinner menu, either. Instead we foraged through the kitchen cupboards for whatever we felt like. I ended up eating Vienna Fingers with milk. Todd ate a can of pork and beans. Kent had some locally-canned chowder. Aaron took a cue from my lunch and ate two PB&J's. And yet, the question now posed by Davy—who ate some frozen vegetables and a fruit cup for dinner, go figure—has probably occurred to each of us. The rules that we semi-seriously live by have taken their toll. But do we really need Brian's permission to watch a movie? An old black-and-white movie from, if memory serves, 1962?

95

"If it's a horror movie," Kent says, "then it's all about superstition and negative thinking." He's claimed one of the best seats, though, at the end of the sofa.

"Doesn't scare me," Aaron mutters. He's pulled in one of the tall, heavy dining room chairs.

Settled on the opposite end of the sofa from Kent, I've filled a glass with ice cubes and look around for the two-liter bottle of orange soda that Todd put somewhere. He's made microwave popcorn too, a bushel of it. Okay, I've kept quiet all day, but now it's official ghost time. "Hear that?" I ask.

The four of them look at me with an implied, *What?*

"Old Joe. I think he's right over our heads."

Much rolling of eyes. *Really, Paul.*

When Davy comes back with his trademark can of Diet Coke, Todd asks him to turn off the hallway light.

Davy looks around as if Todd must have spoken to someone else. "That's the only light on. It'll be pitch dark without it."

"Not quite." eyeing his watch—he thinks he's at Houston Control, for Christ's sake—he completes an imaginary countdown and pulls out the "on" knob of the TV. The screen glows, then resolves into the MGM logo.

"Oh, all right," Davy says. Out goes the light.

Sitting in the dark as the immense outline of Hill House hovers over the opening credits, I have to face it: no matter how many times I watch this movie I get bushwhacked every time. You'd think, now that I've memorized the dialogue and can play back any scene at will just by closing my eyes, it wouldn't affect me that way; besides, the humor, much of it supposedly provided by Russ Tamblyn, is painfully corny, and it's all so dated. Yet, from the first voiceover in which Richard Johnson says, "Whatever walks in Hill House, walks alone," I'm hooked.

"This movie is in black-and-white?" Kent asks. "You didn't tell me that."

"What difference does it make?" Aaron asks, thoughtfully chewing on his thumbnail.

"Black-and-white movies aren't scary," Kent says. "You can't see the blood, or when you can, you can't tell it's blood."

"They used chocolate syrup for blood in *Psycho*," Davy offers. "I read that someplace."

"There's no blood in this one," I say, somewhat impatiently, wanting them to be quiet.

"Yeah, there is," Todd says. He's on the sofa, between Kent and me, leaning so far forward he seems to defy gravity. "Claire Bloom's got her period. You can see it running down her leg."

Davy: "Oh, gross!"

Kent pipes up again, before the opening credits are even finished. "You still haven't told me what this movie's *about*."

Since nobody else volunteers, it's up to me. "It's about a cocky professor who gathers a group of supernaturally-sensitive people together in a haunted house, to see if anything spooky happens." Not bad for a nutshell, though I could offer a lot more about the film, some of it speculation. Is it true, for example, that Theo, the Claire Bloom character, is supposed to be a lesbian? Turns out I don't have to mention it. The minute she appears, in Mary Quant black stretch pants and turtleneck, Kent mutters, "What a dyke."

Seeing her this time around, it does seem pretty clear. She doesn't deliver a single line to Julie Harris without some hidden meaning. And Julie, as Eleanor…what can I say? Eleanor's the heart and soul of the story, unfortunately for her, and Julie Harris's portrayal is the shrewdest I've ever seen. Eleanor is, by turns, pitiful, annoying, sympathetic, perhaps even brave. And losing her mind? Sometimes you think so, other times not.

Oh fuck, here's Luke, Russ Tamblyn's character, carrying on like the Womanizer of the Western World. At one time I thought…well, isn't he gay?

Kent points at the screen, filled at the moment with Tamblyn's puppyish features. "Wasn't he in *West Side Story*?"

"Yeah," Aaron says.

"I always thought he was gay."

Todd clears his throat. Loudly.

"You mean he's not?"

"I mean *shut up, assholes!*"

"*I* thought he was gay," I mumble.

97

Todd gives me a look. He's effectively silenced us, fans and skeptics alike; no one makes another sound till the first commercial break.

Even then we're quiet for a while, watching an ad for a used car lot as if this, too, is part of what we've been waiting for. Finally Aaron slides out of his chair and says, "Gotta pee." He heads toward the dark hallway, then stops. The darkness itself has given him pause.

"There's nobody there, Aaron," Todd says—just the kind of remark that his sarcastic tone was made for.

"Go ahead, turn on the light," Davy says.

I see why Aaron's hesitating: in order to reach the light switch he will have to take at least one step into the darkness that not even the glow of the TV screen can reach. He feels along the hallway wall for it, stretching his arm, just to be sure he can't make it without taking that step. I'm with him all the way, I wouldn't want to take that step either.

"Want me to turn it on for you?" Todd, really sarcastic now.

Aaron mumbles something, takes that long first step. The light is on.

Now, during a margarine commercial, I get a better look at my companions. Really, this is all so painfully familiar, so ordinary. The only uncanny thing that's likely to happen is that I might actually fall asleep sitting here, scary movie or not.

Okay. Aaron's back, and so is the show.

When Eleanor and Theo are trapped in a bedroom while some unseen monster barges up and down the hallway, thumping on the walls to make a sound like the gates of Hell banging shut, I notice, in the corner of my eye, that Davy jumps a little with each *bang*, his fanny nearly leaving the cushion he's so tensely occupying. As for me, I may not be jumping on the outside, but on the inside my guts are pitching and tossing like a ship in rough seas.

Okay, the scene is over now, and there was nothing there, after all, though my mind's ear is replaying the intolerable banging, and my mind's eye is stuck on the moment when the bedroom doorknob rattled and turned, just a fraction of an inch, as the women cowered.

Christ.

Okay, deep breath.

By the time morning comes—in the movie, anyway—my disbelief has not only been suspended, it's been cryogenically preserved—to be thawed, perhaps, sometime in the next century. It's breakfast time at Hill House—time for sweet Eleanor to read the writing on the wall: her name, scrawled in chalk (or, as the professor maddeningly observes, "something like chalk"): HELP ELEANOR COME HOME.

"Oh Jesus," Davy says. Like Kent, he's been both absorbed and restless, his foot swiveling ceaselessly at the end of his crossed leg. "That's it for me. Good luck, you guys."

"Don't be a pussy." Me, surprising myself.

"It's just a movie," Kent says, as if he's been calm all along. "A movie made a hundred years ago."

"Well, I was eight years old when this movie came out," I tell him. "I guess that makes me a hundred and eight. But who's counting?"

"Sorry."

"Shut up, you guys," Todd says.

By the time Russ Tamblyn finds the iron spiral staircase in the library, and makes some foolish dance moves on it (that was a different movie, Russ!), only to have it start...*jiggling* like a live thing...the hair has risen permanently on the back of my neck. At least it should be easier to cut that way.

"You know something?" Kent says. "Brian *wouldn't* want us watching this."

"What difference does it make?"

"Negative thinking. Superstition."

"You guys suck." Me again. Meaning Davy and Kent. Hope they don't take it literally.

Okay, there are a number of things we won't talk about. Number one: how cute Russ Tamblyn is. In fact he was a bit too cute, not rugged enough, to be a 1960s leading man, though today he'd be a breakout star. He'd be showing his butt, too, probably in a romantic comedy with Julia Roberts, the kind that make me want to jump into a vat of carbolic acid.

And we won't, we definitely won't be discussing the fact that old houses are creepy.

Davy is still shaking his head. "I don't know, guys."

"Oh, fuck, go to bed," Todd says. "No one's stopping you."

"Can't we just forget about the movie?" Despite his objections Davy can't take his eyes from the screen. He hasn't made a serious move to get up, either. It's my guess he won't, no matter how scared he gets: he won't want to go upstairs by himself.

As for me, I might not make it to the second floor at all, unless I'm dragged there kicking and screaming. Not that *our* old house is creepy. Embarrassed by the incontinent water stains on its ceilings and unseemly bulges in the walls, humbled by its sagging staircase and the cracks in its settled floors, this house lacks the spectacular ugliness of Hill House and has settled instead for the homeliness of, say, an old relative who's aged gracelessly. There's just something too plain about it to inspire chills.

Then again, there are more frightening sounds than sights in *The Haunting*, and that's one thing this house has plenty of, too—no screams or unhinged voices rambling in the night, perhaps, but still…. Even Brian can't explain what that *rattling* is in the night. We've all heard it. That's where the idea of Old Joe came from in the first place. So no, I'm not going to cut and run either. Sitting on the sofa with one leg under me, I'm settling in for the duration, with the guilty pleasure that comes from caving in to a bad idea. At another time in my life I'd be watching the forbidden movie *and* eating from a carton of chocolate ice cream in my lap.

More commercials. I realize we're not talking anymore during these breaks. Todd doesn't move; he's crouching on the very edge of the sofa like a catcher awaiting a tricky pitch. This gives me a clear view of Kent. Maybe it's the white sweatshirt he's wearing, but he looks…pale. Paler than Davy, who's grasping the arms of the wing chair so tightly that his knuckles might burst through his skin. Paler than Aaron, who's chewing on his cuticles. Paler than Todd, who, let's face it, doesn't ever look pale.

Back at the haunted house—the fictional one, on the TV screen. The plot has thickened. Everyone's been scared witless by now, and the professor's wife, Grace, has arrived unexpectedly. Grace is the type of stone-cold-bitch character that has a bull's-eye painted on her brow: the more she sneers at the others, including her (rather cute) husband, the more likely it becomes that she'll get the shit scared out of her before the next commercial. She plans to spend the night by herself in the stone-cold-haunted nursery, because she's so sure there's nothing there....

Meanwhile the others, having wised up, are spending the night in the parlor on the first floor, while Luke and the professor take turns keeping watch on the floor above. These arrangements are enough to lull the viewer into a false sense of security—*Thank God these imbeciles finally got some sense*—until you remember that, like all characters trapped in scary stories, they have enough weaknesses to ensure something will go wrong. Sure enough, when Luke's supposed to be keeping watch above, he steals down to the parlor to take a swig from a bottle that probably doesn't contain chocolate milk. Just like a man—so fucking lame.

"Asshole," Kent mutters. I cut my eyes in his direction, and damned if he isn't sitting beside me. Where the hell did Todd go? Oh, there he is, in the wing chair. And Davy is now seated on the floor in front of that chair, between Todd's legs. Aaron hasn't moved, but looks tense enough to jump any second.

Soon there's plenty to jump about. The unearthly echoing banging comes back, and we learn all over again how scary a noise can be. When the whatever-it-is reaches the parlor door, we get a new scare: the door starts *bending* from the outside, as if the lurking force has a power over solid wood that turns it into Silly Putty.... Just to see those door panels bulge is nearly enough to turn my sinking fear upside down, into a gorge-rising *ohmigod I'm so scared I'm going to throw up....*

And the funniest thing is, I know how this special effect, one of very few in the film, was done: they used a prop door made of rubber. Yes, a fucking *rubber door*. Yet nothing has or ever will be able to keep me from wanting to throw up, pass out, or shit when those door panels start heaving....

101

Feeling something touch my leg, I nearly jump, then realize Kent has slid his fingers under my knee. The same thing I've done with Eric in movie theaters, sometimes without realizing it. It helps, that animal warmth and pressure on your hand—helps when nothing else will. And it would help me, maybe, to touch Kent's arm. That sweatshirt he's wearing is as tempting as a security blanket, and sensing his firm flesh through it would be better than anything money could buy.

So I move just an inch over, v-e-r-r-y slowly; and while I don't dare let my hand brush against him, I let our sleeves have contact, and there's something even in this, this merest touch of clothing, that's as unexplainable as Old Joe, and just as hard to ignore. Good God, am I getting a hard-on? His hand is now all the way under my leg, but since he doesn't seem to notice it, I pretend I don't either.

Nothing is going to get easier now for the rest of the movie. When a commercial break comes, we're watching the increasingly sleazy used car ads as if they're all of a piece with the scary stuff. I sit through two of these commercials without realizing that Kent has not only moved closer, he's all the way into my space, pressed against me, one arm around my shoulders. The shock of this is nothing that makes we want to disengage him; rather than tell him to unhand me I keep my trap shut. His eyes are still fixed on the screen; he doesn't know what he's doing—just as Davy doesn't know what he's doing, not only sitting on the floor between Todd's legs, but wrapping an arm around each of them. And Aaron—where the hell is Aaron? His chair is empty. From now on, everyone's going to have to get my fucking permission before they move. Oh, there he is, on the other side of Kent, here on the sofa, pressed up against him just as Kent is pressed up against me. There's nothing erotic, nothing suggestive in this needy animal contact, which still does not explain *why I am getting a hard-on.*

Back to the show. The scariest thing yet—more than the bending door, more even than the banging and screaming—is the sight of Eleanor, on the brink of total madness, dancing by herself across the haunted floors of the house, her let-down hair and nightgown swirling about her as she turns and turns…and thinks, according to voiceover, *I'm home, I'm home.* Fear has its own vocabulary, too, and the use of *home* in this movie makes it the scariest word in the lexicon. For people like Eleanor, and—are you ready to face it, Paul?—*people who identify with her,* there is no home in this life or in the next, no refuge or safety or comfort; *there is nothing but torment.* And if we ever thought that we could be loved and safe and free, then what does that make us but *idiots* who *deserve* what's coming to us?

Grace is now missing from the nursery. An all-out search ensues. Eleanor, in the manner of totally-whacked-out fright film characters, has nothing better to do than make things worse. She takes to the iron spiral staircase, that quivering, twanging, *God damned* thing, and it's up to the professor to rescue her, risking his own life…. And rescue her he does, though not before she confronts the gaunt, terrified face of Grace appearing suddenly through a trap door…. It's enough to make Eleanor faint, and us boys aren't doing too well, either. The five of us are crammed together on the sofa now. Kent has both arms around my shoulders, my arms are around his torso, and our legs…like an acrophobic on a ledge, I can't bear to look down to see what our legs are doing. Aaron's on the other side of Kent, and his arms are somewhere in this tangle, perhaps around Kent's waist; Davy's sitting with his head mashed up against Todd's chest, Todd's arms are hugging him, and the face of Todd, who created this mess, is a study in Horrified Second Thoughts, his mouth hanging open. There would be other, much better ways to handle this, not the least of which would be to *turn a frigging light on* so that we wouldn't have just that dreadful, luminous black-and-white photography washing over us, but of course it's too late. A sofa that seats three comfortably is holding five, and yet we're not close enough.

Maybe, maybe that shock moment at the top of the staircase means that the worst is over. The movie does seem to be calming down, and look! Eleanor's even making a reluctant escape, under orders from the professor. Safely loaded into her little car, with a manly, sober Luke by her side, she's going to hightail it down the drive, toward freedom and sanity. Then, before they can get started, Luke leaves the car—he's a nitwit to the end, after all—and Eleanor takes off by herself. A struggle ensues, Eleanor's fighting *something* for control of the car as it careens down the thickly wooded drive. The final scare comes when the figure of Grace in her white nightshirt dashes across the road; twisting the wheel (or having it twisted away from her?), Eleanor crashes into a tree….

Pressed into a corner of the sofa like so much mashed potato, I'm aware that there's been movement around me, a sort of plunging, as if the cushion next to mine has been used as a diving board; and there's Kent, *behind* the sofa now, seeking a further margin of safety. He's standing there, wagging his head and repeating over and over, "Oh shit, oh shit…."

103

Aaron has latched onto my leg. Davy and Todd are twisted around each other like pretzel dough.

The last words of the film's ghostly narration—*whoever walks here, walks alone*—reverberate as "The End" appears, and never have those two words seemed so lame, like an apology that can't possibly cover the damage done. It is *not good* to be alive right now, here in this deathly black-and-white glow; it is *not advisable* to be living in a world where these things can take place; and it would be *just plain stupid* to expect to ever draw another breath that would be free of the enduring chill that's settled into my spine.

And I've seen the fucking movie *a dozen times*!

I turn my head, have to clear my throat many times before I can speak: "Kent? Are you…?"

No, he's not all right. Here is the point where the casual observer could take delight in the irony that Kent, who pooh-poohed the movie from the start, is the one most undone by it. "Come here," I tell him, reaching out. He looks at me as if I'm the very ghoul he's most frightened of. "Kent…?"

Someone has enough presence of mind to turn on the overhead light and switch off the TV. Davy, who has peeled himself free from Todd, says, "Well, this is *great*. There won't be any sleeping in this house tonight." Aaron's typically morose look has taken a turn for the worse. He looks like he's been bitch-slapped from one end of the Maine coast to the other. Todd, our former fearless leader, looks green, and I can only try to imagine what I look like. "Hammered shit" comes to mind.

104

When we've stirred ourselves a bit further, flexing our aching limbs, it seems that, as if by common consent, four of us have decided to become a lynch mob, with Todd as the prey.

Sensibly, he's backing away. "Guys? Don't look at me like that."

"Get the rope," I mutter.

"Hey." Aaron, striving to become the voice of reason. "Look, it's a great movie, okay? It just…does what it's supposed to do."

Even Davy, who has spent considerable time wrapped around Todd like stripes on a barber pole, looks ugly. "That doesn't mean that some rat bastard couldn't have warned us."

"Whoa," Todd says. "I thought you'd seen this before."

"It doesn't matter," I say. "I've seen it plenty of times, and I still want blood. Yours, buddy."

Aaron shrugs. "Okay, I tried. Prepare to die."

Kent approaches Todd with his index finger aimed like a pistol. "The only thing you need to know, fucker, is that whoever walks here, walks alone."

That should have been funny, but it wasn't. The inexplicable sounds of Old Joe have just been joined by a new one—the sound of five men violently wishing that one of them hadn't spoken.

"So that's it," Aaron says, looking at each of us in turn. "That's the scariest part, the 'walks alone'...."

"Shut up," I tell him. "I hear something."

"You'd better not be fucking with us," Todd says, rather cheekily for one who was so recently threatened by a lynch mob.

A series of shivering creaks seem to originate at the top of the house and tumble down through the heating ducts. Old Joe clearing his throat? The looks on the others' faces tell me that they know I'm not fucking.

"It's nothing," Todd says, a bit more sure of himself now. "Every house makes noise."

"Not like *this* one." Kent is hugging his shoulders, though it's now hot enough in this room, I swear, to boil an egg on the throw rug.

"Well, what are we going to do now?" Aaron asks. "We're not going to bed, obviously."

"I want to ask you guys something," Kent says. "Have you been down in the basement? Any of you?"

This remark makes so little sense that we just keep staring at him, waiting for the other shoe to drop. But there isn't one. "I'm serious," he says.

"Why the basement?" Todd asks.

Kent's eyes keep shifting, refusing to look directly at any of us. "Something that dyke character said. About not wanting to spend another night in the house without knowing what's underneath."

Todd is being nice, carefully so, as if Kent might totally lose it any second. "Well, I haven't been down there. Has anyone else?"

Davy and Aaron and I look at each other, shake our heads. I've never given a thought to the basement. And now that it's been brought up, the subject won't go away quietly.

"He's got a point," Davy says. Surprising, because he and Kent were the most scared a few minutes ago. Maybe that's one path to courage—a fear so great that it must be vanquished, no matter what.

"I don't feel any great need to see the basement," I say.

"Me neither," Todd says. "But if you and Kent want to go down there, go ahead."

Kent shakes his head. "It has to be all of us."

"Okay, smoke time." I drag Kent into the den. Cigarettes appear almost magically between our lips. "What's the matter with you?" I ask him in the language of smokers, mumbling while trying to light up.

"Nothing," he mumbles. In a moment he blows out smoke. "But we live here, don't we? So why not look around, anywhere we want to?"

Nothing is good about this, mainly because I agree with him. "Because the door is locked, that's why."

"Oh, bullshit."

"What do you think is down there?"

"Nothing," he says, a little too quickly.

"Talk about bullshit."

Like Brian, Kent can look into me. He's always been able to. "You want to know what's down there, too. I know you do."

"Yeah, I do." I *don't* want to spend another night without having a better idea what's below me, even if it is shut safely away. The feeling agitates me, I'm pacing around just like Kent, wearing a path in the carpet. Is it a good thing, that I'm interested in something beyond what I've been seeing every day for the past few months? Or is it just that I'm fucked up by a movie?

He moves closer. "So what do you think is down there?"

"Oh, for Christ's sake, how would I know? Hill House didn't even have a basement, as far as we know. If there's anything haunting this place it's up here, with us."

Davy and Todd nod their heads in unison when Kent and I return to the kitchen. It's Aaron who doesn't want to go down there. "I don't see why we *all* have to go," he says.

"It's because we don't want you beating off in the kitchen while we're down there," I tell him. "I'm tired of cleaning your jizz off the fridge."

Much eye-rolling on Aaron's part. "Okay, Paul. If it'll shut you and Kent up, okay."

# Chapter 4

**The** preparations take some time. Will we need flashlights? We have some in our bedrooms—they're needed for those dreaded trips to the john in the middle of the night—but we're sure as hell not going up there after them, so I poke around in the kitchen cupboards. "I saw some around here somewhere." Soon we're all looking, pulling open doors till a crash makes us jump.

"Oh fuck." It's Kent, who opened a cupboard only to have a can of cooking spray fall out, making more noise than it was entitled to. "It's okay."

"Wonder what made it fall," Todd says. He hasn't run out of mischief after all. I give him a dirty look.

Because this is, as Brian likes to say, "a man's house," it doesn't take long to round up five flashlights. "What else do we need?" Aaron asks.

Kent disappears into the hallway. A closet door creaks open, then shuts. Kent reappears carrying a baseball bat.

"What the hell?" Todd asks.

"I just want to have it."

I've never seen Kent so serious; I have to look away. It's not the seriousness that bothers me, it's the edge that it gives him, sparking off his sexiness that is always beneath the surface of whatever he does, wherever he is. I always thought he was the kind of guy who knew it, who was cocksure 24/7; now that I see it's not so, his appeal is more powerful than ever.

No one's going to argue with him at this point. "Okay, since you're armed, you take the lead," Todd says.

While none of us has visited the basement, we all know how to get there, from a door off the kitchen. "But the door is locked," Kent says.

"I can open it," Todd says.

So that's what Todd reminds me of: a cat burglar. I see him in the outfit: black turtleneck, black jumpsuit. Scaling a building like a squirrel shinnying up a tree. Another image that, now that I've latched onto it, probably won't go away. He takes out a pocketknife, works a small blade into the keyhole of the old door, and in less than a minute he's able to pull the door open. I'm wagering it wasn't really locked, after all. Its edge is a geological record of eons of paint, more than enough to make a tight seal.

On the inside wall, a light switch. A bare bulb illuminates stairs of unfinished pine. The smell that drifts upward—an ordinary basement smell, damp and musty, redolent of wood and concrete and earth—is more foreboding than it ought to be.

"I've seen enough," Aaron says.

But there's nothing to see, beyond the stairs and the bare bulb, so we have to go down. First Kent, then Todd, then me, then Davy, then Aaron. Who knows when these stairs last saw such action, they're creaking, if not visibly bending, under our weight.

110

"Oh, for Christ's sake." Todd's nice period is over. "What do you think you're going to find, anyway?"

"It doesn't matter," Kent says. "I made a mistake, I should have come down here before now."

"We've all made mistakes," Aaron says.

I give him a look that says, *Can we not use this as part of our lesson plan?*

"Okay, let's go," Todd says.

It's our last chance to say, Forget it. But Kent's not about to. "Okay. The rest of you guys?"

"Oh, why not," Aaron says. "Like you said, there's not going to be any sleeping tonight anyway."

I've maneuvered myself into the middle on purpose, feeling safer there. But that also distances me from knowing what's immediately ahead or behind. That scraping and thumping sound behind me, for example, at the top of the stairs—what the hell is that? Oh, it's Davy, hauling one of the kitchen chairs over to the basement doorway, using it as a prop to keep the door open. "For Christ's sake," somebody mumbles, but I notice nobody's insisting that the chair go away.

At the bottom of the stairs there's a dirt floor, or some other kind of floor that's just dirty; the soles of my sneakers raise a crunch as they touch down. It's an ill-defined space, only teasingly lit by the overhead bulb. The walls seem to be made of the same substance, or lack of it, as the floor, making a dark brown background against which other objects, standing or sitting, look grimy: a huge painted cabinet with glass doors, cardboard boxes of all sizes, a couple of wooden crates. Floor lamps of various heights, modestly low or awkwardly high. A rack of old clothes—you can smell the moldy fabric. Junk is all it is, shit-piled like memories.

"Is this it?" Kent asks. He seems disappointed.

I approach the cabinet, peer through the dusty glass at the shelves loaded with bric-a-brac. Old dishes, it looks like, and figurines and "collectibles," their jumbled order testifying to their lack of interest. A small, familiar detail nags at me from a corner; lo, it's the four-fingered white glove of Mickey Mouse, dressed, my flashlight reveals, as the Sorcerer's Apprentice. I wasn't prepared to find anything so insinuatingly bland; it makes me take a step back, which bumps me against a wooden post that dislodges so much dust I can almost feel it settling on my shoulders.

111

"This place is *nasty*," Davy says, and I can't quite see but can picture him wrinkling his nose.

"What do you expect, for a cellar?" Todd asks. He keeps shining his flashlight around, but its beam is too large for this small a space, it overtakes what can be seen too easily, pins things against the walls like startled specimens. Currier and Ives prints, photographs in old-fashioned oval frames. Sections of a white picket fence, including a gate that leads nowhere. Nothing leads anywhere, this is clearly it—not much of a cellar for a house this size.

"There must be more," Kent says. "I don't even see the furnace."

Todd sends his flashlight beam on its busy way again, bouncing across the walls like a sing-along cue, till I start to feel dizzy, and a little nauseous. I'm about to say, "Enough with the flashlight, already," when he says, "Over there."

Yes, there is an "over there," with a gaping hole that an optimist would peg for a doorway but that I'd prefer to call a portal to hell. It's so *dark* that it completely absorbs our flashlight beams, giving nothing back.

"Let's go," Todd says.

Interesting how Todd has become the leader, as he tends to do, with Kent behind him now, then me, then Davy, then Aaron. Yes, I like being in the middle with warm bodies serving as buffers, perhaps likely to appease The Thing That Wants to Eat Us before it can get to me.

The hole in the wall that is so uninvitingly dark is indeed a short hallway, with nothing but dirt wall on either side, leading to another room of about the same size. And here is the furnace, squatting like a giant singed toad, its grimy ductwork spreading across the exposed joists of the first floor. Nothing else in this particular room except a couple of old bicycles sagging against the wall. Todd is searching, searching, his restless beam dancing like Todd's, the two of them about to give me a headache. "There's nothing *here*," I whine, hoping to create a self-fulfilling prophecy.

112

"Maybe not right here," Kent says. "But there's more."

The next passageway is much longer. Like the last one, it has an overhead bulb with a pull chain. More dim light, more dirt. Okay, we haven't come across anything scary yet, so why keep going? "There's nothing here," I mumble, having accomplished nothing by whining.

Davy, just behind me, speaks up. "That's just the point," he says. "To show Kent that there's nothing here."

"Oh. All right. But how much of nothing do you need to see before…?

"Hey." It's Davy again. "Where's Aaron?"

"He was right behind you." Me, being helpful.

"Well, he's gone…. *Aaron?*"

"So much for there being nothing down here," I mumble. And I'm thinking, okay, Aaron's been eaten, but there's still Davy between The Thing and me. But when Davy turns to go look for Aaron, I have to follow: *I'm* not going to be at the end of the line.

Aaron's in the previous room. He got distracted by stacks of old magazines—mostly *National Geographic.* I understand. Not only am I a bookworm too, but I also had a home, when I was growing up, with *National Geographics* in the cellar. And yeah, I suppose that's where I saw bare titties for the first time—dark, pendulous ones, so exotic as to be out of this world, or at least beyond my imagination. And I recall the sweet smell of the old slick paper, its addictive feel under the fingers. When Aaron says, "I'm taking some with me," Davy sighs, but I understand, I understand.

I let Davy take the lead as we enter the passageway again—I'm not going to be the one out in front, either, now that Todd and Kent are so far ahead.

"Notice anything strange about this passageway?" Davy asks. "*Aaron,* come on! Are you looking at tits? Is that what you're doing?"

"Nothing strange about it," I mutter—this seems to be my new mode of speaking—"except for it being so fucking long and creepy."

"It's *too* long," Davy says. "I don't think we're under the house anymore."

"Why would the cellar be bigger than the whole…?" My question peters out, I guess, because there can be no ready answer, just as there can be no denying that the passageway leads much farther than we ever planned on. Todd and Kent are so far ahead of us that they're just bits of color from here, the maroon and dark green of their sweatpants, the red and white of their shirts.

Davy has stopped. "Why don't we just go back?"

"Sounds good to me," Aaron says. He's brought the smell of old slick magazines into the passageway.

"We can't just desert those guys." I must be saying this out of some sense of loyalty I didn't even know I had. Or maybe it's just curiosity: I don't want them to see something I haven't seen.

"They can look after themselves," Aaron says. "Come on, let's go."

I could head on by myself to join Todd and Kent, but I'm not about to separate myself from any other warm living bodies, not even for a minute. So I don't have much choice but to turn back with Davy and Aaron.

The lights go out.

The darkness is so sudden, so total, that my eyes don't know how to deal with it: they flash on a curtain of red, a sort of **TECHNICAL DIFFICULTIES—PLEASE STAND BY** message, before surrendering to the absence of light. My ears, through shock, may have stopped working for a few seconds; only gradually am I aware that Davy and Aaron are saying, and have probably said several times already, "Shit, oh shit," and "We're fucked."

"Hold on," I tell them. "We've got flashlights." I hope my voice sounds more brave than I'm feeling; I'm all flight-or-fight reflexes, my calf muscles fluttering, heart pounding. Before I can switch on my flashlight I need to reach out to my companions, to make contact, to feel less alone in this darkness of the grave. I find Davy's sleeve and latch on to it. He jumps. "Sorry," I tell him, but his hand is there on my arm, too. And Aaron? "Aaron? Where are you?"

"I'm right here." He's breathing heavily.

Now, finally, it seems we can switch on our flashlights. Mine is a greasy old plastic model, its head resembling nothing so much as a tail-light from some finned auto of the 1950's; its beam, too, is like something from yesteryear, dim and faded: these batteries are on their last legs.

"Fuck," Davy says. "Fuck, fuck." His flashlight doesn't work at all.

114

Aaron's got a fairly good one, he swoops it around to find our faces, trying to avoid our eyes. "Oh hell," he says, shining it back the way we came, which now seems interminably long and uncertain. Looking the other way, we can see that Todd's and Kent's flashlights are working, they look like two sparks from here.

"What are we gonna do," Davy says. It's a capitulation, not a question.

"Take it easy," I tell him, in a shaky voice that gives away the nervous breakdown I'm experiencing.

"This happens sometimes," Aaron says. "We've lost power before. Usually it lasts a minute or two."

*Well,* I want to scream, *so far it's been out for a fucking hour!* But simple nervousness prevails, so much so that I can't speak at all.

"Let's go," Davy says. "Who knows how long these flashlights are gonna last?"

True enough: when I look for Todd and Kent now, I see only one flashlight instead of two. Or maybe one of them has turned his off, to conserve it. That's pretty fucking smart, though there's no force on heaven or earth that'll make me shut mine down, never mind that it's weak as a single birthday candle.

When Davy turns to go back I go with him, my hand that's still clutching his sleeve has voted to stay there. Now Aaron's in the lead, and I'm trying to see where his flashlight beam is heading when the lights come back on. The bulbs that are so widely spaced over our heads are the same as they were before, I'm momentarily blinded before I wearily adjust to how dim they are, after all—how small a shield they provide against, yes, the *darkness of the grave.* That's how I'll always think of this cellar.

This was fucking Kent's idea. I've got an urge to throw him down on the ground and sit on him, and not in a good way. My patience with Davy and Aaron isn't in great supply, either. I'm not holding onto Davy anymore but rather prodding him, my finger at his back.

"Quit it!" he says.

"*Quit it,*" I whine, mocking him.

"I mean it! Quit!"

"*Quit.*"

It doesn't take that long for Todd and Kent to catch up with us. Now we're five again. Aaron doesn't seem to mind being in the lead, which is as good a qualification as any for being there; he could, how-ever, *pick up the pace* a little. We pass through the room with the furnace, the old magazines, and a random sweep of Aaron's flashlight, which he still has on, shows that there are fuse boxes here too. Every-thing in its place, as far as dirt floors and crumbling walls will allow, but I can't wait to get the fuck out of here.

As we move on Aaron's flash picks out other things, too, that we didn't catch the first time around. In the short passageway back to the room we'd first encountered, there are three plywood doors set into the wall, padlocked shut.

115

Kent is nearly panting from frustration and excitement. "What the fuck are *those*?"

Todd shrugs, ever cool. "Storage."

"Storage for *what*?"

I'm about to tell Kent to calm the fuck down when we make eye contact. It's the strangest moment yet, in a night of strange moments; for just a second Kent is unrecognizable to me, someone I've never seen before. It's only my certain knowledge of *who he's supposed to be* that keeps me from losing it, foaming at the mouth, having a panic attack, something. When at last his face settles into a pattern that's recognizable, or nearly so, I can see how, in his agitation, his features were slightly off plumb. I guess it's not unusual for a familiar face to look strange under strange circumstances; the French even have a term for it, *jamais vu*, a distant cousin of *déjà vu*.

"Are you all right?" Todd asks him.

In response, Kent hefts his baseball bat. Another surge of dread: he's going to knock Todd's block off. How ill prepared we've been: we brought flashlights, but never thought to pack a strait jacket. Before I can scream Kent steps around Todd, and I see that what he's really looking at is one of the silver padlocks. It has a screw missing from its hasp. Taking as good a swing as he can in this confined space, Kent bangs the padlock in a way that tears the hasp free, lock and hasp hitting the floor with an unreasonable amount of noise. Kent aims his flashlight, finds that this storage space has its own overhead bulb, and pulls the chain.

Racks, nothing but racks. And in the racks, bottles.

"It's a wine cellar," Todd says.

Kent snorts in disgust. "For fuck's sake."

"Hey." Todd is animated, the first I've seen him like that for a long time. "Let's take a look."

"You know anything about wine?" I ask Aaron.

He shakes his head. "I always got mine at the 7-Eleven."

Kent is agitated. I think he'd rather get out of here than anything, yet he's interested in what Todd is doing, too, pulling a bottle from a rack here and there. "Bordeaux, Merlot, and over here the whites…."

He follows Todd's activity as if he might be expected, later on, to put the bottles back exactly where they came from. "You know about this stuff?"

"I was a waiter when I was in college. I had to learn."

I'm tempted to make a bitchy remark about Todd's college days being far, far behind him, but I'm more interested in the fact that he's setting these bottles aside, as if we're going to do something with them. "Todd…?"

"Cabernet, Zinfandel…."

"Uh, Todd? What the hell are you doing?"

"Well, we can carry at least a couple of bottles apiece, can't we?"

"Whoa," Davy croaks, "you want to take this shit *with* us?"

"It's not ours," Aaron says, though regret seems to tug at the corner of his mouth.

I'm about to second his objection, perhaps a little more convincingly, but something's stopping me. *Not ours.* But if it's not ours, then whose is it? All of this crap, doesn't it have to belong to somebody? It's as if I'm seeing, after all this time, that the world that lies beyond the circumscribed paths that we take in this house, from bed to dining room to living room, really does exist, the evidence of it much closer than I suspected.

All right, I could use a drink. And Todd's answering Aaron's objection, my would-be objection, with the simple words, "We live here, don't we?"

"So what else are we gonna take?" Davy asks. The raspy quality of his voice is getting to me, and I realize suddenly that he's whispering, stage-whispering, meaning for his voice to carry and be kept down at the same time.

"You can talk normally, Davy," I tell him, aware of presenting a challenge.

"Take whatever you want," Todd says, setting aside more bottles. "I don't care."

Davy looks at the bottles, which are hardly appetizing, dusty as they are; but he ends up carrying four of them, two tucked under his arms and two in his hands, his flashlight stuck in the pocket of his sweats. I grab bottles too, feeling their grit against my fingers, their surprising weight, the shift of enclosed liquid as I hoist them. I have no taste for sorting through bottles as Todd has done, but I hope he hasn't pulled a lot of really dry stuff that tastes like vinegar. I should have spoken up in favor of dessert wines. It wouldn't have been more difficult than asking Riley to please remember the peanut butter.

Kent finds the screw that he knocked free from the hasp and replaces it well enough to make it look intact. Perhaps, if no one checks on the wine, there won't be any signs that we've been here…though again I have to ask, *Who is "no one"?*

We make our way back to the stairs. I thought we were each carrying four bottles—except for Kent, who needs one hand for his bat—but Todd the overachiever seems to have six. Let's see, that's…twenty bottles in all? Isn't somebody going to miss this much?

"We can always fill them with water and replace them," Aaron says.

"Only if we can recork them, which I doubt," Todd says.

They're talking as if we really are going to drink all this stuff. I see myself having half a glass of something, preferably on the sweet side, and then no more. Just enough to take a bit of edge off a very edgy night.

When all the bottles are lined up on the kitchen counter, it looks like…a bit much. "Are we going to have to drink all this before Brian gets back?" Davy asks. "I don't even like wine."

"Everybody likes wine," Todd says. "It's just a matter of finding the right one." He picks up a bottle, studies the label, puts it back. Takes up another. "Now, here's a nice light wine. Let's get some glasses."

The glasses aren't exactly wine glasses, and a couple of them are plastic. After struggling with the cork, Todd does the pouring. For all of his finesse he forgot to wipe off the bottle, he hands me my glass with dusty fingerprints on it. It doesn't matter, I'm curious about this stuff, dust and all. Sniffing it, I find it more pleasant than I thought it would be. Fruity, isn't that what the wine tasters say? I'm sure I've heard that word before.

"It's good," Davy says with surprise.

Better than good, it chunnels down my throat into my gut, seeking a warm place to curl up in. Settles down nicely, purring. I drink some more.

"This might be just what the doctor ordered," Aaron says, looking at me—and winking?

"See, one bottle doesn't last long, with five of us," Todd says, opening another.

"Have we got any cheese?" Kent asks.

The dim ceiling light tries, and fails, to compete with the ghostly wash from the fluorescent fixture over the sink. Much too bright, the room shifts unpleasantly whenever I blink. Todd and Davy are laughing together, Aaron and Kent are having a rare exchange. Maybe they've stopped thinking about the movie; I haven't. Because what I want to know is: what am I afraid of? On the first night that something pounded and scratched on the doors of Hill House, Luke and the Professor chased what looked like a dog out into the garden. If that's what the haunting presence really was, some beastie with slavering jaws and an appetite for blood, well, I could handle that. Really, I could stand to be eaten. What's a leg shorn off at the knee, or a little oral disemboweling? That can't be as bad, can it, as…what?

"Paul's in a funk." That's Kent, in the chair next to mine, but I can't look at him; when we were in the cellar there was that moment, as real as any in the movie, when his face changed, when I couldn't recognize him, and I'd like to avoid that again.

"Paul hasn't said anything outrageous for about a half hour now," Todd says. "What's the matter, Paul? Ghost got your tongue?"

I shoot him a look. "What is it with you? Is your constant sarcasm a front for something? Or are you really just shallow and mean?" Rubbing my temples, I finish up weakly: "Inquiring minds want to know."

I don't open my eyes, not wanting to see the condemnation in theirs: *Paul's really done it now.* But what I said isn't keeping Todd from opening another bottle, I hear the *thunk* of a cork pulled free from its glass prison. When I finally do open my eyes, I see that the wine in my glass has changed, miraculously, from white to red. Just as surprising, Kent and Aaron have left their chairs and are talking over by the sink. Time has passed with its usual effrontery, not bothering to get my permission. Todd and Davy are having an animated discussion, Todd still standing at the end of the table, Davy looking up at him…why should he know, or care, that tilting his head at that angle gives him the look of a devotee, or worshipper….

Todd bends down, quickly, and kisses Davy on the mouth.

At least I *think* that's what I saw.

I grab my wine glass—firmly, lest it start slipping about the room, too—and take a deep gulp. *Christ* this stuff is sour, just the kind of wine I never understood the appeal of. So sour I can't believe it, I have to take another gulp. Too much too soon, it insults my stomach, dredging up a great bubble of air that's rising in my throat, I can't help it.

My earth-shaking belch gets attention, four faces, at their various heights and distances, aimed at me.

"Paul's awake," Todd says.

"Paul blew your theory," Davy says to Kent, "that there wouldn't be any sleeping in this house tonight."

I hardly know what to say. Was I asleep? Dreaming? What did I dream—my lashing out at Todd? That forbidden kiss? I'm aware now of having a cranky look on my face, my brow and lips puckered up, my mouth tasting like the inside of my stomach, not good. "Here," Todd says, lowering the bottle at my glass again. "That's the end of this soldier." He holds the bottle up, empty, and I want to ask him things. About that kiss, about that day when I thought I saw him and Davy playing with each other in the hallway. I could do that now, ask him; surely this is as good a time and place as any. It doesn't hurt that he's a bit unsteady on his feet, swaying just past true north, the surface of the kitchen table rearing back from him, I have to grab my glass to keep it from sliding. And take another gulp, while I'm at it. Who gives a crap if it's sour.

*What, what?* Now we've moved, I've gotten up, for some reason, though my feet feel far away from me. Exclamations from the others, rather thin, high-pitched, like chirping. Then Kent's voice, lower but none too steady: "What the fuck *was* that?"

"A sound from upstairs," someone says. Oh, it's me. Did I—we—really hear something?

Aaron, the only one of us still sitting, stares at me. "Should we go take a look?"

"You're not getting me up there," I tell him. Wish I could remember, though, what the sound sounded like.

"It was like, uh, uh, a knocking," Davy says.

"Oh shut up, it wasn't either," Todd says. "It was just the house settling."

"This house makes noise every night," Kent says. He looks at his empty glass, which will not, I predict, stay empty for long.

"*Does* anybody want to take a look?" Davy asks.

"There's nothing to look for," Aaron says, sounding not at all sure.

"Oh, shit." It's Kent, still staring at his glass, which has somehow fallen to pieces on the kitchen counter.

"More where that came from," Todd says, approaching with a bottle; Kent needs another tumbler, but Todd takes it that he needs more wine; he pours, wine running over broken glass. "Oops."

"We're not in any shape to be looking for anything," Kent says. A wine stain runs down the right leg of his sweats, but he doesn't seem too concerned.

"Well, we don't have to stand around here," Todd says. Recovered from his confusion, at least momentarily, he's fetched another glass for Kent and is already filling it. "Let's go see what else is on TV."

"What else" isn't much, till we find an old Joan Crawford flick. It's *Flamingo Road*, if I remember correctly: yeah, there's Sydney Greenstreet, the old queen, playing an evil sheriff.

"Oh, this is good," Aaron says.

"Black-and-white...." Kent moans.

We're piled onto the sofa again, in a crushing configuration that seems to suit our mental and emotional states. Kent is on one side of me, Aaron on the other, and I can't concentrate on the movie at all. It can't compete with the two overheated male presences hedging me in. For some reason I'm obsessed with Kent's waistline—the point where his sweatshirt rides up a little, revealing a wedge of bare skin. I've just got to goose him there, and I do. It's a healthy two-fingered jab that sends Kent rising vertically off the cushion.

"*Ohhhhh!*" he squeals. "Don't *do* that!"

From the other side of Kent, Davy's bleary face appears. "What are you doing?"

"Goosing Kent," I tell him. "He's ticklish."

For some time now a prankster, an impish spirit of pure male energy, has been dying to break loose. Davy gooses Kent's other side. More squeals. More hands. Trembling fingers sprout from hairy wrists

121

to hop all over Kent's torso like fleas on speed. This furious spinning that follows—Kent its screeching hub, the rest of us spokes—can't be contained by the couch, which is being destroyed, its springs creaking and croaking.

*Oof!* I'm on the floor, and Kent's hanging halfway off the couch, screaming for mercy as the others continue to attack his midriff. *Whoosh!* This scene, which I started, now floods me with panic. I'm crawling away, praying I'm inconspicuous, but it's too late. A chorus of cries translates to *Where do you think you're going?* as hands swarm around me, finding what I hoped to God they wouldn't. Oh Jesus, male hands, male hands! They know the true death grip—not a slow and steady throttling but a plucking, probing blur of evil will. The buzz saw chewing up my sides and ribs, making me too breathless to beg, knows no limits: now it's squeezing my thighs and I'm going to fucking *faint!* And…*oh, no*…I find my voice, it's either that or die: *"DON'T!"* Pawing off my sneakers, stripping my socks…. *"DON'T TICKLE MY FEET!"*

Male hands: *don't* means nothing to them. Male fingers: is there anything *worse*? Squeezing my toes in insane variations on *this-little-piggy*, scrabbling against my bare soles, quaking me to the core, splintering my brain…! Thrashing around, trying to morph into a shape that can break the grip of my killers, I stretch my arm out to find something, anything, that I can grab onto to pull myself free. I get hold of one of the little carved legs of the TV console. Amazingly, when I pull on it, the leg seems to meet me halfway. The corner of the set hits the floor. There's a flash, and the noise of the movie is gone, and I'm alive, my freed, tingling feet waving in the air somewhere far to the south of me.

It takes me a while to catch my breath, and even then, when I try to speak, all that comes out are the last trickles of hysterical laughter. *Eee hee hee.* Slowly I raise myself up on my elbows to survey the scene: male bodies in various states of dishevelment flopping around on the couch, searching to find out what just happened.

Lying here, on my back, on the rug, my feet bare, my sweatshirt pushed up into my armpits, is strange all by itself; but there's something more going on, something else has happened to me…oh, I know what it is: a wooden stake has been driven between my legs.

Maybe a vampire was hiding there? I take a look, startled to see that the stake is inside, not outside, my sweats.

Taking a further look, I see that vampire hunting has been epidemic; everyone's got a distended crotch. And I'm not sure, judging by the glazed looks on their faces, that there aren't other ghoulish creatures that need to be exorcised. Crawling back to the couch, I heave myself up onto it, plumping down next to Aaron. His shirt is open, perhaps having lost its buttons in the fracas. "What's going on?" I ask him, and there's something sweet in his smile, something that makes my eyes wander down to his naked chest, soft and fleecy—though not as fleecy as Dwight's. I haven't seen this chest since the day we took down the Christmas tree, yet it beckons like something familiar, as if I might know, by placing my hand on it, what my eyes alone can't find. And how easy it is, settling my hand down just off center, where his heart must be…. It's true: by feel I can tell everything. Nothing on his face, including his smile, changes as I tell him, "It's been you. You've been the one."

He nods.

As if I didn't know, have known all along. And yet I didn't. Those misshapen nights when I was alone, then not alone, then alone again…who could blame me for placing them in the province of dreams, of letting them lie there unexamined? But to know now, to finally know…I let my left hand follow my right. His nipples are soft, delicate. They don't get hard…not right away, anyway.

Next to me, Todd and Davy are kissing. Beyond them, Kent appears, open-mouthed, stripped to the waist, a bottle of wine in each hand. He offers one to me.

123

**Kitchen,** hallway, living room, TV room…we leave the lights on. I flip the switch at the foot of the stairs that turns on the light at the top, and look up, considering what a formidable staircase this is. How come I never noticed it before, and why haven't I ever camped out downstairs instead…? The couch has been pretty accommodating so far; couldn't we…?

Aaron nods, encouraging me on. I don't really want to take the lead, even though it guarantees that I'll have plenty of bodies to fall onto if I slip. But it's my room we're going to, my bed being the largest. Those of us who walk here will not walk alone…or lie alone, for that matter. Taking a swig of wine—it's the vinegary stuff, but I stopped caring about that long ago—I start up, the bottle in my right hand, Aaron's hand in my left. I can't hold the banister this way, but I'd rather hold onto my drink and…my food. Yes, why not refer to it that way? My food, my nourishment, without which I can't live. Kent holds Aaron's other hand, and Todd and Davy complete the links. We weave our way to the top.

I'm not about to let go of Aaron's hand, not even when we reach the top. The procession continues down the hall to my door. "Welcome!" It's a funky mix in here, all right: dirty socks on the floor, and the bed looking none too hygienic, either—not, thank goodness, because the sheets bear visible stains, but because they're so insanely twisted. "Make yourself…*hic*…at home."

So we do. The rest of our clothes come off, not to be folded neatly and stacked on a chair, but left on the floor where they lie, cuffs of sweatpants twisting upward like empty eye sockets, unable to witness what they've left behind.

But I'm bearing witness, to bodies I've dreamed about, fantasized about—Aaron's the one that I've touched but not seen. Could I make up my mind, ever, to dispense with male bodies? Todd and Kent, both slim-hipped and hung; Davy with his sharply defined muscles and white marble skin; and representing the more ordinary, the zaftig Aaron and me, neither of us a world-beater in bodily condition or cock size. But here, in this setting, I can't even look down at my own cock without losing my breath with excitement, as if I've never seen it before. Dispense with male bodies? Oh never, says my member, throbbing like waves on the shore, perhaps motored by the same moon.

The bodies move, agitated, skin growing cold as we stare and stare.

"No, wait, we gotta move the bed."

"Why? Where?"

"*Thwacka-thwacka*, to answer your first question…."

"*Wacka-wacka*?"

"No, *thwacka-thwacka*."

124

"I get it," Kent says. He should recognize the secret language of headboards. "Just move the bed away from the wall."

The bed's easy enough to move, but hello, what's this? Along with a litter of dust kittens, the bared floor reveals my jar of Elbow Grease. We stare as if it holds the key to the mystery of what the fuck we're doing here. The practical side of me perks up, and I take the jar in hand, display it among our circle in case anyone doesn't know what it is, ha ha. And just to add to the deep mix of the moment I ask, "Anyone need a condom?" Looking at the others as each shakes his head, not in the manner of *I don't need one because I'm not going to...*, but in a more furtive way, like altar boys who know they're going to be whipped for spiking the wine but have to do it anyway. Transgression…oh, it's fucking calling *me*, all right, but I don't want to be the first, as if throwing myself onto my own mattress might break its spell. Even admitting that there is a spell to be broken is its own kind of transgression, but in the other direction, the one that would lead each of us back to his own bed. I have to seal our unspoken pact, even if it is like tonguing a sore tooth that's best left alone. "We could," I tell them, "always go back to our separate rooms, to be alone."

"In the night," Kent says.

"In the dark," Davy says.

They're echoing the words of the creepy housekeeper in *The Haunting*, and that seals the deal. Aaron launches himself first, landing in the spot on the left side where I always sleep. On his back, he holds out his arms to me, then widens them to include the group. All for one and all. My eyes are watering from the severe wattage of the overhead light, which promises to be as annoying as those damn disco strobes used to be, but there's nothing for it.

"Should I leave the light on?" I ask.

Four voices: "*YES!*"

Davy turns to Todd and they share a deep kiss. Davy's thighs start to shake. Kent crawls onto the bed, giving me a full view of his ass. In a moment Todd and Davy land together on Kent's other side. I toss the jar of Elbow Grease like a bride's bouquet, and Aaron catches it.

We're crowded, of course. But there are ways, when you're naked and under covers. Aaron has his arm around my shoulders, Kent is plastered along my side like a body cast, and I can tell, without looking, that Davy and Todd are as one. The seismic movement on that side of the bed sets Kent and Aaron and me rocking against each other, and even though my stomach feels a bit unsteady I can appreciate this rocking, this swaying, this coddling together of our naked frames. It's like a mild, adult amusement park ride.

Aaron grabs my dick, and I return the favor. Kent's cock nuzzles my thigh like a horse seeking a carrot. Feverish now, I think—I *know* I can morph, as I tried to do downstairs, into a warm fluid of hands and orifices. Somewhere in my brain second thoughts chase each others' tails, but the gasps and groans issuing from Todd and Davy, and Aaron's excruciatingly light, teasing treatment of my cock, and his hard cock in my hand, and Kent's hard cock, are driving me past the point of any return, or control. My boozy delirium isn't the best condition for ingenious lovemaking, but the point here seems to be sloppiness. Just as we slopped wine into each other's glasses, we slop cocks now; and if it reminds me of pre-HIV days in New York bathhouses, it's without the anxiety that always came with piling up with strangers in a dark orgy room. Here we have the lights on, and I—I *know* these guys.

2:00 by the bedside clock: Aaron's eating my ass while I'm slurping Kent's cock. And Todd is stage-whispering into Kent's ear, "Can I fuck you?" No movement from Todd's other side; perhaps Davy, having been fucked to the gills, has dropped off?

While Todd's fucking Kent, Aaron and I roll around in puppyish play, till he pants into my face: "Fuck me. Please."

It's going to be a trick, in more than one sense of the word, with a vigorous round of intercourse taking place right beside us. Kent's legs are over Todd's shoulders, but I do Aaron doggy style. It's funny, trying to guide it in while the bed is already rocking; now I understand why those orgy rooms had thinly padded surfaces at best. "Hold on, Aar." My inability to hit the target isn't due to any unwillingness from my cock, which is hard as ever despite the late hour and the wine and the stress and the fact that I got sucked off not long ago: and that's funny too, that all these neurons and synapses, as well-traveled as the roads built in ancient Rome, can still carry a buttload of sensation to my brain. So funny, in fact, that I'm laughing when Davy appears in my peripheral vision, on his way somewhere.

126

"You need some help?" he asks, also laughing at the spectacle I'm making of myself, failing to hit Aaron's hole. Lending a hand, Davy helps get my cock where it needs to be. Now Aaron is one busy fuck-ee, grinding his ass up against my groin, pulling me into his nether region like a suction pump. It's so good that I can't keep from coming quickly.

"The reason I got up," Davy says, "I had to pee. And now I've *really* got to pee." His cold feet take mincing steps to the door, where he stops suddenly. "Oh shit, I can't go out there alone."

I haven't shaken the feeling that I'm hosting this party—because it's my bed?—and now that I've let Aaron jack off all over my face I have to tend to this other guest, much as I'd rather not. "All right," I tell Davy, wiping jizz off my chin. "I'll come with you."

"Wait, you guys can't go by yourselves," Aaron says. He's exhausted, his face as red as his dickhead.

"Well, you come too, if you want."

I never understood the logic of this, but there's no way to turn on the hallway light except by the switch at the top of the stairs. So any of us who has to get up in the night, has to take a flashlight with him. I don't blame Davy for not wanting to go alone, or Aaron for not want-ing the two of us to go alone; but it's a bit much when Todd and Kent don't want to be left alone by the rest of us.

"All right, all right! We'll *all* go." I get my flashlight from the night table drawer. Fuck, the floor *is* cold.

"Oh Jesus, *hurry* guys." Davy's hopping from foot to foot. He's got a boner again but it must be a piss-hard, the kind that feels like it's going to start leaking any second.

In the hallway, I'm amazed that any of us has *ever* dared to make this walk alone. Fuck, this place is creepy at night, and the bobbing flashlight is no help where my imagination is concerned: there are *things* just beyond the reach of its beam, even sticking their tongues and fingers into the ragged rim of light, making me switch it restlessly back and forth, trying to catch the rest of them, or at least their faces. "Fuck, fuck, fuck," I'm saying under my breath. The carpet runner is thin, doesn't do much to curtail the cold; and though the hallway is heated it's nowhere near the temperature of the bedrooms, especially my overheated chamber.

127

"My whole adult life, every time I went into a men's room, didn't matter where, I had to jerk off," Aaron's telling me while we walk down the hall. "It was kind of embarrassing. I mean, it always took longer than taking a leak would. If anybody was waiting for me to come out, they must have wondered if there was something wrong with me."

"Jeez, Aar, couldn't you ever hold back?"

"Almost never. All those guys standing at urinals, holding their dicks…it was instant hard-on time. All I could do was duck into a stall before anyone could see how excited I was."

I'm not about to go into what it's been like for me, not because it's different from Aaron's experience, but because it's been similar. Not that I've jacked off that many times in men's rooms…no more than a dozen times, probably…okay, maybe a few dozen times. Of course there are those tearooms where you're *supposed* to jack off, I shouldn't even count those. I'm thinking of those times when it was pretty embarrassing, during a family outing or a lunch with coworkers or—face it, Paul—the one or two times I've jacked off in the men's room of a funeral home or church. I don't think the Unitarians would have minded, though.

It's a relief when we get to the bathroom and turn on the light. Of course the five of us haven't been in here together before, let alone naked. The floor is freezing, we're hopping around in the space between the tub and the sink, not giving poor Davy access to the toilet. He's shrieking, partly from his discomfort and partly from the hilarity that seems to be infecting us all in this cramped cold place. Finally he cries out, "I'm gonna piss all over you guys!"

"Hey Davy." Pushing the shower curtain all the way open, I lower myself to get in the tub. "Piss on me."

"It's no joke, Paul…!"

"I'm not joking." The cold porcelain isn't any joke, either, yet it's funny—I've taken showers in this tub but never lain in it, haven't taken an honest-to-God bath in years. "Come on, Davy, warm me up."

He stands at the edge of the tub, doesn't take his dick in his hand, lets his piss-hard aim itself at my chest. When the stream comes it's hot, shocking, and the part of my mind that wonders what the fuck I'm doing is just the tiny squeaking voice of a mouse in the corner of a room where there's way too much happening for it to make any difference. Piss takes its path down either side of my belly, down my groin, puddling up a bit on either side of me, growing cool there but there's more hot piss to come, wine-piss, Davy's got gallons of it. I'm hard myself but I have to turn over, I want to feel that stream on my back, down my ass-crack.

"Paul's getting into it!"

Todd pisses on me next, his hose letting loose a stream that almost stings with force, and again I'm turning, graceless as only an overweight guy in a tub can be, taking his piss over my stomach and chest and down my back, the backs of my thighs…. The new piss is hot, the old piss is cold, it's a mixed blessing, all right, but I don't give a fuck, what a spot to be in, a bathtub with four guys standing beside it, from here their dicks are the biggest things in the room, two of them pissing on me at once now, then another, and finally Aaron lets loose, aiming at my balls. At the end guess who hasn't released himself yet, it's me, and it's tough because I've got a hard-on too. I get up on all fours, hands and knees in the funky pond of piss, and I'm able to let go that way. My own piss feels strange and good coming through my engorged dickhead.

Time to wash up, in keeping with the demands of good hygiene, not to mention the fact that I stink. Someone thoughtfully turns the shower on, and I'm whooping at the burst of cold water on my back, at another time in another life I'd be pissed as hell but this cold shock is *funny*, I'm wondering how much more I can take, how much more I can feel, my mouth is open wide and I'm laughing, and the water gets warmer and it's not just water, no more pissing as yet because we've emptied ourselves but somebody, somebody like Kent or Todd because it seems like them, has actually brought a bottle of wine into the bathroom, I see the red streaming from the dark bottle and with effort I catch a mouthful of it, make some comment like "fruity and delicate, yet assertive," though no one can hear it but me.

It's crazy, the bathtub is much smaller than my bed but, just like my bed, it's getting overcrowded, there are three of us in it now, Kent and Davy and me in the middle, sitting with our knees hiked up, all wet, and the bottle of officially approved, unscented body wash is making the rounds, making us frisky, slippery, limbs tangling up,

129

and none of this is a good idea, somebody's going to break a bone or a bottle or a cock—but speaking of cocks, I've managed to get Davy's in my mouth while Kent is behind me, his soapy hands finger-fucking me for all they're worth. What with everybody wanting to get into the tub and there being no room for it, I crawl out as soon as I've sucked Davy's load, a mixed blessing of soap and cum. On the floor I'm facing Aaron, who's sitting on the toilet jacking off. "Hold on," I tell him. "I mean, wait." Grabbing the bar of soap from the sink, I'm ready to give him the hand job of his life. "Ooh baby," I tell him as he writhes around, "ooh yeah baby." Someone's behind me, soaping my balls. Then bodies switch places back there. "I've never felt your dick so hard," I tell Aaron. Soapy fingers are at my ass again, probing deep in a way that's telling me there's more to come. "I think I'm about to get fucked." Davy and Kent are making a lot of noise in the tub, reaching simultaneous orgasms through one means or another, or maybe more than one. "I guess it's Master Todd's fat shaft that's going to fuck me." Aaron's trembling so that he can barely stay on the toilet, and now he shoots, I try to aim his dickhead at my mouth but get a *splat* in the middle of my forehead instead. I let go of him just in time to brace myself against the toilet bowl as the big plunge comes from behind, cock filling me to my fingertips. After the first reaction, the tensing up to expel this foreign object from my body, I'm able to relax my startled ass and work with this new rhythm. My head rests on Aaron's thigh where he sits, totally drained, patches of cum in the white fleece of his torso. "Fuck me," I beg. "*Ohhhhh* fuck me to *death*...."

130

Sometime later I'm clutching the base of the toilet bowl while my lower half, featuring my freshly loaded ass, sorts itself out. I'm not sure whether or not I came, but when I turn over my cock is still hard, rising like a hand in the air, a precocious student crying "Me, me, me!" Aaron loses no time getting down on his knees to jack me off. In the tub Davy's riding Kent's cock.

We have cum on our hands and faces, like kids who've raided the jam pantry. The rest of the bottle of wine that found its way to the bathroom has been passed around, finished off. I don't think I'll care if I never have wine again.

"Whoops!" It's Kent, trying to get out of the tub, landing on his ass on the floor.

"I don't feel so good," Davy says. He's still sitting in the tub. It may be my eyes, or the lighting, or anything, but to me his face and chest look mottled, all white and red patches, and I wonder what my own body looks like, but I'm too tired to find out.

"Okay, guys," Todd says. Someone's made him the leader of this expedition. I guess he's got the qualifications: he's tall, he's well built, and he's fucked each of us at least once. Fine with me. If only he weren't reaching a hand down to me, expecting me to get up. "Can't," I tell him. "Too tired. Spend night here."

Aaron's reaching down too. Together, the two of them haul me to my feet, but not for long; I settle on the toilet seat lid, which unkindly kisses my fucked ass. Yes, yes, I see them now, these four naked men, on their feet or struggling to get there. But I see something else, too, that makes little hairs on the back of my neck rise: the bathroom door, standing open revealing the dark hallway. "Who opened the door?" I ask.

Drunken mutterings: what door, where, etc.

"The *door*. I was sure we closed it."

A moment of silence as we look at the open door, the darkness revealed.

"Fuck, it's cold," Davy says. He's got a bath towel around his shoulders, and I've grabbed one too, but they're not doing much to dispel the temperature that's shrinking our much-abused private parts: soon, very soon, we'll be tiny little boys.

"Where's the flashlight?" Todd asks, and the rest of us groan: he's going to make us go out into that darkness. And how should we know where the flashlight is…a search ensues. Aaron finds a plunger, I've got a toilet brush, but…Aaron turns it up, nestled among Kleenex in the oval wastebasket, it must have fallen from the sink. Slowly we pull ourselves together enough to edge out into the hall as a unit.

"What now?"

"Where are we going?"

"Back to our own rooms, or back to Paul's?"

"What's that noise?"

"Shut up."

131

"Well, I heard a noise."

"Shut *up*!"

"I still don't want to be—*hic*—alone."

"Me neither!"

"Well, let's go, then, back to my bed."

The flashlight beam wavers, brushes up against familiar things: the mopboard, the oatmeal wallpaper, the Currier & Ives prints. Nothing frightening in this hallway at all, no matter how long and dark it is. Still we stay pressed together, and when we reach my room we're all trying to squeeze through the doorway at once, no one drawing an easy breath till the door is closed behind us.

# II. Tales My Body Told Me

O C T O B E R ,    1 9 9 8

# Chapter 5

**Lyle** Cook stretches like a cat, elongating as I grow smaller, shrinking in my half-asleep state. *Don't*, I tell him, silently. *Don't wake up. Lie still like me, so still we might not really exist. No Lyle, no Paul. No Mrs. M. pacing the floor down below, wondering what's what. No, no, no.*

*Yes*, his body says, no wider than an exclamation point. He's agile, for a fifty-year-old; I ought to know, I've been impaled on his dick, and vice versa, often enough. I haven't quite got used to his scent yet, but what must he make of mine? Or the scent of this motel room, for that matter? Without my glasses, I can't see much of it, bright as it is with daylight streaming unhindered through the white curtains; but I can smell the saltine breath of unpackaged food, of secrets bursting from waxed paper and cellophane. Cheese puffed and fried. Peanut butter and white bread. Pretzels, graham crackers, glazed nuts. Sodium and sugar tug at my bloodstream; my skin shrinks and responds, shrinks and responds like the waves, like the shore that exhales its own musk of shell and sinew rotting under wet sand.

Tales my body tells me, lies fed by rhythm, nourished by the buried.

Lyle brings his face close to mine—like me, he's helpless without his glasses—to see if I'm awake. His heavy lidded gray eyes are startling. For some reason they make me think of the way his cum tastes, like bitter coffee.

"Yeah, I'm awake," I tell him. It's time to reach for a cigarette, but I can put it off till I see what he's up to. Or up for. Already my body is pinging, my right side all touchy from having him near.

Still he stares; and I'm about to say, "What the hell are you doing?" when he asks, "Do you love me?"

Those gray eyes: perhaps they have their own scent. God knows the rest of him does. Not something I *can't* get used to; just different, that's all. One of the endless variations on the male scent, mysteriously sweet for something so close to sour.

"Fuck you," I tell him.

"First you have to say you love me." He cracks up, snickering through his nose.

"Christ." I roll to the side, pull the pillow over my head. "Tell me you're just a bad dream."

"Dream? I'm your worst fuckin' nightmare!"

He pokes me, a finger here, a finger there, and I'm laughing and going *ow, ow, ow* in a way he finds amusing. "Oh, God damn you!" I tell him. "Fuck you to hell!"

"Been there, done that."

I feel him shifting, though God knows he's light enough, he could do somersaults without making the bed creak. "Ow," I say again, in surprise because he's got his head between my legs, licking my balls. And I'm thinking, Mrs. M., Mrs. M., whatever time it is, I hope it's too early for you to be knocking on my door, wanting to make up the room.

Mrs. M., aka Mrs. Munson, didn't know what to make of me on the night I showed up here, wet as a wharf rat. She wanted to know where I came from, and why, but I shielded my expression as best I could under my dripping baseball cap: my answers weren't likely to satisfy her. Standing in the dimly lit lobby of the Sand Dollar Motel, in a puddle of my own making, I pulled out my wallet to show her my driver's license. She looked at the tiny picture, looked at me, looked at the picture. Why would a man with a Kansas City address suddenly show up on the Maine coast in the off-season, asking about weekly rates?

"My mother's dying," I told her. In truth my mother had died years ago; this was a shameless play for sympathy. I needed some, having driven all the way from wistfully-named Portland International Jetport in a rainstorm, in a Neon with sluggish wipers. The immaculate little woman in a cardigan, fake pearls, and eyeglasses with frames shaped like tailfins made a perfect *O* of her red-orange lips and eased the registration card toward me. She hadn't yet answered my question about rates, and I had the uneasy, giddy feeling that she might let me stay for free. It didn't matter, every other motel in the vicinity was closed for the season, turning shuttered eyes to the sea. I wasn't about to go searching for another haven.

"Why *do* you stay open past Labor Day?" I asked her.

She shrugged. "Somebody has to."

Did she get a close enough look at my luggage tags to see that the name on them—Eric Silverman—was different from the one on my driver's license? My own bags are so old they wouldn't survive a cab ride, let alone a flight. So it's been the practice, with Eric and me, that I'd use some of his luggage when we traveled. Except, of course, that now "we" are not traveling. I've left him, or he's left me. Hard to tell which, since we haven't actually confronted each other.

During my first several days in Two Piers I learned what the twelve-step groups mean by "one day at a time," only with me it was "the next few minutes at a time." If I could get up in the morning, swing my legs over the edge of my squeaky bed, pull on my khakis and a shirt and sneakers and take myself downstairs to the lobby for a cup of coffee that tasted like hot varnish, then I was doing pretty well. Other days I stayed in my room till hunger forced me out—that, or Mrs. Munson, making her rounds. If I hadn't appeared by one o'clock in the afternoon, I could count on her knocking at my door and calling, "Mr. Lavarnway? Mr. Lavarnway, you in there?" I keep asking her to call me Paul, because I can't stand the way she croaks out *Lavarnway*, her voice rising on the last syllable, making it a bird call. "Yes, I'm all right," I called back, sometimes with my head still under the sheet, in denial of daytime. Sometimes I only made it as far as the desk that faced the heavily curtained window. Poor thing, it was so spindly, with a dark finish intended to make it look like real wood, only nobody'd had his heart in it. The chair was another spin-

137

dly thing, made more to be looked at than sat upon, though it wasn't much to look at either. Anyway, I'd sit in the chair and lay my head on the desk, one side of my face pressed into its stickiness; when the tears began I'd let them roll, pooling up on the wannabe wood grain. Of course my nose was running too, leaving a grosser, slicker pool next to the tears. When my neck began to ache I'd turn my head to the other side. Leak, trickle, turn, and my back began to stiffen, but still I couldn't get up. By the end of the afternoon my entire head as well as the desktop would be soaked, my eyes blurry with the mucus of grief.

During these long periods of shut eyed suffering I saw Eric as I hadn't seen him in years. He appeared as a cherished specimen of wildlife appears to a painter: in a clearing, in a ray of sunlight, caught in a moment of awareness and grace, shorn of rough edges. A direct delivery from God. Yet it wasn't so much physical beauty I was seeing, and the light wasn't really as it appears in a painting, readable and directed. This Eric's glow came from within, blending with his features until I couldn't tell anything—not an ear or eyelash or fingernail—apart from the whole, from everything he meant, everything I'd ever felt about him.

Then he was gone, and I was staring as only a person with his eyes closed can stare, at nothing—nothing real, anyway, nothing that could make a difference now. And my body, like an idiot, kept pumping out tears and snot.

During the night I'd wake a few times, disoriented, unable to place the darkness of this room, the sound of breakers. And I knew—at least a couple of times I knew—that I'd been dreaming of Richard Roscoe. His shaved head, his pecs, his dick. How was it that my dream life was now managed by torturers? When had my subconscious given away the store? And just as I realized there'd been some mercy after all, that I hadn't had to look at Richard's eyes with their bright green pleading, I was seeing them, memory rushing in like a sketch artist with a hateful knack for detail. It was no news that memory could be cruel, nothing to make me slap myself on the forehead and say, "I never *knew* that!" Yet I could have cut off my own dick, if that would also guillotine the recent past.

Sometimes it was close to two o'clock in the afternoon when I finally left my room. Once I walked to the little post office to send a postcard to Eric with nothing but the Sand Dollar's phone number on it, just so he would know where I was. That errand took the wind out of me, I had to go back to my room and cry some more. But most days when I left my room I headed for the diner next door, a whitewashed old rail car with a long counter and a few booths. The menu item I liked best were the buttermilk pancakes, which they served with a blueberry compote, thick and gluey. Blueberry pie filling, no doubt, straight from the can—a Paul Lavarnway meal if there ever was one, especially if you added half a pot of black coffee. Like the motel, the diner was quiet in the off season, its ICI ON PARLE FRANÇAIS sign now propped in a corner, the migration of French Canadians having ceased after Labor Day. The short, stocky guy who worked the counter, about my age but (I hoped) more grizzled looking, showed none of the curiosity that kept Mrs. M. going, and I was able to eat my meals in peace.

Afterwards I strolled along the beach, probably appearing, as beach strollers do, not to have a care in the world. *To not have a care in the world*: I'd recently read in the newspaper that, according to those who decided such things, it was now okay to split infinitives. If you read it in the paper, it must be true.

**As** Lyle licks my balls they begin to feel fat, like rising dough. My cock exposes more and more of itself to the air, like a throbbing newborn filled with want. Holy crap, I *do* want him, as much as I did last night. Reaching, I knead his shoulders, thin as wings; stroke his hair, long and shimmering. Desire keeps shoving me, I want to speed up this porno flick, knock out every other frame. Then his hair brushes my thighs and I think, *aahhhhh, why hurry?* His fingers are at my ass, plying my crack, and again there's not enough time, I have to have him *now*.

139

Who wants this shameless writhing need for a man? Who *wouldn't* want it?

Up on his knees, he brings his face close to mine again. "Tell me you love me."

"Fuck you!" I scream. "Fuck you to fucking hell and beyond!"

He laughs through his nose. The head of his cock taps against my ass, a planet seeking entrance through a keyhole.

I met Lyle at my brother Glen's house, in the Rosemont section of Portland. For many years my brother had worked as some kind of City Hall bureaucrat, until he was able to take early retirement at the age of fifty-one. Whatever his job had been, I could only be sure that, knowing Glen, it had added nothing positive to the delicate balance of kindness in the world. But his house was a grand and innocent-looking thing, the kind of house that 1960s sitcom families lived in—big and white, with bay windows and dormers, a gently rolling lawn. The whole neighborhood had that complacent, proud-of-itself look that spoke of insularity, a united stand against the forces of nature, of change itself. I'm not sure I could survive in such a neighborhood, so aggressive in its fresh paint, gleaming windows, and neatly clipped grass. As a domestic aesthete I'm a ne'er-do-well, more at home in the eclectic midtown neighborhoods I had known in Kansas City or my old East Village tenement in New York.

No sooner had I parked, mindful of the proximity of my rented tires to the immaculate green hem that served as a curb, than Georgie, my brother's beagle, came leaping down the lawn, howling in glee. I didn't have a chance to speak before he was on me, claws scrabbling against my jacket, pinning me against the car. Nothing for me to do but wait for my brother to rescue me—which he did, half-loping down the lawn on his long legs (how come he got the long legs and I didn't? Is there just one pair to a family?), smirking as he called off his mutt. "He's happy to see you," Glen said to me, the closest Glen would come to telling me that he felt that way too.

Inside the house, passing through the crowded kitchen and dining room to the living room with Georgie lunging at my heels, I found Mark sitting forward in his chair with his elbows on his knees, leaning into the TV as if he were confiding in it. "Hey, there he is," he said, turning towards me. His smile was quick, bright, nervous. "And, oh God, you brought the dog from hell with you…Georgie, get down, *down*."

"Georgie, get down," my brother said, coming in behind me.

Was I expected to sit? I chose the edge of a loveseat. Signs of Glen-as-decorator were everywhere. For a person who totally lacked senti-ment, he had an eye for coziness and intimacy—the frilly loveseat, the inviting corner. And I had to admit that the rooms weren't crowded, after all; it was the crowdedness of the walls that gave that impression. In the living room there were more small framed watercolors and photographs than I could count, acquisitions Glen had picked up at street fairs and flea markets, estate sales and thrift shops. All innocu-ous, nothing harsh or controversial to offend the eye. Then there were the houseplants, way too many of them, yet each in its way essential. Lush, lovingly cared for, they revealed another side of Glen.

"You know," he said—still standing, shifting his weight from one leg to the other—"we weren't expecting you."

"Oh?" What the hell? Had he already forgotten our phone conver-sation? I certainly couldn't; it had taken me days to work up to it. My dread at the thought of seeing my brother or my aunt had kept me from calling, while my guilt at not letting them know I was around told me that I *had* to call. What a bitch, this ping pong match be-tween dread and guilt. Finally, to put myself out of my misery, I had picked up the phone and called Glen.… "You said dinner, didn't you? Friday night?"

"Well, today's only Thursday."

Oops. Any chance that I might have been able to practice mind-over-matter in my brother's house vanished as my body took over, my throat stopping up, my face turning a hot red.

"It doesn't matter," Mark said, not taking his eyes from the TV.

Glen said nothing, letting the awkwardness build to a deafening roar. I had to leave, but how? I couldn't just bolt from the room. I had to hand it to Glen, he'd placed me in a ridiculous position in record time, unable to leave, unable to stay. And it wasn't even contempt that was keeping me pinned there; it was indifference, my brother's secret weapon.

He could have stood there forever, enjoying my mortification; but the doorbell rang, and since Mark was still glued to the TV Glen had to answer it. It was my chance to get up, to make my way to the door with apologies, but somehow I couldn't. Christ, what a masochist.

Voices came from the direction of the back door, and a tall young man appeared in the doorway. He didn't make a sound, and I wondered briefly if I'd made him up. Then I noticed that he wasn't young after all. It was his general outline, his slenderness and shoulder-length hair, that had fooled me. As he came closer I saw that his hair was gray. His face had seen some years, most notably his eyes, which seemed to have a permanent squint behind the thick lenses of his glasses—the squint of a miser, a malcontent. Someone who would feel at home in my brother's house. But it was Mark, tearing his eyes away from the TV screen, who looked at the newcomer with some fellow-feeling in his eye, the kind of twisted bonhomie that only two misanthropes could share. "You're late," he said.

"Fashionably so."

Glen returned to the living room, looking from the guest to me. "You've met before, haven't you?"

"No, I don't think so," I said.

"I'm Lyle. Lyle Cook." He stepped forward with an outstretched hand. It's always good to meet a fairy with a strong handshake. "Mark's told me a lot about you."

Mark? Not Glen? It figured that my brother's partner would tell someone else a lot about me; I wasn't sure if Glen himself even knew much. I ran through some of the safe, trite things I could say to Lyle, like "Only good things, I hope," but the lightning speed of my mind was as usual betrayed by my body. My throat remained stopped, so I just sat, sliding farther back into the loveseat, wondering if Lyle could mistake my blushing for something less embarrassing, like sunburn. Meanwhile my brother crossed the room to a recliner that had seen better, pre-Georgie days; and I realized, with a start, that Lyle's only choice for a seat was next to me. He settled down, his narrow butt hardly making a dent. I shrank as far as I could into my corner, which wasn't far. Mark was in his TV trance again; my brother had settled into a gloomy, self-absorbed moment; and I still wasn't up to saying anything. How much like a family we were—guarded, reserved, speechless, like the family I grew up in.

142

It was Lyle who again broke the silence. He leaned toward me, as if we were farther apart than we were, and said, "You're from Kansas City."

"No, I'm from around here, originally."

His eyes shifted toward Mark. "Mark and I go back a long ways together."

"I'll say we do," Mark said grimly, not taking his eyes off the TV set.

So Lyle really was Mark's friend, not my brother's. Maybe that was a point in his favor. "Did you grow up," I asked him, "in Two Piers, like Mark?"

"Yup. Still live there."

"With his mother," Mark said, looking grimmer than before.

Okay, I got it. These two related by expressing comic disgust with each other. At that supremely depressed moment I felt I could use a relationship like that, where all was irony. "You," I said to Lyle in mock horror, "live with your *mother*?"

"And sister," Lyle said with some satisfaction, as if he'd trumped me.

"Don't you have a boyfriend?"

"Nobody steady. Nobody I could set up house with, like Ozzie and Harriet here."

I was beginning to like him. "They're quite a pair, aren't they?"

"They still fuck like bunnies," Lyle said loudly, getting a rise out of no one. The way Lyle and I had been left alone in *our* little world made me feel as if we were on a blind date. I hadn't mentioned anything to my brother about leaving Eric, and was wondering if I'd ever get up the nerve to do it when the doorbell rang again. Georgie took off, howling, and my brother, grunting and moaning, hoisted himself out of the recliner to follow. Pretending interest, I followed too, needing a break from the close quarters I was sharing with Lyle.

Glen was ushering two women into the kitchen. "C'mere," he said, in my direction. "Meet Herb and Jonna."

*Herb?* I'd heard all sorts of lesbian monikers, but this was a new one. The two women were about my brother's age—it's easier to tell with lesbians, who tend to scorn the makeup tricks of straight women. Under their parkas, which they piled into a chair, they wore checked flannel shirts and blue jeans. Herb, not surprisingly, was the one with her hair cut short—almost shorn off, in the crew cut style butch women were favoring lately. If this weren't a queer household

I might have mistaken Herb and Jonna, even without hearing their names, for a straight couple. It was only her hands that gave Herb away, smallish ones with clear polish on the nails. Jonna was the one with long hair, though there was nothing feminized about it; she looked shaggy, the way long-haired guys used to look before men's hairstyling became popular. The two of them shook hands with me as my brother made introductions.

Georgie had followed me to the kitchen, and kept jumping up on me. My thighs and calves were being reduced to raw hamburger. Somewhere nearby—I couldn't even remember where the bathrooms were—a toilet flushed. Then Lyle came into the kitchen, wiping his palms on the seat of his jeans. Talk about long hair—his was immaculate, as evenly trimmed as a thoroughbred's tail. He approached Herb, took both of her hands in his, and kissed her on the cheek. He did the same with Jonna. His smile seemed devoid of what I was already thinking of as his trademark irony.

My brother finally noticed that his dog was trying to shred me. "Georgie, *stop it!*"

I'd never heard Glen discipline the dog so sharply, and to my surprise he got down and slunk out of the room, keeping close to the floor.

Mark appeared in the doorway. "We're going to invite Paul to stay, aren't we?"

Glen hadn't thought of this option, I could see it in his face. "Oh," he said. "Well."

"Actually, I have to be leaving," I said. I didn't have enough epidermis left for another Georgie attack, and there were too many people here for me.

"Oh, come on," Mark said. "We've got plenty. Besides, these girls don't eat much." He threw a fake punch at Jonna's shoulder. She laughed. Like Herb, she was about twice his size, and it would take more than a punch to bring her down.

"Yeah," Herb said, frankly studying my face, "why don't you?" She had an *I'd like to ask you a lot of questions* look, possibly because she'd never known Glen had a brother. Old friends, new friends, it didn't matter—having a brother wasn't something Glen would mention. To be fair, neither would I.

I looked at Glen, who met my eyes reluctantly. "Well," he said, "we don't want to hold you up if there's something you've got to do, or someplace you've got to be, or maybe you've already eaten and you're not hungry. But of course you're welcome to stay."

I laughed. When did I decide that my brother's lack of grace, not to mention his unwillingness to simply have me around, was funny? "Oh, okay," I said, "since you insist."

Now that the spell had been broken, we could all move. "We're only having leftovers anyway," Mark said, "nothing fancy."

"Do you mind if I smoke?" Jonna asked, retrieving a pack of cigarettes from her parka.

Glen looked at me and turned even more pale than usual. He had never let me smoke in his house. "Oh…sure. Go ahead. We've got an ashtray someplace, don't we, Mark?"

And so began one of the more elaborate household rituals of the late twentieth century: the non-smoking hosts' search for an ashtray.

"Maybe in the hutch, in the bottom drawer?"

"Maybe in the junk drawer in the little white table?"

"How about in that cupboard, on the top shelf…? No, way in the back."

"What was it, anyway? One of those little plastic ashtrays?"

"No, we had a real glass one…we had it out Christmas before last, when what's-his-name came over."

Trying to be helpful, Herb joined in the search, but couldn't do anything but spin from one corner of the kitchen to the other as Glen and Mark shouted conflicting directions. Meanwhile Jonna, far from being embarrassed, winked at me as she took a seat at the table, a cigarette hanging from the corner of her mouth. I had a cigarette between my lips too, and we wagged them at each other like two naughty boys waving their pee-pees.

"So," I asked her, "where do you all know each other from?"

"We used to be neighbors of Glen and Mark's, when we lived over by Danforth Street."

"I remember that neighborhood. There were some beautiful apartments there."

"Reasonable rent, too. But we outgrew it, and when Herb's mother died she left Herb her house…."

145

The search for an ashtray ended in a compromise. Mark slid a tiny white saucer, the kind used for a demitasse cup, between Jonna and me. Of course, once it had been sullied by ashes it would never again be of use *as a saucer*. The two of us lit up, feeling naughtier than ever.

By the time Herb and Jonna and Lyle and I had debated the pros and cons of living in the city versus living in the country—the women taking the lion's share of the discussion—Mark and Glen had warmed up several platters of food and were bringing them to the table. Mouth-watering aromas had preceded the turkey, dressing and sweet potatoes; sometime recently Glen and Mark had had an old-fashioned Thanksgiving style dinner, with Thanksgiving now only a month away. Rather than get grumpy over my brother's forced hospitality, I counted my blessings as I forked up slices of juicy breast meat. Herb cracked the first "breast meat" joke before I had even filled up my plate. After that there were only sounds of eating, lots of them, till Herb announced, "Listen, you guys, I've been going through the most amazing thing."

Jonna chimed in. "You won't believe this."

"You mean," Mark asked, "you finally had the surgery?"

Herb held up her middle finger while she finished chewing. "You've heard about all this stuff about 'recovered memory,' right?"

"Aw, I don't believe in that," Glen said.

"What about it?" Mark asked. His lips seemed to be working against the smile he usually wore.

"Hey, listen," Herb said, "I didn't believe it, either. But it was like this: I woke up one morning—or I was half-asleep, half-awake—and I *remembered*…no, it was more like I *saw*…. Jesus, it's so weird to talk about." She shifted in her chair, as if she needed to get into just the right position to speak further, and moved her hands, modeling something in the air, something larger than she was. "I saw this man coming towards me…only it wasn't *me*, the 'me' I am now…I was just a little girl. And this *man*…."

Okay, nothing personal, but the way she said "man," with its unmistakable subtext of *vermin*, gave me a start every time I heard it. So often lesbians talk about men as if nobody else knows what they're really like, when in truth we've *all* had our hearts or souls bitten by a

146

rabid rodent or two. So I tried to listen compassionately as Herb described how she had been repeatedly raped by her own father, starting when she was only four years old.

"Four years old?" my brother asked. "How can you remember anything from when you were four? I can't."

"Some people can remember when they were *born*," Herb said. "It's all in here." She tapped her index finger against her temple so hard that it made a sound, like thumping a melon. "I've been having these marathon sessions with my therapist, and you wouldn't believe the stuff that's been coming out."

"I already don't believe it," Glen said, glancing my way as if he expected me to second his opinion. But more than anything I felt embarrassed by Herb's story, then embarrassed by my own embarrassment. I looked at the table, at the turkey bones lovingly picked clean, the quietly congealing bowl of gravy. At least Herb had refrained from telling the bulk of her story while we were in the midst of stuffing ourselves; but if the dinner hadn't been spoiled, then something else had, something as huge as the creation myth Herb had sculpted out of the air. Perhaps life itself could be spoiled, if it offered nothing more than the bleak prospect of always being haunted by memory, even just the *threat* of memory. They have a point, those pundits who claim that we aren't doing any better, mentally or emotionally, after a hundred years of psychotherapy.

While Herb was in the midst of responding to my brother, in calm tones—absorbed in my funk, I wasn't really listening—Mark bolted from the table. His years of running had served him well, he crossed the living room and bounded upstairs in what seemed like three strides. I looked to my brother, who only raised an eyebrow in Mark's direction, as if to say, *There he goes again.* It was so much like Glen that I found myself taking it personally, having spent more of my life than I cared to think about with that eyebrow aimed at me. So I excused myself and followed Mark upstairs.

I was only seven years younger than my hosts, but in terms of gay life theirs was a different generation, one that believed in maintaining separate bedrooms for appearance's sake. I'd never been in either one, so when I saw Mark sprawled face down across his bed, the soles of his sneakers facing me, I hesitated to go in, and felt a bit queasy when I finally did, as if I were breaking some privacy barrier.

Mark rolled over to see who had come in. "Oh…it's you."

"What's the matter, hon?"

"I'm just not in the mood"—he ran the back of his hand across his nose—"to listen to some old dyke talking about how she'd been raped as a kid, that's all."

That remark was like a gunshot, coming from someone so gentle. "What's wrong?" I asked him. I was speaking to the back of his head, since he had rolled over again. I went around to the other side of the bed and sat on its corner as if I were sitting on eggs. I didn't need any recovered memories to tell me I'd always been attracted to Mark. His room attracted me, too, even if it did resemble a sports-crazy high school kid's idea of a sanctuary, with football posters and pennants on the walls. His love of sports was something Glen didn't share, so he had to keep it to himself. I had no love of sports either, but I could see it as a way of paying homage to male vitality. Mark was young for his age and his own vitality fairly hummed. Should I dare put a hand on his shoulder? Was I staring, now, at the fine hairs on the back of his neck? Where was my common sense, or whatever it was that should be telling me what to do next?

He rolled over again, looked up at me. Started to speak. What stopped him was Lyle, making another untimely entrance. He looked at Mark, looked at me, and without a word plopped his narrow ass on the bed. "Hey," he said, shaking Mark's shoulder as if to wake him up. "What's the matter?"

148 The two of them exchanged a look, furtive but unmistakable. They both knew what was the matter, but weren't about to say anything—not while I was in the room. It was too much for me, the emotional equivalent of the huge meal we'd consumed downstairs. I backed out of the bedroom, blaming myself for not seeing that it was a bad idea to come here in the first place. The last thing I saw, before feeling for the staircase railing, was Lyle's eye. His right eye, drooping, *winking* at me. It was the wink of a marionette: nothing else in his face moved, no other muscle, just that eyelid.

Weird, weird! That settled it, I was getting the hell out. I'd thank Glen for dinner, do a nice-meeting-you with Herb and Jonna, and

grab my coat, all in one smooth motion. But another surprise await-
ed me in the kitchen: my brother was sitting at the table all by himself.
The dykes and their parkas were gone.

"I told Herb she was full of shit," Glen said. He sucked gravy from
his thumb.

That was my brother for you. He didn't even ask about Mark. But
soon enough there were two sets of heavy footsteps on the carpeted
stairs. Whatever was in that charged look that Mark and Lyle had
exchanged, it wasn't there now in the way Glen and Mark looked at
each other. Meanwhile my face was burning again. It was that god-
damned *wink* that Lyle had given me. It could mean only one thing.
Yet it couldn't mean…*that* thing. Could it?

"What happened?" Mark asked, looking around as if there might
be lesbians hiding in a corner.

"I told Herb she was full of shit," Glen repeated.

That settled it: I was on Herb's side. If I thought I could catch up
with them I would have gone and apologized for my brother. It would
be the first time I ever apologized for him, but not the first time I
should have. He didn't know remorse—its bitter, grungy taste, like an
old penny under the tongue.

Mark sighed, taking his seat again. "I have to admit I'm kind of
glad they took off."

"What's the matter with you, anyway?" my brother asked, as if he
had just recovered the memory of Mark's leaving the table.

"Nothing's the matter," Mark said, crossing his arms to give himself
a hug.

It took me a moment to realize I was holding my arms in the
exact same way. *Nothing's the matter* was something I could say, too;
but it seemed as if every word and gesture I'd made during this fore-
shortened evening had signaled distress. It didn't matter, nobody
here wanted to see my flares and red flags. I looked at my watch and
feigned surprise. "Oh, look at the time. I really must be going."

Glen was out of his chair like a shot. "Don't let us keep you, if
you've got things to do."

Lyle extended his hand. "Nice to meet you." We shook again, only
this time he gave me the old "queer's handshake" that had been so
popular in high school—the one where you tickled the other guy's

149

palm with your middle finger. Startled, I watched for something to happen again in his face: another wink, something. Instead there was only his poker face, giving the lie to the joke between our hands.

"You know where your jacket is?" Glen asked. He wasn't about to see me to the door.

"Don't worry, I can find it," I said, not taking my eyes off Lyle.

My coat was in the small pantry between the kitchen and back door, perched uneasily on a tall stool. I lifted it, then let it drop. I'd been craving some time to myself ever since I stepped into this house, but now that I had it I could only kick myself for doing everything wrong. I hadn't even mentioned Eric. "Oh *fuck*," I said, as tears filled my eyes. I turned to shut the kitchen door behind me and there was Lyle, stepping in to join me, pulling the door closed behind him. Did I have to explain my weird behavior? What did I owe this guy, with his wink and his high-school handshake? Moving into my personal space, he hummed, actually *hummed* as his face came closer to mine. It was the kind of hum I'd make in the presence of a rich dessert: *mmm-mmm!* How weird, how inappropriate!

His mouth found mine. Unbelievable, that he could be so pre-sumptuous, so aggressive...that he could have *so much* tongue! It was time to slap the shit out of him, but instead my hand came to rest on the side of his face, which he hadn't shaved in a couple of days. When the kiss finally ended, and he said, "I'm dying to know if you've got a hairy chest," I made my own *mmmm* and slid open the middle button of my shirt. His hand was rough as his face, its slow drag through my chest hair one of the most.... "*Ohhh*," I sighed.

150

"*Ssshh*," he said, giggling.

What the hell, I let loose: "*OHHHHH!*"

"*MMMMMMM!*"

"*OHHHHH...!*"

Both of us giggling now. How could we help it, Glen and Mark were right on the other side of that door. Heaving with laughter, my shoulders clinked against jars of peaches and apricots. Lyle kicked over Georgie's bowl of kibble. Having outgrown our space, I grabbed my coat and he found his—only a light denim jacket, what was he thinking?—and we burst out the back door, down the narrow con-crete path to the front of the house. Small floodlights illuminated the clapboards, reminding me that this was the hallowed ground of the middle class, where I might intrude from time to time but would never belong. Behind my little Neon was his car, a red Volkswagen that had seen better days. Its inside, I wagered, would smell of sea and sand and neglect.

"I'll follow you," he said.

He didn't know where I was staying, or if I was alone, but his statement had its own logic. As I unlocked my door the wind brushed my wet cheeks, and I realized I really was crying. Or had been, or was about to, or all of the above. It didn't matter, I had to keep going. But the tears didn't stop as I drove, leading us south through Portland to Route One. Could Lyle see my red eyes in my rearview mirror whenever we passed a streetlight? Why didn't he just veer off, turn around, before I had a chance to trash his life? By the time I reached the long, straight stretch of road that passed by the salt marsh, I was crying too hard to drive and had to pull over. Traffic was scarce on the narrow road, not a single light shone across the marsh. A sense of isolation struck my spine like a sudden chill. I was alone in a haunted space, bereft of human companionship, susceptible to spirits. Yet there was Lyle, his car pulled over beside mine, its flashers on. Part of me wanted to open my window and yell, "Go away!" But another part of me was keeping busy, unlocking the passenger's side door so Lyle could get in.

"Hey," he said.

He brought the smell of the marsh in with him—cord grass, salt grass, mysterious nourishing mud. There wasn't much light except for our flashers, but I sensed his hand stirring near mine. The kindness of strangers: there was no such thing, not when a stranger wanted things from you in return. But when his hand rested on my shoulder I let it stay, and started talking, and told him pretty much everything.

When I finally stopped, he had only one question: "Do Glen and Mark know that you broke up with your husband?"

This was good for a double handful of fresh sobs. "Oh…Glen… *fuck* Glen!"

His hand moved to my leg, just above my knee. "What I can do?"

151

I stole glances at him, his face hidden in shadow. If he just wanted to get laid, he would have taken off before now. And if he really was being kind…but the chances of that weren't great, either. I shook my head, not knowing what to say.

"Do you want to be alone tonight?"

Again I shook my head, giving the honest answer.

**In** my room, Lyle sat in the spindly deskette chair and crossed his legs at the knee. There's a soft spot in my heart for the affected mannerisms of certain gay men who perform them without thinking, just doing what their bodies tell them to do. And I've got another soft spot for the way Lyle was dressed, in white sneakers, blue jeans, t-shirt, and denim jacket. I dressed that way, too—like someone half my age or younger. Even Glen and Mark were the sneakers-and-jeans type. Gay men get away with it more easily than straight men do, I don't care what anyone says.

"Look," he said, "I don't want anything deep from you, and you don't want anything deep from me. This is what it is, that's all. If you can deal with it, great. If not, tell me and I'll leave." He looked around, eyes darting nervously over some of the room's lived-in features, its air of occupancy and decay, not unlike that of a sickroom.

I barked out the cold, unattractive laugh I'd developed lately. "Well, you're the one who came on to me, remember? I didn't even find you attractive, to tell you the truth."

He looked around some more, creases deepening on either side of his mouth. The boxes and half-consumed bags of snacks on the top of the dresser, table and desk testified to a degree of sloth and gluttony that he'd never seen before. Or maybe he'd just never been in a stranger's motel room before; it was possible. "Well," he said, "I mean…Jesus, what are you doing here?"

"What do you think I'm doing here?"

He glanced nervously at the door. Not for nothing was Norman Bates the boogeyman of choice for the latter half of our century: he took the private pain of the psychopath off the movie screen and into our mom-and-pop Sleepy Havens. No one was safe, not even in the friendly off-season inn down the street. Would Norman have taken pity if he'd known his victims were as miserable as he was? Leaving the question alone for a moment, I went into the bathroom to pee.

It was a long one. When I came out Lyle was stretched out on the bed, naked. He'd turned the TV on, and was aiming his scowl at the screen. Judging by the yammering and applause, it was a talk show he was watching. It was only after I'd got naked too, and had stretched out beside him, that I said, "What the hell do you think you're doing?"

He didn't take his eyes from the TV. "You want to throw me out?"

"No." His refusal to look at me was an invitation to look at him. Naked, he seemed less skinny than he did when dressed. "Not bad, Lyle," I could have said, especially when I got to his dick. Rather homely when flaccid, both too red and too pale, I could now see its expanding possibilities. "I don't want any funny stuff, either," I told him. "No hearts and flowers. Let's just use each other, okay?"

In the morning I'm contemplating my jar of lube, the Elbow Grease that Eric and I had shared. This transgression, the theft of that jar from its place of honor in our bedroom, wasn't too much of a stretch: I'd used the stuff for many a solitary jack-off session, when sex with Eric just didn't come often enough. Two of Lyle's long, skinny fingers appear, dipping into the jar. He smears some on me, which means I can be content to lie back and let him ride. Impaling himself on my dick is no big deal—literally—but what it does to his dick is nice to see; it bobs up like Nessie taking a breather from the Loch. I've always attracted men with big dicks—or does it just seem that way because I'm so ordinary in that department? I'll have to remember to ask Lyle, he'll tell me anything.

After I come he scrambles forward, grabs hold of the headboard and shoves his cock in my mouth. I get a spirited face-fucking, helped along by the fact I've got two fingers up his ass, still slippery from my dick. His cum, it turns out, tastes better when I've already got morning mouth. Now he's turning around, sucking my dick while I finger and lick his hole.

Later I'm asking him: "Is your dick as sore as mine?"

And still later: "Hey, it's Friday. Don't you have to work today?"

"My days off change a lot. This week I'm off Thursday and Friday."

153

It's embarrassing, insofar as anything between us can be embarrassing by now, that I don't even know what he does. "And your job is…?"

"I'm a nurse."

"Really?" That gets me sitting straight up in bed as nothing else has. "You? A nurse?"

"A damn good one, I might add." He's lying on his back, speaking to the ceiling.

I swing my legs over the side of the bed. My feet are cold, so I look for socks among the tangle of clothes. "Do you work at the Medical Center?"

"No, I do home health."

I try to picture him in whites. Showing up at someone's door, saying, "I'm your new nurse." It's not easy. I find my socks, which are all I need to get me to the bathroom. As I pass the deskette I grab a fistful of graham crackers. They have the kind of sweetness that sneaks up on you, and more than anything else I've eaten lately they remind me of my childhood.

Which reminds me of the dream I had last night.

Okay, now I've got an agenda, if Lyle's interested. Or even if he's not.

**The** Neon seems less lonely with Lyle in the passenger's seat—not that he looks any more comfortable than usual, his right hand on the grip above the door as if it might fly open any second. "Where are we going?" he asks.

"I had a dream last night about the ugly place were I grew up, in South Portland, so I'm taking you there. You'll enjoy that. Wouldn't anyone?"

A layer of gloom hovers over our heads like cigarette smoke. We take the Pine Point Road to Dunstan Corners, turn right onto Route One. Past the salt marsh again, past Scarborough, where my aunt lives. We're traveling north, up the map, but it feels more like a descent, through layers of memory. Neighborhoods unearth themselves, their names familiar and yet mysterious, because I never knew where they came from. Only the numb habit of repetition makes them resonate: Thornton Heights. Cash Corner. Now, Cash Corner is an intersection where three streets come together, and on a paved triangle barely large enough to hold it sits the Tastee Freez, a childhood standby. I pull in without a second thought.

"They used to make these freezes," I tell Lyle. "Kind of like milk-shakes, only with seltzer in them, so they're thick and fizzy at the same time. Nothing like them in the world."

Now that we've parked, he lets go of the hand grip, reluctantly. "You eat a lot, don't you?"

He often seems to speak without moving his mouth. It's a disquieting habit. Though I heard him the first time, I have to ask: "What did you say?"

"I said, 'You eat a lot, don't you.'"

"Oh, is this some *gay* thing, where you just can't help commenting on my weight? Because to tell you the truth, you don't do a whole lot for me, either, in the light of day."

He digs in his pocket for change. "Get me a small cone? Dipped in chocolate, if they still do that."

"All right." I wave off his handful of coins. "Never mind, I've got it."

I didn't know it would be so painful, trying to explain to the young black woman behind the counter what a "freeze" is, or what I remember it to be. "Put seltzer, or soda water in it," I tell her, and she just looks at me, the whites of her eyes showing all around. Well, bless her heart. Not many years ago it would have been unthinkable for a black person to be working in this neighborhood. As a first-generation Tastee Freez African-American she has earned her startled demeanor. She ends up handing me a concoction that I take with a smile, even though it looks like a stagnant mud puddle. It's an unseasonably warm day, and Lyle's cone is dripping from under its chocolate shell by the time I get it to him. Funny how he asked for the chocolate dip "if they still do that." Poor guy, he doesn't get to the Tastee Freez any more often than I do. He takes the cone as if he hasn't handled one in a long time, turns it around as if it has an on/off switch somewhere. One of the drips reaches his knuckle even as he pokes out his tongue to catch it. I sip my drink, which is awful. The seltzer makes it fizzy but also tasteless. It's the only chocolate drink I've ever had that seems to need salt. Lyle makes more of a mess, his

155

tongue still lagging behind falling pieces of chocolate shell. Who'd believe he's gay, with such an inept mouth?

"So," I ask, "what else do I need to know about the end of the world?"

The topic came up the night before, after our first fuck. Lyle claimed to know twenty different ways in which the world could end. The first—I could have guessed this one—was asteroid impact. He told me about the Kuiper belt, a band of some 100,000 ice balls somewhere beyond Jupiter, each one more than fifty miles in diameter. The belt spits out those ice balls frequently, and if one of the larger ones hits Earth, it's all over.

"Gamma ray burst," he says now. "Ever hear of that?"

"Sounds like something out of a comic book."

"Or a movie, right? Guess where these bursts come from—galaxies far, far away. They're caused by the merging of two collapsed stars."

"Oh, so it's a love story."

"There might be one about to happen nearby, or there might not. Dead stars are impossible to see out there."

"So, suppose it's happening nearby...?"

"These bursts can have ten quadrillion times the energy of the sun. It would fry our atmosphere, destroy the ozone layer."

"So then the sun could kill us."

"Skin cancer. Even worse, it would destroy the plankton that form the basis of the food chain." At the word "food" he looks rather pointedly at my crotch.

"Have you always been, like, horny as a seventeen-year-old?" I ask him.

He tugs at his own crotch. It's time to peel out, before we start molesting each other in the parking lot of the Tastee Freez. I wad up what's left of his cone in a handful of napkins, and hurl the rest of my drink in the trash barrel, hoping I won't be hurling it again later on.

More neighborhoods. Mill Creek, Knightville, Meeting House Hill. Where did these names come from? Well, Meeting House Hill has a Congregationalist church on it, the selfsame one where my mother taught Sunday School many years ago. No doubt about it, I'm homing in on the old neighborhood, a stone's throw from Willard

Square. Not that anyone's likely to be impressed, least of all Lyle, but here it is: Sagamore Street.

Number 12 sits at the top of the hill, not far from where the street dead-ends at an overgrown field. As you approach, the house seems to perch on the horizon. A typical two-family clapboard, with bay windows in front and, on the driveway side, what used to seem like the world's longest flight of stairs leading up to the second floor. It's the color of the house that I never get right in my memory: a light gray, not much more than a dirty shade of white. On overcast winter afternoons the house was the *same exact color* as the sky, its outline a mere pencil sketch against the gloom; but put a fistful of thunderheads behind it, a truly stormy sky, and the house took on a completely different color, the faintest shade of blue.

The other houses on the street as I used to know it ranged from the Castonguays' neat Cape Cod across from us to the Clarks' ramshackle mess with its sagging porch, holes punched in the wooden latticework around the crawl space as if someone's head had been rammed through it. Stray cats and dogs circulated through the junk, the old tires and mattresses in the side yard. Then there was the sprawling three-story house on the corner, a yellow-and-brown monstrosity that the neighborhood kids wanted nothing to do with—it made you feel deeply troubled just to walk past it. We always kept to the opposite side, as if that could make a difference on a narrow street with no sidewalks.

I pull into the driveway of number 12. There are no other cars around. Perhaps we look conspicuous, since the thick lilac bushes that once stood between our house and the next, a white one-story that I could only remember as belonging to a Mr. and Mrs. Brown, are gone. Only a straggly line of dead grass separates the two properties now. I can see through the Browns' window (which can't possibly still be the Browns') with disturbing ease. Lyle is restless, crossing his arms on his chest, rubbing his kneecaps, staring at the floor. Yet after a few minutes a kind of peace descends, even if it is a gloomy kind of peace. School's not out yet, so there are no kids jumping into piles of leaves, splitting open the spiny husks of horse chestnuts, finding different ways to torture each other on the asphalt. No bullies, no whiners, no fat little Paul Lavarnway.

Yes, Paul was always a butterball. Almost as soon as he started school the other kids learned to single him out for being different, to call him names and push him off the sidewalk. They hated his body but couldn't wait to get their hands on it, shoving, pulling, poking, tripping him up, beating him down, stealing his glasses and even his shoes, someone holding them aloft like a prize while others pinned him down and tickled him.

But in contrast to Paul, that sad lump of a specimen, there was… Gary Castonguay. I hear him again in my dream from last night: *So what about your dad?*

Little Paul, surly and bored: *What about him?*

*Did he bring home a sword? My dad's got a Japanese sword.*

I ask Lyle, "Have you ever tasted a young boy's skin? When you were a young boy yourself, I mean."

He looks at me as if I'm up to something. "I guess."

"Ever know certain boys that you liked a lot and didn't know why?"

"Sure I did." He moves his knees apart, just a little.

"You wanted to touch them, and you didn't know why that was, either."

"Uh-huh." His knees spread a little wider.

I don't need any more of an invitation. I undo his belt, open his jeans, and his cock springs up obligingly. I lean down and suck. If the spirit of my younger self is around, I hope he's watching me blow a guy in his driveway.

Just a few more sucks, and Lyle's slightly bitter cum fills my mouth. It takes some effort to stay with him, his hips are writhing so. But I don't lose a drop, don't even have to wipe my lips afterwards—that's a clean suck job. He wipes his own mouth, though, with the back of his hand, as if he's been drooling.

Upright again, I find the lever that lets my seat recline, giving Lyle better access to my swollen crotch. "Jack me off," I tell him.

He frees my dick from my dampened jeans and sets in, using thumb and one finger at first, then two fingers, then three…each guy has his own way of playing this particular instrument, who could ever get tired of hand jobs? Meanwhile I'm watching the second floor of the gray house, remembering out loud: "Low plaster ceilings, rooms always dark in the daytime…oh, Christ, that's good…cold floors, cracked linoleum, old braided rugs…yeah, just like that…furniture warped and sprung, the sofa sagging where I liked to sit and read…oh yeah, jack that dick…the bedroom Glen and I had, with the high lumpy beds, and the corner windows you couldn't open in the summer because of the bees…oh, man, work that cock…."

I put out a lot of precum, Lyle's fingers are good and slick. And he's using his free hand on my balls, bless him, doing things only gay men know how to do. I'm happy to let my gloomy memories melt down as I heat up. Poor planning, though, means my handkerchief is still in my hip pocket when I shoot all over the place.

"Oh, shit!" Lyle jumps back as if my cum is burning him. There's a grin on his face, though, deepening the creases even as it makes him look twenty years younger. "Jesus Christ, you shoot like a teenager!"

I grin back at him. All of sudden the afternoon seems to be waning, though it's barely two o'clock. I pull myself back together, tucking my t-shirt into my much-abused jeans, and start the car.

"So where are we going now?" he asks.

"Oh fuck, I don't know."

We climb up Pillsbury Street toward Willard Square—how quaint these names sound now. Along the way Lyle offers to fill me in on more ways the world could end. "Where did I leave off?"

"Gammy rays."

"Gamma bursts."

"Whatever!"

"Next up: collapse of a vacuum."

"Who was it who said that nature abhors a vacuum?"

"Galileo."

"Oh, quick answer. Of course you could be 100% wrong."

"I could be, but I'm not."

"Did you have a father?"

He snorts, as if I just made a bad pun. "So they tell me. I never knew him."

"So it's always been just you and your mother and sister?"

A pause, too long not to be meaningful. "I had an uncle," he says finally, and I glance over and see he's speaking to the window. It's time for me to say something; why can't I find words? We ride in

159

silence for the several miles that take us to Scarborough. "This is where I went to high school," I say, taking the turn. The old building is gone, the new one unrecognizable—less homely but more institutional looking, as if an old jail had become a new prison. But the parking lot is still located on the west side of the school, and there is still a soccer field beyond it, where Paul used to stumble around during gym classes. That's not what I wanted to remember by coming here. What do I want? Not more silence from Lyle, that's for sure, so I snap at him: "For Chrissakes say something."

He looks at me, sneering—or rather snorting, sucking up snot. I'd rather he wiped his nose on his sleeve, but I'm not about to say anything because there's a chance that he's been crying. "So," he says, "did you have a shitty time in high school, like I did?"

"Yeah, like everyone did."

"Ha! Don't you believe it. For some guys those were the best years of their lives."

"I can't see how, unless there were some hot circle-jerks going on that I didn't know about."

"Probably were."

"So what did you do in high school?"

He looked out his window, though there was nothing to see but an expanse of empty parking lot—emptier than I would have expected, since school just let out an hour ago.

"Were you doing your uncle?"

How quick he is, pinning me up against my door, his fists filled with my jacket. Any other time, with any other man, I'd be babbling—*I'm sorry, I didn't mean anything, please don't hurt me.* But I'm strangely relaxed, even with his sour face breathing into mine. Let his fists do what they want, I don't care. Even more strange is the smile tugging at the corners of my mouth, because at last I got to him. I touched a nerve.

160

Too late, he sees that I've won something—exactly what, who knows—and he lets me go. Retreats to his corner, his shoulders twisted away from me.

"Do you want to go home now?" I ask.

I can barely hear him: "Let's go home."

We've gone a couple of miles before I ask, "Do you want to talk about it?"

"Jesus fucking Christ! What, you want me to *confide* in you? Who the fuck do you think you are?"

It's my turn to be hurt, but I can feel it again—the small bitter smile, the facial equivalent of a pebble in my shoe. "I often wonder that myself."

He curls back into his corner, as far as his seatbelt allows. I'm hoping he'll come back to life by the time we reach the Pine Point Road, but no such luck. My tiny smile curdled some time ago; there's a familiar tingling behind my eyes, and I'm going to start crying if I don't pull over *right now*.

Another view of the salt marsh from here, but since it all looks the same to my untrained eye—colorless reeds, accidental channels reflecting blue sky—we might as well be back on Route One. Lyle's still not looking my way, and yes, there's a great heaving sob inside me that's just dying to burst like a bubble. Maybe I can forestall it if I just tell him I'm sorry. But just as I'm about to manage those two words he cuts me off.

"He killed himself."

Oh. I take a deep breath that my lungs want to reject, there's too much emotion pressing on them. Now I can say "I'm sorry," but instead of an apology for my fucked-up behavior it'll be the sympathy card that's never enough. So I still can't speak until he breaks the tension again.

"That's what they say, anyway."

A truck passes too fast, rocking the little car. I wish it would suck me into its draft, tow me along to wherever it's going. If Lyle confides any more he'll end up hating himself for it. Hating me, if he doesn't already. I start the car, pull onto the road and drift for a while, past a canning plant with its smell of clams. Look, Paul: it's all over with this guy. Go back to your crackerbox prison now, close the curtains, have a cry.

When we reach the Sand Dollar and he still hasn't said any more I don't know what to do but pull into what I've come to think of as my personal parking place, the one nearest the stairs. On the way I spot Mrs. Munson on the front deck, fishing around in the mailbox. It's way too late to be checking the mail, but from her vantage point she can see whether I'm alone and, if I have someone with me, whether he accompanies me upstairs.

"Miserable nosy bitch," Lyle mutters.

He makes no move to unbuckle his seat belt, but the fact that he's spoken gives me some hope. Hope for what, Paul? Do I want him to stay, after all? And what's with his comment? Did he and Mrs. M. have a run-in at some point? Still tongue-tied myself, I get out and start up the slightly springy wooden stairs.

In a moment the car door slams, then I feel his weight added to the stairs.

When we're in the room he closes the door with a *whump*, locks it, puts the chain bolt on, and zings the curtain shut. "There's not going to be anybody passing by," I point out, "unless you're worried about the miserable nosy bitch."

He slumps into the chair next to the dresser, against the wall. It's as spindly and uncomfortable as the deskette chair, but it's got armrests, and allows him to prop his feet up on the end of the bed. This blocks my way to the bathroom, but for the moment I don't mind. "As long as we're going to be private," I tell him, "we might as well get naked. Or should I go down and get us something to drink from the machine?"

"Oh, sit down."

I've never seen his face this sour. Okay, so he's finally going to let me have it, then be gone. Only I'm still not ready for it. "Why don't you tell me what it is?" I ask him, trying to strike a balance between an apology, which he wouldn't accept, and any breach of our pact not to get too deep with each other, which I've already broken.

He looks around with his mouth clamped, as if he's searching for a spittoon. Then he takes a deep breath, tilts his head back against the wall. "His name was Winslow. Win. Uncle Win."

I make a little sound, the kind you make when you don't want to make the wrong one.

"He died in 1964."

Do the math, Paul. In 1964 you were ten years old. Which means that Lyle was, at the most…fifteen?

"I guess I shouldn't say he died. He disappeared."

162

This is what I get for letting my thoughts wander for just a second. "What?"

A sigh. "He just disappeared one night. No one ever saw him again."

"I'm...sorry."

We sit for a while in an uneasy funk of grief (his) and morbid curiosity (mine). I'm trying to think of something to say to pull us out of the murk when there's a knock on the door. Well, damn Mrs. M. after all—she *is* a miserable nosy bitch. The door doesn't have a peephole, so I try to see her by peeking through the curtain, but the angle's wrong. Great security. Suddenly very peeved, I unlock the door and yank it open so fast it draws an audible draft into the room. It is a woman standing there—a young woman, I guess, with freckles. Do older people have freckles? I can't remember.

"Shit," she says—nothing personal, just startled.

"Fuck," I tell her. "You scared me to death."

Her long hair is the color of half dried sand, parted in the middle. She keeps plucking strands of it, pulling them back so they won't blow in her face. "Is my brother here?"

"You've got the wrong room." Odd, since this is the only occupied room, as far as I know. Then I see my error: just as I'd thought at first sight that Lyle was much younger, I've made the same mistake with her. She's older, maybe older than him—and he does have a sister, doesn't he? I start to correct myself, but she's leveling a gaze past my shoulder, right at Lyle, who's squinting at her.

"Don't say anything," he says, and I realize that's aimed at me, because now he's shouting at her: "What the fuck are you doing here?"

She turns to me, taking the opportunity, as any sibling would, to complain about her brother to a third party. "I told him you don't do things like this, you don't just shack up with a total stranger in a motel room."

I look back at Lyle. His contempt for her is almost visible, like a mist. "I don't need checking up on," he says, "so get your fat face out of here."

Oh, that was good, *fat face*—a true sibling insult, mean and unfair. Her face, like her body, isn't even slightly plump, let alone fat. She'll

163

become an interesting-looking old person, while I'll grow all turkey-necked and jowly, like Alfred Hitchcock.

"Well," she says, "as long as I'm here, you might as well ride back with me."

"Whatever we're doing," I ask, "can we make it quick? It's getting cold, standing here with the door open."

That wasn't an invitation, but she steps inside.

"How did you even find me here?" Lyle asks.

She rolls her eyes. "God, this is the only place that's *open*. And Mary Munson knows who you are."

Oh, so it's Mary, is it? Mrs. Mary M. and I will have to have a little talk.

"So what the fuck do you *want*?" Lyle asks.

My head is just starting to hurt. "Look, this is getting really boring, so if you're going to shout at each other, go somewhere else."

She looks at me as if for the first time. "Oh. I guess you're not some kind of serial killer or crazy person, are you?"

"Not yet."

"This is my sister," Lyle grumbles.

"Thanks," I tell him, "I figured that out." I squint at her, Lyle-like. "Do you have a name?"

"Celia," she says. "Do you have a name?"

"Paul."

"Let's go," she says to her brother, as if "Paul" meant "goodbye."

"I'm not going anywhere."

"You'll miss dinner."

164

"So fucking what?"

"Well, fine!"

Somehow I feel I have to see her to the top of the stairs. The two of us shuffle down the breezeway. The yellow lights are on, which I guess Mrs. M. puts on solely for my benefit. "Don't worry," I tell her. "This isn't anything…serious." She gives me a look, a kind of caregiver look, and I ask, "Are you a nurse, too?"

"I'm a hairdresser." The wind is stronger than ever, and she's both holding her hair away from her face and displaying it, as if "hairdresser" calls for a visual aid. "Look, don't pay any attention to him, okay? And don't let him out of your sight. Please."

Her instructions, contrary as they seem, make a kind of sense. "Don't worry." As I watch her pick her way down the stairs, I wonder why I care. Maybe it's the way she said to her brother, *You'll miss dinner.* My brother, my only sibling, never said anything like that to me.

# Chapter 6

**It** takes some effort, in the off-season, to find dinner around here. The diner closes early, so after an evening of outlandishly piggy sex Lyle and I set off in search of pizza. The pizza that we end up with has onions and green peppers on it, per Lyle, and over the course of the night it comes back to visit me more than once. Each time I get out of bed, muttering about heartburn, going to the bathroom for some of the antacid that I drink like milk, Lyle doesn't seem to notice. He doesn't even change position during the night, while I toss and turn enough for twenty sleepers.

It's still pitch black outside when his watch-alarm sounds. He turns it off, clears his throat like someone about to spit, then croons, "Good morning. Tell me you love me."

"Christ! What *time* is it?"

"Almost five."

"Are you out of your fucking *mind*?" I snatch back the blanket he's taking too much of, trying to keep it around his shoulders as he sits on the side of the bed.

"I'm working the 7-to-3 shift. Have to get home, clean up, make myself look like a nurse."

"Well, I agree it would take a long time to make yourself look decent. Maybe you should have got up at four."

"Hmm. If I thought I looked like *you* in the morning, I'd shoot myself and get it over with."

"Your sister told me not to let you out of my sight."

"You could come over to my patient's house with me, but it's a dump. Oh, I forgot, you already live in a dump."

"I tremble to think of what your idea of bedside care must be."

"Please. This guy is old as the hills. Older." He gives up the blanket at last, finds his jeans on the floor: I hear his pocket change jingling. "Interesting thing, though. He knew my uncle."

I remember Celia's advice to not pay attention to her brother. Still, it's worth noting, even to my sleepy mind, that he's mentioning his uncle again. "Does he talk about your uncle?"

A flapping sound: he's shaking his shirt out before putting it on. "He doesn't talk too much, and I can't understand him half of the time, but it's been…interesting. He's got a picture on his wall of the two of them, when they were both on the Two Piers police force."

"Your uncle was a *cop*?"

"For several years, back in the forties. His flat feet kept him out of the army."

My eyes close, and I start to…drift. Could go back to sleep in a matter of seconds. Then I wake up, startled by something, I don't know what. Time has passed—not much, yet there's some light in the room now, enough to show me that Lyle's still getting dressed, fetching a stray sock from the foot of the bed. I know what startled me: the thought that, for the first time in two days, I'm going to be alone, for several hours at least. "Hey," I ask, fully awake, trying not to sound desperate, "are you coming back after work?"

168

"Ohhh…I don't know."

"Come on." I'm sitting up, the blanket across my own shoulders now. "Who knows, I might break down and tell you I love you."

Even without my glasses I could see a look of suspicion on the fuzzy plain of his face. "I'll call you," he says.

Oh fuck, he's going to do it, let himself out into the dawn. "Wait!" Trying to throw the bedclothes off, I find that some of the sticky messes we've made have glued the sheets together. By the time I've worked a leg free, he's gone. Nothing to do now but to go back to sleep, back to my schedule of staying in bed till noon. Lyle's pillow still smells of his sleeping head; I clutch it to me, rocking back and forth till sleep comes again.

I finally break down and call Lizzie, my aunt who has always refused to be called "Aunt," to let her know that I'm nearby. She's cautious with me on the phone, as if she doesn't trust my voice and won't be sure it's me till we meet in person. So we make arrangements and I meet her at The Coast, a restaurant that will soon be closing for the winter. It's a huge place that looks like a hangar, with fluorescent lights lining the curved ceiling. The floor is cement, with endless rows of picnic tables. The smell of grease in such chilly air reminds me that the last breath of summer has long passed. Lizzie, who normally hates seafood, likes the shrimp here because they're small and breaded and she can pop them into her mouth without having to look at them. I like the shrimp, too; it's as close as protein can get to greasy junk food. What with the soggy fries, also served in a pint-sized carton, I should have heartburn in about an hour.

For a heavy woman Lizzie looks small, sitting with her elbows on the picnic table, eating shrimp with a plastic fork, stabbing them as if they might still be alive. "So what's up?" she asks.

It's startling to realize I haven't anything to say. It would have been nice, since we hadn't seen each other in six years, if I could have been prepared, even if it meant bringing along notes on index cards. "Oh, nothing," I tell her. It sounds unconvincing, even to me.

She takes a sip of lemonade, frowns at it, sets it down. "What'cha been doing?"

"Nothing. Staying in bed, mostly."

"You know, you don't look so good."

Her tone is so serious that I have to look up from the shrimp that I've practically buried my face in. "I'm all right."

She looks at me with blue eyes that have grown more and more pale with age. Good God, does that happen? Does aging leach the color from your eyes? My mother's eyes at the end—they were pale too, like pencil marks not quite erased. My mother never "knew" that Glen and I are gay, and Lizzie has never known either. But they knew that Glen and Mark lived together, in a way that could only mean one thing; and they knew that Eric and I were well established, too. The

169

lies that have characterized our family life have a gentling effect: everything falls softly, and nothing ever hits the mark. I try on a smile. "Everything's okay," I tell her. "Everything's under control."

"Well...." Still staring into her cup, she says, "I talked to Eric."

"*What?*" I hate the expression she's wearing now, her I'm-just-an-innocent-little-girl look. "You *called* him?" A chill runs down my spine, only it's more like my stomach, which, so lately warmed by shrimp and fries, is now an icebox.

"No, he called me."

A family bursts into the room—young mom and dad and three small children, all fair hair and ruddy cheeks. They collide with a picnic table just across from us, kids scampering all over it while the parents take off their coats and run their fingers through their long hair. How do you not take it personally, the sudden appearance of strangers during a private moment? Another argument for becoming a recluse—except that recluses don't get blueberry pancakes or fried shrimp. "He called you?" I asked Lizzie. "He called *you*? Why would he call you?"

"Why do you think? To see if you were all right."

I can sense that she's looking directly at me, wanting to find my eyes, to ask the same question: am I all right? But all I can do is look at the plain cement floor that seems so familiar, the background of my life. When my voice comes out it's a low growl: "Well, he could have called me. He has my number."

"No, I don't think he could have," Lizzie says. "He didn't sound like he knew what to do."

"So what did you tell him?"

"I told him that, just from talking to you on the phone, I didn't think you were doing too good."

I break away from my new friend, the cement floor, to glance at my other new friends, the fair-haired family of five, and see what the ruckus is about. The parents—who look too young, really, to have three children, however small—are standing at the order window, and the kids are running, one or two at a time, between Mom and Dad and the table, shouting out the different things they want to eat. Everything in their world depends on getting what they want, and I remember how childhood is like that. Silently I encourage them:

think up what you want, kids, everything possible, even impossible. Go ahead and ask if they can make you a root beer float, or strawberry milk, or French fries that are crinkly instead of smooth.

"You're not doing too good, are you?" Lizzie asks.

"No," I tell her, lapsing into the family vernacular, "I haven't been doing too good." I peek into my French fry cup: there are three small, soggy ones left, each crumpled into a different position, like accident victims. I sure eat a lot of really unattractive food. "So what difference does it make?"

"I think he'd like to talk to you, Eric would."

I frown at her. "Never mind what you *think*. What did he *say*? Did he *say* that?"

She looks away. "He didn't say much. You haven't said much, either, not really."

"Well, what do you want to know?" My voice grows, booming in the mostly empty room. "That I slept with another man? Is that what you want to know?"

Now comes a silence even louder than my voice. I steal a glance at the young family. They're not tearing their hair out over what I just said; the parents have placed their order and they're all sitting together, or at least the parents are sitting, refereeing as the kids climb on the table or run up and down the aisle. Anyone who fears for the survival of the nuclear family need only stand outside of one, looking in. This little group is invulnerable, living in their shell. Perhaps it's like the barrier between Lizzie and me: there's no way for me to talk to her about being gay. The way hasn't been invented yet, and it would take someone smarter, less emotional, and more coherent than me to do it.

171

When I finally look at her again she's staring out the window, though there's nothing to see. It's dark now, and the owners, just a couple of weeks away from closing, are already saving money by not turning on the parking lot lights. "It's a dirty little town, Two Piers," she says, and I know I'm in for one of her rambling monologues on local history. She knows, or claims to know, where the bodies are buried, which skeletons are in whose closets. She talks about greed and corruption, not with contempt, but almost wistfully, as if she's missed out on something. Tonight's lesson has to do with political rottenness in a seaside town, with "that Judge, what's-his-name, who had everybody in his hip pocket, including the cops." I gather up our empty cups and take them to the white trash barrel which, in summer, would have been surrounded by yellowjackets. On my way back to the table I'm nearly mowed down by the blond bunch, all five of them racing toward the window where their food is ready. I mutter under my breath, "Jesus, watch out for the old queer, why don't you."

Lizzie's looking for something in her handbag, or maybe just giving her hands something to do. Looking up, she smiles at me, very briefly; and it occurs to me, as happens on rare occasions, that Lizzie loves me. She loves me without quite knowing who I am, or what, if anything, I want out of life. She loves me even though she probably has more problems than I do. I guess I love her, too, even when she exasperates me.

"You've got to have somebody, Paul," she says. "Everybody's got to have somebody."

I take her arm to help her up, which gives me an excuse not to face the mild hope in her eyes, and we shuffle through the screen door into the parking lot. I'm muttering again: "*Damn*, it's dark." Good thing there are so few cars, that makes it easier to find Lizzie's without actually being able to see it.

Suddenly, just as she finally fits her key in the lock, the outside lights come on with a kind of *puh!* sound. They're tall, tall fluorescent lights, the kind you see at a ball park, throwing several acres of ground into sharp relief. "Jeez, now I'm blinded," I tell her, covering my eyes. Okay, so the owners haven't turned the parking lot lights off for the season after all; they just neglected to adjust the timer for the earlier darkness of October.

172

**On** my way back to the Sand Dollar I'm trying to digest fried food and the fact that Eric called Lizzie. I should have asked more questions about what he said, should have wrung every word out of her. Her take on it, obviously, was that I should call him. That won't happen. If I did call, and I got the answering machine, my head would explode. It's all too easy to remember what it felt like, calling him from that pay phone on Blue Parkway. What would I say, anyway?

My self-imposed exile has rendered discussion obsolete. We belong to the past.

Trying to think of other things leads to thoughts of other men. Richard Roscoe. Lyle Cook. These guys have tugged me around like puppies wrestling with a stuffed animal. I bear their teeth marks. My seams are torn. I end up focusing on Lyle because he's the one I haven't given up on yet, even if I do keep seeing Richard's faded red truck everywhere I look.

I turn down the street where Lyle and his sister and mother live. He pointed out the house as we passed it the other day, a two-family not much different from my boyhood home on Sagamore Street. Same bay windows in front, same porches, same weather-beaten look despite coats of paint. You could easily pass it by without noticing it, especially on this street where there are blocks of such houses, separated by narrow driveways and, here and there, a side street that's not much wider. It's only eight o'clock, but most of the houses seem dark, including Lyle's. The only sign of life is a blue glow in one first-floor window. Come to think of it, I'm not sure if Lyle lives downstairs or up. I approach the front door warily, in case a guard dog or some other menace launches itself at me from a dark corner of the yard.

The names taped next to the first- and second-floor doorbells are too faint to read, so I just push the bottom one. The blue TV-glow may mean that someone has fallen asleep with the tube on; I might get yelled at.

The front door swings wide, sucking a chilly draft around me, and my mother stands there, scowling in her myopic way, her pale blue eyes trying to fix on me even as her frown gets in their way. The terror of recognition lasts only a split second, but it's enough to take several years off my life and plant a few more white streaks in my beard. "Oh, it's you," she says, causing an aftershock that nearly sends me running; this is just what my mother would say. Translated, it means, *Oh, it's you—not the person I was waiting for.*

This person retreats into the hallway, leaving it up to me whether to follow. So I do, if only to hear and see more of her, and hopefully put to rest any lingering notion that my mother's alive and living in Two Piers. The hallway leads to a kitchen so yellow it hurts my eyes, even though the only light comes from a dim overhead bulb. A lone

173

teacup sits on the table. Mrs. Cook—if that's who this is—picks it up and takes it to the sink. Her bulk shifts visibly, painfully from one leg to the other, yet she moves quickly, as if to get the pain over with. She turns and leans against the sink counter, stands rubbing her right shin against the back of her left leg. It's my mother's *I've-got-to-pee-so-make-it-quick* pose.

"I'm sorry to bother you," I said. "Are you Lyle's mother? Mrs. Cook?"

"Well." She sighed, giving up on trying to place me. "I don't know who *you* are."

"Excuse me. I'm Paul Lavarnway. I'm a friend of Lyle's, sort of."

She shakes her head, not at me but at a far corner of the large room, past the table covered with yellow oilcloth and the counter where canisters with bright yellow tops are lined up by height, to the yellow wallpaper with its pattern of red roosters. "I wish I'd never had kids," she says. Words taken from my mother's mouth! I feel like telling her to knock it off, an impersonation shouldn't be *too* perfect. "Goddamn ungrateful, don't ever think of anybody but themselves…."

"Uh, is this a bad time?"

She raises a hand, swats at her right eye. "Jesus." Stomps to the far end of the room, looks around, stomps back. "I'm tired." Leans against the sink again, right shin rubbing her left calf exactly as before.

"Well," I say, "I'm sorry, I was just dropping by to say hello to Lyle."

She looks at me differently now, her eyes searching. "You know where he is?"

My face is turning red, as if she's caught me not knowing something I'm responsible for. "No, I thought he might be here."

"Goddamnit to hell."

As she sucks in her lower lip and chews on it, I'm ready to give her lifetime tenure as Evvie Lavarnway's representative on earth. Who else could ever be half as good? "Sorry I missed Lyle," I tell her. "So he didn't say where he'd be?"

"If I had it to do all over again, I'd *never* have kids."

I could ask if Celia is home, but her line of thought doesn't encourage me. So I ask her to mention to Lyle that Paul stopped by, and without waiting for her response I duck into the hallway, then out of the house.

Not a soul on the streets as I drive the mile or so back to the Sand Dollar. To the east, the sea and sky are one in the darkness. It's life at the beach as I imagined it, a horizon full of nothing but solitude, silent as the grave. On the radio I find a station that plays lazy jazz standards. I recognize "One More for the Road," one of Lizzie's old 78s that I played to death on my little record player at an age when I was supposed to be listening to "Tubby the Tuba" and "This Old Man." Of course I didn't understand the song at all. When Bing Crosby got to the lines about the man having found a torch that had to be drowned before it could explode, I had a picture of a man holding a bomb with a lit fuse, running toward the water, any water. Since there was no **BANG!** at the end of the song, I figured he made it.

I drift a little toward oncoming traffic and get honked at by a speeding pickup. Focus, Paul, focus! Getting lost in thoughts of the past—childhood interpretations of torch songs, no less—can lead to a head-on crash. Still, I wonder what I liked about that song that I couldn't understand. All I can think of is that, at the tender age of six or seven, I could identify with the world-weariness of the singer—a feeling that became a constant in my life, a part of the equation that never varied.

At the Sand Dollar, Mrs. M. has turned on the **NO VACANCY** sign so she won't be disturbed. As I climb the stairs to my room, singing under my breath—*This torch that I've found*—I see no signs of life on the beach, no fires or strollers. Familiar old depression tugs at my eyelids, offering oblivion, the chance to open my door, fall onto the bed and seek relief in sleep without even taking my sneakers off.

Oh fuck, there's someone outside my room, leaning on the rail. Lyle? No, soon enough I can see it's Celia, her face turned away from the glaring yellow light bulb. Her leaning posture reminds me of her mother; she seems resigned to waiting, and when I call her name she only turns her head a bit. I open my door and wave for her to follow me in. The bed has been made by Mrs. M, but nothing has been done to the floor in too long, the crumbs are getting out of control. They start collecting on my socks as soon as I kick my sneakers off.

175

Celia's like a toy with a new battery, perky and noisy. "So where is he? Why didn't he come home for dinner? He's *never* done this before, not without calling. I was pounding on your door earlier, I thought you were both in here...."

"Hey, take it easy." I rub my eyes, willing sleepiness away. "Give me a break. I haven't seen Lyle since he went to work this morning."

"Fine, but where *is* he?" she insists, as if I've failed to address the issue.

"I really don't know, Celia. I just found out myself that he wasn't home, when I stopped by to say hello."

"Oh, God. My *mother*." She turns away, makes some odd, swinging gestures with her arms, a sort of calisthenics of frustration. "I'll never hear the end of this."

"So what can I do to help?" I'm aiming for a weak, teeny-tiny voice, half hoping she won't hear me. I can't imagine doing anything but flopping down on my bed—unless it's having a snack first. My stomach growls, wanting sugar.

"Look. It's like this." She pats the air in front of her, like a bricklayer smoothing mortar. "I don't care that he missed dinner, which my mother thinks is a capital crime. But he didn't even *call*. He's never not come home for dinner without calling. And then it got later and later. He's *never* done this before."

"Well, he's not a kid. You're talking about a fifty-year-old man. Some of us do a few crazy things in our middle age.... You want some Oreos? Hurry, there's not many left."

"That's it. I'm going home." But instead of turning on her heel she takes a slow look around, her eyes widening. "God, what a mess this place is!"

Okay, I just made a similar observation myself a moment ago. But I *had* gathered up the cum rags and let them soak in the sink, not wanting Mrs. M. to find them. Plus I'd carried the pizza box and some other trash down to the dumpster myself. I'm pretty sure the place no longer smells of corn chips and cum, mozzarella and smeared asses. "You should have seen it this morning."

"Did he say anything before he left?"

"Of course not," I say.

"What did he tell you?" Crossing her arms, responding not to my words but to what must have been some look on my face.

All I can remember are his remarks about his patient...*He knew my uncle*. But he didn't say anything that *meant* anything. "I don't have anything to tell you, Celia. I'm sorry."

She tilts her head, pulls back strands of hair that threaten her left eye. "I wish I knew...."

"You wish you knew what he sees in me?"

She takes a step back, startled that I could complete her thought so accurately.

I take a step forward. "It's like this, hon. I'm a bear. A big old hairy bear. A recognizable gay type, highly coveted by some. By the way, are you a lesbian?"

Her jaw dropped. "That is absolutely none of your business!"

"Aha! You're a lesbian."

"I'm sorry I came here!" But her steps to the door are slow, and instead of storming out she has to turn again, facing me as if I were a spoonful of necessary medicine. "Will you help me?"

I'm moving too, toward the dresser with its comforting array of boxes. "You ever have these? Little graham crackers shaped like teddy bears? They even come in chocolate...."

"Paul...."

"Of, if you're more of a salty snack person, there's some corn chips and pretzels left."

"Paul!"

"*Mmmph.*" My mouth is filled with teddy bears that will soon soften, offering up the blessed relief of sugar and chocolate. I sip some flat Diet Coke to help them along.

"I wanted to ask you...nicely...if you'd help me look for him."

"Uh...." My mouth, temporarily free, waters for something else. I grab a handful of chips. "What can I do?"

"If you'd come with me...."

Sighing, I sit on the edge of the bed and pull my sneakers toward me. If she's going to be so serious about it, I don't have any choice but to help her. "What if he's still at his patient's house? Maybe something came up and he had to work a double shift."

177

"No. He came home after work. I…looked in his room." Her hesitation explains that this isn't supposed to happen. "His smock was there, with his name badge and his pager."

I finish tying my sneakers, look for my jacket. I had it on a minute ago, where could it have gone? "I still don't know what I can do to help you."

"Just come with me."

"All right." There's my jacket, on top of the TV for some reason. "But I want you to understand something. Lyle and I don't 'mean anything' to each other. Okay?"

She looks at the bed. No traces of Lyle and me remain, nothing to show that two men who don't mean anything to each other could generate a hell of a lot of heat. But Celia seems to see beneath the bedclothes, catch a glimpse of what must have been. She shakes her head, by way of saying "Okay, but it doesn't make sense to me." That's good enough.

We take her small blue pick-up. I ask where we're going, but she's too agitated to finish a sentence: "I think we ought to…it wouldn't be a bad idea, just to rule it out…we could try, anyway…."

She drives down the strip toward the amusement park, hangs a right at the arcade called the Palace Playland. I didn't think there was anything else in that block but souvenir shops, closed up now; but there are cars parked diagonally to the curb, near a place with no sign outside and no windows, except for a small square pane bearing a neon beer logo. After we park I ask her, "Is this a gay bar?"

"To find a real gay bar you'd have to go into Portland, which Lyle wouldn't do, not by himself. He used to come here, though, a long time ago." She's turned the engine off but her hand lingers on the key, as if she might change her mind any second. "I don't want to go in there, I really don't. I don't want to find him in there."

"All right, I'll go in."

"No." She glances at herself in the rear view mirror, as if to see how afraid her eyes look. From what I could see by the streetlight, they look very afraid. "Lyle's been sober for over two years. Hasn't touched a drop."

"Oh. Well, maybe that's all the more reason why I should go in there alone."

With a contrariness that I'm starting to get used to, she opens her door and strides across the sidewalk, leaving me to hustle to catch up with her. She precedes me into the warm, humid, smoke-filled hole; it's like walking into a lung. A reminder, if I needed one, why I haven't been inside a bar in years. The booths looks grimy, and the bar itself, along the opposite wall, is sparsely populated but bears a full complement of half-empty glasses, wadded-up napkins and overflowing ashtrays. The bartender, whose figure is too much like mine to justify the tank-top he wears, is sweeping up, or pretending to, his long greasy hair swinging in front of his face. He glances up at us briefly, his droopy eyes expressionless, as if we're just fellow pedestrians on a crosswalk, not valuable customers. How valuable we're going to be I don't know, since I don't feel like drinking. Or, I don't know, what the hell, maybe I do. A beer wouldn't sit well with the chocolate graham crackers and greasy shrimp, but they're not sitting well by themselves, anyway. I pull out my wallet and turn to ask Celia what she'll have, but she's gone. The bartender fills a plastic tumbler for me—apparently only mixed drinks come in a real glass—and pinches the two dollar bills I give him by the corners, as if the ink is still wet.

I take a walk, a very short walk, down to the other end of the bar and back. It gives me a chance to see who's sitting in the booths, but the few figures I can make out through the smoky haze are all hunched into themselves. All I know is that none of them is Lyle.

Celia pops up by my elbow. "Let me have a sip of that," she says.

I hand over the tumbler. "I was going to ask you if you wanted something, but you disappeared."

"I was checking the men's room."

179

"For Chrissakes, Celia, I could have done that."

She ignores me, walks slowly toward the back while scanning the booths, taking a closer look than I had. Someone in the very back booth makes her quicken her step. "C'mere," she says, snapping her fingers at me as if I were a dog. "Sit."

I slide into the booth, even as she disappears again. The man who's sitting here alone doesn't even look up from his drink. Something about him, though, makes me wonder if I've seen him before, especially when he raises his head. For a boozy moment—after just one tumbler of beer!—I'm not even sure if I'm in Two Piers or Kansas

City, which means that the man across from me could be anyone I've met over the past fourteen years—friends of Eric's, co-workers, social acquaintances from the Kansas City Couples group, even my first husband—everyone I've abandoned or driven away. He could even be—couldn't he?—Eric himself, summoned forth by my desperate need to see him, made vague and ghostly by his desire to keep away. "Sweetheart." My cheeks burn; did I say that out loud? "Sweetheart." Whatever has loosened my tongue, it's not about to stop. "Come back to me."

His laughter brings me back to my senses—if you can call it laughter, that sputtering and snorting and heaving. It's nothing like Eric's hearty laughter, and certainly nothing like Eric himself, this creature that I zero in on, narrow of eye and long of nose in a parsimonious-looking way, that nose too thin to admit more than a whisper of scent, which then must travel a long, cruel journey to the brain. He has a cowlick peeking slightly above the crown of his head, and the mere shadow of a chinstrap beard. He's either squinting through smoke, or has a naturally squinty eye. Seeing me studying him, he laughs again. It sounds like strangulated snoring.

I decide to be offended. "The least you could do," I tell him, "is buy me another beer."

He snorts—in disgust, I suppose—and slides out of the booth. I figure I'll stay for a slow count of ten, to see if he comes back. And son of a gun, he does, with a fresh beer as heady as a daydream. Part of the foam spills over as he sets the cup down, and I catch it with my finger.

"You're funny," he says, straight-lipped.

"Did you practice saying that in front of a mirror?" I ask. "It's not easy to say 'You're funny' without smiling. Unless you really don't mean it."

"I guess I don't mean it, then."

*Well, in that case, why don't you leave?* I'm *that* close to saying it. But then I'm the one who sat down with him, not vice versa. Which, in an equally perverse way, gives me the right to start grilling him—especially since we've decided that I'm not amusing. "Hey, is this a gay bar, or what?"

Now he smiles. "It's whatever you want it to be."

"Oh, we're playing that game, are we?" I squint, trying to match my left eye to his. "Why don't you tell me your name?"

"Call me Richard." He leans closer. "You're strange, you know that?"

"Ah, now we're getting somewhere." I take a healthy gulp of beer—jeez, half of it gone already. "I've got a reason for being here, and it's not what you think. I'm looking for Lyle Cook."

Some kind of scuffle erupts nearby, making him lean in even closer to be heard: "Yeah, I saw you come in with his dykey sister."

"His dykey sister might be more of a man than you are, Ricardo."

He laughs his strangulated laugh. "Spoken like a real queen."

The haze of smoke is getting to me; I want some of the real thing, not just secondhand. "I'm going to smoke." He doesn't object, so I light up. The smoke and the beer make a seductive combination, like smoke and coffee. Like smoke and *anything*. "So where is he? Lyle, I mean."

"How would I know?"

"Well, you're sitting here in your usual spot, you've seen all the regulars come and go…."

"Hmmph. Like you know everything."

The noise of the bar swells and recedes, almost with a regular pattern, like waves on the beach. Time, on the other hand, passes quietly, in the background. The bitchy give-and-take of Richard(!) and me isn't much different from the bitchiness that seemed to keep Lyle and me together. I remember the nature shows that Eric loved to watch on Sunday afternoons: you'd see a couple of bear cubs or something, apparently trying to maul each other to death, but really just playing. That's what Lyle and I did: we played, sometimes with claws exposed. And it was sweet.

This new friendship I've struck up is something different. During our halting, sputtering conversation I make reference to his cowlick and squinty eye, and he makes some choice remarks about my weight. And there comes a time—how long after?—when I look up and he's gone. In front of me sit a few plastic beer tumblers, some of which have been used more than once. It's not like me to be drinking so much, but at least I've had a somewhat amusing conversation in a

181

bar, and that's a rare thing. I'm halfway disposed toward just sitting, waiting to see if someone more interesting comes along.

No such luck. Celia falls into the seat opposite mine, takes a good look at me and snorts.

"That must be the snorting seat," I tell her.

"God, have you been *drinking*? You're a lot of help!"

"As a matter of fact, I was talking to this guy...." The room seems brighter, the smoky haze luminous. I shield my eyes, like a drunk in the noonday sun. "This guy Richard, I was asking him if he'd seen Lyle...."

"Richard? Oh, he's a great one to talk to. Did he try to recruit you?"

"Well, it's a little late for me to be recruited...and anyway, this was your idea, wasn't it?" I stifle a belch, none too successfully.

"Shit. I've talked to everybody in here. Nobody's seen him." She slides out of the booth like butter on a griddle. Taking off without me, no doubt. I try to follow her with my eyes, but I'm just a bit woozy.

Now she's back, tugging at my sleeve. "Let's go, let's go."

"Ow, ow, ow." I hitch myself painfully along the leatherette bench and out of the booth.

We're outside, in the unseasonably warm, humid night. I'll be running my air conditioner later on, probably to the disgust of Mrs. M. Maybe she'll snort at me.

"It's totally unbelievable," Celia says. "I called my mother just now, and he's *still* not home."

"Do you fear"—another belch—"foul play?"

"Hush your mouth." She raises a hand, about to hush it for me. "I'm going down on the beach."

Doesn't going down on a beach get you a mouthful of sand? I'm about to ask, but she's already gone. Probably just as well. My "foul play" question wasn't tactful either. "Paul, you suck," I tell the weathered clapboard side of the bar, as if it holds my reflection. Then I follow Celia, or what's left of her: a shadow disappearing just beyond the streetlight. "Hey, wait." My stunted steps jiggle the loose fat above my waistline, my breath comes hard. I should be in my room, with my junk food and cold sheets, I'm of no earthly use to anyone. Now I have to laugh, seeing how *silly* it is that I should keep going so long after my spring has wound down, my batteries drained. Yet I keep going, and going, and gradually my head clears a bit. There's a grim purpose, after all, in the way my stubby feet keep lifting up and setting themselves down, one slightly ahead of the other. No use pretending I'm not afraid, but so fucking what? I'm going to see what comes next.

Celia crosses the beach under the pier—not a path I like to take, the sand here always cold, the wet pilings clammy to the touch. I'm glad to get past them, and to see that Celia has stopped not too far ahead, near where the sand meets the grass line that forms a little ridge. She sits down with her back against it, facing the sea.

"Sorry," she says, her long hair whipping around her face in the wind. "I don't really know why I had to come down here. I'm just… frustrated." I can't see her face very well as her hand keeps moving up to it, tearing at the strands of hair blowing into her eyes, her mouth. "You don't have to stay here with me, I'm all right. I come down here this late all the time."

The beach is spooky at night, all black-and-white, breakers charging in like ghosts on a rampage. Horizon gone, nothing out there but darkness incalculably deep. I'm not about to leave her alone, and don't have the energy to walk all the way back to the Sand Dollar anyway. "I'll stay for a little while," I tell her, sitting down hard on the sand beside her, feeling the shock from my tailbone to my fuzzy head.

We don't say anything, not for a long while. The ridge, comfortable to lean against, shields us from the wind. The sound of the surf becomes one with the white noise in my head, lulling me to sleep.

183

When I wake I find that even my face went to sleep. It's stinging with circulation now, the way numbness wears off after seeing the dentist. Am I imagining it, or is the sky a little lighter, suggesting a horizon line? Having slipped down from the ridge, Celia lies in the sand in a fetal position, her windbreaker covering her shoulders and most of her head. Though I haven't made a sound—nothing that could be heard over the wind and water—she stirs.

"Where am I?" she asks—humorously, but only partly so.

"On a long night's journey into day," I tell her. "Go back to sleep."

"I can't, I'm awake now." She wriggles around into a sitting position, keeping the windbreaker wrapped tight around her. I ask if she's cold. "No," she says. "It's just that…." Suddenly she's crying. I can't see her face very well, but her sobs make her head jerk like a barking dog's.

"It's all right, hon," I tell her, more than a little terrified. Maybe it's a pre-programmed male response to a crying female, but I *have* to calm her down. "Celia, it's all right."

She lets the windbreaker slip down, freeing ends of her hair that whip in the wind. "*Nothing's* all right." She takes a deep breath, as if that will help her stop crying; but it only leads to an explosion when she finally lets it go, bawling.

"Lyle's okay, Celia. He is. I know he is." Does anyone ever believe talk like this? When we hear it in the movies, we know what it means— that the missing child has definitely drowned, the detective's partner has for sure been murdered, or the sweet old lady has totally breathed her last, smiling in her sickbed. But I can see that the characters who babble soothing words are also trying to reassure themselves. I'm not ready to believe that anything serious has happened to Lyle, not by a long shot; and by gathering Celia into my arms—she's so thin, so angular, it's like holding a kite—I'm seeking comfort too.

We hold each other for a while. Yes, there's a dim line of light along the horizon, and the sky's no longer a void but a soft gray ceiling. And I can see that Celia's eyes are red and swollen.

"What are you really doing here?" she asks. "Why did you come here, anyway?"

184

"Oh, it's a long story." I lean back against the ridge and wonder how I could even begin to tell it. But the morning still lay beyond the horizon somewhere, we're both awake, and there's nothing else to do; so I tell her the story, as best I can, of Eric and me, and Richard Roscoe, and how I threw my life away.

But what she really wants to know is, why did I choose Two Piers to come to? I explain that the little town is close to where I grew up, to my remaining relatives…but not *too* close. Besides, I always loved the beach, and the amusement park. I tell her how I remember the pier—she does, too—when it was still its original length, and there was a big aquarium at its end. And there was the Noah's Ark funhouse, and the Aladdin slide, neither of which I was ever brave enough to take on. There were the battered onion rings and the French fries that scalded the tongue, and the caramel corn, and the pizza. We recall the fire that destroyed the huge wooden roller coaster, and the winter storm that swept the aquarium out to sea. "Kind of a fitting end to an aquarium," she says.

By now daylight has come, the sky overcast but recognizable. The water, though still dark, is more blue than black. "What would happen now," I ask, "if we went back up the street? Would anybody be stirring, or is it earlier than we think it is?"

"I have no idea. I'm never going out without a watch again." She stands up—feeling achy, I can tell, just as I do when I straighten my legs—and slaps sand from the seat of her jeans. When she offers me a hand to help me up I don't hesitate to take it. My knees are petrified, refusing to bend, forcing me to stagger a bit. Or is that the effect of last night's beer?

"Thanks," Celia says. "Thanks for staying with me, talking to me. I'm sure Lyle's fine, it's no big deal."

I smile at her. "Things always look better in the light of day."

Instead of stepping up over the ridge, which would take us to a side street, Celia heads down the beach the way we came, and I follow. Later I will see her in my mind's eye, her hair flying, open windbreaker flapping as she followed the gentle slope of the sand toward the tall dark pilings underneath the pier; and I will imagine myself doing what I did not do then, calling her, stopping her in her tracks, sending her off in another direction before she could get close enough to see, wrapped around a piling like a huge clot of seaweed, the dead body of her brother Lyle.

# Chapter 7

**A** couple of days after Lyle's funeral, I get out of bed. It ain't easy.

Sometimes, in my dreams, Lyle and I are on the beach alone. He's waving his arms and describing something that's about to happen in the sky. I don't understand exactly what he's saying, but it seems that the end of the world is coming very, very soon. It's already happening; as soon as I look away Lyle disappears. I know where to find him, though. He's under the pier, lying face down in the wet. His hair is tangled in the pilings. I take scissors—Celia's scissors—and start to cut him free. But each time I release a strand of hair from a piling, another wave comes along, wrapping the other strands more tightly than ever.

Well, Lyle will just have to wait. He'll have to wait, that's all, because Eric's coming to pick me up. I'm supposed to meet him on Main Street, in front of the Palace Playland. He'll be driving our new car, and he'll be taking me…someplace. Someplace where we can take a last look around before the end of the world.

In another dream I'm up on the pier, and I see Lyle go over the end. Yes, it happens just the way they said: he's drunk, and leaning too far over the railing, and…whoops, he's gone. Hitting his head on the edge of the pier as he falls. It's the blow that kills him, not the water.

187

After the funeral I took a cue from Lyle and got my own bottle of liquor. The whiskey burns going down and knocks me out for hours at a time, dependable as a sleeping pill. It has a pleasant, dulling effect on my few waking hours, too, which are mostly spent going to the bathroom and yelling at Mrs. M.

*Mr. Lavarnway, are you all right?*

*Bitch! Whore! Slut! Leave me alone!*

*Mr. Lavarnway, are you going to open—?*

*Cunt from hell! Fuck off!*

Really, Paul, are you sure this ever happened, or is it just another dream? Hmmm, don't know, though I swear I've got a clear memory of squatting naked on the carpet, surrounded by trash and a slick pool of vomit, yelling at Mrs. M. as she taps on the door. After what seems like the longest time, she goes away.

The room reeks of puke and booze and dirty linen.

Have some more whiskey.

My brother doesn't call, but Lizzie does. She asks if I knew the boy who fell off the pier. I tell her to leave me alone, goddamnit. And Chrissakes, he wasn't a boy, he was fifty years old. Yes, she says, wasn't that an awful thing, they ought to do something about that pier.

As if it would make a difference. As if he wouldn't have found something else to fall off of.

No, it doesn't pay to answer the phone. As for the knocking on the door, well, there's nothing you can do about that. Especially if it's not Mrs. M. But who is it now, knocking with an urgency I've never heard before?

"Paul? Hey, Paul, you okay?"

A deep male voice, not unfamiliar. Gets confused with the sound of the breakers, though. Fading in and out. I turn the TV on. A black-and-white set—no frills here, by God—so I look for a black-and-white show. An old movie, maybe. Son of a gun, there's Humphrey Bogart, on Channel 8. He doesn't look any better than I do.

"Paul! Hey, Paul?"

Maybe it wasn't a good idea, turning on the TV. Better to be quiet, pretend I'm not here, but it's too late now. Christ. But whoever's at the door, maybe he can tell me what movie this is. *The Big Sleep? In a Lonely Place?* I wrap a blanket around me before I open up.

It's Mark Rodgers, my brother's long-suffering partner, standing there. He's wearing what looks like his high school letter jacket, it must be over thirty years old. That's Mark all over: all he has to do is touch up his hair a bit, and he can pass for a kid. A boy.

"Paul." He's affronted, disgusted by my appearance, the smell of the room behind me.

It's an overcast day, looks like winter, but there's still way too much light out there for me. "Come in," I tell him, my eyes smarting, "or go away. In or out, take your pick."

"Paul...."

"One thing, though. This is a pants-free zone. You come in, you take your pants off."

Mark removes his baseball cap as he crosses the threshold. "Jesus."

"Is he here too? I hope he brought his own bottle...."

Mark sniffs the air. "What's that? Whiskey?"

"You want a shot? There's a tumbler in the bathroom."

"No, thanks."

Oh, that's right, he's a teetotaler. "So, to what do I owe this visit?"

"I didn't get a chance to talk to you at the funeral."

Yes, the funeral. Damnedest thing I've ever seen, held at the local Unitarian Church, where Lyle was something of a regular. I'd expected your standard sanctuary; instead there was a rather bare carpeted room with a double circle of chairs. A raised platform in the center held some of Lyle's possessions. That was it. Not even a closed casket, let alone an open one. People sat here and there along the circle, some in the inner row, some in the outer. Where was I to sit? I hardly belonged in the inner circle, did I? His mother was there, barely recognizable in a dark gray dress, uncomfortable-looking where it stretched over her hips. She clutched a black handbag as if she feared someone might try to take it from her, and the only part of her that moved was her trembling chin.

Next to her sat Celia, in a black skirt and white blouse. The two women seemed no more connected than strangers on a bus. I sat as far from them as possible, in the outer circle. Mrs. Cook's outfit, uncomfortable as it looked, couldn't have been worse than mine: I was

189

wearing the only decent pair of dark slacks I'd brought with me, and I'd had to pour myself into them.

The minister, if that's what she was called, wore black slacks and a navy blue cable-knit sweater. There was nothing ecclesial about her, I only knew she was officiating because she nodded at all who entered, her hand sweeping the circle of chairs, letting them know they could sit anywhere. She may have been the youngest person there. Most of us, so loosely affiliated that we had nothing to do but look at each other, were in our forties and fifties. When I saw another familiar face I nearly cried out: it was Mark, sitting about a quarter-circle from me, removed from Celia and her mother but also in the inner row. He saw me at the same moment, and nodded. He was wearing the same semi-casual dark as most of us, but he'd forgotten to remove his Red Sox baseball cap.

The minister did not sit in a chair herself but rather half-reclined on the carpeted platform, as if she were about to take a sunbath with Lyle's effects. She stayed in that position as she began to speak to the ragged circle around her. As soon as she mentioned "celebrating the life of Lyle Cook" the tears came, and I was glad I'd remembered to scour my suitcase for a clean handkerchief. I didn't know what grieved me most: the way he'd met his end, the fact that I'd never see him again, or the way the two women he left behind were obviously suffering. Celia had been crying so much that it seemed the hot tears had partially melted her skin; her face drooped alarmingly, making her look even older than her mother.

After the minister's remarks, which I heard practically none of, it was time to sing a song. The hymnals that had been placed on our chairs were the usual dusty tomes, no doubt filled with the Protestant dirges I'd known as a youth. But to my surprise, the selection she had us turn to was "Morning Has Broken" by Cat Stevens. Cat Stevens? In a *hymnal*? Perhaps the Unitarians were onto something. Unfortunately, this particular song was damned hard for amateurs to sing. Our voices strained, wavered, broke—did everything but carry the tune.

The minister explained that the rest of the service would consist of "a few words" from those who wanted to open their mouths. Testi-

monials, the ways in which Lyle had "touched our lives." I closed my
eyes, swayed a bit in my chair as a wave of fatigue swept over me.

"He was a good nurse," someone said.

Murmurs of assent. I opened my eyes to see who had spoken. A
younger man, blond, wearing blue jeans and construction boots.

"He took care of my partner…toward the end," he added. "I'll never forget…how good he was."

That was the Lyle I'd never know—Lyle of the white smock and
hypodermic, who knew his way around a blood pressure cuff, knew
how to look into someone's eyes to see how well he was doing.

"He was a good brother." It was Celia who said that, it couldn't
have been anyone else; but I could swear that raspy croak was not
her voice, and that it came from a different direction. "He never hurt
another living soul." When I dared to look her way her eyes were on
me, erasing all doubt, if there'd been any, that she blamed me, somehow, for his death.

And I was left, through the next several comments that were made,
with this nagging voice in my head: *say something, say something*. But
say what? That I liked the way he handled my dick? I looked at Mark
again. Hard to tell if he knew that Lyle and I had been banging each
other. I was startled, though, when Mark opened his mouth, as if he'd
read my thoughts and was about to spill the beans.

"I knew Lyle most of my life," he said. "He was a good friend. We
used to clown around, pick on each other, say things…it didn't mean
anything, it was just our way of being friends." He said this last to the
small display of possessions in the center. For the first time I took as
good a look at them as my seat in the outer circle allowed. A book,
opened to show glossy black-and-white photos; his high school
yearbook, no doubt. His current nursing license, in a 5"×7" frame. A
modest stack of CD's. Another book, a dogeared copy of Robert Per-
sig's *Zen and the Art of Motorcycle Maintenance*. And look, Richard
Brautigan: *Trout Fishing in America*. A red t-shirt with the name of a
bowling alley on the back: so he'd been on a team at some time. Yellowed post cards, a tiny Eiffel Tower from some long-ago trip to Paris.
Was there anything that an old boyfriend had given him? Perhaps
that was a taboo subject, even after death, with his mother sitting
there. During a sudden silence I opened my mouth. A sound came

out, like the squeak of an old drawer sliding open. But the drawer was empty, so I shut it.

At the brief gathering afterward, in the lobby, Mrs. Cook turned away from me as I patted her shoulder. I managed to take Celia's hands and press them between my own, though she tried not to look at me either. Since then I haven't seen or heard from either of them.

"Look," Mark says now, finally closing the door behind him.

"No, you look. Pants off." I take a step back, trip on the hem of the blanket, and sit down hard. Which would be embarrassing if Mark weren't taking his own fall, tripping over an errant can of Pringles, landing on top of me…. "*Oof!*"

"Damn, Paul…!"

The blanket falls completely off the bed, and soon both of us are entwined in it. The more Mark tries to kick his boots free, the more wrapped up he becomes, thrashing us both around till we smack into the dresser. A pitter-pattering like rain falls on us.

"For Christ's sake, what is it?"

"Goldfish. Cheddar ones. I like to eat them with butter toffee peanuts. Get that cheesy-nutty thing going."

"God*damn*it!" Another thrust against the dresser, and something more like hail comes down. "What the hell…?"

"That would be the butter toffee peanuts."

"Great. Now I'm getting peanuts down the back of my neck!"

"That's okay, you can eat them when you get home. Or Glen can eat them, whoever gets there first."

"Paul…." Free at last, Mark gets to his feet, shakes himself like a dog. I can practically hear the peanuts rattling against his backbone. "I've got to sit down." He takes the deskette chair.

I'm content to remain on the floor, wrapped in the blanket that's now ripped in a couple of places, nothing serious. "Well, thanks for dropping by, Mark. But you're really interfering with my pity party, especially if you won't eat."

Not in response to me, but rather absent-mindedly, he picks up a few of the crusty peanuts from the dresser top and pops them in his mouth. "I wanted to ask you something."

I stick my bare foot free of the blanket, rub it up against his calf. "I thought I'd never see the day. Eight inches, Mark. Extremely versatile. And I'm only lying by two inches."

"God*damn*it, Paul." Now he sounds like he really will lose his temper. "Listen to me, please! I know that you and Lyle were…kind of close, near the end."

"I guess we were, if you could call two guys 'close' who had a… what? Forty-eight-hour fling?"

He tracks down a few more peanuts. Son of a gun, he likes them. "Did you meet his mother?"

"I'm afraid I did."

"Yeah, well." How like a kid he is, making himself small in the chair, cringing as if Mrs. Cook herself were in the room. "She doesn't like me at all."

"You're in safe company, she doesn't like anybody."

"Celia never liked me much, either."

"Well, Celia's a special case. You have to—what? Get to know her? That sounds funny, coming from me. You've known these people most of your life, haven't you?

"Yeah. So this will sound funny, too: I want to ask you to do something for me, over at their house. There's nobody else I can ask."

**During** the daytime there's plenty of parking in front of the Cook house, though the absence of cars gives it a lonely, shunned look. I sit in my car with the radio on, not listening to a word of a call-in talk show. I don't know how long I'm going to sit here. At least inertia has its attractions, being a distant cousin to oblivion. "Oblivion," I say aloud, promising myself to look up the derivation of that word sometime. Soon I'm letting my eyes close. It's my favorite oblivion, the nothingness of sleep, calling to me.

I've almost nodded off completely when the front door of the house slams. Upstairs neighbor, old man in a parka, scrabbling down the steps. He doesn't glance my way, and there's no reason why he should. Still I feel…affronted? That's not right. How about plain damn lonely, ready to disappear from the planet if I don't have some human contact soon? I'm not looking forward to this errand, but

193

the alternative—returning to my wall-to-wall grave at the Sand Dollar—turns my stomach.

I get out of the car and clamber up the porch steps, my legs cramped from sitting so long. I can't remember if the doorbell works or not so I pound on the door, loud enough to rattle its glass pane. If Mrs. Cook is home alone, it could take her a good long while to answer, so I wait a couple of minutes before pounding again. The inside door opens, as if I just found the right combination of knocks. "Hi, Mrs. Cook."

She's just visible on the other side of the storm door, the hallway dark behind her. "What do you want?"

"Remember me?" Cheerful, like an idiot. "I'm Paul."

She lifts a hand, rubs the side of her face. Maybe she was sleeping. "What do you *want*."

"Can I come in?"

She brings her hand down, turns her head slightly—holding back an impulse to spit at me? Poor thing. I had thought, on first glance, that she was a dead ringer for Evvie; but the truth is that Mrs. Cook is even homelier. Her white hair looks stiff and hard and dry, standing out in planes over her ears and the back of her neck. "I don't care what you do," she says. And she's gone, stomping back down the hall on her stiff legs.

This is as close to being welcome as I'm going to get, so I open the storm door and follow her through the foyer into the flat. She heads toward the kitchen, just as my own mother would, crosses directly to the sink filled with suds, stands there with her back to me. Shimmies as she scrubs a plate, the way my mother used to do, the hem of her thin housedress swaying.

194

I take a seat at the table, as if…what? I'm going to be offered a cup of coffee, or better yet, cookies and milk? It's amusing, this sense of hopeless expectation, if only because it's so familiar. Recognizing an old feeling is as close as I've come lately to recognizing an old friend. But my smile only meets it halfway, lifting one corner of my mouth. I clear my throat and try to say something. "Uh…how are you doing, Mrs. Cook?" I learned from Lyle's obituary that her first name is Maud, but I'm being personal enough calling her "Mrs. Cook," especially since she doesn't call me anything at all.

"Goddamn good-for-nothing." A saucepan lid clatters into the drainer.

"I was wondering, are there any errands you needed run?" I'm speaking loudly, assuming she's hard of hearing—or selective of hearing, as my mother used to be. "I'm here, I've got a car, not much to do. Need anything from the store?"

Something else hits the drainer. She pulls the plug, grabs a towel from a hook on the side of the refrigerator to dry her hands, rubbing and rubbing, her hands fighting with each other under the cloth. When she's done she stares into a corner for a moment, her lips moving slightly, little puffs of air coming out, like whispered curses. Suddenly I need to know what she's saying, it's as if the wisdom of the universe is leaking away with no one but me to pay heed.

"My mother was a lot like you," I blurt out.

She looks at me, finally—or rather at my feet, under the table. "So what."

"She was lonely and disappointed," I tell her. "And mad." In the lexicon of my family, *mad* always meant angry, not crazy. Crazy Maud might be, but I'm not about to call her that.

"What do I care about your mother."

That was my mother's trump card, what it always came down to— that she didn't care, about me, or my father, or Glen, or anybody. A wickedly efficient defense: if you don't care, then you can't be hurt. "I'm just saying," I tell her, "that maybe I know a little bit about how you feel." I'm speaking, not to the Maud Cook whose son has just died—I can't claim to know what that feels like—but to the Maud that Lyle had known. "My mother was surrounded by people who didn't live up to her expectations," I said. "Didn't even *try.*"

Maud's chin trembles. Quick as a flash she makes eye contact with me, then looks away. "You're better off if you expect nothin'," she says.

"Ain't it the truth? Expect nothing, or expect the worst. That way you're never disappointed."

She raises a hand to give one eye a good rub. "You can't count on nobody, that's for sure."

And so we trip, hand in hand, down the path of depression. I wasn't my mother's son for nothing; besides knowing every step of

195

the way, I can quote chapter and verse on the trials of living a worthless life full of worthless people. Maud takes a step closer to the table, reaches out to lean on one of the captain's chairs, her other hand on the small of her back.

"Sit down with me, why don't you," I tell her.

She looks wary, the wrinkles between her eyebrows deepening, as if I might turn out to be an insurance salesman after all. But she pulls a chair out and sits, if only because she's been on her feet too long. Clears her throat the way my mother always did when she sat at table. A polite "ahem, ahem," it was a way of changing gears, putting on politeness for the sake of company. I can see my mother's hands, their skin shiny, spotted with age, moving above the surface of the table, adding milk to her tea, grasping the salt and pepper. I'm glad that Maud, for now, is keeping her hands in her lap.

"Where's Celia?" I ask. "Is she working this afternoon?"

She nods, but her mind is on something else: she's squinting as if to see a thought better.

"Are you thinking about Lyle?"

She takes a deep breath, starts to speak. Stops and starts again. "Doesn't do any good to think, does it."

I keep my voice low, like a confidant. "He was a disappointment, too, wasn't he."

She traces a pattern on the Formica tabletop with her finger, its nail yellowed but strong. "It wasn't his fault."

"Whose fault was it? His father's?"

"He never knew his father. He was better off for it, too, believe you me." She glances up at the dim yellow light over our heads, not caring if some half-hearted deity overhears her. "You don't have any say over how your kids turn out. You think you do, but you don't."

Her tone says that's her final word on the matter. I wondered how Maud and Lyle had managed to co-exist for so many years in the same house; after all, she knew he was gay, had witnessed his comings and goings. That's where my case was different: I was pretty sure my mother knew I was gay, but she pretended not to know. She would have made no comments—none aloud, anyway—about how I had "turned out." And I was sure that she, like Maud, would not take any blame for it. "Lyle was a good kid, though, wasn't he?" I asked,

196

wanting suddenly, desperately, to hear her say something good about him.

No such luck. Her finger picked at the surface of the table, though there was nothing to pick at—no stain or hardened spill, not so much as a stray grain of salt. "It could have been different," she said.

"What could have been different? People are what they are, you can't change it."

"You don't know what you're talking about." She pushed back from the table, giving an extra shove as if she could send both table and me flying. In the blink of an eye she was across the room, dampening a dishcloth, wiping the countertops, the surface of the gas stove. All the while she kept up her end of a mad little monologue, muttering just loud enough for me to hear now and then. "Coming into my house...asking *me*, like I knew anything. Like I ever had a say in anything."

"Okay," I said, pushing my chair back. "I'm sorry I bothered you. I just wanted to ask.... Lyle had something I gave him, and I'd like to get it back, if I could."

Now she was at the sink, sprinkling liberal doses of green powder over the white enamel. She wasn't muttering anymore, and her silence was the oppressive kind, meant to harm as much as any words could. I had grown up around a lot of that silence.

"Could I just, maybe, look in his room?"

She was using too much of the powder; it was nipping at my nose, and must have been stinging hers. I could have gone to Lyle's room myself, but I wasn't sure where it was, and I really wanted her approval first. It was unfair, the way I'd been playing her as if she really were a carbon copy of my mother; if they were alike at all it was only because they were of the same generation of beaten-down women who had been given so little and then told they had to like it. It makes me think again of Winslow Cook, Lyle's uncle—of that same generation, but empowered by his gender. What was the connection between him and Maud? I ask her, "Was Winslow Cook your brother-in-law?"

Before I even get to the word "brother" she's facing me, and if her old sour frown disturbed me before, it weakens my knees now.

"I *said* I never wanted to hear that name again in this house! You...."

197

She's got that dishcloth balled up in her fist, and comes at me as if to hammer it into my face. Grabbing the front of my shirt, she starts to shake me, the way a dog would shake a rat. It's the last piece to fall into place, if I want to complete the comparison with my mother: she also had this strength, angry strength. Flailing around for something to hold onto, I grab the edge of the table. *This is sickening, sickening.* Now she raises the cloth with its green powder-paste, and she's going to rub it into my eyes....

The edge of the table with its slippery Formica doesn't give me much of a purchase, but it's all I've got, so I pull, pull the table right away from the wall, so hard that the teapot slides off onto the floor with a crash that seems out of proportion to its size. Maud releases me, steps back from the tea spreading across the linoleum. I've got to run, but now my heart is beating so hard it really alarms me, I don't know if I can make it to the door. More likely I'm going to die, right here. "Now you've done it," I tell her, rubbing, rubbing my chest through my shirt as if I could erase the panic and pain.

"Good for nothing," she's saying, "good for *nothing* good for *nothing*...." She heads for a narrow little closet by the stove, pulls out a mop and bucket. Plies the mop, a self-wringing kind that twists in her hands to deliver the tea to the bucket. Not for nothing is she a product of an older, self-denying generation: she wants to kill me, but her kitchen floor comes first.

Impossible as it seems, I'm calming down. As she empties the bucket into the unused half of the double sink, I rise from my chair on legs none too steady, each of them wanting to run off in a different direction while the knees complain, *We're not strong enough yet.* But I'm more determined than ever to look at Lyle's room. "Ahem," I venture after a minute or two has passed, one of those stage-whisper throat clearings. "Ahem, ahem."

She looks at me over her shoulder, twisting her head as far as her fat neck will allow, then returns to washing dishes without a word. That sideways glance, offering a glimpse of only one of her eyes, tells me that she hasn't forgotten I'm here. But it also seems to say something else—that I've hurt her somehow. It's in her slumped posture, the petulant tilt of her head: she's waiting for something, most likely an apology. I'm going to have to get used to that idea, that I'm the one who has to apologize to her. "Mrs. Cook?"

She hears, but doesn't acknowledge. For no other reason than to safeguard my sanity, I've got to stop making so many comparisons between my mother and this woman; but really, how much like Evvie she is, even when she's sulking. Especially when she's sulking. So I know enough to wait past the point where a pregnant pause would end before I say again, "Mrs. Cook? Uh...I'm sorry I upset you."

She shrugs as if she's trying to shoo a fly from her shoulder. I wait, determined not to speak again until she does. This afternoon could wear on into the evening, if it hasn't already.

There's a commotion of keys from the hallway door, and in a moment Celia bursts into the kitchen with a load of plastic grocery bags, their loops wound around her reddened fingers. She stops so short when she sees me that a couple of the bags nearly spill. Opens her mouth, but nothing comes out. With two heaves she gets the bags onto the kitchen counter, pulls her fingers free and rubs them.

"No gloves?" I ask her.

She blows warm breath into her fists, rubs her palms together. "Didn't think I'd need them." She opens the bags, peels the tops down to expose a loaf of bread, stalks of celery, bananas. Maud is still at the sink, hiding, pretending, sulking.

I tell Celia, "I thought you were at work."

She glances in her mother's direction—not too fiercely, in case it might bounce back. "I lost my job."

"I'm sorry."

"Doesn't matter." Celery and milk go in the fridge, bread in the breadbox, canned soup and vegetables in the cupboard near the stove. "I got your saltines," she says in Maud's direction, setting the white box squarely down by the sink. Apparently saltines are a sore subject. My mother loved them, used to spread them with margarine; but that thought doesn't stay with me long because I'm picturing Eric and me coming home from the supermarket, hoisting plastic bags onto the stovetop to unpack them, crisscrossing past each other to store things where they belonged. Eric likes to do the refrigerator stuff, hunkering down in front of the meat and vegetable drawers, while I deploy the canned goods and paper products, following a pattern never consciously set but precise as a blueprint. How does it happen that domestic chores get divvied up, along with a hundred other things, with no exchange of words? Watching ourselves, Eric and me, doing the groceries, balling up the plastic bags to stuff in the trash can—it's like watching a film clip of extinct tribal rituals, never to be fully explained or understood.

At a loss herself, Celia looks at me and says, "How are you?"

"I'm all right. How have you been doing?" Oh fuck, she's already told me she's lost her job, how well *could* she be doing?

She sits across the table from me. The back of that chair is turned to the wall also, so like me she faces outward instead of facing the table. We must look like bookends, one fat, one skinny. In spite of everything I sense a warmth in her presence, something nameless and welcome.

"I don't know what to tell you, Paul," she says. "I think my mother's going crazy, and maybe I am too."

It doesn't seem to matter that her mother can hear her, and in fact Maud shows no reaction, just makes repetitive motions over the sink. (My mother uses one of her sharp, shiny nails to pick at a stubborn flake of pie crust, while nearby, Eric wipes down the counter where the half-gallon of milk had sat—the plastic bottles always seemed to come wet, like new babies. Who's crazy? Who's to say?) "You've been through a lot," I tell her.

She pulls her long hair back into a ponytail. "It's not over, either. Everywhere I go, there's still people telling me how *sorry* they are."

I turn my hand over on the kitchen table. My palm is red where I've been gripping the edge. "That's all they know how to do, Celia."

"And yet." She drums her fingertips on the table. "Are they really sorry, or secretly glad that something has happened to take their minds off their own troubles?"

"I know that makes it worse, that it was a news story and so it's not going to go away for a while. Not completely, anyway." I hear these words and wonder who's speaking them. I yearn for some small intimacy, even if it's hardly more than small talk; then I lose my sense of self as soon as it begins. Maybe some people were never meant for socialization, even of the simplest kind. An extinct tribe.

"If only...I don't know. Did you just get here?"

"A few minutes ago. I wanted to see how you and your mother were doing, and to ask if I could get something from Lyle's room."

"Oh." She couldn't be more surprised if I said I was looking for the Holy Grail. "His room?" She chews it over for a few seconds, then looks to her mother, who's finished with the sink and is now wiping around a set of tall aluminum canisters. "Ma, can I have the key to Lyle's room?"

No response. Maud's in her own dimension, we're in ours.

I whisper to Celia, "Do you know where the key is?"

"I can get it." Wanting, like me, to waste no more time, she gets up, crosses to the cupboard beside the stove. The inside of the cupboard door bears a row of cup hooks holding a variety of keys. Celia chooses one and says, "Let's go."

I follow her down a dim hallway to a door at the end. She stands there, rubbing the tarnished brass key as if to summon something forth—a genie, a piece of magic to make the recent past go away, return the key to Lyle's pocket as he lives and breathes and manages his private life. She takes a deep breath, as if there might not be any oxygen in there. The lock gives way with a solid click, like a tumbler in a safecracker movie.

The room is smaller than I expected—the high ceiling adds to the narrow effect—and prodigiously messy, with papers, magazines, dirty linen, and candy wrappers all twisted together as if a tornado had come through. If I'd had any taste for this errand it's gone now, I have no will to confront a life that ended too soon, before any of its odds and ends could be sorted out, made clean, put to rights.

Celia steps carefully into the room. Not a square inch of carpet is visible, so it's not a matter of moving from one clear spot to another, but rather having to decide what to step on. I try to match her tracks as if we're picking our way through snow, and touch her elbow lightly: "Was it always like this?"

"Yes." She shakes her head sadly. "This is my brother's mess."

It seems like a violation—as if I haven't violated enough already—to look at the bed, but I have to. It's as narrow as an army cot, the kind of bed that announces *whoever sleeps here, sleeps alone*. And it's the only neat thing in the room, its covers pulled taut. I look at Celia, who's trying, as I did, not to look at the bed.

201

"What are you trying to find?" she asks.

"A photo album, a small one. Pocket-sized." This is as much of the truth as I'm going to tell her. If it's not enough, and that breaks the deal, then so be it.

But all she says is, "I wouldn't know where to start." She's distracted by the mess, the futility of looking for anything in this roomful of mysteries.

"With the drawers, maybe?" It seems preferable to having to touch the stuff on the floor. I don't even want to touch it with my sneakers, so I pick my way carefully over to the tall, cherry-stained dresser. It takes the two of us, each tugging on one of the brass handles, to get the top drawer to yield, with a painful squeak: it's so stuffed with papers that they expand as we force it all the way open, forming a convex heap that will make it impossible to shut it again.

"Good God," Celia said.

"Did Lyle save everything?"

"I didn't know he was this much of a pack rat."

We sift through a pile of letters and school papers that go all the way back to sixth grade. No matter where I put my hands they seem to be somewhere they don't belong. Instead of trying to deconstruct the pile piece by piece, we lift sections of it to see if we can spy the brown cover of the photo album. Nothing doing. I straighten up slowly, my back stiff. "This is going to take a while."

The posters on the walls show rock bands whose very names disturb me: Foo Fighters, Smashing Pumpkins, Counting Crows. I look closer, at one of the albums advertised: *Mellon Collie and the Infinite Sadness*. I saw that CD among Lyle's possessions at the funeral. I ask Celia, "Do you like these groups?"

She looks at the posters as if she's never seen them before. "I don't know, I'm more of a New Age freak myself. That *Mellon Collie* album, Lyle used to play it to death." She nods toward something against the farthest wall that I didn't notice before—odd, because in this room of cast-off clothing and mess, a room that might have belonged to a teenager, it's the one authoritative object: a sound system, components encased in a tower of tinted glass. Several tiny red and green lights appear here and there among the controls, as well as a couple of digital time displays. I look for speakers, and finally spot four black hexagons, one in each corner of the room.

"Whatever you do," Celia says, "don't touch it. He has a fit if he thinks anyone's touched his sound system. He doesn't even want Ma to dust it."

She lifts a hand to her mouth, suddenly aware that she spoke of her brother in the present tense; I wipe off whatever look is on my face—surprise and dismay, it feels like—but can't stop myself from turning red. I look down and away from her, at the floor: part wastebasket, part bulletin board, it holds concert flyers, copies of *Rolling Stone* both old and new, loose pages from alternative newspapers, movie ticket stubs, picture postcards.... All I want to know is where the pictures are, and the clutter is taunting me, daring me to chase the wild goose. Without much heart in it I say, "Let's keep looking."

Celia sits on the edge of the bed, facing away from me. Her shoulders sag, and with her hair thrown over one shoulder I can see part of the back of her neck, the skin smooth, unmarked, so pale. "Look," she says, turning toward me, "I don't know if I can go on." Her eyes narrow, she even raises a fist. A tear, just one, rolls down her right cheek. I lean forward, put my hands on her shoulders and pull her toward me. My hands seem to press against skin and bone and nothing else. Suppose I were in her place, and someone I loved died...all right, suppose Eric died. And some fat, foolish stranger came along, wanting to rifle through his things. I'd be mad, too—more than mad. But Celia's fist has unfurled and she's giving me a tentative embrace, her hands light as wings against my back.

"You don't have to do this," I tell her. "I'll search a little more by myself, if you don't mind."

She shakes her head at me, her mouth partly open. "I don't know what to make of you."

"I don't know what to make of myself. But you can trust me, honest."

She gets up, takes another look around the room. "Stay a little while, if you want to. Truth is, nobody's going to spend much time here. I won't ever sort through this stuff, and my mother won't, either. She made his bed, that's all she could bring herself to do."

I jump up as if I've sat on a skillet. It was Maud who made the bed, a mother's last gesture, and I've been sitting on it. Perhaps the unmade bed had contained some imprint, however faint, of Lyle's body, and Maud couldn't bear to look at it. There is certainly something rude, something *hurtful* in the way that Lyle's several pairs of sneakers, scattered throughout the room, still hold the shape of his feet.

Either Celia has aged in just a few minutes, or I'm seeing her more clearly—the crow's feet at the corners of her eyes, the shape of her mouth where it won't rebound from anger and grief. "I'll be out there," she says—nodding at the door, not looking forward to it—"if you need me."

"Thanks. I hope...." She's gone, closing the door softly behind her, before I could finish my platitude, whatever it was going to be.

Looking around, I see the room has changed with her absence: each bit of clutter, every detail of Lyle's personal life reproaches me, denounces me as the worst kind of intruder, ready to rape and pillage someone else's life with no regard to privacy, no respect for the dead. A wave of nausea sweeps over me, and I have to sit on the edge of the bed again. As the nausea passes I tell myself to get organized. First, finish the dresser drawers. With a lot of grunting and shoving I manage to close the drawer we already opened, then pull on the one below, working up a sweat as it yields a half inch at a time. It's crammed just as full as its upstairs neighbor.

Searching the dresser drawers takes so long that I'm surprised Celia hasn't reappeared to check up on me. I've squeezed the third drawer shut when I notice the small desk that sits beside the dresser. It's small enough to be a child's desk, requiring a child-size chair. The chair, if there was one, is gone now. But what kind of child's desk is this? Its one drawer, a square one fitted beneath the desktop on the right side, has a *lock*. I sit back on my aching haunches and study the keyhole. It looks like a serious lock, and when I tug on the drawer's knob I meet a resistance that says, *Don't even think about it.* Celia might know where the key is hidden, or at least could help me look for it; but instead of calling out to her I perch on the edge of the bed again—this transgressive act is becoming easier and easier—and give the matter some thought. The key has to be in a place where no one would dare look for it. Under the bed, taped to the box spring? Or—how about that sound system that no one was allowed to touch?

I approach the cabinet warily. Touching the upper corner of the glass door makes it swing open, soundlessly, bringing the components and their lighted displays into sharper relief. Without thinking I touch the nearest **POWER** button. The next second I'm several feet across the room, scared senseless by a deep voice booming at me from all four walls. My hands fly to my ears, but instead of flattening them to my head my fingers make little ineffectual cages. No matter how much it hurts I'm afraid *not* to hear the earthquake voice, perhaps the very voice of God Himself. Then a different kind of fear, of disturbing not only the whole house but also the whole neighborhood, has me leaping back to the **POWER** button, pressing it again with a badly shaking finger.

The silence that follows is just as eerie as the booming voice was. Though there's nothing stirring within sight or hearing—what little hearing I've got left—there's still something, some disturbance in the air that presses on my abused eardrums, runs a cool finger up my spine. Maybe it's the approach of Celia and/or Maud, roused by the racket, ready to throw me out into the street. But seconds tick by and nothing happens, and I wonder for the first time if Lyle's spirit might be hanging around. Maybe it's incensed that I dared to power up his system, maybe it wants to send me packing. It's true that if there was ever a time to stop, this is it. How simple it would be to return to my motel room and junk food, there to remain till my bill gets so high that even kindly Mrs. M. will have to throw me out. What am I waiting for?

205

Carefully I peer around the back of the stereo cabinet. A tangle of cords leads to a power strip on the floor, its amber switch glowing. I turn it off with the toe of my sneaker. Robbing the system of power gives me a sense of empowerment, as if I could even switch off Lyle's spirit at will. Reaching into the cabinet again, I gently lift the top component, the FM tuner. Part of me is desperate to know what I think I'm doing, while the other part, the busybody part, calmly looks underneath the tuner. No key on the cabinet shelf, no key taped to the side.

I move down to the next shelf, home of a CD player. I can't lift it very high, what with the shelf above it, and the amount of light that gets in there is stingy; but I manage to get a look, and also feel under the machine and run my fingers along the cabinet walls.

The next shelf holds a dual tape deck, an older, larger beast. I have to get down on my knees for this one, and again find nothing. It's pointless to go on, but an inner need to finish the job keeps me going, because *finish the job you start* is part of my absurd work ethic. Too bad it never did me any good; I never did become a star athlete (my father's wish) or a doctor (my mother's) or a decent partner (Eric's).

A turntable sits on the bottom shelf. Apparently it was never used, not in this spot anyway, since there's no room to raise its tinted plastic lid. In fact there's no room to lift the turntable at all, so I can't look under it either. I scan the cabinet walls on either side, and while I think I see something on the right, the light's so poor I can't be sure. When I stick my hand into the narrow space my fingertips feel a change in texture, from wood to paper. They trace the outline of what must be a very small manila envelope taped to the side, while my fevered brain asks *Clever? Or stupid?* The envelope isn't that far into the cabinet, and is placed so that its flap can be opened without having to remove it from the wall. *Clever? Or stupid?* Even my far-from-agile fingertips find it easy enough to remove the small key.

I take no time to wonder whether the key will fit the locked desk drawer. I just want to *get it over with*, so I fit the key in, turn it, pull the drawer open before I have a chance to think it over again. The first sight to meet my eyes is a set of glossy full-color male genitals, the glamour-porno kind that look like they've never been used for anything and are waiting to be broken in. Lyle didn't save porno magazines, just pages cut from them, making for a more compact, denser stash. From the first handful I take out it's clear that his taste in men wasn't far from my own. He liked them dark and on the hairy side, and favored glowering, intense stares over coy come-hither looks. Yet they're all the same, these models, whether dark or blond—they're what you want but can't have, and don't really exist except in dark, wet places of the mind, or soul, or wherever mute desires make their home.

As I dig through the pile I feel more and more like a ghoul, an erotic grave-robber. I'm glad, at least, that the pictures don't arouse me. Even dumb desire has to draw a line somewhere, and I'm not about to jack off in a dead man's bedroom. The pictures are changing, though, as I get deeper into them, from full-body pictorials to shots of genitals only—all shapes and sizes and colors of cock, proudly erect or getting there. It's the bomb-shelter, time-capsule version of porno—you can't keep everything, just what you need most.

Some of the pictures are frail, they've been handled many times. The finish is worn from some of the glossy-magazine cutouts, while those printed on coarser, more porous paper have picked up the grime and smear of excited fingers. Some have a torn patch on them, or a missing corner, where I guess they got wet and had to be whittled down, lest the whole pile start sticking together. The number and variety of "just cock" pics don't surprise me, but the size of some of them does, no bigger than a thumbnail. A few fall to the carpet, near my aching knees. Not wanting to interrupt the search, I try to keep track of the fallen ones in the corner of my eye. There's no way I can put them back in the same order, but at least I can be sure that I put them *all* back, safe from Celia's and Maud's eyes.

As I get deeper into the drawer it becomes more obvious that the album isn't there, but I'm determined to look through everything just to make sure. I start removing handfuls of pictures, making it easier to get to the bottom, where the drawer's bare wood looks back at me like a reproach. Just to be double sure I remove everything—and now I see the white letter-sized envelope stashed at the very back of the drawer.

I open the flap, which is not glued down, to find the pocket-sized photo album, the kind with cellophane sleeves, each large enough to hold a snapshot. Mark didn't tell me what the album contained, but he must have realized I'd peek. Opening it at random, I look at one picture, then the rest. In faded black and white, bearing the uneven gloss of early Polaroids, their subject matter is always the same: an older man—he must have been much older than Lyle when these were taken—in various stages of undress. In the first picture he's wearing only an open flannel shirt and reclining in an armchair, his head flat against the back of the chair, the rest of his body tilted toward the camera—which couldn't have been far from his spread knees, judging by the way his erection fills the picture plane. It's huge (as any erection would be, from that angle) and dark, a stiff, sharp-edged shadow next to his faraway face, which is somewhat blurred. The next photo is the same except that the man is caressing his hard-on, his fingers curved tenderly, as if they were clutching the neck of a violin. There are a dozen more photos, and the first two served as a good introduction to them, because they're all about the guy's cock, whether he's lying naked and spread-eagled on a bed or standing up, fully dressed, his erection poking from a partially zipped-up fly. His face is sometimes blurry, sometimes sharp, but either way there's no mistaking his glee, his love of exposing himself to the lens and, no doubt, to the person—the *child?*—whose hands hold the camera.

I take a closer look, at the face this time. A white crew cut, a large nose, wide mouth. I'm sure this was Lyle's uncle; and that gives these snapshots, these warped moments in time, a value they don't deserve.

I put the photo album in my pocket, lock the desk drawer and put the key back. Step out into the hallway and close the door behind me. No sound or light comes from the kitchen or living room. Celia might have gone to her own room, but I don't know where that is and have no taste for exploring. I'm not sure I want to see Celia, anyway—or anyone else. I grab my jacket, which I had left in the kitchen but now hangs on the hallway coat tree.

There's not a soul on the street, either on the sidewalk or driving by. I get in my car and review my options. For the first time in my life I'm not hungry, and I don't want to go back to my room. I'll have to see Mark sooner or later, so I might as well get it over with. Besides, Glen will be embarrassed if I show up at dinnertime, so that's another incentive.

It's starting to get dark by the time I've driven the ten miles to Glen's. His pickup isn't parked in the driveway, but there are lights on in the house. I'll have a rare opportunity to visit with Mark alone. And there he is, peering through the glass of the side door, unable to see through his own reflection who's coming up the walk. When he opens the door his face breaks into a smile that seems so strange on the face of someone who lives with Glen.

"Paul! Come in, come in. Glen's not here, he took Georgie to the Promenade for a walk. They'll be back soon, though."

"Well, that's all right. I'm dropping in unannounced, after all." As casual as I sound, at least to myself, my brain is buzzing. "I've got your pictures."

He claps his hands together and rubs them briskly. "What can I offer you? We've got Coke, and Diet 7-Up—that's what your brother drinks these days—and there's booze, of course."

"I'll have some of that 7-Up, I guess."

Wearing thick gray socks and no slippers, Mark half-walks, half-slides to the refrigerator. Watching him take out drinks and ice, I notice the little tonsure on the back of his head, no larger than a quarter. His hairline has receded, too, making him look less boyish, a little more like forty, though he's really fifty. What would it be like to lie about your age and get away with it? It's out of the question for me, I wouldn't even try it. Mark could, though. Pouring Coke for himself, his arm slips, leaving a bubbling puddle on the counter. "Oh." He slides around, grabs a couple of paper towels. "We don't like spills in this house, oh no we don't."

"Can I help you?"

"No, that's all right, I got it." He cleans up the spill and scores three points on the kitchen wastebasket before I can take a step toward the counter. He pushes my glass toward me—it actually slides along the counter, as if it it's been freshly waxed and polished, like the linoleum.

"Thanks." From my right-hand pocket I take out the photo album, place it on the counter. It falls open to a shot where the presumed Win Cook is smiling, laughing. It would be an ordinary picture of an amused older man if he wasn't naked, his boner filling half the picture frame. The picture on the opposite page also shows his face, but in a different light: eyes closed, mouth wide open, brows knit. It's the unmistakable, half-pained look of a man who's coming, or is just about to come. Somehow his big dick has escaped the picture plane, he only appears from the chest up; but of the two facing pictures this seems the more private, more intimate—an image torn from the gay collective unconscious. "Was this Lyle's uncle?"

Mark bites his lower lip.

209

"Why is it so important for you to have these? To keep Lyle's family from finding them?"

He shakes his head, and I'm starting to wonder if he's lost the ability to speak when he finally says, "These are my pictures." Always pale, he manages to turn a shade paler.

"Do you want to talk about it?" I back off a couple of steps, giving him room in case he wants to leave the kitchen, sit somewhere else to talk.

He can't move, can't take his eyes from the album. He reaches out, turns the pages slowly. "We started playing games with Lyle's uncle when we were pretty young." Not quite crying, he dabs at his eyes and nose with the back of his hand. "How young? Maybe ten, eleven?"

"Oh, God."

"See, he used to look after us, after school, because Lyle's mother was working and my parents were working. We'd go to his house. I think the very first afternoon we were there he stripped naked and started chasing us around."

I take a step back. Several more steps would get me to the door, and my feet are all for it. "You don't have to talk about it, if you don't want to."

"No, no. I *want* to. Because…it was fun. We never knew a grown-up to do the things he did. The things he let *us* do. We were running around naked, too. We knew it was bad, we just didn't know it was *sinful* bad. Or maybe we did. Christ, I don't know.…"

I lean forward to pat his shoulder. "I'm sorry."

"No, no." He gulps back sobs, making horrible hiccupping sounds; he'd be better off letting himself go. "I *want* to talk about it, because… we didn't know it was dirty, not at first. At first he'd get us—all three of us, I mean—kind of wrestling around and tickling each other. It was…I'd never seen a man's body before, or even another boy's, that's how sheltered I was. I don't think Lyle ever had either, he didn't know…about the secret parts."

"How long did this go on?"

He shrugs. "Two, three years, I don't know."

"Were there any other boys involved?"

"No…unless he saw them when Lyle and me weren't around, and I doubt it. He couldn't have been *that* horny."

I hear Glen's truck pull into the driveway, and much too soon he's there in the doorway. Mercifully, he's left Georgie outside. "Chrissakes," he says.

"Take it easy," I tell him. "Mark doesn't feel good."

Glen snorts. "That's nothing new."

"Well, then, you should know what to do."

"Well…."

Mark turns toward his partner, all trace of teariness gone. "I'm all right," he said.

"You're not staying, are you?" Glen asks me. He wears his wide-eyed *you're trying my patience* look, which is similar to, but not quite the same as, his *I wish you were never born* look.

I ask Mark, "Do you want me to stay with you for a while?"

"No, I'll be okay." He smooths his hair, checks his collar button. "I'll walk you out."

When we're halfway to my car he says, "You know what's really goofy? When it all finally stopped, and we weren't seeing Lyle's uncle anymore, I…*missed* him. I wanted to be with him again. I don't think I ever got over it." Two large tears fell, one from each eye, running a race down his cheeks.

"Use my handkerchief, it's clean," I tell him, wishing I'd thought of it earlier. "I didn't get to know Lyle very well, but he may have felt something like that, too—nostalgia for his uncle, I mean. Did you notice that the album seems to be missing two photos?"

He flipped to the front, where two of the cellophane sleeves are empty. "Yeah, I did. I don't know why. It was full when I gave it to him last. We…sort of swapped it back and forth." He wiped the corners of his eyes, blew his nose. "He just disappeared, you know, Win did. Killed himself, a lot of people thought. Lyle and me, we'd stopped seeing him some time before that. You know why? I mean, why things stopped when they did?" He laughed just enough to blow spittle from his still-wet lips. "We quit because Lyle and I turned fourteen. He never said it in so many words, but we'd gotten too old for him."

There's nothing to do with a statement like that but let it fall, flatten against the pavement, and slither quietly away. It takes a couple of minutes, during which the sky clicks a few shades darker. I'm thinking, with a sickening feeling, of that time in the high school parking

211

lot when I asked Lyle about doing his uncle. That now seems like the least proud moment of my life. I want to take it back, do it over, along with a million other things. No: what I really want is to back to my room and mope over my whiskey. But first I have to ask Mark what I couldn't bring myself to ask Celia: "Mark, do you think it's true that Lyle got drunk and fell off the pier?"

He looks alarmed, as if he's fearing for my sanity. "What do you mean, do I think it's true?"

"Well, he was sober for a long time, wasn't he?"

A shrug. "Anybody can fall off the wagon, Paul."

"Yeah, but to fall off the wagon *and* fall off a pier…?"

Another shrug. "Lyle always had rotten luck."

Okay, I could twist that around and take it personally—like I was Lyle's next-to-last piece of rotten luck. But I've got one more thing to ask Mark. "Do you know who Lyle's last patient was? I mean, do you know his name, did Lyle mention it to you?"

Again he's looking at me as if I'm a strange specimen indeed. Still, the question doesn't just die. It hangs around, because Lyle's last patient, whoever he was—or *is*, I should say, since as far as I know he's not dead yet—knew Lyle's uncle, and Mark's got nude pictures of that same uncle in his pocket. There's probably no connection, no sense to be made of anything here; but Mark's look begins to soften, as if he has to agree, in spite of himself, that there's some plausibility here, some reason why he should answer me.

**J o h n** Toomey lives in a cottage on a side street leading to the public beach, not far from the Sand Dollar. Has this little white house, with its weather-beaten paint and sagging porch, ever seen better days? It looks as if it were built to sag, its natural posture a kind of slumped repose. A path of flagstones, some tilted, some nearly covered by earth, lead to the porch steps. I stride up to the screen door as if I own the place, and when I've pounded on the frame a few times and there's no answer I pull the door open, its spring twanging, and step inside.

The living room has fat plush chairs—one dark red, one purple—with lace antimacassars on their arms. They face, at an angle, a huge console TV, equally out of date. A coffee table, its varnish cracked, holds an assortment of magazines fanned out in a neat semicircle, like a hand of cards. If the room reminds me of anything, it's the waiting room of the family doctor we had when I was a kid. His office was in his home, which wasn't unusual back then, and I remembered sitting in a chair like these, dreading a vaccine or a booster shot.

The room beyond is a dining-room-cum-office. The lid on the roll top desk is open, revealing many pigeonholes filled with papers. The dining table holds piles of stuff—junk mail, receipts, and small devotional magazines. Ah, *The Daily Word*. I used to subscribe to that myself, back in my metaphysical days. I move toward one of the two small windows in the room, to raise the yellowed shade so I can see better. I barely touch it and it springs upward, making an ungodly noise. It's as if I've stepped into a Warner Brothers cartoon, the room about to come alive with hyperbolic sound effects—creaking floor boards, chiming clocks, and perhaps from the kitchen a teakettle hooting like a factory whistle. But in a moment there's just silence again, and dust, and the inevitable grains of sand underfoot. The window looks out toward the beach, the sea a brooding blue.

To be a spy, to break and enter—even though the door was open— suits me. I consider the dark hallway that must lead to the bedroom. Isn't this just like a relationship? You start out formally, at the front door, and work your way in, exploring intimacies along the way. At last you're in a dim room, a bedroom with the shades drawn, and you're not at all sure how you got there.

And when someone else appears at the front door, it scares you to death.

The twanging of the spring on the screen door alerts me. By the time the door slams I've retreated from the bedroom, where my eyes didn't have time to adjust to the darkness, back toward the living room. A real snooper, a genuine breaker-and-enterer, might have hid in a closet or a dark corner; but I want to see who's there, and to have him see me.

It's a man—a young man? The sunlight is behind him as he stands in the doorway, I can't see his face very well. He hasn't had a chance to get his bearings—to realize there's an intruder in the house. In his right hand he clutches a bottle of Coke and a white paper sack, and nearly drops them when he sees me.

"Who the hell are you?" he asks. "What are you doing in here? I wasn't gone ten minutes."

"Well, you should have locked the door."

"Is he all right?" He tosses the bag and soda rather carelessly onto an overstuffed chair and heads for the darkened hallway. I follow him into the bedroom, noticing again its smell of ointment and rubbing alcohol and perspiration. He switches on a bedside lamp. The old man lies sleeping, his breathing making only the slightest sound even though his mouth is open. The young man—a nurse, obviously, Lyle's replacement—does some minor fiddling with the bedclothes and steps back. Then he motions me from the room, making sweeping gestures with his hands, as if I belong in a dustpan. I follow him back toward the front of the house.

"Gee," I said, "do you always leave the door open when you go to lunch?"

"If you're selling something, I'm going to throw you out on your butt."

He has shoulder-length, rather greasy hair—is this the standard among male nurses now?—and his chin is a little on the weak side for one who makes threats of bodily harm. I can't make out the name on the badge he wears, just the R.N. after it. From what I know about male nurses, there's a better-than-excellent chance that he's gay. "Would that be John Toomey back there?" I asked.

"Well, this is his house, who else would it be?" He crosses his arms over his white smock, a defiant gesture somewhat spoiled by the way his voice breaks into a whine: "Look, are you selling something or what?"

It's too much fun asking questions, I can't stop: "Did you know Lyle Cook?"

His shoulders slump. He runs a hand through his hair, pats his breast pocket. "God, I wish I had a cigarette."

I offer my pack. "Here you go."

"No, I don't smoke when I'm on duty. I try not to, anyway." Another shoulder slump. "Oh hell, okay."

We light up, fueling the camaraderie of those who share nicotine-delivery systems. "My name's Paul," I said.

"I'm Danny." He lets go a long stream of smoke. "So what the fuck are you doing here?"

"This was Lyle's last patient. I just wanted to see him."

"So you just walk into somebody's house?"

"Only if some dumbfuck nurse leaves it unlocked."

Danny finds an ashtray, sets it on the coffee table. "I still don't get it. Mr. Toomey, he's pretty much out of it. So what's the point?"

"Fuck if I know." Suddenly I'm very tired. If I'm going to be a sugar junkie for the rest of my life, I'll have to start carrying some with me, to avoid the lows. "Hey, is he gay?"

Through nothing but having a smoke together, Danny and I have already acknowledged each other as members of the club, so my question doesn't surprise him. "I highly doubt it. He was a cop."

"A cop? Here in Two Piers?"

"Yeah…. Oh, Jesus!" He's remembered his lunch, which he grabs from the corner of the chair. "I hope the olive oil didn't get on the upholstery." He pulls a white waxed paper bundle from the bag. "Italian sandwich."

For some reason it hasn't occurred to me, during my exile, to indulge in an Italian sandwich, one of the staples of my childhood. Meat, cheese, tomatoes, pickles, salt and pepper and loads of olive oil—I didn't learn until I went away to college that in other parts of the country they were called "submarines" or "hoagies."

"I got everything on it," Danny said. "You want some?"

"No, thanks." The only thing that stops me is the green peppers, which don't like me. "What's wrong with Mr. Toomey?"

"What *isn't* wrong with him? His whole system is shot, poor guy. It's comfort measures only, at this point."

"Does he get round-the-clock care?"

Danny's mouth is a little too full; a speck of diced onion falls to the carpet. "Yeah. I'm strictly first or second shift, though. No nights."

"Does he have any family?"

"Nope. No friends, either, that I know of." He swigs from the plastic Diet Coke bottle, his Adam's apple working double-time.

"Can I talk to him?"

His drinking has been so intense, it takes him a moment to catch his breath. "If you can wake him up, you can." He checks his watch. "He'll have to wake up soon, anyway, I have to give him meds at one."

"Does he have lunch?"

"I wish to hell he would. He refuses everything I try to give him."

I enter the darkened bedroom one tiny step at a time, as if Toomey may have left his bed and is hiding in a corner, waiting to pounce. But the old man isn't going anywhere, and as my eyes adjust to the dimness the details of a sickroom raise their homely heads—the cluttered bedside table, boxes of tissues, and glasses half-filled with water, small bubbles clinging to the sides. The hospital bed is so high and white it seems to be offering the old man's body up to heaven. I stand by its head and watch Toomey, sleeping with his mouth slightly open, lips puckered inward. His false teeth lie at the bottom of a glass that sits by my right hand. I pull the hand back, as if they might bite. Feeling foolish through and through, I know I can't try to rouse this poor old man. I *am* tired—tired of myself. It would be easy to develop chronic fatigue, with or without sugar lows: I've got no present, no past—not one I can deal with, anyway—and I'm on my way to becoming a John Toomey, dying alone in a hospital bed, in a rundown house, with a greasy nurse. *If* I'm *lucky.* How did I manage to enter this house as if I belonged here, as if I could do any good? All I want now is to leave as gracefully as possible.

On the other side of the window from the sickbed, the wall is covered with photographs in dark frames. Women of forty, fifty years ago, their hair short and marcelled, with bangs that seem carved from wood; men wearing the cocky smiles of simpler times. Or were they? In a spot of honor, at eye level, is a group photo in a long oval frame.

> *Town of Two Piers*
> *Police Dept.*
> *August 1940*

Reaching carefully over the glass with the false teeth, I turn on the bedside lamp. Toomey doesn't stir. Returning to the picture, I try to find him, but can hardly read backward from his old dying face to the bleached-out features of the young men with hairless faces, the outdoor picture so bare of shadows it must have been taken in the noonday sun. I can spot Win Cook, though: third over from the left in the second row, above the row of cops who are kneeling on the ground. Younger than the Win I saw in the old Polaroids, he's still recognizable, mainly due to his big nose and wide mouth—features that also remind me of Lyle.

I step back from the picture. Afterimages of white faces swim around as I blink. Turning to the bed again, I see John Toomey is awake—or at least his eyes are, aimed at the ceiling. His mouth is still slightly open, his breath whistling. I sit on the three-legged stool that Danny must have placed by the side of the bed, the better to lean gently into the old man's field of vision. I stay quiet, just let my face hover, not too close, until his eyes move. Then I ask, "John?"

Toomey grunts, which shakes his frail body like a sneeze. His tongue is thick in his mouth, there's white matter collected at the corner of his lips. I find a swab on the table, unwrap it and soak it in a water glass (not the one with the teeth). At the touch of the swab his lips move slightly, taking in some water, causing a few drops to spill from the mouth like tears from a great dark eye. There's not much hope of talking with him. He's too far gone, like my mother when I last saw her.

But he surprises me. He blinks, once, twice, and his rheumy eyes slide in my direction. I take the swab away and he coughs, like an ancient engine coming to life. The sound brings Danny to the doorway. As much as I want to talk with Toomey in private, I can hardly ask the nurse to leave us alone, and it might not be wise anyway, just in case.

"John?" I ask. "How are you feeling?"

"*Eh.*" He goes on to sound out vowels—*Uh, Oh, Ee*—and I don't know if he's trying to form words of if this is just part of his waking up process. I look at Danny, who shrugs and shakes his head. Now the old man gets testy, his tone and volume rising, tracing the curve of a question I can't quite make out. I look to Danny.

"He's asking, 'Who are you,'" Danny said.

Not knowing how well the old man can see, let alone hear, I lean a bit closer. "John," I said, "it's Win. Win Cook." I glance at Danny, who's frowning. "Remember me?"

"*Ooh?*" Who?

"Win. Remember me? We worked together."

Now he says something like *Oh Christ*. Agitated, he moves his arms, sliding his elbows toward the head of the bed to try to get some leverage, raise himself up.

"Easy, take it easy there." He hasn't raised himself far, but I bunch up his pillow so it will keep supporting his head. Danny still stands in the doorway, frowning, his arms folded across his chest. If he knew how much I'm bluffing, winging it, playing tricks on the old man, he'd probably throw me out. My tricks aren't very clever, though—relying as I am on the old man's inability to tell whether I'm forty-five or eighty.

There's *something* that he recognizes, I see it in the way his eyebrows come together, a shrewd discerning wrinkle between them. "Ihn?"

"That's right. Win. Remember when we were on the force together, before the war?"

His eyes narrow. He breathes through his mouth, harshly, for what seems like a long time.

"You and me, John," I tell him.

"*Ihn?*"

"That's right. Remember the times we had?"

He turns his head to the side, away from me, straining the cords of his neck. Eyes still narrowed, he utters some sounds that are conversational in tone. As his mumbling gets softer I'm afraid he's drifting off to sleep again. "John!"

His mumbling gets louder, he moves his head from side to side. I've seen all I want to see of his hairless yellowed scalp, mottled with age, and especially his eyes, which begin to resemble twin configurations of evil. The next time he looks at me he stretches his lips in a grin. He's harder to understand than before, but keeps repeating one phrase. At last I know what he's saying: *Right in the head.*

"That's right," I said. "Right in the head. Remember those times?"

"*Hehhhhhhh.*" The fingers of his right hand, the one closer to me, curl into a weak fist. Now his tone is bitter, punishing, he'd spit out words if he could.

Danny is standing on the other side of the bed, ready to intervene in whatever voodoo I'm practicing. At the same time he's interested. "I've never seen him like this," he whispers.

I raise a finger to my lips—*Shhh!*—and strain to hear what the old man is saying. "Help me, Danny," I whisper.

Danny leans closer, strain showing on his face: this is against his better judgment, maybe he should have thrown me out after all.

Toomey's bitterness gives him strength; his sounds are, if not clearer, louder: "*Uhn eye eer!*"

"What is that, Danny? What is it?"

Danny bit his lip for a moment. Then he said, "Down by the pier."

"Hey John, what happened down by the pier?"

"*Ah er eh in!*"

"Danny?"

"*Ah er eh in....*"

"What is it, Danny?"

"Jesus Christ." Danny raises a hand to his mouth. He looks pale, even in the dim light of the sickroom. "I think he's saying, 'Bash their heads in.'"

Yes, I'm beginning to understand old John better myself. Perhaps it's not just a matter of hearing—it's a matter of hearing what I'd rather not hear. Once the flinching is over I find I can move in on the old man, even bring my face right down to his to ask, "Who was it, John? Whose idea was it to bash their heads in?"

Oh, those eyes, those weak blue eyes surrounded by mottled yellow and red—how they slide toward me, bearing everything I've ever feared: the power of the privileged—of those who, secure in their righteousness, would bash the world to pieces. And to add insult to the assault, John chooses to speak no more to me. Instead he purses his lips in a grotesque imitation of a kiss. As I back away from the bed he continues his pantomime, his pursed lips carrying a puff of air each time he aims them at me, blowing kisses in the most hateful parody of affection I'd ever seen. I look to Danny to see how this is affecting him, but he's already gone.

219

I find him in the living room, standing at the window with his hands clasped behind his back. Having become some kind of expert in non-verbal communication, I can see by the set of his shoulders that he's sorry, very sorry I came here. I let myself out as quietly as I can, easing the screen door closed behind me till it shuts without a whisper.

**L u n c h** at the diner, a walk on the beach, a long nap. In the evening I go out for pizza. It's after nine when I get back to the Sand Dollar. Mrs. M. has dimmed the lights in the lobby, but the lights over the outside stairs are brighter than anything else in the neighborhood. I can tell by the sound of the surf that the tide's coming in. The crashing waves always seem louder at night, but tonight they're outdoing themselves. It'll be a welcome sound to fall asleep by—though I'll have to accompany it with whiskey, as I did this afternoon, to keep away thoughts of *down by the pier, bashing their heads in.*

The message light on my phone, a small red bubble to the upper left of the keypad, isn't blinking. It's the first thing I check whenever I enter the room, on the off chance that Eric might have called. By now it's become an irritating habit I'm trying to break, so I curse myself more than the phone as I lean against the desk to take my sneakers off.

The phone rings, nearly startling me off the desk onto the floor. That would be Lizzie, of course, and I'll have to give her some excuse for not calling in the past couple of days. Nothing comes to mind, and I'm tempted to let the phone ring till she gives up. But I'd feel guilty about it afterwards, so I pick up on the fourth ring.

It's Eric. I sense it before I can even make out the first thing he says, whether it's "Hello?" or "Paul?" or "Fuck you." It's as if the breath he takes before he speaks is enough to clue me in. I can say only, "Oh," and "Oh" again as I sit on the edge of the bed, twisting the phone cord with my left hand.

"I'm here," Eric said. "I'm in Portland."

"Oh!" God, it's as if one of the crashing waves just burst into my room. I'm engulfed, swept away, unable to talk or think. After a moment I realize there really is a roaring in my ears that's not coming from outside, and expect my head will start hurting any second. "I don't know what to say," is what finally comes out of my mouth.

"Are you surprised to hear from me?"

"Well, God yes! I knew you had my number, but…hearing your voice…." Oh fuck, I'm going to cry. A whole crying *jag* is speeding from my chest to my throat, and my sinuses are tingling like a numb limb coming back to life. "Honey." Can I make myself believe *that's* what he said when I picked up the phone? "Honey…."

"Look, I need to talk to you."

I'm making noises that sound, from my end, halfway between gurgles and sobs. His voice is so familiar and so distant at the same time! But that's how he always sounds on the phone—more formal, more self-conscious than he would in person. Meanwhile Paul, who's supposed to be so good with words, can't put two of them together to save his life. *I don't know what to say* is still all I can think of, and the fear of sounding like an idiot makes me choke. At last I manage to whisper, "Excuse me," and pour some water from the ice bucket I filled this morning. My right hand is shaking as badly as my left; spilled water beads up on the desk top, the beads also shaking, uncertain whether they should stay where they are or leap back in the bucket.

When I manage to speak again I surprise both of us by asking, "Where's Maddy?"

You'd think I just spoke in a foreign language, he takes so long to answer. "Well, where *would* he be? He's at the vet, I boarded him there."

"Is he all right?" Yes, God, I have to choose *now* to talk about the *cat*.

"Of course he is."

His stern, annoyed tone is unlike him, yet it's the first thing to convince me that this really is Eric on the phone. When exactly did we have our last conversation? Could it have been in our living room, in what seems like eons ago, when I stuttered and stammered and nearly broke down because I was on my way to see Richard Roscoe? Responding to my silence, Eric goes on to ask, "Should I call back later?" All I can do is cover my mouth with the palm of my hand, squeeze my cheeks together to keep from shouting or screaming or moaning. Which gives him the opportunity to ask another question: "Are you alone, Paul?"

It's a question filled with hurt, and it's all it takes to kick off my crying jag. I'm barking sobs into the phone, reaching for my handkerchief, realizing I left it with Mark. The only substitute within reach is the facecloth under the ice bucket—wet, but it feels good on my face.

How awful my sobbing and snorting and gagging must sound over the phone—amplified, distorted, even worse than it would sound in person. Realizing this only makes me cry more. Pulling myself together isn't an option, it's more like a figure in the distance waving a hankie, bidding goodbye.

When I finally calm down enough to *listen*, I hear Eric crying too, expressing his tears in quick intakes of breath. Encouraging as this seems, it also scares me; if he gets too upset he might *hang up*, he might *go away*. "Don't!" I cry.

"What?" he asks, his voice trembling. "Don't what?"

"Don't hang up!"

"If I were going to hang up, I would have done it by now!"

There it is again, the scornful tone that's so unlike him. But it takes no more than a half-second of soul searching before I realize he's speaking like *me*—Paul the impatient partner, always ready to scold, to ask the rhetorical question as if it were my task in life to teach, not by example, but by ridicule (*"Well, where would he be?"*). If I'm feeling alone and frightened now, I wonder how many times I've hidden behind a book or newspaper and made him feel small with my words. I cry harder, howling into the phone, my chest hurting.

"Paul, listen!" He speaks slowly, as if he's repeating himself, and he probably is, has probably been saying *Paul, listen* for a good half hour while I've barked like a seal, screeched like a peacock, and hooned like a humpbacked whale. "Paul, you have to leave that place."

Well, if he means my motel room, with its half-empty boxes and bags of junk food, he's right. It's a wonder I haven't drawn ants, or even mice. Are there mice near the beach? I have no idea. But I owe it to Mrs. M. to say something nice about the Sand Dollar. "It's not bad, Eric." I blow my nose into the facecloth. "It's relatively cheap, and clean."

"You need to get *out* of that town, period! It's dangerous."

"Dangerous…?"

"That guy who fell off the pier. The way they've been talking about him, on the news…was he gay? Do you know?"

Is he asking me about Lyle? Does he *know about* me and Lyle, and is there any way to explain it if he does? "He was…just some guy who got drunk and fell off the pier."

222

"I wonder if it was really an accident."

Oh, Christ. "What do you mean?"

"You know what I mean, Paul."

So he's back to scolding. If I had any pride, any sense of self-worth, I'd speak up like a man, scold him right back. Instead I'm whining, like a child who's peed the bed: "Well, what do you want me to *do*?"

"I don't know—"

"Where *are* you?" The realization comes again that Eric's not speaking from within my poor febrile brain, as he's been doing for weeks; he's not fifteen hundred miles away, but *within reach*—in Portland, he said! Filled with dread and longing, I understand now why women in old movies are always swooning and fainting. Wasp-waisted heroines in hoop skirts, falling backwards into the arms of the nearest surprised males—has it never occurred to anyone that these women are *nauseous* with love and fear? It's not that their dear hearts are overflowing with emotion, it's that their shrunken little stomachs are *churning*, as mine is now. It's all I can do not to say to Eric, "I think I'm going to pass out. Or throw up. Or both."

But I must have said it anyway, because now he's firing questions at me: Am I lying down? Do I have any water nearby? Have I eaten lately? The question about eating is downright funny. But the question about lying down reminds me of his are-you-alone remark. "Yeah," I tell him, "I'm lying down. With a lifeguard, one of those guys with great abs who sit in the tall white chairs. He'd say hello, but his mouth's full."

"Well, it wouldn't surprise me."

"Listen, you!" Where is it coming from, this *anger*, this sense of how unjust it is that I had to put up with crap, anybody's crap, least of all Eric's? "Cut the sarcasm. I've suffered enough, okay? Take my word for it, you'd be *happy* to see what I've been going through. It would do your heart *good* to see how I've been sitting here with my face buried in snot...."

I stop, not because I feel like it—having rediscovered the joy of infliction, I could prance all night—but because Eric is crying again. His staccato inhaling sounds are like the snapping of a window shade. By now I really am lying on my bed—the cord isn't really long enough but the phone skittered obligingly across the desktop—with

223

my eyes closed. I'm waiting for Eric to either stop crying or to *start* crying as I had done, sounding like a chorus of zoo animals. Waiting, tight-lipped, to hear *him* say how much *he* had suffered. But I can't stay quiet for too long, because he still hasn't answered my question. "Eric, where…are…you?"

He sniffles, snorts, pulls in one more deep breath. "I'm at the Holiday Inn on Congress Street. We always liked Holiday Inns."

Did we? I guess we did. We never got much more adventurous than the AAA guide book recommended; and there's that gene we inherited from our parents' generation that makes us think that a name brand actually means something. But when I try to picture Eric staying alone in a hotel room, name brand or not, I can't. He could get lost searching for the ice machine, and never find his way back. He could misread the thermostat and freeze himself into a popsicle. He could run afoul of thieves and adulterers…like me.

"Sweetheart," I tell him, "Come and get me!"

**Eric's** coming to get me. Not just coming to see me, but coming to *get* me, to take me away, take me home! Now this little room that's been home for an eternity seems eminently disposable, something to crumple up and throw away without a second thought. All I have to do is get my things together. "My things, my things!" Forgettable as this room may be, I've wormed my way into its nooks and crannies well enough, judging by the disposition of my belongings. When did I empty my suitcase and place socks, underwear, and shirts in the dresser drawers? When did I hang slacks in the closet? I can hardly get my suitcases—Eric's suitcases—open fast enough, and it takes will power to keep from rolling all of my clothes into a great crushable ball and pitching it in. Where does this heated desperation come from? Am I afraid that Eric might change his mind? Well then, isn't it possible that he might not show up at all? I look to the door and, as if it might help, hurry to open it, to let the October chill in. Eric, my door is open! I know you won't fail me!

I'm in the bathroom, screwing tops onto tubes and jars, when I hear a noise. Eric's here, he's pushed the door open so wide its knob kissed the wall. "Oh, baby!" I cry out, hurrying to wipe some toothpaste residue from my fingers before I hurl myself into the room, toward my future.

I skid to a stop well short of the door. My eyes are playing tricks on me, for that's not Eric who stands near the foot of the bed, his chest heaving from exertion and emotion, arms waving as if he's about to lose his balance.

It's Richard Roscoe.

I'm struck dumb.

"I had to find you," he says.

I thrust my hands out, forbidding him to come closer, to make himself more real. He's a full-blown hallucination, that's all. I won't even speak to him. But then he takes a step closer, and I can't help myself. "How?" I ask him. "How did you find me?"

He takes another step. Now we're separated only by the width of the bed. "They told me at your job that you were out of town, and I figured you'd come up this way. Your brother told me where you were staying."

"My brother...." Yes, Glen would be easy to find, he's the only Lavarnway in the book. And yes, it would be just like him to tell a stranger where I was staying, then forget to mention it to me.

"I've been working up the nerve to do this." His hand clutches at his chest—he wears a fleece-lined jacket over a t-shirt, I've never seen him so covered up—as if his heart is skipping beats. "I didn't know.... I wasn't sure...."

"How could you just show up here? Why didn't you call first?" I'm expecting, as he becomes more real to me, that I can turn him around, start him on the right path. That was all I ever wanted to do with him, get him *started* right.

"I...couldn't. I just couldn't." Overheated with emotion, even with the door still open, he tugs at the collar of his jacket. "To have you tell me on the phone that you didn't want to see me...."

Well, how would it have gone, Paul? Would you have told him that you didn't want to see him? Yes, I would. Because he's right, hearing him on the phone is nothing compared to seeing him like this. That navy blue jacket he's wearing, fit for winter—it's so new it hasn't lost its stiff, hanging-on-the-rack look; he bought it just for this trip. For me. I'm sagging, ready to collapse onto the bed. Not a good idea!

225

I swerve off, take a step towards him instead. He follows up with steps of his own. Now his hands are gripping my upper arms, he's as real as real can be, his eyes, his scent. Robbed of all strength, I sit on the edge of the bed. With his own kind of gracefulness, so unexpected in a man of his build, he turns and sits, still holding me, his face above me now; and I can see everything—the hope and torment that brought him to this lonely place, the tears starting to grow as he holds what he's traveled so far to find.

"Oh, baby," he keeps saying, "oh, baby…."

I lean back, almost lying down as his face comes closer. Now that he's become real, and I recognize his warmth, his grip, his eyes and mouth, his full lips gathering themselves together for a kiss…what am I going to do?

Another sound, from just outside. I look up, half expecting to find Mrs. M. standing in the yellow light of the open doorway….

But of course it's Eric who stands there.

Richard follows my eyes, and lets go of me so fast that my head and shoulders bounce on the bed in a way that might, in another context, be funny. He gets to his feet, backs away from me, even as Eric, who hasn't quite entered the room, starts to back up also. I need to be there, right in front of him, explaining everything, taking that *awful look* from his face, the look of the betrayed. I call his name, but my voice is only a squeak.

Eric points a finger at Richard. "You," he says.

Richard raises the back of his hand to his eye, as if Eric has just spat in it. "Are you…?" He rubs both of his eyes, and when he takes his hand away they're wet. "I'm…sorry. I didn't know…."

"Eric!" I get to my feet, which are none too sure of themselves, and hold out my arms.

Eric backs away, coming up against the breezeway railing. The awful look on his face hasn't changed.

He turns.

And runs.

With a squawk I launch myself after him. How small he already appears, down at the end of the breezeway, almost to the stairs. "Eric! Don't leave me!"

Now Richard's coming through the door right behind me. "I—I'm sorry," he says, turning in the opposite direction from Eric's flight, toward the stairs at the other end of the breezeway.

"Richard! Don't...!"

It's too late. They're both gone. I sink to my knees on the cold cement and grip the wrought iron railing. Too weak to pull myself up, barely able to raise my eyes toward what this night and my life have converged into: a darkness that spreads everywhere and holds nothing, nothing at all.

# III. A Tale for the End of the World

FEBRUARY – MARCH,
1999

# Chapter 8

**All** plans for not-sleeping aside, the five of us have drifted off, a pile of wine-soaked brains, tangled limbs, and spent dicks. I have, at the moment of waking, if it can be called that, a memory of piled-up sleep, warm bodies and cold feet, sour wine breath, and the kind of exhaustion that won't let you move, not even when you've got some-body's hair in your mouth. Stretching, I can't quite reach the clock without disturbing everybody. A collective groan rises at the specter of daylight. 7:15 is too early to get up, on a Sunday anyway, but then I recall that this is the day Brian gets back. Like our sleep-stiffened limbs, the events of last night aren't sorting themselves out too well. All I remember are little flurries of activity—in the TV room, the basement, the kitchen, the bathroom—that each left its own brand of mess behind.

231

And something else. I can't quite name it, but it's there: something new on my mind. Even newer than last night's debauchery, though the two aren't unrelated: there was something about waking up with flesh in my face—Kent's flesh, to be precise, his shoulder pressed against my nose—that sent me a message. Of course it won't come back to me while I'm trying to think of it. As soon as I have a quiet moment to myself…. "Come on, guys"—I pull my foot free from where Davy, intent on going back to sleep, has pulled it up to his head like a pillow—"we've got to get this place back in order."

Todd sits up, yawning. "Anybody's head hurt?"

"Mine does, a little," I tell him—surprised, now that I think of it, that it doesn't hurt worse.

"A wine hangover's the worst thing in the world, but it's mainly cheap red wine that'll do it. What we drank last night wasn't cheap."

"Well, I'm not cheap, either," Kent says, his voice grating with the morning hoarseness a smoker can identify with, "but I still feel like shit."

When I finally manage to get both feet on the floor, I pull on some briefs and thick socks, all I'm going to wear till I get some coffee in me. Still no one else is out of bed. It was Todd, if I remember correctly, who led us through the various excesses of last night; leave it to luck that I have to be the one to lead the reconstruction. "Okay," I grumble, "I'll make the coffee."

The necessary first stop at the bathroom, and I'm confronting myself in the mirror. This room never gets much natural light, but I'm reluctant to flip the switch: dim as it is, there's something going on in the mirror. Easy enough to attribute it to my slightly aching head, or my aching ass. Too much wine, too much cock. When was the last time I felt this spent, my little willie barely up to the task of conveying piss to the toilet bowl? I can just manage to pee while keeping my face in the frame of the mirror. No wonder I look older today, my hair so gray.

My hair—since when do I have shoulder-length locks?

I jump, stuffing myself back in my briefs, reaching too late for the light switch. Oh, much too late, for even as I throw it and my own face comes to light, I can still see the ghost that confronted me in the mirror: it was no Old Joe or Hill House specter, no figment of the imagination. It was Lyle Cook.

For the first time since I came to this house, the body that keeps washing up on the shore in my dreams has a name.

**Later** that day, Davy appears in the living room doorway and announces, "Brian's gone."

Exhausted from all of the cleaning we've had to do, the rest of us are sprawled across the furniture, reading ex-gay stories. How we seem, at these moments, like geeks who think it's cool to hang out at the library. I look up and say, "Yes, honey, we know."

Davy swallows, a blip in his Adam's apple. "Is anybody going to listen to me besides Paul? Because the truth us, Paul doesn't listen."

Todd doesn't miss a beat. "Did you say something, Davy?"

"Brian's gone."

"Yeah, we know."

"To Nantucket."

"Fuck it."

"Fuck you."

"Fuck *you*!"

"Not if you don't come to bed *right now*!"

That rejoinder raises a weak giggle or two, but we're in late-afternoon mode, no more likely to get excited about anything than the winter sunlight that paws the wall like a weak kitten. I've been melancholy today, anyway, thinking about Lyle. Only gradually, over the course of what seems several minutes, does it occur to me to ask Davy what the hell he's so excited about.

"Brian's *gone*! I looked in his room. Everything's gone."

"What?"

"All his *shit* is *gone*."

"That's not possible."

Davy would know, though; he's been in Brian's room before. "Come and look," he says.

Aaaauuuugh, I hate getting up. The story I was reading was get- 233 ting good, too: Steve and Linda, the ex-gay and his bride, were about to embark on their honeymoon, which meant there would be much hinted-at sex in some pleasure destination with palm trees and wide beaches. The moral of these stories always seems to be: leading the straight life can get you to Jamaica. "If I have to go all the way upstairs," I announce, "then you other guys are coming too."

"*Aaaauuuugh*," Kent goes. He gets to his feet, followed by Todd, who gives a heavy sigh, and Aaron, who has a headline on his forehead reading **ROOMMATE FILLED WITH DREAD; FEARS WORST.**

"Come on." I offer him a hand.

"This is bullshit," he mutters. I feel his resistance, too, yanking my shoulder as I pull him up, then land a good-natured slap on his butt.

Davy is first up the stairs, then me, then Todd and Aaron and Kent. Okay, I'm distracted by Davy's butt, he's the only one of us whose ass looks good in sweatpants. So when we reach Brian's door, I'm unprepared. Just unprepared, that's all, for whatever's coming next.

"Look," Davy says.

Sure enough, the attic room is bare. There's something in the air that takes me back to my college days...the ghost of a fragrance... patchouli.

Todd: "Are you sure this was his room?"

Davy points. "There was his futon, over there. Even the crucifix is gone."

I wasn't sure I believed the crucifix part in the first place, yet there's the shadow of a cross on the otherwise faded wallpaper. Odd how a trace of something carries the impact of the thing itself.

"What the hell?" Kent asks.

He's turning in circles, trying to take in the whole room at once, as if Brian might be hiding in a corner. I'm near the window now; the world we've shunned for so long seems to take an interest in us, pressing its gray cataract against the pane.

"What are we gonna do?" Davy asks.

Well, it's not like we're a basketful of kittens abandoned on somebody's doorstep, for Chrissake. Yet we move closer together, just as those kittens would upon facing the strangeness of the world outside.

234

I'm shoulder-to-shoulder with Todd. Something's happening, I feel the tension in him. I could reach out—almost—to stop him from whatever it is he's up to, which turns out to be...grabbing the sides of his sweatshirt and stripping it off over his head. I catch a whiff of his deodorant stick, something with lime. A glimpse of his appetizing chest, those demitasse nipples.

Someone lets out a breath. The room grows warmer by the second. Kent is next to strip his shirt off. Its fleecy lining releases a few puffs of lint into the air. More male underarm scent. (When was the first time a boy took his shirt off for me? I honestly can't remember.) It looks like the last one bare-chested is a rotten egg, so Davy strips next. Aaron and I look at each other. Shrug. Predictably, I have trouble getting my shirt off, should have removed my glasses first. Aaron helps me, pulling from above while I struggle within, and my half-nakedness pops into the world like an ungainly newborn. Aaron is the only one of us wearing a button-down shirt—easier to remove, and the unbuttoning itself provides a little something extra.

(Okay, I remember. His name was Jay, and he was hardly a boy. Older than me. I was twenty-five, and had just pulled the rug out from under my life by admitting my gayness—first to myself, then to a roomful of horny guys at a homosexual watering hole. Jay was the first to put his tongue in my mouth. It introduced me to men as a matter of scale: if a tongue could feel that big inside me, then what about…?)

Standing shoulder to shoulder, in a circle, facing outward, we kick or toss our shirts to the nearest corner. Someone lets out a breath.

(Jay didn't take his shirt off for me, I took it off, while he was un-buttoning mine. It's a wonder we didn't tear some buttons off. Prob-ably at that moment we were weak, having lugged our passion from the bar to Jay's car to a suitably distressed motel. In his car I could hardly breathe, being so close to him as he drove. Painfully erect in my jeans, I felt not so much sexed up as transformed, transmigrated into a different species, one with an exoskeleton. Should I take my dick out while he was driving, or leave it in? Out, in, out, in? I slid close enough to lay my hand on his crotch: he was mutating too, I discovered, as we swerved across several lanes.)

Okay, let's try switching species. Think of Steve and Linda, under a lanai on a wide, white beach. They've had their first hinted-at hon-eymoon sex, and now they're basking under a sun that belongs exclu-sively to them. Having oiled each other up, they lie hand in hand. His body—big surprise—is easier to picture than hers. In fact, the more I concentrate on her, the harder she tries to slip away.

And then I see Lyle. His thin body, how agile it was.

Now Todd is reaching for the waistband of his sweatpants, grip-ping it so tightly his hands are fists, and…in one smooth motion he's pulling them down, disengaging his feet from the cuffs. He's not wearing underwear, and his cock and balls are bobbing, swaying, catching the melancholy light of the attic room. He stands with his hands behind his back, only a twitch or two of his cock revealing that it means something, his showing his nakedness this way.

Finally Kent says, "Well, hell," and strips off his own sweatpants. Unlike Todd, he's wearing tighty whities, which get stripped off too and added to the pile. Looks like the last one naked is a rotten egg, and once Davy's stripped bare it's down to the two heaviest of us, Aaron and me. I kick my sweatpants into a corner, and miss. Look down at my toes, which look like poor abandoned things on the gray painted floor.

Aaron takes a deep breath and pulls his sweatshirt off. Slides his sweatpants and underwear down. It's only when his pale, pale foot approaches mine and nuzzles it that I realize we're all standing in a sort of circle. On my other side Kent's lean left foot sidles up, full of grace.

Hands and arms slide across shoulders. Somewhere a sob collects and releases—from whose mouth I can't say. The circle sways, we pick up our feet and we're turning, making the floorboards creak, past the shadow of the crucifix on the wall, the spot where Brian had lain in his untroubled sleep. Faster now, and someone's giggling—oh, that's me—and we stop just short of falling.

This was the place where Brian had *lived*. Slept. Walked around nude. Pleasured himself. (Maybe.) And we're naked, naked and dancing. If Brian is gone for real, let's remember this: not the things he said, or his patience, or kindness, or the blissful look on his face, but the Brian who was forever a secret, Brian the subject and object of fantasy. Brian with a hairy butt crack, Brian with a dick that could raise its head in an almost intelligent way, like Lassie when Timmy came whistling. Brian with a neatly trimmed, ginger-colored bush. "Oh, Jesus," I whisper, as our circle contracts. Aaron nuzzles my shoulder like a cat; Kent springs a boner against my thigh. My own cock grows heavy: oh, that familiar quickening of the flesh.

Meanwhile the light in the room clicks down another notch. Which means time is passing.

"If we could do anything now," I ask, "then what would we do?"

We pull each other down to the floor.

**Later,** we're crouching at the window in Davy's room, which looks out toward the street. Watching for Riley's white van to arrive, as it does every Sunday at this time, just before dark. We're touching, each hand on a shoulder blade or ass.

"He's not coming," Aaron says, for about the twentieth time.

"Shut up," Todd says.

"If Brian's gone, then Riley is, too."

"That doesn't follow," I say, as if we're discussing a geometry theorem. But the truth is, who the fuck knows? I'm as anxious as anybody, just as likely to heave a sigh of relief when Riley appears. And I do.

Straining, we can just see him opening the rear doors of the van, taking out six plastic sacks of groceries.

"I hope he remembered the Bisquick," Aaron says.

Okay, I was thinking the same thing. Bisquick, and peanut butter. It's Todd who finally voices the question that should be on our minds: "Should we ask him?"

None of us has more than a nodding acquaintance with Riley. Personally, I wouldn't ask him for the time of day. He looks Neanderthal to me, a bit too ready to reach for the nearest club. Yet I've seen and noted the way his body shifts in his overalls.

"He might not be the best person to ask," Kent says.

"He's the only person there *is*, fuckwad."

It's not going to happen right now, anyway, because we're not about to confront him in our nakedness. I rub my hands across the gooseflesh on my upper arms; like a country with all kinds of topography, the house has a wide range of temperatures. Davy is humming a little tune, something he does now when he gets nervous. Riley puts the groceries away—the knocking around in the kitchen, barely audible up here, makes me think of Old Joe—and trudges back to the van.

The kitchen is the same as we'd left it, except that the refrigerator is fuller, the cupboard groaning with cans. There's nothing else, no note. Perhaps we're not supposed to have discovered yet that Brian is gone, that he's *gone* gone.

Out of nowhere I announce, "Let's pretend there's nothing wrong."

237

"How the fuck do we do that?" It's Todd challenging me. "Think about it. Somebody's been in this house, somebody took all of Brian's shit from his room, and we didn't even *know* it."

He doesn't expect me to have an answer to that, but I do. "Oh, it's just Old Joe. Old Joe took Brian's clothes."

A corner of Davy's mouth turns downward. "Paul...."

"Typical ghost shit."

"Don't," Aaron says. Rubbing the gooseflesh on his shoulders, though it's warmer in the kitchen than it was upstairs.

"I get it," Todd says, no closer to smiling than the rest of us. "We just have to push on."

Kent shifts his brown eyes around. "I'm going back to the living room."

It might be practical to put some clothes on, but I'm not going to suggest it. I'm tired of always being the one to put forth new ideas.

**T h e** following afternoon finds us in our customary places in the living room. It's time for the ex-gay hour—only an hour, come on, it's the least we can do. I'm reading aloud. *"The human potential for change has barely been explored during the course of mankind's history. The phrase 'scratching the surface' acquires new meaning when we realize how much of the mind is never put to work...."*

I look up to catch Todd yawning, scratching his balls. We still have not managed, since our group striptease in Brian's old room, to put any clothes on.

*"It is the human propensity toward mental laziness that accounts for the failings that constantly assault us. Crime and perversion flourish in the absence of hardworking thought. Fortunately, we have developed exercises that can help prepare the mind for the work it is meant to do...."*

"Prepare my dick," Davy says, grabbing said dick, wagging it a little.

"Prepare my rectum," Kent says. He's stretched out on his belly, on the braided rug.

"Who wants to do some mental exercises?" I ask.

Four middle fingers are raised.

Still, we keep reading.

**Still** later, still in the same positions in the living room. Dozing off, all four of us. Last night we all piled in my bed again. Despite our crowded condition we managed to get more sleep, though I woke at one point to a gentle rocking next to me. Kent was jacking off against my leg. I reached down for his fat warm cock, and the next thing I knew someone mumbled "Group handjob," as if this were a regularly scheduled event. Before long we were all glued together, the way I used to glue popsicle sticks together when I was a kid, building a fort. Now I wake up in the wing chair bringing a half-dream with me, on the topic of fucking Kent—no doubt inspired by his prepare-my-rectum remark. It takes me a moment, though, to realize what woke me: a slamming sound. I look at the others and they're just as startled.

"The front door," Davy says.

My heart picks up a beat, because this can only mean one thing, even though none of us dares to say, "Brian's home."

Yet the heavy steps approaching us aren't Brian's, nor is the voice that booms in our direction. "Men!" it says.

We look at each other. Whoever it is, he's calling our name, our new and ancient name. Calling our calling.

"Men!"

Is anyone else thinking that he must have the wrong house?

"Men!"

Suddenly we jump, as if we're all controlled by the same switch. I grab the old afghan from the back of the sofa and wrap it around my midsection. Kent rolls himself up in the braided rug. Aaron pulls the cushion from the wing chair, while Todd and Davy cover their crotches with the round pillows from the loveseat. Thus upholstered, we must make quite a sight—more startling, perhaps, than five men sitting around naked—to the stranger who appears in the doorway.

239

He's relatively young, his dark crew cut and the razor-sharp crease in his khakis attesting, perhaps, to military service. A long, thin nose and one squinty eye, the left one. He takes us in, and in the firm straight line of his lips there is both resignation and resolve, tinged with sadness.

"Looks like we got a lot of work to do here," he says.

**10:00** p.m. Dinner and chores over, Kent and Aaron and Todd and I are sitting in the living room, looking at each other as if we're already the strangers we're meant to become. Harmon, our new leader, is somewhere else at the moment. And Davy...?

There he is, in the doorway. "Harmon's gone," he says.

This is much too much like the Brian's-gone scene that played out yesterday. "Cut it out, Davy," I tell him. "It's not funny."

Davy shrugs. "He got in his truck and drove off. I saw him through the kitchen window."

"He won't be gone long," Todd says.

"Did anyone see him bring in a suitcase, or a bag of any kind?"

"Nope."

"Nope."

"So he's not staying the night."

"He'll be back," Todd says. Maybe he's going to say more, but doesn't get a chance to, because Davy has crossed the room in about two steps and is covering Todd's mouth with his own.

"Don't," Todd says when his mouth is free again. "Don't." Looking Davy right in the eye. "Don't." But their hands are locked in an embrace, fingers in tight weave.

I'm moved to make an announcement. "It's time for bed. Who's with me?" Kent takes one of my outstretched hands, Aaron the other. Todd and Davy follow us toward the stairs, sidling along slowly, wrapped up in each other.

**Morning,** about two weeks after Harmon's arrival. When my alarm goes off the second time I'm out of bed in a flash, leaping into my sweatpants and t-shirt like a superhero leaping into his costume. Peeking through the curtain to make sure the outside world is still there—not that it makes a hell of a lot of difference.

Tripping down the hall with the nonchalance of a soldier in peacetime. Leaping steps barefoot two at a time down to the kitchen, where I am, yes, the only soul stirring. Firing up the coffeemaker, crouching in my chair for my morning meditation.

I am in control of my destiny. No one can make me stray from the path that belongs to me. No thought, no action can touch the reality of my Self. I am secure.

240

At seven o'clock sharp, Harmon lets himself in through the kitchen door. "Morning, Paul."

"Morning, Chief."

"You've got coffee going, great. Where are those lazy bastards?"

"Not present or accounted for. At least not yet."

Harmon stands with his hands on his hips, staring out the window above the sink. "Christ," he says, "it's a beautiful day. And there's no time to waste. Go get 'em, will you?"

"Sir, yes, sir!"

Up the stairs the way I came down, two at a time. Davy's room is first. I wake him up in the accepted manner, taking a pillow that's fallen to the floor and whomping it on his chest. "Up and at 'em, you worthless piece of shit."

He leaps, coughs, covers his eyes as if he could bring back the night.

"You don't want to be the last one down, do you?"

Somewhere in his phlegmy head that strikes a note. No, to be the last one down is not a good idea. He swings his legs over the side of the bed and stands, a bit shaky after—what, maybe two hours of sleep?

On to Kent's room. He's sleeping on his side, cradling his pillow with both arms. How precious. I pick up the wooden paddle that leans against the wall and whomp him one on the backside. This does the trick so well that he seems to levitate off the mattress, the sheet sliding away from him; and there he is, sitting naked on the edge of the bed.

"Fuck's sake, cover yourself up."

Shaking his head, moaning, not yet aware of where or who he is. Finally he grabs the sheet and covers his crotch. "Sorry. Rough night."

"How so?"

Is that some kind of sideways smile he's giving me? "Asshole's sore. And that paddle didn't help any."

"You'll be sore all over if you don't get moving. Harmon's here."

On to Todd's room. He's lying on his back, his mouth open. I can't reach his backside with the paddle so I give him a sharp poke in the

241

ribs instead. Startled bolt upright, he swings his legs over the side of the bed. Keeps himself covered, but he can't stop wincing.

"What's the matter with you, for Chrissake?" I ask.

"My dick's sore."

"Shut the fuck up!" I swing the paddle as if to connect with his shoulder; he twists away. "Harmon's here."

He reaches to the floor to retrieve his clothes. I'm gone.

Aaron's room is last, down the corridor past my own door. I grab his paddle but, curiously, I can't seem to use it. He's sleeping on his left side, his features so relaxed and innocent he could be an angel lying there. I want to touch his face, to feel the contrast between his overnight stubble and smooth brow.

That way madness lies.

Finally I lean into his ear and yell, "*WAKE UP!*"

He rolls across the bed as if he's rolling downhill, twisting up in the sheet and blanket, thumping over the side onto the floor. "Ow," he says. "Ow, ow, ow...."

Christ, what a whiner. "Shut up!" I tell him. "You can't sleep all day! Harmon's here."

He looks around, the corners of his mouth sagging in dismay. I stand looking at him a moment longer than I should. "Move it," I tell him. "*MOVE IT.* You don't want to be the last one downstairs."

As it turns out, Todd is the last one downstairs, dressed, like the rest of us, in sweats and a t-shirt. Davy has already shoveled scrambled eggs onto our plates.

"Okay, men," Harmon says. "You know what to do."

242

Todd takes his seat. Obediently holding his wrists together behind him, he lets me tie them tight without complaining. Then I backhand him across the side of his face. Oh Jesus Christ it feels good.

Todd stays tied up as we eat breakfast. Afterwards he inclines his head obediently, licking our plates clean. There's something obscene in the way his tongue works up a lather of egg scraps and bacon grease. I'm tempted to tell Harmon about Todd's comment when I got him up—"My dick's sore"—but I know I won't.

Glancing up suddenly, I connect with Aaron's eyes. And sad, somber eyes they are, too: hazel eyes, predicting a storm.

**And** at the end of the day....

At the end of the day, we march up the stairs, single file, to my room.

The sweats and t-shirts that we tugged into place that morning come off.

For it's true: Harmon does not stay the night, as Brian used to do.

At first we didn't believe it. But the room that was Brian's remains untouched, and Harmon leaves not even a toothbrush in either of the bathrooms. When he turns off the kitchen light, letting himself out the back door at 10:00, that's the last we see of him till morning.

It's a tight fit, the five of us in my bed, and we're more than a little funky after a day of push-ups and sit-ups, the discipline for various infractions.

*"Todd, looks like you ain't got any underwear on, under those sweats."*

*Todd would rather be anywhere else right now. "Sorry, I didn't have any clean—"*

*"Drop and give me fifty!"*

*If there was any doubt that Todd lacked underwear before, there's none now as he performs pushups with his package nearly brushing the floor.*

*"What are you looking at, Lavarnway?"*

*"Nothing, sir!"*

I'm the first to get in bed. Todd falls across my midsection, knocking the wind from me. "Sorry," he says, "I tripped." Before I have a chance to speak there's Kent on one side of me, Davy on the other. And Aaron...where's Aaron? Oh, those must be his pale, pale feet angling toward my head. "Hold me," he says, meaning "Hold my dick." I can reach it by scooting down a ways and throwing my arm across Kent's body. Now I have Aaron's stiffening prick in my hand and my mouth on Kent's button mushroom of an organ. It's a grower-not-a-shower, and will soon be too large for my mouth.

Greased fingers are working my asshole, their sign-language announcing the approach of a blue steel boner—Todd's, I would imagine, since he has to top *everybody* during the night, like he has a quota to fill. Studboy, fuckboy, his thrusts make it hard for me to perform my sucking and jacking with much exactitude, but that's okay. This

243

is sex as chaos theory—we all reach our destination, but perhaps not in the way we imagined. What began as a neat, efficient knob job has become a slob job as my fucked body pulsates, arriving and withdrawing like a stop-motion wave; but the arrhythmia is exciting, unpredictable, and I'm not going to let go, not of Kent's cock or Aaron's. Davy, he of the greased fingers, is at my side, reaching beneath me to jack me off. His fingers are cold, their touch achingly erotic.

"Fuck me!"

"Jack me!"

"Suck me!"

The headboard plays its old *thwacka-thwacka* song. Though the quantity of flesh has multiplied, I'm taken back to the bed of Richard Roscoe, who got such a bang out of jack hammering my butt. Fucking me like there was no tomorrow—which might have been a clue that there really *was* no tomorrow, not for us. The sharp pang of nostalgia gets my butt moving, no longer a passive object but a sex machine in its own right, meeting each of Todd's strokes halfway. I've had to let go of Aaron's cock, but Todd's taken over, giving him the kind of ham-handed jackoff he craves so; and since it's no longer practical for me to be blowing Kent I've taken hold of his cock with my right hand and won't let go.

Jacking, fucking and quaking, we're like one animal that's about to spurt through five orifices, and it's hard to tell who comes first. There's Todd's cry, but at the same time Aaron is showering us with jism—no wait, that's Kent's jism too. Then I'm shooting, spraying like a rabid cat. Davy rolls over with a handful of my cum, which he applies to his rod. It takes him less than a dozen strokes to get off, splashing me from armpit to waist.

244

Todd is panting, there's sweat on his brow. It's our task now to stroke and soothe him till he's ready for his next performance. What a prize animal he is, there ought to be a blue ribbon around his neck. I caress him softly, run my palm across his big brown nipples. Farther down, Davy is kissing Todd's thighs.

I call out to him. "Hey, Davy."

Davy gets up on his knees, and lo, he's hard again.

"Davy's next," Kent whispers.

Staring at Davy's cock, Todd inflates also. Even as I marvel at the length of his fine young rod, I scoot back, moving on my hands and knees, to the edge of the bed, then off the bed—Christ, the floor is cold! Yet in my overheated condition it feels good. Kent and Aaron are off the bed too, Kent opposite me, Aaron at the foot: when Todd and Davy fuck they need as much room as they can get. Todd rears up on his knees, slips both my pillows under Davy, whose calves are now resting on Todd's shoulders. It'll be a tight fit, a tight fuck, yet varied as hell: Davy may be on his back now but he'll be spinning before long, with Todd sweating like a juggler trying to keep six plates in the air. Aaron and Kent and I watch from the floor with our eyes just above the edge of the mattress; the day may come when the action gets so frenzied we'll have to wear safety goggles.

I love to watch Davy's face while Todd is fucking him. Do I look like that, too, when I'm getting fucked? Am I capable of showing such slack-jawed rapture? Todd is slack-jawed also, his eyes squeezed shut, as if opening them to see the angel impaled on his dick might make him come too soon. Not surprisingly, Aaron has moved from the foot of the bed to kneel at my side, and he doesn't have to tell me that he's aching for yet another hand job. I grab hold of him—no need to even spit in my palm, we're all slicked-up for the night—and give him the grip he likes. By now his dick knows our hands so well it could read our fingerprints.

Now Davy lies on his side as Todd pumps away. They look like they could fuck that way for hours; but no, here they go changing positions again, and by some miracle Todd's cock never leaves Davy's ass as they reconfigure themselves so that Davy's on top, his head thrown back, his slightly curved dick pointing up, up, mimicking the path his jizz will soon take.

"Oh Christ," I'm saying.

"Oh God," Aaron's saying.

He's jacking me off as I jack him, and it's *so* sweet. Kent, perhaps lonely on the far side of the bed, creeps up onto it, lies beside but not touching Todd, and pumps his cock. Note to myself: I will have that cock in my mouth again before morning.

When Davy arches his back, semen spurts from his prick all over Todd's chest and shoulders. Now Todd digs in, his thighs shaking as

245

he pumps the dazed Davy, and Todd comes too, with unmistakable anguish and joy.

We're all back in bed just in time, the cold floor was refreshing but now my feet are freezing. I brush them, unintentionally, against Davy's side, making him squeal. Todd is still lying in the middle, and Kent is still beside him, though now Kent is whispering into Todd's ear. I can't make out what he's saying but I know the drill, know that it goes something like this: *I watched you fucking Paul and Davy and I want it, too. I could see what your cock felt like and I want it so bad. I'd do anything just to have your cock inside me. My ass is so hot right now that it's fucking burning, burning for your hard dick....*

Todd loves dirty talk like nothing else on earth. Listening to Kent with his eyes closed, he can't help but squirm; and the miracle we're all watching for—the resurrection of Todd's cock—takes place on cue, the organ merely nodding at first, and then, like a dog sensing something in the air, stretching its neck, higher, higher.... Kent can't resist reaching for it, letting his fingers play lightly along its length. Todd is moaning, and Kent is too, they've abandoned their native tongue for this moan-language that's better at telling how they feel, what they want, and what the immediate future will bring.

The future is now. Kent swings himself up and over Todd, and with the practiced hand of a man who's spent a good part of his adult life getting fucked, he guides Todd's pole up his burning hole. What a fucktoy Kent is, as agile as Davy; but he has to have his dick done at the same time, too, so Aaron takes care of it, caressing that slippery pole as only a man obsessed with handjobs can. Left to ourselves, I ask Davy if he'd like a rim job. He backs up over me, lowering his slick crevice toward my tongue.

Sometimes it's three o'clock, sometimes it's as late as four or five when we finally pry our sticky parts loose from each other. I'm so totally fagged by then that I'm thanking God I'm already in my bed, I don't have to go padding off down the cold hall as the others do, to their separate rooms. Todd has the farthest to go and I don't know how he makes it, fucked out as he is. Maybe I should offer to change rooms with him. We'll cross that bridge if and when we get to it.

I set my alarm to go off at six, as usual. It'll be agony, forcing my-self out of bed while my body cries out for more horizontal time. But the alternative, being the last one down to breakfast, isn't so attractive either.

**T h e** next time a guest comes for breakfast, again on a Sunday morning, I'm ready. I get up in time to shower and dress beforehand, and there are no butterflies in my gut as I descend the stairs. It's a great improvement since Kent paid his guest visit, which seems like ages ago.

The first to join Harmon, I help him with the preparations. "Hey, Harmon," I ask, getting a carton of eggs out of the fridge, "tell me something, whatever happened to Brian? We were never told."

He looks at me, and just the way his stiff black eyebrows move, crowding toward each other as he frowns—oh, here are the butterflies in my gut. Then he grins and, still grinning, draws an index finger across his Adam's apple, accompanying it with a kind of growl that represents, I guess, the sound of someone getting his throat cut.

Oh. Okay. I take eggs out and return the carton to the fridge.

Kent appears, wearing black slacks and a white button-down shirt fastened all the way to the collar. Is this ecclesial-looking outfit a nod to the Sundays he left behind, somewhere back in the world, or is he just making an effort to look nice? Probably the latter. Look at me, in black Dockers and a navy blue button-down shirt. I've even trimmed my beard and shaved my neck. But this is no nod to Sundays past; when I lived with Eric I was a pure slob, never bothering to change out of the sweatpants and grungy t-shirt I'd slept in the night before.

"A late one," Harmon says, sweeping his spatula toward the kitchen clock—meaning the guest, not one of us. The last-one-down rule doesn't apply on Sundays. "It's not going to hold us up, though."

"I have a question," Todd says. He actually raises his hand. "If we get a new housemate, where will he stay? In Brian's old room?"

That's the second mention of Brian this morning—not a good idea. But Harmon is smiling. "I was just getting to that. There's an announcement to make: Aaron's going to be leaving us."

Todd and Davy glance up quickly from their plates. Aaron has been quiet and still is, turning his hangdog expression toward Harmon.

247

"We'll miss you, Aaron," Harmon says, "but we won't be sad about this. It's a victory when a man heals, when he's ready to go out and live his life the way nature intended, goddamnit."

All eyes are on Aaron, who looks as pale as Kent. And is his lower lip trembling?

"Yeah," Harmon goes on, "we know you're going to miss us, too." His bonhomie strikes such a false note that I have to suppress a laugh. "But with everything you've got to look forward to...."

Such as? Wife and kids. A normal life. All memory of this place shut out forever. My fingers tremble as they touch my knife, my fork.

When the doorbell rings, Harmon folds his napkin and places it beside his plate. "Excuse me."

Someone whispers a crack about Harmon's "Sunday manners." Otherwise we're quiet as we spread butter on pancakes, sprinkle pepper on eggs, and glance at Aaron almost shyly, as if he were new. And in fact he is new. He's the healed Aaron, the Aaron who's going out into the world to live. Gone are his tearoom days, slogging from one shit-smelling paradise to the next, seeking the ultimate handjob. His brow looks heavy, he can't seem to stop squinting with anxiety, and his every jerky move makes it evident that he'd rather be anywhere else than here. That makes him a member of the club, as far as I'm concerned; but it's his reason for not wanting to be here that fills me with envy. More than anything else, I want to know what it's like, to have changed. Completely. Forever. And I'm not likely to find out, not from him. Bright as he is, he's also the least articulate of us.

248

There's Harmon in the doorway, with the guest right behind him; and though I can see only a portion of the stranger's head—one eye, a wedge of forehead and hairline—over Harmon's shoulder, I'm so sharply reminded of Eric that I drop my fork. Fortunately it falls into the napkin on my lap, so I can return it to my plate in less than a second, with no one noticing. But they'll have to notice that I'm blushing, the rims of my ears starting to burn in what also seems like less than a second. I don't look up again as Harmon and guest move into the room.

"Everybody, this is Daniel. Daniel, meet Todd, Davy, Aaron, and Paul."

I nod without looking up, then think better of it. This is exactly how I don't want to behave. I lift my gaze toward the familiar faces, then toward the guest who hasn't yet taken his chair.

I drop my fork again. This time it lands on the linoleum. How can I help it—this new guy is Eric. And yet he's not. He's slimmer, for one thing. And his hair is a lighter brown, and he wears it parted on the side, as Eric never does. And he's clean-shaven—no mustache, no goatee. It's my own fault. I've been thinking of him too much, lapsing into memories of the lazy Sundays we used to spend together. My own fault, my own fault. And I can't avoid thinking of him now, as I avoid looking directly into those eyes which are disturbingly close to me.

"How do you do," Daniel says.

Oh, Christ, is that Eric's voice? But I can't be sure of the accent, not till I hear more. Closing my eyes briefly, I will my pulse to slow down. Are the others noticing me? What can they be thinking? What am I supposed to think, reacting this way to the presence of a male stranger?

"Sit down, Daniel," Harmon says, clapping him on the back. "Join us. No need to be shy."

Daniel murmurs "thank you"—again, not enough for me to be sure of his voice—and takes the empty seat.

"Now, you're not going to tell us you've already eaten," Harmon says, resting a hand on Daniel's shoulder.

Daniel smiles, shakes his head, spreads his napkin over his lap. "Pancakes are my favorite."

I sit, head bowed, eyes closed, no longer focused on how I must look. This is Eric's voice. How could I not know it, even in my sleep, distorted by the peculiar acoustics of dreams?

"So where are you from, originally?" Todd asked. His faux sarcasm makes it sound like, So, where are *you* from?

"Argentina," Daniel says.

Before I can stop myself I raise my head, my voice cracking from stress and a dry throat as I ask, "Argentina? You sound more like an Ecuadorian."

249

Daniel doesn't even blink. Instead he breaks into a wide grin. "That's amazing! I was born in Ecuador, as a matter of fact. You really know your accents!"

I look at him, then look away, replaying the glimpse I've just had of Eric's smile, his eyes. "Daniel" wears glasses different from Eric's, larger, rounder, with plastic tortoiseshell frames; but the eyes are the same...or are they?

"So what...what's your profession?" I ask.

"Oh, I've been a teacher for many years," Daniel says. "But now I'm taking some time off, just for myself."

"Did you teach around here, Daniel?" Harmon asks. He's back at the griddle, pouring out more batter, sucking a bit of it off his thumb.

"Yarmouth," Daniel said.

I wonder how extensive his background check was. It would be easy enough, wouldn't it, to find out if Daniel really was a teacher in Yarmouth? But the background check can't be too extensive, if no one's supposed to know you're here. There are too many people on the outside, too many well-meaning but thoroughly wrong-headed friends and relatives who might try to intervene, which would be disastrous to the healing process.

So it wouldn't be that difficult for Eric to make up a story and get away with it. Still I can't be sure. Being ninety-nine percent certain means nothing, with that other one percent hanging around. I force myself to look up again, to watch the others busily plying knives and forks, swigging coffee, their conversation a bit more animated than usual.

250

"I just can't," Daniel was saying. "I can't believe these programs really work."

"Most of them don't," Harmon says. "The so-called 'faith-based' programs don't work, because they're built on phony religious principles. Here we don't talk about God, we only talk about the power of your own mind." Harmon smiles, tapped his right temple with his index finger. "And it works. Ask these guys."

Daniel looks at me, right in the eye. His hair's not only lighter in color, it's longer than Eric usually wore it. I remember photographs Eric has shown me, taken years before we'd met; it was this Eric in those photos, slightly slimmer, clean-shaven, with longer hair, plastic-rimmed glasses. Yet even this direct eye contact leaves me in doubt. There's nothing to those eyes beyond size and shape and color—no acknowledgment, no hint of recognition. Meanwhile, I'm giving myself away with each breath I take. Disturbed, frightened, mystified—how can I not show it? I pass a hand over my forehead and find it warm, too warm to be healthy.

Fortunately the agony soon ends, Harmon gets up to take Daniel on a tour of the place. I don't even know how the conversation turned out, which of us gave testimonials. Maybe no one did, we're all looking sheepishly down at our syrup-streaked plates. I shake my head, trying to snap out of it. Focus, Paul: don't forget the real bombshell of the morning, the news that Aaron is leaving.

"Aaron," Davy says, "we…we wish you all the best."

"Well," Aaron says, barely loud enough to be heard, "it's a mutual decision, mine and Harmon's."

I want to ask, Then why do you look so miserable? Instead I ask him, "Where will you be going?"

"Back home, I guess. To stay with my parents for a little while. I can't go back to where I was living before."

A couple of us murmur, "Of course not," the rest of us nod.

"How soon do you have to go?" Kent asks. I look at him, as usual, with a certain amount of doubt in my heart. I can't help it. If Todd has the gay speaking voice, Kent has all the mannerisms—he practically twitches with them: the fluttering fingers, the tossing head, even the way he moves his shoulders.

"In a couple of weeks, I guess," Aaron says. He still looks so miserable. "I'm going to miss you guys." He stretches his hand out on the table, palm down, and a couple of the others pat it in an abrupt, self-conscious way. As if to draw the attention away from himself, Aaron asks, "So, how about this guy Daniel?"

"He…seems sincere," Davy says.

I pull into myself like a turtle, listen from deep within my shell.

"How did somebody from Argentina end up in Maine?"

"How did any of us end up here?"

"I like his accent."

"I always wanted to learn Spanish."

As usual there are no comments on the new prospect's physical qualities. The most offhand remark, the mildest compliment could have a construed meaning. It's okay to like an accent, but not a voice; okay to like the sincerity in his eyes, but not the eyes themselves. In my reverie I try to reconstruct Eric's face, sketch in precisely those details that are now taboo. I have a feel for his eyes, eyebrows, nose and mouth, the smooth pale planes where his sideburns were shaved off, something I once had trouble getting used to. Now this man here today, this Daniel, doesn't have Eric's pale skin. Instead his cheeks seem rosier—or is that a result of the lighter hair? Is that why people lighten their hair, to make their faces look less pale? Fuck, there's a whole world out there, a whole universe of information on looks, all the tips and tricks I never heard or listened to. What an unconvincing queen I've made, I don't even know how to wear my hair.

Not so Kent, with that alluring wave across his brow, his trimmed eyebrows, his mustache that he also keeps trimmed now, I've noticed, with nary a stray hair. He looks at me, peering into my shell: "Are you okay?"

"Better than okay," I reply. Brian always encouraged us to say that; who knew I'd ever feel nostalgic about it?

Kent's lively blue eyes don't move, yet they seem to be dancing, almost glittering in the sunlight streaming in through the windows over the sink. Oh, I'm a sucker for eyes, always have been—but why am I noticing them now more than ever?

Harmon and Daniel return, and yes, it's all his fault, that Daniel, for making me think of Eric and of the past, the dark and dangerous past. I'm going to spend the rest of the day doing not-thinking-about-it exercises, willing myself to be free. It's not too early to begin right now.

# Chapter 9

**After** a day of studying, meditating, and visiting different sorts of corporeal punishment on each other, we can't wait to start rubbing skin to skin again. While I'm kissing Todd tenderly on the cheek I slapped that morning, someone else is caressing my ass, which felt the tip of Harmon's steel toed shoe that afternoon, for what reason I can't remember.

These are the memorable times, the only real times, and everything else takes on an aura of unreality.

**Lying** in bed with Todd, Davy, and Kent, talking about giving Aaron a proper sendoff. I'm trying to remember what we did for Dwight when he left.

"Was it a party or something?" Kent asks.

Surely there was something—a toast with sparkling apple juice in plastic tumblers? But I can't come up with it.

It's Davy who remembers: "We never got a chance to do anything for Dwight," he says. "He left earlier than expected. We just got up one morning and he was gone."

Of course. How could I forget that all of a sudden there was no more Dwight? I remember sitting at breakfast, staring at his empty chair, thinking that the only trace of him left was the shallow cra-

253

ter his fist had made on my bedroom wall. I even had some dreams about his departure which were, in their own way, as disturbing as my dreams about that night on the beach, the dead body of Lyle Cook rising and falling in the shallow surf.

**I** pull Aaron aside. "So why are you leaving?"

He shrugs. "Harmon says it's time. I've been here longer than anyone else."

It's strange: we know so little about each other. And doubly strange, now, to have Brian gone: he seemed to know everything. "Are you going back to...?" I want to say "hairdressing," but somehow I can't.

"I'm still a barber," he says, somewhat defensively.

"Do your parents know you're coming home?"

He looks so unhappy. "If I just show up on their doorstep, they'll have to take me in."

I can't say what I'm expected to say: *I'm sure you'll be happy.*

**D a n i e l,** taking his own look around the house, steps into the den.

"It's smoky in here," I warn him.

"I don't mind."

Oh, doesn't he? Asthma is one thing Eric can't hide. "Do you have an inhaler with you?" I ask, hoping to catch him off guard.

"Inhaler? What for?"

He's got his game face on, no doubt about it. "So," I ask him, "are you moving in?"

254

"I will be," he says without much conviction. "As soon as I can. Just have to pack up my clothes and things."

"You don't need much." Should I take a calculated risk? I decide to go for it. "We tend to run around naked when Harmon's not here."

This shakes him. "I don't...?"

"What the hell difference does it make?" I ask him. "We're all guys."

He shrugs. "Oh. Okay. I...don't have a problem with that."

I see him, seeing me. He doesn't know what to make of me, either.

**Todd's** tied to a chair, his shirt open. "Okay, men," Harmon says. With a towel he picks up a knife that's been resting on a stove burner. We watch as the knife approaches one of Todd's large, soft nipples. "You think a man's nipples are something to play with, son?" Harmon asks.

"N-no, sir," Todd says.

"You've got 'em, though, ain't you? Look at these big brown suckers."

"Please don't touch me," Todd breathes.

"*WHAT?*"

"Please…sir, don't touch me."

"Shut up!"

God forgive me, I'm getting hard.

**Todd** and Davy and Kent and I are in bed. Todd has a bandage on his chest. I wonder what his nipple looks like.

Aaron's in his room down the hall.

"It's different," Kent says.

He's lying naked on his belly and I'm on top, nibbling his ear. Licking behind it, then the back of his neck. I know what he means but I'm ignoring it. I can make him ignore it, too.

"You know what I mean?" he asks.

"Mmmph." Between his shoulder blades now, running circles with the tip of my tongue, brushing gently with my mustache.

He takes a deep breath. Sighs. "It's not the same."

Okay, I give up. I need a gulp of water, anyway, from the tumbler of water on my nightstand. Of course Kent's right, it's not the same without Aaron. Especially when we know that Aaron's only just down the hall.

He hasn't been sleeping with us, anyway, over the past few nights, but he said it was because he had a cold. Now that we know he's leaving, it's not as if he's just a few doors away, sleeping off the sniffles; he might as well be on a different planet.

What I'll miss about him: he was always up for something. His cock was dependable. Only a few days ago I gave his thigh a surreptitious squeeze at the breakfast table, and sensed the twitch of that tireless member. Always dying for a hand job, he gave pretty good

255

ones, too. I never minded fucking him, either, though Todd was his preferred choice. Of all of us I'd say that Kent had the least connection to Aaron, the least attachment; yet here he is, getting all moony because Aaron's leaving.

"Let's go get him," I suggest.

"What? You're crazy."

"All right, look. A few nights ago he was the same as always, horny as a hound. Then suddenly he's leaving. What changed? What happened so fast? And when?"

By now he's rolled out from under me. His serious brown eyes blink at me, once, twice. "You don't remember when Dwight left?"

That's Kent's peculiar obsession, he's asked me about it a hundred times, even though my answer is always the same: "I told you, there's nothing to remember. He was just gone one morning, before the rest of us got up."

Startled, as if he's just heard this answer for the first time, he cuts his eyes toward the four corners of the room. Looking for an escape?

"Okay," I tell him, "let's go."

Would Todd and Davy want to go with us? At the moment Davy's giving Todd a blowjob, a slow one. More and more, lately, they seem to be crossing the fine line between having sex and making love. The rapture on Davy's face in particular, as he lies there with his lips around Todd's German helmet—it's almost too private a joy to be witnessed. So I'm just as glad to be leaving them, although, by the time I've grabbed my flashlight and Kent and I are padding along naked down the hall to Aaron's room, I find it was a mistake not to put socks on—beneath the thin runner the floor's like ice.

I'm rubbing one foot with the other, awkwardly, as we stand before Aaron's door. No light steals through the drafty jamb, and no sound. Kent and I are holding our breath, as if enough stillness could create the stir we're listening for. Finally I have to tell myself to breathe.

"He's asleep," Kent whispers.

Yes, I'm hoping the same thing. But I'm not sure, any more than he is. Anxiety collaborates with the cold, raising more gooseflesh: I'm all bumps.

"Are you thinking what I'm thinking?"

256

Yes, of course, it's occurred to me: Aaron's already gone. I turn my flashlight off, since I don't have the nerve to throw open the door and shine it in. But I make enough noise with the doorknob to rouse Aaron, who is there after all, making the bedsprings jangle as he stirs. "Who is it?"

"It's just us," I whisper. Silly, there's no need to keep our voices down. God knows we've been making enough noise at night, these past several weeks. Yet try as I might, I can't raise my voice. "Kent and Paul."

"What are you doing here?"

Has any one of us ever asked that question of the others? It makes me feel so lonely, in addition to being so freezing fucking cold…. I have to do what any toddler would do: leap across the room and into bed with the grownup. And Kent's right behind me.

Now, this is a trick. It's only a single bed, after all, and a stingy one at that. There'll be no stretching out side by side by side. We're more like a shape-shifting triple decker, Kent and I spinning around the big warm nucleus of Aaron. I didn't know I was going to feel this needy: I want to be hugged and fucked, sucked and suckled. Aaron's moving too—how could he not, with two cold bodies pressing against him—but I have to admit the bitter truth: he's here against his will, or *we're* here against his will. Something in the very turgor of his skin says that everything's changed. And yet—*there*, now—we really have done the impossible, we're side by side by side, even if half my ass is hanging out in space. And we're quiet, as if the three of us, by being still, could transport ourselves slightly back in time to when we were five-in-a-bed. Aaron's rod would cooperate, I *know* it would, if only… if only I dared move, which I don't. Instead I whisper, "Aaron?"

"*What.*" Sounding more annoyed than anything else.

"Want a hand job?"

Silence—for more than a moment, more like a minute. At last he says, "What else you got?"

The impertinence, so unlike him, comes from a place filled with pain. And when I ask myself, what else *have* I got, I come up so empty that I have to gulp some chill bedroom air to keep the tears down. My left arm is thrown across Aaron, my hand grasping Kent's upper arm, while my other arm is trapped between myself and Aaron and is

257

rapidly turning numb. Kent's right arm is clutching me, just beneath my shoulder, and it's this more than my own grip that keeps me from tumbling to the floor.

What else *have* I got?

Don't go, Aaron. It won't be the same without you.

Don't go. Maybe Todd and Davy will get married, and you'll miss it.

Don't go. Brian may come back someday.

And Dwight….

At last it's too much, the pressure of our three bodies trying to keep together in such a tiny space. I feel my grip on Kent slipping, as I slip from his. With a cry, almost a sob, I let go completely, to be treated to a short drop that feels like a long one, my ass on the unforgiving floor. A similar tumble has taken place on Kent's side of the bed, I hear him cussing softly. My eyes have adjusted so well to the darkness that I can make out the room's two windows, barely perceptible owing to curtains much heavier than mine: they are like the whites of the night's eyes. Their blind stare makes it easier, somehow, to ask the question that's burning in my gut: "Aaron? What happened?"

Even the slightest pause seems longer in the dark. "Shut up," he says. "Nothing happened."

Clear enough, yet the tearfulness of his voice wants to open a door, so I keep going. "Just a few days ago everything was the same as always." Yes, Paul, that's you, using the word "always" to describe this place. "What happened?"

"Harmon says it's my time to go."

"How come?"

"I've been here longer than the rest of you guys."

"Quit saying that!" Another spurt of tears, because he's making this place sound like…a prison. "The thing is…are you…healed?" For the first time in—oh, how long?—I have to face the fact that healing isn't something we just talk about in abstract terms. It's…possible.

"I…I think so."

This makes me sit up. The windows, the sclera of the night, shift their positions too. "Well, Chrissakes, Aaron, you shouldn't have to leave unless you're sure."

"I'm…sure."

258

Poor Aaron, he's physically incapable of lying. His voice box, tongue and teeth just aren't up for it. Even his lungs won't cooperate, they barely give enough breath to push his words a few feet through the static-free night air.

Or is it just that I don't…want to believe? "Kent? Are you still there?"

A sigh. "Still here." Still on the floor, like me.

"Do you think it's possible, after all?"

"If I didn't think it was possible," he says, "then why the fuck would I still be here?" Unlike Aaron and me, he doesn't feel the need to stage-whisper. His normal speaking voice sounds like a peal, a call to arms.

And it makes me afraid, because our cynicism is what's linked us together, Kent and I.

"What about you?" he asks me.

"I…I think Aaron's crying."

Sure enough, a sound almost like chirping, but in this case sobbing. By instinct I reach up, try to find his hand. But my fingers only bump against his covered body, which shifts, his crying muted as he turns away from me.

"Aaron…."

"Leave me *alone!*"

A sob catches in my own throat. I get up to leave, balancing carefully because, goddamnit, now my right foot has gone to sleep. Where did I leave my flashlight? Feeling along the top of the desk, my hand bumps up against something that gives way. A stack of books tumbles to the floor, raising an unholy racket.

"*Leave me alone!*"

I want to ask Kent if he's coming with me, but I don't have the nerve. I guess I don't have to, I hear him getting to his feet. Another sigh brings him closer.

"Careful," I tell him, "there's books…."

"I know."

I want to take a book with me. It's silly, but I do. I might never see this room again, and if I do, it may be someone else's. So I grasp the nearest cloth cover, its straight edges reassuring. The binding rests in my palm like a body, heavy yet familiar.

259

"Let's go, I'm fucking freezing." This from Kent, and he's whispering at last.

Back in my room, Todd and Davy lie adhered to each other like layers of lasagna, fast asleep. Kent tumbles onto the bed, then me, and I'm still holding the book, which for some reason wants to assault him, its corners poke him every time I move. All I can say is, "Beg your pardon, beg your pardon," with some irony that he wouldn't catch: for what I picked up in Aaron's room was *The Canterbury Tales*, and I have it open to the famous woodcut of the Pardoner. The one lost soul. If I were able to reach into the book and touch this miserable creature, I'd tell him that I understand.

Sometimes a lost soul is the best friend a body can have.

**Two** mornings later, Aaron's gone, just like that.

And later that day, Daniel's moving in.

**The** new configuration: Todd and Davy and Kent and me and… Daniel, sitting by himself in the wing chair while the rest of us pile onto the sofa and loveseat. Harmon's in the wooden chair in front of the bricked-up fireplace. Seen from a slightly removed angle, this might look like an interrogation scene. Certainly Daniel looks uncomfortable, adopting the classic body-language defense of legs crossed, ankle on opposite knee. What can't be seen—or maybe it can, just not as clearly—is that Paul is uncomfortable too, and wishing that he could just disappear into his corner of the loveseat.

260

It's easy enough, here where the light streams in behind Daniel, rendering his face nearly invisible, to believe that he doesn't look like Eric, not at all. Nevertheless, I've been avoiding him. What's the alternative? To approach him and ask, "Hey, are you my former partner of ten years?" That question lies in a no-man's-land of impossible queries.

Not that the impossible doesn't happen regularly around here. This morning when I woke up, I found Davy and Todd bundled together on one side of the bed. The animal comfort that they took in each other was obvious in the way that the side of Davy's face was pressed into Todd's chest, but now there was something else as well, something more tender. On the other side of me Kent woke up, lay there scratching his balls for a minute or so, then left the bed. The large red numbers on the clock read 5:50, just ten minutes from alarm time. I fetched my glasses from the nightstand and took a focused look at Davy and Todd. The corners of their mouths were turned up, as if they had found something, not in their sleep but outside of it, and had managed to pull it partway into their dreams. I cleared my throat, not wanting, somehow, for the alarm to wake them, to see them startled. After a couple of throaty *a-hem*'s their eyelashes fluttered. Before their eyes were fully open Davy raised his head, Todd lowered his, and they entered the kind of liplock that you'd expect to see in—what, honeymooners?

It happens again, at dinner: I look up from my Manwich to find Todd and Davy staring at each other. Staring into each other's eyes, actually. Damned odd behavior. I want to clear my throat then, to break it up, whatever "it" is. Instead I steal a guilty glance at Daniel, who's absorbed in some rant of Harmon's. Suddenly I want Daniel to look at me; I *will* him to glance in my direction, but it doesn't work. Instead it's Harmon who cuts his eyes toward me, and I see he's expecting me to follow what he's saying, as if he's been speaking to both Daniel and me all along.

"Those God-and-the-Bible programs are bullshit," he says, for the hundredth time. "Once you start restricting yourself to literal interpretations of the scriptures, you're screwed."

I'm tripping on the consonance of *scriptures* and *screwed* and thinking, *I've got to get out of here, right now.* "Sorry," I announce, pushing myself back from the table. "I have to see a man about a dog." These archaic expressions, picked up from my parents' generation— how much longer will anyone be able to understand me? Kent's already giving me odd looks, as if half of what I say doesn't make sense. But in Daniel's profile there's some acknowledgment, as if he knows what I'm talking about, will always know. I slip behind Todd, glance at Davy, glassy-eyed and simpering, and take the stairs two at a time. Lock myself in the bathroom, and burst into tears.

Can they hear me down below? There's nothing I could do about it, I'm sobbing the way a little windup dog barks. When the sobs die down I spend some time blowing my nose and mopping up my face with a half roll of toilet paper. No one taps on the door. By the time I

261

come out, Harmon has left for the night. I know this because, when I go to my bedroom, Todd and Davy and Kent are in my bed. All six eyes are on me as I breeze into the room, take my dopp kit from on top of the dresser and breeze out again. Back in the bathroom, I look frankly at myself in the mirror and wonder how the guys kept from screaming when they saw me. *Peace out,* I tell myself. *You're tired, Paul. You're exhausted. No one could experience what you've gone through and* not *be exhausted.* And no one could understand this, either…except maybe Eric. I hurry to brush my teeth and wash my face. Somewhere I've read of some terrible disease that can make you bleed through your eyes, and I seem to be headed in that direction, having used more than my quota of tears for the month. The next time I see the boys I want to be halfway presentable.

I get back to my bedroom to find them lying there as I left them, on their backs, the sheet pulled up to their noses. Papa Bear, Mama Bear and Baby Bear, snuggled tight in the one bed that's just right. With Aaron there too, as well as me, it used to be crowded. Yet I miss him. Now there's no one else to take the up tiny space he didn't fit into, except…Daniel, down at the end of the hallway. Does he know that we're all in here every night? How could he not know? He's probably heard, if not witnessed, the daily six o'clock exodus. And what's he doing while we're pig-piling the night away? Draining himself of the evil spooge? This situation takes me way, way back—to elementary school, when the new kid on the playground was either invited to shoot marbles or chased into the woods after class let out. Maybe… maybe we should invite Daniel to shoot, if not marbles, then a few wads. I peek out into the hallway, which is forbidding as usual.

"Paul, come *on,*" Kent says. "We're tired."

"Fuck you."

"Not if you don't come to bed *right now.*"

If I don't speak up…. "Hey, why don't we ask Daniel if he wants to join us?"

The three of them look at me, each with his mouth hanging open in the exact same way. It's like watching the gay men's chorus. Silently they close their mouths and look at each other. Okay, I get it: these three naked guys—each sporting a semi, if the topography of the sheet is any indication—are fully aware of how it looks, this schizo life they're leading: queer by night, repaired by day. The split gets to me, too. We got here through a maze of conscious and unconscious decisions that would be hard to replicate. Do we know Daniel well enough to assume that he could, or would, do the same?

The answer being no, at least as far as I can tell, I decide it's time for some investigating. The truth can be arrived at through plotting, scheming and, if necessary, lying. Over the next couple of days I develop a plan, and Davy, a serious backgammon player, reluctantly agrees to participate. On Sunday afternoon he'll challenge Daniel to a game. If Daniel is really Eric, he won't be able to resist a chance to play; but if he does resist, Davy will suggest something else. While the game is proceeding I'll sneak into Daniel's room, to see what I can find out about him.

It's a simple plan, with relatively few moving parts, and it works quite well, at least at the beginning. I'm in the living room when Davy broaches the subject of backgammon, and Daniel perks up—exactly as Eric would, upon finding a new opponent. The backgammon board that's stored on top of the bookcase has had a rough life, judging by its three scuffed corners and one missing one—chewed off, apparently. But all of the black and white discs are accounted for, as well as the dice; so when the boys are engaged I make my exit, feigning a headache and the need to lie down for awhile.

The neatness of Daniel's room testifies to his recent arrival. No odd bits of clothing have accumulated in the corners, and his desktop is bare. I ease open his top dresser drawer to find neat piles of Calvin Klein briefs in various colors. Does Eric favor Calvin Kleins? Well, yes, but that's not—hello, what's this? In a corner of the drawer, under some socks, my fingers meet up with a hard plastic cylinder. Pulling it free, I nearly drop it as soon as I see it. It's a white inhaler like the one I've seen Eric use for his asthma. Azmacort, it says, and I'm wondering if that's his brand. Where are the rest of his medications? Cholesterol, blood pressure, allergies…the bottles must be around somewhere, and prescription labels don't lie.

I'm easing open the second dresser drawer when there's a knock at the door. My heart leaps against its cage—is this the fatal heart attack that's been lurking in my future? But I come to my senses in a second

263

or two: Eric wouldn't knock on his own door, he'd breeze right in. So I open up, and there's Kent. "Can I help you look?" he asks.

What's the best way to tell him to fuck off without hurting his feelings? "I don't…." I begin, but before I can finish he reveals his true agenda. It's the way his hand works under his t-shirt, lifting it a bit, revealing his creeping Charlie. How many times have I seen him make that gesture, which he always ends by working his fingers under the waist of his sweatpants…. "Oh, I get it, you're horny."

"I just thought…you know…doing it in the new guy's room might be kind of hot."

"With Harmon still here?"

Kent's eyes are hopeful. With Aaron gone, and Todd and Davy paying more and more attention to each other, he may be expecting more from me. It's true that our sexual activity has never crossed this threshold before, and while I'm still telling him in my mind to fuck off, my dick is saying something else. But no, this mission is too important. "This is serious," I tell him, doing my best to scowl.

"I'm serious too." There he goes, sliding his sweatpants down. No underwear—an infraction!—and his cock is anxious to say "Hi," like a latecomer to its own party.

"We could get caught," I remind him, in a lame tone of voice that doesn't begin to put a sensible damper on the occasion.

"I *know*." Having kicked off his sneakers he's naked from the waist down, and in one graceful move he strips off his t-shirt too. This is Kent as I love to see him, all right—naked and randy, his cock in full play mode.

264

"It's not a good idea, not a good idea at all." I slide my sweatpants down. How many times have we been warned against letting the little head control the big head? How many times have we heard, here in this very house, how important it is to not listen to the little head *at all*? I set my glasses on the desktop and pull off my t-shirt with a groan of despair: so this is how it is. We'll be fucking on the front lawn next, in the snow.

Gently sliding my hand around his dick, making just enough contact to make him gasp, fitting my mouth over his: oh, let me not wonder, at least not now, why another male body should speak to mine.

Kent's shuddering all over, as if my tongue, all by itself, could make him explode. Is there anything better than this?

The bedroom door opens.

Heart attack number two. I was right, wasn't I—Daniel wouldn't bother to knock at his own door. Visibly startled to see two naked men standing in a puddle of their own clothes, he rocks back a step, as if he's thinking he entered the wrong room. Rocks forward again, dismissing that notion. Back again: the most sensible thing is to run away, to pretend he never saw this. Then forward: what the hell, this is *his room*. I've snatched my glasses from the desk and put them back on so I can see his face. It's all there, not so much in his expression as in his lack of one: he already knows what's been going down around here. And who's been going down.

I look at Kent, who regards Daniel with equal measures of fear and curiosity. Yes, this is also how it must be, that even the fear of being discovered—surely one of our oldest, deepest fears—can't cancel out the sexual charge that comes with it. As for myself, I can tell that I'm just about to give in to the decadence of the situation, and damn the consequences. Nero fiddled while Rome burned; me, I'd be fucking and sucking on all seven hills.

So I make the invitation: "Uh…care to join us?"

The look on Daniel's face is something I'll never forget. If I wanted proof that he's not Eric, here it is, for Eric would never *ever* look at me with that kind of contempt. Oh, he *couldn't* look at me like that, no matter what I've done!

Could he?

Daniel steps back and slams the door. I feel that slam as if it connected with my face, which is burning with shame and need.

**"Okay,** perverts. It's time you started looking like men."

It's Sunday morning, breakfast time. Nobody's tied up, the last-man-down rule not applying on Sunday; but that doesn't mean we're not on the edge of our seats, expecting Harmon to try something. His looking-like-men comment, all by itself, is enough to make the hairs stand up on the back of my neck—prophetically, as it turns out.

We're getting haircuts. This afternoon. In the old days Aaron would give each of us a trim now and then, using an ancient set of clippers that belonged to the house. Since he's been gone we've started look-ing…yes, a bit shaggy. But the haircut session itself is only part of the news.

"It's a woman who's coming in," Harmon says, a smile creaking across his face like an opening door.

We steal glances at each other: a woman? Has a woman ever set foot in this house before? So far we've seen only the two-dimensional kind, in the men's magazines that are faithfully delivered to our front door, the subscription labels still bearing Brian's name. Those glossy ladies with their spread thighs are meant to represent the deepest of intimacies, but I'm never able to do more than glance at them. Lov-ingly photographed though they may be, their peach-colored forms don't do anything more for me than the car ads do. My comrades share this lack of connection. One afternoon when we were all read-ing I looked up to find Davy frowning at a centerfold spread out on his lap. Unaware that anyone was watching, Davy grasped the maga-zine and gave it a clockwise turn, as if the picture might finally make sense if it were upside down. I burst out laughing, of course.

But to be confronted with an actual woman….

Is there anything to be nervous about?

At the appointed hour I'm on my way down the second floor hallway when Kent steps out of his room and asks me, "How do I look?" Well, he looks the same as I do, in the standard house attire, sweatpants and t-shirt, no flannel shirt since the house feels warm-ish today. But his clothes are, like mine, freshly laundered. Todd ap-pears and, neat as he always is, there's something more careful about his appearance, too. Oh, his t-shirt is tucked in. Lastly there's Daniel, who's also neat as always but may have just washed his hair, or at least wet-combed it, sweeping it back from his face in a way that reminds me of You-Know-Who. He hasn't spoken to me since he caught Kent and me in his room.

We wait in the living room for *the woman* to arrive. Harmon seems no less nervous than we are, peeking through the curtains every two minutes. Now and then I meet the eyes of one of the others, and we smile a little crooked smile. Good God, you'd think we were waiting for a whore to arrive.

When the doorbell rings Harmon is right there at the front door. "Hi," he says, taking hold of the woman just above the elbow, guiding her in as if she can't see. At the moment I can't see, not very well: she's just a shadow against the bright daylight. There's something familiar in her silhouette, though, and when the door has closed and she's moved to the center of the room, I see who she is: Celia Cook. Even if I didn't recognize her I'd remember her gesture of raising a hand to her face and pulling back strands of her long fine hair before speaking.

"My," she says, smiling, "what a group of handsome young men."

Oh fuck, was she *paid* to say that? And look at the five of us, sitting here grinning like idiots. Before Harmon can come forth with his military manners Todd's out of his seat: "Let me take your coat, ma'am."

"Call me Celia," she says, shrugging out of her parka. Her smile is so much the same as she aims it at each of us, I can't tell if she recognizes me or not. Just as well if she doesn't: I'm different now from the messed-up Paul she met months ago. Okay, maybe no less messed-up, but different.

Todd is holding her by the elbow now, exactly as Harmon did, leading her to the kitchen while Harmon follows, smiling like a proud father, breaking composure only long enough to mutter "Get off your asses" to the rest of us as he passes through.

"Okay, who's first?" Celia's set up at her station, a kitchen chair with a sheet underneath to catch the falling hair. Another sheet is ready to be spread over whoever takes the chair. Could anyone miss the symbolism here, and are any of us prepared to be tucked between two sheets by a woman?

"I'll go first," Todd says, Alpha male that he is. Perhaps, in his imagination, he and Celia have already set up housekeeping and are churning out babies, one-two-three. Davy looks alarmed as Todd assumes the position, and it's more than he can do—more than I can do, for that matter—to watch as Celia fusses with the sheet around his neck. Taking up the clippers at last, she sets them buzzing—an angry sound. I seem to recall being frightened when I had my first haircut. Tired of standing in a corner, I'm on my way to take a seat at the table when Todd cries out, "What are you *doing*?"

267

He's taken his hands out from under the sheet and is feeling the back of his head. From my angle I can't see what she's done back there, but I can see that a surprisingly large thatch of Todd-hair has fallen to the floor. Celia, looking as alarmed as Todd, turns to Harmon. "Didn't you tell them?"

Harmon laughs. A rare sight at any time, it's rarer still to see him this amused, truly tickled by a situation that's just beginning to dawn on us. "Sorry, boys," he says, wiping a corner of each eye. "I guess I forgot to tell you: you recruits are getting your heads shaved!" More laughter, his mouth open so wide I can see his molars, two gold crowns gleaming.

**When** it's over and Celia has left, we're appalled and dismayed by the sight of each other, yet unable to split up, to go to our separate rooms and nurse our shorn scalps.

As if something worse might happen if we don't stand together.

Our naked heads make us look both older and younger. Older in the face—any wrinkle or blemish or rough patch of skin is more visible with no hair calling attention to itself—and yet younger overall. And there's something erotic in the image of the freshly shorn recruit, a man beginning his initiation into the ways of the world. Yes, yes—initiation, breaking in, becoming a strong young cock. Just as I can't stop passing my palm over my scalp, marveling at its total nakedness, I want to touch these other heads, too. I see us in bed, Todd and Davy and Kent and me, bald heads bobbing as we split into two teams of sixty-niners, racing toward climax. I haven't forgotten Daniel, either, though he stands apart from the rest of us. His bald head makes him look more vulnerable, more confused. When I put a hand on his shoulder he glances back at me, seems to consider for a second before roughly shaking me off.

All right. Whatever. Jamming my hands into the pockets of my sweats, I find the small folded note that Celia passed to me as I got out of the chair. We were shaking hands, and she was looking me in the eye, doing such a perfect job of not knowing who I was that I felt compelled to show no recognition either. And the paper that she pressed into my palm was, no doubt, her version of a business card or some other advertisement. Even now, discovering it anew, I can take

268

or leave the thought of opening it; it would be just as easy to pitch it in the trash.

Of course, a second later my fickle mind is swinging in the other direction, and I unfold the note, keeping it palmed so no one else will see.

> *I think the Judge is behind all this. You need to get out* **NOW**.

I don't know what's more disturbing: the message, its brevity, or the fact that she neither addressed nor signed it. There's a randomness to it, like the message inside a fortune cookie: it can't be meant for me. Okay, she mentions a judge, and a judge has been mentioned before…by Lizzie, I think. But the idea of getting out **NOW**…. Where would I go? And what could be so threatening in the immediate future?

I slip my hand back into my pocket, re-depositing the note. At the same time I meet a glance from Harmon, unsmiling, more than halfway toward that point of displeasure when he'll have to take his temper out on somebody. I rub my head and darken my own expression, as if the haircut-cum-humiliation has done enough to beat me down for one day. When I look up again he's left the room.

**Of** course it has to happen: the night when I forget to set the alarm.

I'm the first to wake up, panicking because it's lighter in the room than it should be. I grab the clock, hold it right up to my nearsighted eyes.

The house rules have grown more strict. No longer are we allowed to shower and dress after breakfast; now we have to be dressed and ready for inspection when he sets foot in the door, at 7:00. Which means I have to set the alarm for 6:00 at the latest, in order for all of us to have time to jump in the shower.

And it's now 6:45.

Before I sound a cry of panic I put my glasses on and re-check the time. "Oh, Christ!"

Davy, who ended up sleeping at my feet like a cat, stretches and frowns. "What's up?"

269

Todd, on my right, rolls over and throws his arm across my chest. Reluctantly I slide out from under it. Only Kent is still asleep. Uncovered, on his back, his slim, hairy chest rising and falling, his morning erection lying on his belly.

I clear the cobwebs out of my throat and announce, "We're in deep shit."

The only way we can be presentable when Harmon appears is to double up in one of the showers, triple up in the other. We have to improvise, there being no time to draw straws—and imagine how *that* would turn out, the mass dissatisfaction, the amount of discussion it would take to make five queens happy. Somehow it works out that Todd and Davy and Kent head for the second floor shower. Daniel and I will have to share the first floor shower, off the hallway by the kitchen.

I go down to his room to get him, remembering to pull on my pajamas first. Anyone else's door I'd enter without knocking, but his pulls me up short. I tap, politely at first, then more urgently as no answer comes. "Daniel? *Daniel?*" Finally I have to peek in. At the same moment I see his bed is empty, a groan and rattle coming through the walls tells me he's already there, in the downstairs shower. Well, of course: since when does he depend on me to get him up? I'll just have to jump in there with him, he'll understand.

It's not easy, though, even after I've entered the bathroom without knocking. Daniel's in the shower, all right, his body appearing in vague patches through the translucent shower curtain. I'm squinting, trying to configure these distorted glimpses into…something more familiar. I'm on the verge of calling Eric's name, just to see if, in a moment of watery confusion, he'd reply. Instead I clear my throat, not wanting to startle him. It also seems like a good idea to flip the light switch a couple of times.

That does it. A muffled "What?" comes from the tub.

"Daniel, I'm coming in. Don't worry, I won't touch you."

"Into the *shower*?" Peeking around the curtain, his disgusted face seems to hang before me for a second; his bald head adds another layer to the Eric/not-Eric conundrum. But there's no time to argue. No time for my usual confusion, daydreaming, or fucked-upedness, either. I strip my glasses off and toss them on the counter. "Please

270

please please," I'm saying, grabbing the curtain, shooing him back with my free hand, stepping into the tub. The water's tepid, the best we can get with both showers running at once; still I'm begging for it, while he hugs his shoulders and shrinks as far from me as the tub will allow. He's talking too, and what with the noise of the spray I can barely make him out:

"...*away* from me...think you're *doing*...?"

"Please, it's an emergency!" I try to duck under the showerhead, but he blocks me with an elbow. "Just let me get a quick rinse!"

"...*out* of here...*pervert!*"

"Yes, yes, I'm a pervert, but don't let me be a dirty one, please?" I'm sticking out my neck, rubbing behind my ears.

"...on your *ass*...serve you *right!*"

"Can't I borrow the soap for a *second?*" Ducking lower, trying to sneak under those damn elbows. "At least let me have some runoff!"

He's trying to slap me now, but I've got a secret weapon: my butt, which I use to back him into a corner. For a second, before he gets his hands around my neck, I get the benefit of the full stream. Ahhh....

Suddenly we're dancing a desperate dance, for something's gotten into the stall and it's stinging us all over. Screaming, Daniel crosses his arms on his chest and tries to push past me, but I'm screaming and pushing too, and it takes me a second, which seems like forever, to think of grabbing the showerhead and aiming it against the wall. It was blisteringly hot water stinging us, something that's not supposed to happen, unless....

Unless someone turned on the cold water in the kitchen.

Shrieking, out of fear this time, I hop out of the tub, grab my glass-es, run down the hallway and up the stairs. Todd and Davy and Kent are streaking down the hallway ahead of me in a mad dash for their rooms, laughing the dizzying, hysterical laughter of children being chased by the boogeyman, knowing they'll get caught any second. The same hysteria is rising in me: I'm going to shriek in the other direction, to my room.

But there's Daniel, coming up the stairs as if there's no hurry, a towel around his waist.

"Are you all right?" I ask him.

"You almost killed me!"

271

"No, no, it wasn't my fault the water got so hot! Harmon must be here…." There's no way I'm going to make him happy, and I wonder why I'm even trying, under this dire circumstances. Why, for that matter, am I still standing here, as if I can't bear to leave him? "Are you all right?"

"*No* I'm not all right, how could I be, with you…*attacking* me…."

"Oh Christ, we're doomed." There I go, giggling nervously, I can't help it. "Harmon's here, and we're fucking naked. We've got to get dressed."

I'm still dripping, and starting to freeze. Without a word Daniel takes off his towel and hands it to me. It's had a fair soaking by now but is still better than nothing. I don't know what throws me off balance more: his unexpected kindness or the fact that I'm seeing him naked for the first time—the shower didn't count, since I had my glasses off. This ought to be a big deal, since it's my chance to compare his body with Eric's, to make sure they're not one and the same. But I don't have the heart for it. This is *not* Eric. Besides, he'd go into full-scale homosexual panic if he thought I was looking at his dick. The best I can do is sneak a glance at his right hip, where he ought to have a birthmark the size of a dime.

So. There. I've looked, and he doesn't have it. End of story, Paul. Get dressed now.

Without a word I start down the hall to my room, and nearly get creamed by Todd, Davy and Kent, who have thrown on clothes. "You guys!" Todd hisses. "Hurry up!" They practically tumble down the stairs.

272

Socks, underwear, sweatpants, t-shirt. I wipe my water-spotted glasses with a handkerchief and take off. I'm going to be in for it, if I'm the last one down. So why am I hesitating at the top of the stairs? Waiting, pacing, wondering if Daniel could have got dressed before me? Glancing down the hall, I expect him to appear, any second now. I count to ten. Okay, *now*. Finally he does appear, walking—having given up, like me, on running a useless race. I hope he appreciates that I'm waiting for him. Really, he should try to like me, I'm willing to try to like him…until I notice what he's wearing, dark green sweats and a light blue t-shirt that are identical to mine. "Oh, for Christ's sake! Did you have to put on the exact same outfit I'm wearing?"

"I didn't know what you were going to wear," he mutters. "Anyway, it's too late to change now."

When we get to the kitchen, three pairs of eyes turn toward us from the table. Harmon is standing at the stove. Glancing in our direction, he says, "Well, if it ain't fuckin' Tweedledum and Tweedledee."

"Don't read anything into this, guys," I say. "We didn't dress alike on purpose." We're in trouble, though, and soon enough we're tied to our chairs, back to back. My throat is parched, but it's no good asking for juice, I'd get it thrown at me.

"Here, Paul, have some juice," Todd says, and *splat*, here it comes. There's something incredibly nasty about orange juice when it's running down your face.

"Some coffee, too," Davy says. Fortunately it's not too hot, he uses a lot of milk. Dreary, though, and nauseating, the converging streams of juice and coffee on my phiz. Can I blame Davy, though? I would have done the same to him.

Kent dips his fingertips in his orange juice and flicks them toward Daniel, spattering his face with sour drops. Better than getting it poured on you, I guess. Meanwhile Todd, using his spoon as a catapult, has landed a glob of scrambled eggs on my forehead. Maybe it's only right that I'm getting the major share of the abuse, for the secret reason that I was the one who forgot to set the alarm. Which doesn't mean that Daniel's not upset, I can feel his anxiety. If he were Eric, he'd be crying right about now: it's the kind of situation, where he's helpless and bullied, that gets to the core of him. *Don't cry*, I'm thinking, as if there's still a possibility he might be Eric. But when the tears come, they're mine, for what feels like a shitload of reasons. Odd, the taste of salt with the juice and milky coffee.

Harmon draws near, making poor-baby, tsk-tsk noises. Announcing, as if he needed to, that the worst is yet to come. "Aw, what's the matter, sonny?" He backhands Daniel across the face. I hear it and feel it, the force nearly enough to knock both of us over. After an initial cry of surprise Daniel is silent. The blow has knocked his glasses off. Davy retrieves them from the floor; miraculously they're unbroken.

I'm awaiting my turn, the sting that will continue to burn my cheek for a half hour. I've got my eyes clenched shut against it, as if

273

that would do any good. But before Harmon can approach me the phone rings. I open one eye to see him put his hand on the receiver of the kitchen extension, glance at us and seem to think better of it, then pick it up anyway. He doesn't get a chance to say hello, just stands there listening while a voice yaps at him. Hard to make out any words, but it sounds like Riley's voice.

Harmon hangs up the phone with unnecessary force. "Okay, men, you're on your own for the rest of the day. I've got a meeting to go to."

Is this a trick? More of the psychological kind of punishment? None of us makes a sound, and I don't open my other eye till Harmon's got out his heavy jacket and is putting it on. With a hearty wave of good-bye he leaves through the kitchen door.

Todd, Davy, and Kent look at each other. Then Kent snaps to attention, remembering that two of us are tied up. He loosens our ropes easily enough, and I grab a fistful of napkins, hand half to Daniel. "How's your face?" I ask him.

"It's all right," he says. He looks at the napkin he's blotted his face with as if there might be blood on it. His cheek bears Harmon's four-fingered imprint.

Oh, if this was Eric, and I thought someone had hit him…. I want to help set him to rights, but there's not much to be done—we've dabbed at the coffee and juice stains on our t-shirts—and, somehow, not much to say. But I do think to ask the others: "What did Harmon do when you guys came down this morning? We were *all* late, after all."

274

Shrugs. "Nothing," Kent says.

"Isn't that kind of strange?"

The three share a look. Yes, it's strange—almost disappointing. Even negative attention is missed, if it's all you ever get. Harmon has taught us to thrive on it—the slap, the scrape, the first-degree burn. We nurture ourselves by night, and by morning we're ready for more, from Harmon and from each other. Just like men.

Todd and Davy are whispering again, as they tend to do a lot these days. I look on with a kind of sad nostalgia, remembering when we were all for one, one for all. When Todd clears his throat and says, "I have an announcement to make," I'm not even surprised.

It's Davy, though, who pushes back his chair and stands. "We're leaving. Todd and me."

Okay, now I'm surprised. "Leaving? As in running away? How do you know it's safe?"

Dead quiet. With that question, which just popped out of me, I've voiced what we've all been thinking, what's been on our minds ever since Harmon first showed his stubbly face here: there's danger in the air. Grave danger.

Todd stands up and takes Davy's hand. They look like two schoolkids who are just about to skip down the road together. Yet there's something in their clasped hands that even I can't make fun of.

Kent looks from them to Daniel and me, his eyebrows raised, questioning.

Daniel answers. "We'll all leave."

"Wait, wait, wait," I tell them. "This is serious."

Todd and Davy look at me patiently, but with resolve. The lives they're meant to lead are ticking away somewhere, unheard and unseen, like clocks in vacant rooms. It's time to find them again.

# Chapter 10

"**O u r** suitcases have to be somewhere," Daniel says.

"I wouldn't bet on it," I tell him. "How far would we get, anyway, carrying suitcases?"

"For God's sake! You keep talking as if somebody's going to hunt us down and kill us."

How can I tell him that it's Lyle Cook I'm talking about, and the note his sister pressed into my palm? "You don't know what I know."

"So tell me."

We're in my room. Daniel sits on the edge of the bed, his arms crossed on his chest. He still doesn't like me, but we've joined forces because Todd and Davy and Kent have gone to their rooms and neither of us wants to be alone. "We could die."

It's all he can do not to sneer. "Who's going to kill us, Paul?"

Todd and Davy pass by the open door. If I'm not mistaken, each of them has a paper sack. "Wait," I call after them. In the hallway, I catch them at the top of the stairs. "Wait." What does this scene remind me of? Oh, it was that day when I was in their position, at the top of the stairs, and they stood about where I'm standing, fooling with each other in the hallway. Suddenly everything that's happened since then comes whirling toward me. "Wait," I tell them, steadying myself against the banister.

277

"There's nothing to wait for."

That was Kent, coming up behind me. And he keeps going, toward Todd and Davy. He has a book in his hand…thin black cover, pages edged in red. "A Bible?" I ask.

Kent turns to face me, fishes in the open neck of his shirt, and reveals something I've never seen him wear before, a gold chain with a cross on it. "I'm a minister."

"You…?"

"MCC, baby."

I couldn't have seen it before. Left to my own devices, I wouldn't see it still, or guess it in a hundred years. It's so obvious now, though: there's Kent extending an arm toward Todd and Davy in a ministerial gesture if I ever saw one, urging them, *herding* them down the stairs.

"What now?" It's Daniel, behind me, sounding morose.

I shrug at him. "I guess we're going to have a ceremony."

**"And** do you, Todd, take this man…?"

They're standing together, Todd and Davy, in front of the bricked-up fireplace, and Kent is facing them. In a small group like this, everyone serves in some capacity; Daniel and I seem to be witnesses, standing too close to be idle spectators. Todd and Davy look at each other, blinking through tears. Their smiles are tentative, crooked. Everything is hopeless and loony. There's not a dry eye in the house.

And Daniel is holding my hand.

He must have taken it when my mind was otherwise engaged, as happens frequently. My hand, which has spent a good part of its life in Eric's, called no attention to what was happening, preferring to curl up quietly, like a cat in a favorite spot. How could I not have noticed his hands before—definitely Eric's hands, fingers widened in the middle from years of knuckle-cracking? How could I not have known his feet, especially when I saw them this bathroom this morning—fleshy feet, not a tendon or metatarsal showing, the shy curve of his toes, the little nails like afterthoughts…and flat, those feet, flat as griddles?

While Todd and Davy kiss, I cut my eyes toward him. Yes, we've joined wavelengths at last, our peaks and valleys matched: he's watching me too, his hand squeezing mine back. And we're talking without speaking, as in the old days.

*What are you doing here?*

*I came to get you out of this place.*

*How did you find me?*

*Everyone knew bits and pieces about what might have happened to you—your aunt, Glen and Mark, Mary Munson, Celia Cook....*

*But that day when you first came here, how could you not show that you knew me?*

*I'm not sure anymore that I ever knew you.*

That last comment is breathed into me as he relaxes his grip, letting cool air brush my palm. No, not everything is known. Or reconciled. Or possible.

"Here," Kent is saying to the newly joined couple, "this is for both of you." He takes off the chain with the gold cross. Todd takes it, stares into his palm, asks, "Are you sure...?"

And as if there always has to be at least one hysterical person at a wedding, I'm suddenly launching myself across the room: "Don't go! You *can't* go...!"

How tenderly Todd touches my face, allowing me to lean on him, press my face against his chest. "Paul," he says, "you think too much, feel too much...care too much."

"What if Harmon's watching? What if Riley's out there, in the van...?"

"We can't just stay here, Paul. You know we can't."

They have their winter coats, at least, which have been hanging in the hall closet since the one time we used them, on Christmas day. Unable to wait another second, Davy turns the knob that opens the deadbolt lock. We all draw deep breaths, as if we're about to enter an alien atmosphere.

But the door won't open.

"Let me try," Todd says. He makes sure both locks are unlocked. Still the door won't budge. He steps back, blinking. "It's got some kind of lock on the outside." His expression is similar to what mine must be—the look of the betrayed, horror softened by a touch of foreknowledge, the small mute thought that something like this— yes!—was bound to happen.

279

So we've taken a step, and it's all downhill from here. I hardly have the heart to follow the others to the kitchen, where the back door is just as intractable.

"I guess there's no point in trying any of the windows," Kent says. He looks down at the Bible still in his hand, seems surprised to find it there. He lays it on the corner of the kitchen table.

"We just need some tools," Todd says. "Maybe in the basement."

"I don't remember seeing tools in the basement," Kent says.

"We saw something else, though," I point out. "That long passage. Leading somewhere, away from the house."

Kent starts looking in the corner of the kitchen where odds and ends tend to pile up. "Where's my baseball bat?"

**"Jesus** Christ!" Okay, I suppose I should stop talking like that, now that I know about Kent. But I can't help it, the basement seems so much colder now. I feel it as soon as we open the door.

A little more confident than we were on our first visit, we take the springy unfinished stairs down to the first room, and find again the passage that leads from there. We've got our coats, and flash-lights, and Kent carries his trusty baseball bat, but that's all we have; what we really need are caps. Todd and Davy left their paper bags of possessions behind, preferring to travel as light as possible. As we pass the banged-up door to the wine cellar, I can't help but ask Todd, "Want to grab a few bottles?"

"What are we doing?" Eric asks, right behind me. He's on the verge of tears, his voice trembling. But he's filled with anger, too; I can feel it pushing him onward—pushing too close, in fact.

I snap at him, "Don't step on me!"

"Step on you? I ought to strangle you!"

"What happened to that moment of tenderness we had up there?"

"Ow!" he says. "You could at least *tell* me when you're going to stop!"

"That's it, up ahead," Kent says.

The passage, he means—the long one. "But where does it go?" I ask.

"My guess," Kent says, "is that it leads to the Judge's house."

280

That gives me a shiver that has nothing to do with the cold. "The Judge? Why are *you* talking about a judge?"

"The Judge ran this town for decades. He had power over everybody."

"Who are you talking about?" Daniel asks.

"Judge Whistler," Kent says.

Oh.

*Oh.*

The slow, dial-up connection I have with my memory has been iffy in recent times; still I see something I didn't see before, when I replay those few minutes I spent in John Toomey's sickroom. We were discussing the bashing in of heads, and when I asked Toomey who was behind it, he pursed his lips in that disgusting parody of kissing....

Unless he was really *whistling.* Or trying to.

"But that guy"—I find myself tugging on Kent's shirtsleeve, the better to get his attention—"he can't still be around. The Judge."

"Don't be too sure."

My knees are shaking, making it an adventure just to take one step after another. I've passed the point where I stopped on my earlier visit here. Now the passage takes a sharp turn. And another. Finally we come up against a plywood door. There's a padlock to keep it shut, but the lock is open.

We're in a different basement now. Pulling the string of the dim overhead bulb reveals a cement floor. The air's a bit warmer, the space itself more crowded. Pieces of heavy old furniture, a large table holding oak chairs upside down, legs in the air. Stacked wooden crates filled with books, old appliances, the odds and ends of the ruling class. From somewhere I come up with a word: "Orts."

Kent sweeps his flashlight around, illuminating corners. "This is the Judge's house, all right.... What did you say?"

"Pelf," I announce. "Fenks. Sordes."

"What language is that?"

"Very old English." A shiver runs up my spine. "Words for refuse. Leavings. Excreta."

"Whatever, Paul...."

"Can't you smell it? There's something sour in the air."

No one else will admit to it, but I think we're all sensing it. Something not right, something that poor air circulation alone can't explain. Farther along we reach a stairway, steal glances at the top; but we're not about to go up there.

"Are there windows…?" Kent asks.

Yes, there are windows, small two-paned rectangles above eye level, but they're walled in, revealing nothing but gray bricks.

"Look," Eric said, "there's another doorway."

A doorway without a door, leading into another room. Eric finds the pull-chain for another dim overhead bulb. This room is narrower, much narrower…or rather the walking space is narrow, leading between what looks like huge storage bins built of plywood, fastened shut with small padlocks. Then the space opens up again, we're in a room of uncertain dimensions.

"Not much in here," Todd says, shining his light around.

True, the cement floor is bare, except for one shoe lying on its side. A lonely thing, adding to the emptiness of its surroundings. Todd picks it up, brings it close to his light, nearly drops it. "Oh!"

Kent was close enough to see also. "Oh, no…."

Davy doesn't have to get closer to know: "It's Aaron's."

"No!" It's me, hanging toward the rear. "Let me see."

It would be hard not to recognize this trainer, uglied up with turquoise, pink, charcoal gray, and apple green latex. They're the ugliest trainers I've ever seen, and how cruel that seems now, when I'd so much rather *not* remember them. Because the presence of that shoe here, now, means….

282

"He never left here," Kent says.

Yes, there's that. And more. The presence of that shoe, left behind the way a cat might leave behind a morsel of mouse, tells me we're moving in the wrong direction. We need to get out of here just as badly as we needed to get out of East Oak House. My feet are already retreating, nearly tripping over each other as they back toward the door. But no one else moves, so….

Kent has found something else on the floor: a plain matchbox. He picks it up, shakes it; something inside makes a sound, but it's not matches. He slides it open and, with shaking fingers, removes a man's gold ring. The matchbox falls to the floor. Shining his light on the ring's inner surface, he's on the verge of discovering something… then he's gone, even his light is gone, as if a trap door has opened up under him.

"Kent?" Todd kneels, finds Kent on the floor, on his side, in a fetal position, his head shaking with the turbulence of what he knows.

"It's true," he says. "It's true."

Davy and Eric are behind me, having half-consciously begun their retreat, like me. But Kent is pulling me forward again. It's true: what a piece of luck to find something true when the chips are down. So I'm looking at the ring, which Todd has taken from Kent's palm and is holding up to his flashlight. It's a challenge with eyes like mine, but yes, I can read the inscription:

**WITH ALL MY LOVE, KENT**

Kent is still moaning, "Oh, it's true, it's true…."

"Kent?" I kneel beside him too. Who wouldn't be alarmed, seeing him like this, who wouldn't press his hand against his flushed cheek…. "Kent?"

His voice, barely audible, carries tears: "He never left. Dwight. He never got out."

I remember the day, Kent's first day, when he asked me if I had ever seen anyone leave the house—any of the program's graduates, that is. The ex-gays, the brethren. His question seemed strange at the time, but it had to stand in line with a whole lot of other strange things, waiting for an explanation that might or might not come someday. Now it's here: Dwight was Kent's partner; somehow Kent traced him here, lied his way in so he could find out what had happened to him. And instead of moving forward he got tripped up, waylaid, seduced, confused…just like the rest of us. The time that passed in the outside world moved so slowly, so lazily here.

The pills helped, no doubt. Scrambled up time, so that my early days here, and what immediately preceded them, were always fuzzy. Now, in its delicate, circuitous fashion, memory *unspins* its sticky web, letting me work my way back.

It was that hideous night when Eric and Richard ran from me, both of them—ran from me and each other as I fell to my knees in the yellow light of the Sand Dollar breezeway and begged them not

283

to. Later, because I *could not* be alone, I walked to the odd little bar on Main Street that Celia had taken me to. My plan was to drown my sorrows in alcohol, and it would take a lot of it. Fortunately I wasn't put off by the snappish, surly bartender. I took the first of what promised to be many cups of draft beer from him and headed toward the last booth on the left, what I thought of as the gay section. There was no one there, and that was ideal: I wanted to drink alone.

No such luck for long, though. I was on my third beer, the room growing increasingly dim, when there was movement across from me, a jostling of the table as some unwelcome souse made himself at home. "Unwelcome souse," I muttered, to no effect. I looked into the darkness, and looked again: there was a man with long hair like Lyle's, only it was red hair, and he was younger. With a kind face.

"Well, hello," he said, every bit as if he were expecting me—or as if I were expecting him, had been waiting all my life just for him to come along. "My name's Brian," he added.

So what, I wanted to say, but checked myself.

"Can I get you another beer? It's on me."

From that point on he was my obedient servant, entertaining me with beer and all kinds of stories that kept the time passing. Exactly when he moved on from simple narratives to extravagant promises I couldn't say; but somehow he managed, without too abrupt a transition, to lean across the table and make the extraordinary claim that he could free me from pain. What a come-on! And it got better: as the night wore on and I got so full of beer I could hardly move, he made more and more sense. His words ate away at the image I had of Eric, horrified, accusing me with his eyes, then running off. They picked their way through my brain, his words, turning this and that into puffs of smoke, and yea, it was all good. I could hardly refuse when he stood and took my hand, led me from the bar back to the Sand Dollar to "get my things." I scribbled a note of farewell to Mary Munson; she had a credit card imprint from me, with the amount left open, so I wasn't stiffing her. Still later, in his office at East Oak House, Brian composed some notes on his old manual typewriter, with the help of my drunken mutterings—notes to my brother, aunt, and Eric, simply stating that I was going away for a while. I signed them as if they were perfunctory agreements that didn't even bear reading.

*Now these pills, Paul, are to help you sleep.*

Sleep? I was half passed out already. But I took the pills, my new little friends, and they did help me sleep. I must have slept for several weeks, for the next thing I knew it was Christmas, and an awful lot of my memory had gotten bored and taken off, to look for new prospects.

Now, in the corner of my eye, I catch Davy, visibly shaken like the rest of us, looking from Eric to me and back again. "What is it with you guys?"

I'm following another sound—the beating of my heart, which fills my inner ear. Since my body is taking over anyway, with its own sounds and impulses, I let my right hand rise of its own accord, reaching for Eric. He comes to me instantly, is in my arms even as I'm thinking *Wait, it's going to be strange holding him again.*

"Don't tell me you guys *know* each other?"

It's not so strange holding him, after all. The body has a better memory than the brain. "We sort of knew all along," I said. "Well, I knew and I didn't know."

"Now do you remember how it was you ended up here?" Eric asks.

"I ought to remember, it was the night you left me."

"*I* left *you*?"

"Well, that's what happened! You saw me with Richard, but that didn't mean anything…."

"Funny, it meant a lot at one time! Enough to make you lie to me."

I press my fingers against my temples and yearn for a place to sit down. "Speaking of lying, how did you manage the birthmark thing?"

"I'm wearing a little bandage over it, that's all."

Yes, a place to sit down, if only for a moment, would be so nice right now. I lean my back against a crate, which helps. "I still don't understand half of what's been happening here."

"I wouldn't mind understanding a few things myself," Davy says, hugging his shoulders. He looks longingly toward the next room, where Todd is sweeping his flashlight around, searching for more horrors. A sudden cry alerts us: he's found one.

"Oh, God," Eric says, "what now?"

285

He takes a faltering step, but I've got my hand on his arm. "Wait. Wait wait wait. Suppose we find something down here...really horrible?"

I hope it's just the dim light that gives a menacing cast to his features, as if he could change back into his Daniel-face any second. "I'd say we already have."

"Don't, Davy." Todd's standing in the doorway, holding out his palm. "Don't come in."

"What is it?" I ask.

"Paul...."

"Don't bother warning me, I have to see." I give Eric's shoulders a firm squeeze, as if that might help to hold him in place. "Wait here."

Kent is still on the floor, crying, with Davy attending to him. Todd is none too steady as he slowly raises his flashlight toward the far left-hand corner of the room. The beam reveals just the tips of two boots that seem to be hanging in midair.

"It's Harmon," Todd says.

"Show me."

"No."

I take his arm myself, bring the unwilling light up: yes, it's Harmon hanging there, some kind of rope around his neck—hard to see, the way it cuts into his flesh. And his face...his face is something no one should see, not with his mouth like that, his swollen tongue protruding, his squinty eye closed forever. Whoever set up this horror exhibit did a first-class job.

286

And it's funny—so funny I forget to laugh—but only now that I've seen Harmon's death mask do I realize I'd seen his face before I had even heard of East Oak House. It was on the night that I visited the bar for the first time, the night when Celia and I were looking for Lyle. It was Harmon, introducing himself as Richard, who shared that boozy interval in the booth with me. His hair was longer then, allowing for the cowlick that became, in my memory, his defining feature. I remember what Celia said to me about him, too, later on: *Oh, he's a great one to talk to. Did he try to recruit you?* So Celia knew about East Oak House, even then! Too bad she didn't know what a death trap it is.

"Let's get out of here," Todd says.

We help Kent get to his feet. I don't know where everybody thinks we're going, but I plan on scooting back to where I came from, the house we lived in, even if it means having to break windows to get out of it. If only my knees weren't shaking.

"Hey, guys!"

Now what? That voice from the not-too-distant past seems to be coming from above, up the stairs; and yes, there's light coming from that direction too.

"Come on upstairs, guys," Brian says. He's smiling, as if he's inviting us to toast marshmallows around a fire.

**Judge** Whistler's den—I guess that's what this is—has dark wood paneling, lots of books, hunting scenes on the wall, and trophies: a moose head, a many-pointed buck. An enormous desk, a cherry-stained monolith that doesn't suit Brian at all, he looks like a child sitting behind it. He can't stay still in the swivel chair, keeps slightly rocking back and forth, or twisting side to side, adding to the child-like effect.

Riley is in the room, too, looking, when I first spot him, like another piece of taxidermy, a bear in gray overalls rearing up on his hind legs. He wears his usual expression, which is more like no expression at all, a flat affect simply announcing, *Yeah, this is me. So what?*

"Hi, guys," Brian says. I hope he won't have too many more opportunities to offer that insipid greeting. "Sit down."

There are five straight-backed armchairs in front of the desk, as if we were expected. Well, of course we were. The chairs turn the room into a kind of court, a place of judgment. By taking seats we're collaborating somehow in a persecution, admitting that we have no choice. Eric and I are side by side, but I feel the loss of him all over again, because I would so much rather not have him here. It would be better, for his sake, if we still had fifteen hundred miles between us.

Todd clears his throat. "Can we settle some things?"

*Bam!* The sound is like a gavel pounding, but there's no gavel. I lean forward to see what Brian used to make that sound, and see nothing but his bony hand flat on the desk. He raises it, his forefinger settling on Todd. "You're not setting the agenda here."

"We've had enough of your agenda," Todd says, his tone more sad than anything. Is he feeling that everything is his fault, even as I sit here blaming myself? We're so anxious to take on guilt, the one-size-fits-all emotion.

"Look," Brian says, "It's kind of unusual to dismiss everybody at once, but we're sending you home."

"You mean, you're closing the house?" Davy asks, even as I'm thinking, *For Christ's sake, don't you know what 'sending you home' means?*

"It's not my decision," Brian says. "The house belongs to the Judge."

There are sounds coming from the door behind and to the left of the desk. A rattle, a creak. Perhaps it will start bending, like the door in *The Haunting*—how tame that movie seems, in light of everything. This door, now: it opens inward, and a man, an ancient man in a wheelchair passes through, pushed by a male nurse in whites. I wonder briefly if the nurse might know Danny, John Toomey's nurse. Or if he knew Lyle. But my main source of wonder is the old man, sitting directly in front of us now, his hairless head half disappearing into a pillow, his face totally without color except for his deep brown eyes, the strongest evidence I've seen that eyes don't lose their color with age after all. They move, those eyes, right and left, but his lips look sealed.

"Can he speak?" I ask.

"He's a hundred and three years old," Brian says. "He can speak, but you have to be close. Isn't that right, Judge?" Brian leaps from his chair at the desk to put his ear up close to the Judge's lips. "The Judge wants to know who you are. So: Paul, Kent, Todd, Davy, and...?"

"Eric," says Eric.

"Daniel," say the others.

I raise my hand. "Sorry, there's been some confusion, especially on my part. This is Eric, the man I've been living with for ten years."

Brian starts to hike his fanny up on a corner of the desk, thinks better of it, glances at the Judge, then tries again. Being half perched there seems to bring him back into full counselor mode. "It would have been so much better if you guys had chosen to heal. Really." He presses his fingertips together in that here-is-the-steeple gesture we know so well. "But you were weak-minded, so you didn't."

"Oh, bullshit, Brian." I'm rubbing my face, rubbing my eyes as I speak, wishing I could erase all of this, including myself. "When have you ever managed to 'heal' anyone?"

He rises to his full height, once again the Brian we've known. "I healed myself," he says quietly.

Even here, with the air so thick with emotion I can hardly breathe, Brian calls on my deep sense of mischief. "Oh, Bri," I tell him, "how can you say that? How can you deny what we meant to each other?"

"That's not funny, Paul."

Squinting at him with freshly rubbed, bleary eyes, I see Brian as I knew him at East Oak House—at the kitchen stove, in his office chair, in the living room, officiating over our confusion, adding to it whenever possible. "I'm not trying to be amusing, Bri. I'm perfectly serious, just like you were when you were down on your knees, sucking my dick."

"Stop it!"

"But it was even-Steven, wasn't it, because I went down on you, too. I licked your ginger-colored bush…."

"That's enough!"

"I remember your perineum, Bri. How many guys have said that to you? I treasured that patch of skin, white as the driven snow. I even spoke to it. You said you could feel my words traveling right up your spine."

Brian has become a little too purple to speak. I glance at the Judge, and he, too, is showing some color at last; but the way his brown eyes are shifting and circling now does not look good. The nurse has left, perhaps to get some medication.

"So, what now, Bri?" I ask. "You kill us, like you killed Harmon, and Aaron, and Dwight, and who knows how many others?"

"That's not funny either, Paul."

"Good, we agree on something." I'm wondering, for the first time, if it's possible that he doesn't even know what's been going on. "What happened to Harmon?"

Brian shrugs. "He took over for a while because I needed a break. I still do, I'm really exhausted. But his methods were a little too…ex-

289

treme. What's that, Judge?" Again he places his ear close to the old man's lips. "'Intolerable,' the Judge says."

"Do me a favor? Let's ask the Judge about Winslow Cook. I have a feeling there was some connection there."

Brian narrows his eyes at me and shrugs, just briefly, as if trying to dislodge a fly from his shoulder. It's something he does when he's frustrated—or suspicious. "Who is Winslow Cook?"

The Judge's eyes are on me, for what seems like, in this charged atmosphere, a solid minute. Then he switches them to Brian, summoning him to lean down for another ear-against-lips session. Another minute seems to pass before Brian straightens up.

"He says thatWinslow Cook was his son-in-law."

"Son-in-law? Was he married to Maud? Is Maud Cook the Judge's daughter?"

Again Brian bends low, to hear the whispering. The Judge has an afghan tucked around him, covering even his hands; suddenly I'd love to know what they look like. "The Judge says that history's been rewritten, it doesn't matter now."

"No, I'll bet it doesn't, especially since Win Cook was a pedophile who liked boys. I suppose he was also Lyle Cook's father, though Lyle was never allowed to know it. That was merciful, considering Win seduced him."

It's unusual for Brian to look as uncertain as he does now. Perhaps he's wondering, finally, if he wandered into the wrong room. When the Judge gestures with his eyes, he bends again to listen. "The Judge says you're speaking lies, vicious lies."

290

"Is it a lie that the cops used to bash queers and throw them off the end of the pier? Who knows how many men disappeared that way? Because back in the day, before the storm of '79, the pier was a lot longer. Any dead body pitched off its end would be swept out to sea. I bet that's what happened to Win Cook, finally, wasn't it? And when the time came to kill Lyle...."

Brian is standing in front of me, now, trying one last time to act like a counselor. "Paul, you need to be quiet now. You're not helping, with all this crazy talk."

How right he would be, if he didn't know what we know, hasn't seen what we've seen. "My God, Brian, you really don't know, do you? What do you think happened to Harmon?"

"He's gone, I do know that. Riley drove him to the bus station, and that's the last we'll see of him."

"No, it's not." I feel almost sorry for him now. "Go down the basement stairs, Bri. Take a flashlight with you. Turn right at the bottom, look in big room. In the corner."

"There's no point—"

"They *killed* him!" It's Davy, who's been quiet up till now. He's on his feet, driving his clenched fists against his thighs. "They *killed* him, you idiot! Just like they killed Aaron and Dwight and the others! Go! Go look!"

Brian glances at Riley. So do I. The big lug is still standing at the rear of the room, in front of floor-to-ceiling bookshelves filled with the words of the law. He holds something I've never seen him with before: a gun, some kind of revolver hanging from his right hand, pointed at the floor. It looks no more out of place on him than a trowel or a flashlight would.

The gun makes Brian hesitate, but only for a second. He crosses the room, toward the short hallway, takes the basement stairs in what sounds like a few long leaps. I wonder if Harmon looks even worse by now; and when the scream comes, I do feel sorry for Brian, who just possibly might not have known any better than to do what he's done.

The Judge doesn't look very well. He parts his shriveled lips with great effort, turns his head side to side, seeking air. He may not even be able to hear me speak, but I have to: "Lyle came here, didn't he, because of the accusations John Toomey was making, in his off-kilter way? Toomey used to be a cop, he knew all about what you had the cops do, what you let them do. Lyle confronted you about Win, he showed you two of the snapshots he had. He accused you of having Win killed and thrown off the pier. It made you furious."

While I was talking the nurse returned, with two prescription bottles in one hand and a glass of water in the other. No, this is not a nurse from an agency. He's a private nurse, has probably worked for the Judge for many years. Living this sheltered life has given him a sense of privilege. It shows in his posture, in his calm deliberation as

291

he turns to me and says, "I can assure you that Lyle Cook was a very, very vile man."

I acknowledge him with the briefest of looks; I have a few more words for the Judge. "So you had Riley kill Lyle, after getting him liquored up first. Bash his head in, and then…what? You probably have a lot of ways to dispose of bodies, but Riley couldn't resist throwing him off the pier, just like his father. Only the pier's shorter now, and instead of being washed out to sea, Lyle ended up on the beach."

"It's an obsession with the old gentleman," the nurse says. By many standards, he's an old gentleman himself; only his proximity to the Judge makes him look younger. "The whole idea of a world without queers. Can you imagine what a boon that would be to all mankind, to the very evolution of the species?"

"Not to me," Todd says. "It would mean I'd be sucking off straight guys, and I *hate* that."

The nurse, whose name I will never know, ignores Todd's intrusion. He asks me, "What do you think? A world without queers."

"I don't know anymore what I think, but I'll tell you what I'd like." The upholstery, the rugs, even the soft leather book bindings seem to be working against me, soaking up my energy, my voice; I try to speak up. "I'd like to see a world of six billion individuals, no one of them like any other. Six billion minorities. Each with a different skin color, a different belief, a different language, and a different gender."

The nurse wiped a drop of water off the Judge's chin. "And how could such a world function?"

"It probably couldn't, not even for a day. But just once, for a brief time, no one would have to feel lonely because he was different from everyone else."

"Aha." The napkin that had patted the Judge's chin was placed in a white pocket. "The Judge would say that's the kind of sentimentality the world needs less of."

The door to the basement slams. Brian must be back now, and yes, here he comes, dragging his feet. "Brian, are you all right?" I ask him.

He starts to speak, then clamps his hand over his mouth, as if he might throw up. Judging by the stains on his shirt, he probably did throw up, downstairs.

"Oh, Brian, please don't tell me you didn't know what was going on all this time."

"We're supposed to cure 'em, and if we can't, get rid of 'em."

That was Riley, speaking for the first time. We look at him as if we weren't even sure he *could* speak. "Some of them pay," he says. "They pay a lot—or their parents do—to have 'em either cured or killed. That kid Aaron, his father said it didn't matter if we ended up killing him. He said as far as he was concerned, it'd be the same thing as the abortion that should have happened twenty-seven years ago." No one would accuse Riley of having a sense of humor, but damned if that last remark didn't bring a grin to his face.

"Oh, no," Brian says. "No, it was never like that." He gets to his feet, turns to Riley. "Tell them the truth."

Riley, however, shakes his head, grinning all the while. "I'll do better than that," he says. He raises the gun, takes aim at Brian, fires.

Brian falls. Screams follow, including my own.

"I got a bullet for every one of you," Riley says.

I'm drenched in panic sweat. My neck is too weak to hold my head up, I have to tilt it back against the chair cushion. I ask Riley, "Aside from the fact that the whole idea is insane, could you ever claim that you really *cured* anyone?"

Riley smiles his crooked smile. "Cure 'em or kill 'em—it don't matter to me."

First my neck wimped out, now my knees are shaking again.

"Well, I think it sounds like a good idea."

I nearly get whiplash, turning so fast to stare at Eric. Did he really say such a thing? It would have made just as much sense coming from the mouth of a hunting trophy—the buck with the dusty antlers, the tired-looking moose. But yes, it's Eric who's staring at me defiantly, his trembling lower lip the only sign that he's quaking inside. I ask him, "How can you say that?"

"Well, *my* life would have been a lot better if I wasn't gay. For one thing, I never would have met *you*."

So. More than the threatening presence of Riley and his gun, of the Judge and his nurse...more than the horrible truths that have just come to light...it's Eric who will strike me down, reduce me to a whiny little playback machine: "Never would have met...?"

293

"My life would have been better, all the way around. I might have even had something to show for it—children, maybe, or a love relationship that *meant* something."

"Oh, honey." Whatever I do right now might be the last thing I ever do, but does it have to be…tears? "It's meant something, believe me…."

"*Believe* you? How can I ever believe you again?"

"Oh, baby…."

"This is how it is," Riley says.

I'm moving, out of my seat, standing to face Eric and grab his shoulders, as if I can shake some sense into him, or at least get him to stop saying horrible things. But as soon as my hands touch his shirt he brings his own hands up, pushes against my chest with a force that sends me toppling backward, nearly falling over a corner of the desk.

"This is how it is, all right," Riley says. "The Judge always said so. This is what it's like when two queers say they love each other. It ends up like this, just like this."

Finding my feet again, rubbing the spot where the corner of the desk jabbed my butt, I challenge Eric. "Stand up. I won't let you…*sit there* and talk to me like that." Again I reach for him just as he does stand up, knocking his chair back and pushing me again, harder. This time my shoulder hits the wall, and suddenly I *know*, as if the impact has knocked some sense into me: I know what Eric's doing. "All right," I tell him, "if that's the way you want it," and I go after him. I'm going to tackle him, even though I've never tackled anyone in my life; but he jumps forward, puts his hands around my neck. I grab his forearms, try to pry his hands away. From the corner of my eye I see Kent leave his chair, back away from us. I get my mouth close enough to Eric's ear to whisper, "*I know what you're doing.*"

"Bastard!" he says.

We're locked together, his hands at my throat, my hands on his arms, but that doesn't keep us from moving, swinging around in a mad dance, nearly falling over Kent's chair, toppling it instead. I sensed the others—Brian, Todd and Davy—moving toward us, but cautiously. "You're the bastard!" I yell, finally breaking Eric's grip, putting a vise on his wrists and lifting them over his head. "You...*sorry excuse* for a man!"

And all the time I'm thinking, as much as my sweating and heaving will allow, trying to project my thoughts into Eric's head: *I know what you're doing, good for you, I never would have thought of this, creating a diversion....* As ugly as he looks, snarling like a rabid dog, I never stop silently praising him.

Until he spits in my face.

"God *damn* you!" I almost lose my grip on him. Then I've got hold of his right forearm with both hands and I'm swinging him around into my vacant chair, which takes flight, hitting Riley in his midsection, causing him to drop the gun. Swinging again, I throw Eric into the wall.

"Cocksucking *queer!*" he yells—spitting again, because his lip is split and he's got blood in his mouth. Here's a man I've seen nearly cry because he cut himself shaving, bloody in the mouth now and wanting more blood—making me want more, too, more blood, more hurt. He lunges at me so recklessly that it's easy to sidestep him. He lands on the carpet, rolls over and nearly knocks me down.

"Get up, you sorry son of a bitch." I grab his upper arm, try to pull it from its socket. He gets to his feet but I don't let go, and before he can get his balance I swing him around again. Riley has retrieved his gun, it's time to get rougher. I pick up one of the fallen chairs—it's heavier than it looked, and it didn't look light—and heft it over my head. I'm about to heave it in Eric's direction when he makes his move. He's never played football either, but he has some instinct for tackling; I'm stupefied to see him spring, his feet actually leaving the floor just before he hits my midsection, his arms wrapped around me as we fly backward, into the French doors and through them, onto the snow.

295

The snow isn't like snow at all, I don't even feel the cold. Maybe I'm dreaming all this. Maybe it's not deep snow I'm stumbling through but rather bedclothes twisted around my ankles as I thrash through a bad dream. But it's only taking me a few seconds to feel the sharpness of the air, that's all. It stings my bare scalp, and takes my already failing breath away as I run down the lawn. For a long moment I don't know where I am or what I'm doing.

Now comes another gunshot. I look back, terrified at what I might see. There's Eric, his face bloody, barreling along behind me. Has he been shot, is he about to collapse? I wait till he's was almost past me before I let myself run again. By then Kent and Davy and Todd have nearly caught up with us too, all of us panting and heaving, now in sync, now separately. I could throw up—would like to throw up—but I can't stop, and my stomach has nothing to offer anyway.

I've seen so little of this neighborhood, this town; but there's a car at the curb that I recognize. It's Lyle Cook's Volkswagen, and Celia Cook is getting out of it. Police sirens wail in the distance. I finally stop, only halfway down the lawn to Celia but unable to lift my feet one more time. Eric calls out to her one heavy huffing word at a time: "What took you so long?"

The Judge and the nurse and Riley are nowhere around, no doubt they're trying to make it to the back of the house, hoping to escape that way. But it's too late, two police cars are already pulling up to the curb. My breath begins to slow down at last, and I realize I've been panting from panic as much as exhaustion. Now my feet can feel the cold. I look at Eric and tell him, "You were so good. You knew what to do."

His face is raised, as if to help stop the bleeding from his lip. He gives me a look of such complexity—of such anger and fear and open-mouthed bewilderment—that it makes everything around it go dark. I'm sinking to my knees, stretching out in the snow.

# Epilogue

**The** Couples Group party this month is being hosted by Jorge & Dean, who live north of the airport. Driving past the long-term parking lots, I half expect some barrier to rise up from the road, as if the boundaries of our existence are as limited as a housefly's. Instead we keep going, farther than we've ever gone before into the suburbs north of Kansas City.

Our relationship keeps going also, Eric's and mine. Y2K has come and gone, and the world hasn't ended; it seemed so unlikely, in spite of the panic around us, that it wasn't worth breaking a sweat over. Nor have we succumbed to a renegade ice ball, or gamma ray burst, or any of the other catastrophes on poor Lyle's list. Now we keep our eyes on the foreseeable future and what it will take to get there. We keep "lucky" things around the house—the little wind-up toys that we've collected, gifts from friends and acquaintances, Pride Day souvenirs, and mementos from our few travels together, including a sand dollar from the beach at Two Piers. These things crowd the tops of bookcases, the huge oak coffee table in the living room, the edges of the kitchen counters. We even have, on the living room wall, a beautiful imagining, in oils, of what a gay angel might look like. Every time I look at it I think of Dwight, and of Aaron—both of them so pale and fair.

At the end of last year, just before Christmas, part of our luck did run out: we lost Maddy. Maddy—short for Amadeus—had been slowing down for a while, spending more and more time on our bed. The beginning of the end came one evening when Maddy appeared in the living room and tried to jump up on the sofa between us, only to slip and fall to the floor. To see this kind of failing for the first time is to deny it, or at least call it a one-time occurrence, never to happen again. But he stayed in his fallen position, making us realize he was too weak to move. I brought his food and water bowls in from the kitchen and he ate and drank. His thirst and appetite were reassuring, but they also confirmed that he would have liked to visit the kitchen but was too weak to make it.

When we took him back to the vet, to the fancy clinic in Johnson County where there were animal specialists from surgeons to radiologists, a shadow on the ultrasound hinted that his pancreatic abscess may be coming back. This time we vetoed surgery, not wanting to put him through it again. We took the chance that he might *not* be seriously ill and ran with it, and for a while he really did seem to be better. Then the weakness came back, and he collapsed while trying to get out of his bed in the living room. We took him in, just wrapped in a towel—there was no point in using the carrier—and left him for a couple of days of treatment and tests. We were able to visit him, sometimes having to wait a few minutes while they put a new arrival in its cage, or finished giving some dog or cat an injection or infusion. The beautiful gray-and-white fur on his underside had been shaved for the ultrasound, his bare pink belly hung down. We unlocked his cage and brought him as close as possible to us without disturbing his IV line. He looked bewildered, but his appetite was still good, and the IV antibiotics had brought his minor fever down. They decided to keep him one more day while they adjusted his insulin level, and then we could take him home.

I should have known, when the vet called us in the middle of that night, that Maddy was about to go. He had suddenly become very anemic, the doctor said; they were having to watch him very closely, that was all they could tell us for now. Incredibly—or so it seemed later on—Eric and I went back to sleep. It wasn't much more than half an hour later that the final phone call came.

**T h e** last photo we took of Maddy shows him perched on an otto-man, near the fireplace. Behind him hangs the Christmas card that Todd and Davy, who now live in Connecticut, sent us. We also hear from Kent, very occasionally, via e-mail. He has a congregation in a suburb of Boston.

**W e** turn off I-29 onto a smaller highway, which leads to the atten-uated two-lanes of the countryside. The sky holds more stars than we're used to. The vast fields show no signs of life except for an illumi-nated silo or chore light here and there. Suburban sprawl is taking its first baby steps where Jorge & Dean live, in a housing development complete with cul-de-sacs and a swimming pool.

The house, with the standard bay window and cathedral peak over the living room, has a slapped-together look. You can picture it and twenty clones being built in a day. Jorge & Dean are a young couple, and they've made it a party house, with soft, cream-colored modular furniture, black-light posters on the walls, and huge stereo speak-ers duct-taped to the living room rafters. Music blares, salsa and hip hop.

There's a flight of stairs leading up to the kitchen, which overlooks the living room—a handy arrangement if you want to toss beers down to the TV area rather than carry them down the steps. Men are bunched in little groups on either side of the L-shaped kitchen counter. Some couples, including Eric and I, tend to stick together through these gatherings, while others separate immediately, never rejoining till it's time to hunt for their Tupperware containers and say their goodbyes. I envy and fear the more gregarious couples, and feel absurdly grateful if they speak to us. It's so much like high school. The distant past isn't so distant, if you can still break a flop sweat at the prospect of not fitting in.

Eric sets down our Tupperware bowl filled with fruit salad. Bolder than me, he begins to thread a path through the groups while I fol-low behind. Some men nod hello, others want hugs and kisses. That always surprises me, but I hug and kiss along with the best of them, slobbering on the cheeks of guys whose names I can't remember. Thank God for the nametags, which, for this party, are shaped like sombreros. Mine says **PAUL / ERIC** on the brim, Eric's says **ERIC / PAUL.**

It's not an all-male party, after all. One of the few regularly attending lesbian couples is here, Shari & Desi. Shari's nametag has only her name on it, though, and Eric and I ask simultaneously, "Where's Desi?"

"Oh, she had a family thing to go to," Shari says. "Her brother's getting married and the rehearsal dinner's tonight."

"Another man bites the dust, huh?" Eric says.

Shari rolls her eyes. "You should see the bride. Johnson County high society. Her family doesn't know what to make of Desi and me. You notice I wasn't invited to the dinner. Oh well!"

I like Shari. She has a voice that projects so that you can hear it above all others in a crowded room, yet she tends to be a little withdrawn, like me. If we'd known each other in high school we probably would have been best friends, two wallflowers hanging out together at the dances. She turns now to help Jorge, who wears an identical potholder mitten, take a pan of enchiladas from the oven. We move on to say hello to Stan & Mike, and Tom & Tom, and Harvey & Stu. Eric finds the drinks and is pouring us each a Diet Pepsi when I stumble upon the kitchen table, which was hidden by the group standing around it.

There's a new couple here, sitting at the table. It was probably Dean, with his fussy host manners, who insisted that they sit down, though nearly everyone else is standing. The man with the shaved head is facing away from me, but when several men standing closest to him burst into laughter, he looks around, laughing also, turning in the chair to see how far the laughter extends. He's comfortable here, he's looking for more people to enjoy. I look as friendly as anyone else, and he reaches out to me for a handshake.

It's Richard Roscoe. I have the advantage, because he doesn't recognize me immediately—I've lost weight over the past year or so—but it's no fun; the split-second is coming when he'll know me, and his expression will sour. Okay, I'll have to take my lumps. There's no reason why he should be glad to see me, considering I didn't even call him when I returned from Maine last year. He'd gone to extraordinary lengths to find me in my self-imposed exile, to make sure I was all right; and even though he ended up running away, I shouldn't have repaid him with silence.

Yes, here it comes: his beautiful eyes change as he recognizes me, and his smile fades. He starts to say my name, then stalls. All that comes out is "*Puh.*" Only the handshake we've engaged in is still going on, as if our hands are acting independently.

"Richard…."

Our hands slide apart, finally, and he raises his, palms out, to keep me from saying another word. He brings his other arm around, and before I know it he has both hands spread outward, inviting me to hug. It's as awkward as a hug must be when one person is sitting and the other standing, but it's therapy, the way the puts his arms around my waist. Without thinking I plant the briefest of kisses on the top of his head.

"Paul," he says, getting it out this time, making it a name he can say with no regrets. "I want you to meet somebody."

I recognize his younger, darker-skinned partner and his brilliant smile—Michael, another Metro bus driver. I look for Eric, over by the drinks, so I can wave him over and introduce him, too.

**The** enchiladas were great, and now Jorge & Dean have tied a piñata to one of the living room beams, and we're taking turns trying to break it open with a baseball bat. The catch is, we have to do it as couples, blindfolded, holding the bat with hands bound at the wrists. The yellow papier-mâché donkey is tough, and though some couples have managed to land some square blows it's barely cracked. Now Eric and I have a turn. We move to the center of the group for the blindfolding, and to have our wrists bound together with a scarf, my right to his left. I'm thinking hard about the best way to do this—maybe we should swing at the count of three—when Eric, without warning, raises our arms to swing. We're not ready, we're nowhere near ready, but I have to follow him. What choice do I have, bound together as we are?

**Wayne Courtois** was born in Portland, Maine, and currently lives in Kansas City, Missouri, with his longtime partner.

A graduate of the MFA Program at the University of North Carolina-Greensboro, Wayne is author of the memoir *A Report from Winter* and the erotic novel *My Name Is Rand*. His short fiction has appeared in journals including *The Greensboro Review* and *Harrington Gay Men's Literary Quarterly*; in the webzines *suspect thoughts: a journal of subversive writing* and *Velvet Mafia*; and in anthologies such as *Of the Flesh, Love Under Foot, Best Gay Erotica, Out of Control,* and *Country Boys.* Nonfiction work has appeared in *I Do/I Don't: Queers on Marriage; Walking Higher: Gay Men Write about the Deaths of Their Mothers;* and *The Lost Library: Gay Fiction Rediscovered.*

Wayne has served on his local Ryan White Planning Council, and as a grantwriter in the nonprofit sector he has helped to raise millions for HIV/AIDS services, hospice care, and the arts. Contact him at waynewrite@gmail.com.

Lightning Source UK Ltd.
Milton Keynes UK
UKOW051925140213

206316UK00001B/94/P